"I never miss an A[...]
—Julia Quinn, *New York* [...]

"Treat yourself to [...]
from a most ta[...]
—*Romance Reviews Today*

"For fabulous Regency flavor, witty and addictive,
you can't go past Anne Gracie."
—Stephanie Laurens, bestselling author

PRAISE FOR ANNE GRACIE'S NOVELS

Bride by Mistake

"The always terrific Anne Gracie outdoes herself with *Bride by Mistake* . . . Gracie created two great characters, a high-tension relationship and a wonderfully satisfying ending. Not to be missed!"
—Mary Jo Putney, *New York Times* bestselling author

"Another [of] Ms. Gracie's character-rich, fiery tales filled with emotion and passion leavened by charm and wit."
—*Romance Reviews Today*

The Accidental Wedding

"With her signature superbly nuanced characters, subtle sense of wit and richly emotional writing, Gracie puts her distinctive stamp on a classic Regency plot."
—*Chicago Tribune*

"Anne Gracie's writing dances that thin line between always familiar and always fresh. She is able to take a Cinderella story with all the inherent—and comfortable—tradition, mix in a few recognizable elements, add a dash of the unexpected and a sprinkling of the unpredictable, and come up with a luscious indulgence of a novel . . . *The Accidental Wedding* is warm and sweet, tempered with bursts of piquancy and a dash or three of spice. Like chocolate and chili, this novel is your favorite comfort food, with an unexpected—delicious—twist."
—*New York Journal of Books*

continued . . .

To Catch a Bride

"It was loveable and laugh-out-loud, full of heart and of memorable and interesting characters." —*Errant Dreams Reviews*

"A fascinating twist on the girl-in-disguise plot . . . With its wildly romantic last chapter, this novel is a great antidote to the end of the summer." —Eloisa James, *New York Times* bestselling author

"One of the difficulties of reviewing a favorite author is running out of superlatives. An Anne Gracie novel is guaranteed to have heart and soul, passion, action and sprinkles of humor and fun." —*Romance Reviews Today*

His Captive Lady

"With tenderness, compassion and a deep understanding of the era, Gracie touches readers on many levels with her remarkable characters and intense exploration of their deepest human needs. Gracie is a great storyteller." —*RT Book Reviews* (4½ stars, Top Pick)

"Once again, author Anne Gracie has proven what an exceptionally gifted author is all about . . . Absolutely one of the best romances I've read this year!" —*CK2S Kwips and Kritiques*

The Stolen Princess

"Gracie begins the Devil Riders series with a fast-paced and enticing tale . . . Captures both the inherent tension of the story and the era with her hallmark charm and graceful prose." —*RT Book Reviews* (4 stars)

"Anne Gracie's talent is as consistent as it is huge. I highly recommend *The Stolen Princess*, and look forward to the rest of the series." —*Romance Reviews Today*

"Anne Gracie always delivers a charming, feel-good story with enchanting characters. I love all of Ms. Gracie's stories and *The Stolen Princess* is no exception. It stole my heart, as it will yours." —*Fresh Fiction*

Berkley Sensation titles by Anne Gracie

The Merridew Sisters

THE PERFECT RAKE
THE PERFECT WALTZ
THE PERFECT STRANGER
THE PERFECT KISS

The Devil Riders

THE STOLEN PRINCESS
HIS CAPTIVE LADY
TO CATCH A BRIDE
THE ACCIDENTAL WEDDING
BRIDE BY MISTAKE

The Chance Sisters

THE AUTUMN BRIDE

THE

Autumn Bride

ANNE GRACIE

BERKLEY SENSATION. NEW YORK

THE BERKLEY PUBLISHING GROUP
Published by the Penguin Group
Penguin Group (USA) Inc.
375 Hudson Street, New York, New York 10014, USA

Penguin Group (Canada), 90 Eglinton Avenue East, Suite 700, Toronto, Ontario M4P 2Y3, Canada
(a division of Pearson Penguin Canada Inc.) • Penguin Books Ltd., 80 Strand, London WC2R 0RL,
England • Penguin Ireland, 25 St. Stephen's Green, Dublin 2, Ireland (a division of Penguin
Books Ltd.) • Penguin Group (Australia), 707 Collins Street, Melbourne, Victoria 3008, Australia
(a division of Pearson Australia Group Pty. Ltd.) • Penguin Books India Pvt. Ltd., 11 Community
Centre, Panchsheel Park, New Delhi—110 017, India • Penguin Group (NZ), 67 Apollo Drive,
Rosedale, Auckland 0632, New Zealand (a division of Pearson New Zealand Ltd.) • Penguin Books
(South Africa), Rosebank Office Park, 181 Jan Smuts Avenue, Parktown North 2193,
South Africa • Penguin China, B7 Jiaming Center, 27 East Third Ring Road North,
Chaoyang District, Beijing 100020, China

Penguin Books Ltd., Registered Offices: 80 Strand, London WC2R 0RL, England

This is a work of fiction. Names, characters, places, and incidents either are the product of the author's
imagination or are used fictitiously, and any resemblance to actual persons, living or dead, business
establishments, events, or locales is entirely coincidental. The publisher does not have any control over
and does not assume any responsibility for author or third-party websites or their content.

THE AUTUMN BRIDE

A Berkley Sensation Book / published by arrangement with the author

PUBLISHING HISTORY
Berkley Sensation mass-market edition / February 2013

Copyright © 2013 by Anne Gracie.
Cover art by Judy York. Hand lettering by Ron Zinn.
Cover design by George Long.

ISBN: 978-0-425-25925-2

BERKLEY SENSATION®
Berkley Sensation Books are published by The Berkley Publishing Group,
a division of Penguin Group (USA) Inc.,
375 Hudson Street, New York, New York 10014.
BERKLEY SENSATION® is a registered trademark of Penguin Group (USA) Inc.
The "B" design is a trademark of Penguin Group (USA) Inc.

PRINTED IN THE UNITED STATES OF AMERICA

10   9   8   7   6   5   4   3   2   1

ALWAYS LEARNING   **PEARSON**

With thanks to my friends—the Maytoners—as always, for sanity, support and laughs when I need them most.

And with gratitude and many thanks to my readers.

Prologue

"And what am I to do on the occasion? It seems an hopeless business."

—JANE AUSTEN, *PRIDE AND PREJUDICE*

London, 1805

"I'm sorry, my lord, but there's nothing left."

My lord. Max Davenham still couldn't get used to being called that. Lord Davenham was his big, hearty, larger-than-life uncle. But his uncle was dead and Max, the heir, was now Lord Davenham.

Then the import of what Harcourt and Denton, his uncle's lawyer and man of affairs, were telling him filtered through. "What do you mean, nothing?" His uncle was a rich man; everybody knew that.

Harcourt spread his hands in a rueful gesture. *"Nothing."*

"Less than nothing," Denton clarified. "Your uncle sold off everything that could be sold off, mortgaged the rest and borrowed as heavily as he could."

Max struggled to take it all in. His uncle had died just over a week before, of an accident in the hunting field, but no one seeing him in action could possibly have suspected there was any shortage of money. At the time of his death he'd been hosting a large, lavish house party.

"He died in debt?" It wasn't really a question. Since the news of the death, Max, who'd been finishing his final year at school, had been approached by an endless stream of tradesmen demanding payment, dunning him for what his uncle had owed. Some of the sums were enormous.

"A great deal of debt," the lawyer agreed heavily.

Max speared his fingers through his hair. "What a damned, bloody mess!" Nobody reprimanded him for the bad language. He was a schoolboy no longer. He was Lord Davenham, and he was entitled to swear, to take his seat in the House of Lords—and to bear the responsibility for the huge financial mess his uncle had left behind.

"Thank God for my aunt's jointure. At least she won't be caught up in this mess." His aunt was the only daughter of the Earl of Fenton. The late earl hadn't much liked her marrying a mere baron and on her marriage had set up a generous trust to provide for her in widowhood.

There was a short silence. Harcourt gazed fixedly at his fingers. Denton fiddled with the documents that lay before him. Neither one met Max's eye.

"That's gone too?" Max said incredulously. He didn't understand much about trusts, but he'd always believed—in fact, he'd overheard his uncle say once—that it was damned well unbreakable. Obviously he'd found a way.

He looked at the two men in front of him. "So what must I do?"

"Everything that remains must be sold off."

"Everything?"

Both men nodded. "Everything," Denton confirmed. "Davenham Hall—"

"The home estate?"

"Everything," Denton repeated. He consulted the list in front of him. "Davenham Hall, the Cornish mines, the hunting box in Leicestershire, the Sussex properties, the manor in Norfolk, the London house—"

"The London house? But that's my aunt's *home*." Aunt Bea hated the country. The loss of the country houses wouldn't bother her in the least, but . . .

Max's brain was spinning. How had nobody seen this coming? Taken steps to prevent it?

He shook his head. "I don't mind selling off the other properties, though I'd rather we tried to keep the home estate if we possibly can, but I won't allow the London house to be sold."

"I'm afraid you have no choice, my lord."

Max frowned. "But where would my aunt live?"

Harcourt said apologetically, "Perhaps with relatives?"

Max was appalled. Aunt Bea? His magnificent, outrageous aunt, a leader of the *ton*, living on her relatives' charity as a poor relation? He couldn't imagine it. It would kill her.

"Impossible. There are only a few distant cousins left," he heard himself saying.

Denton leaned forward and said firmly, in a voice not untinged with sympathy, "You haven't understood, my lord— *everything* must be sold, and even then there will be debts—big ones."

Max slumped back in his chair. "You mean I'm ruined?"

"Utterly."

There was a short silence.

"Did my uncle not realize?" From all Max could see, his uncle had been spending money like water up to and including the day he died. No, not spending money—running up debts.

The silence thickened and became awkward.

Denton broke it. "He knew he was ruined, all right. He'd known for years—we tried again and again to make him understand, but . . ." He shook his head.

Harcourt, the lawyer, hesitated, then said delicately, "Your uncle did, however, ensure he had paid all his gambling debts before he . . . died. He died a gentleman."

Max stared at him, realizing what the man was telling him, what nobody had told him before now—the reason for the wild, lavish house party, the last drunken, reckless out-of-season hunt, where his uncle, always a noted horseman, had taken greater and greater risks, putting his horse at any barrier, heedless of any danger until he'd come off at the last fence, slamming headfirst into a stone wall and breaking his neck.

The bastard had *known*. He'd gone out on a drunken spree, escaping the mess he'd made. Paying only his gambling debts— his so-called debts of honor—*honor!* Max snorted. Leaving the mess to his wife and his eighteen-year-old heir.

He forced his fists to unclench. "Does my aunt know?"

Harcourt shook his head. "She knows nothing of this."

"Her jewels might secure a—"

"Paste, my lord," Denton said sorrowfully.

"Paste?" She'd brought a fortune in jewels to the marriage.

"Lord Davenham had them copied, all but a couple of her rings—the ones she never takes off."

"Does she know her jewels are paste?"

"I doubt it."

"So we're ruined, indeed." There was a long silence. Max's brain was reeling. Only a few weeks before, his biggest problem was whether he'd pass the Latin exam and whether his cricket team would win the cup. Now . . .

He rose and paced about the room, trying to make up his mind what to do. He didn't seem to have much choice. But he wasn't going to take the advice of Harcourt and Denton—not completely.

He squared his shoulders and resumed his seat. "Very well, sell off everything except the home estate and my aunt's house in London."

"But—"

He held up his hand. "I won't allow my aunt to be rendered homeless and dependent on the charity of relatives. Retaining her London home and securing her an income is my first priority."

"But—"

"And if I can possibly hang on to Davenham Hall, I will. If you can, rent it out to someone; if not, close up the house and rent out the land to local farmers."

"But, my lord—"

"I do understand the gravity of the situation," he assured them. "But the home estate in Devon has been the heart of my family for generations and I'm going to do my damnedest to hold on to it. Sell off everything else; make sure you get the best price you can. Be discreet; once the vultures scent blood they'll peck the carcass to bits. And part-pay the noisiest of the creditors first; it might give us some breathing time."

The two elderly men exchanged glances and seemed to come to some unspoken understanding. "Very well, my lord, but the sale of the properties won't begin to cover all of the debts. How will you—"

"I'll borrow."

Denton said in an exasperated voice, "My lord, the banks won't lend you a penny. Don't you understand? You're *ruined*."

Max clenched his fist. "I am *not* ruined yet! And if the banks won't lend me the money I need to secure my aunt's future, I'll find it elsewhere."

In an urgent voice Denton said, "Don't do it, my lord. You don't know what you're getting yourself in for. You spoke of vultures, but private moneylenders are worse than vultures."

Harcourt added, "He's right. Remember your Shakespeare— they might lend you the money, but they'll demand their pound of flesh."

Max stood. "Then if that's what it takes, so be it."

Chapter One

*"Give a girl an education and introduce her properly into
the world, and ten to one but she has the means of settling
well, without further expense to anybody."*

—JANE AUSTEN, MANSFIELD PARK

London, August 1816

S he was running late. Abigail Chantry quickened her pace.
Her half day off, and though it was damp and squally and
cold outside, she'd taken herself off as usual to continue her
explorations of London.

Truth to tell, if her employers had lived in the bleakest, most
remote part of the Yorkshire moors, Abby would still have removed
herself from their vicinity on her fortnightly half day off. Mrs.
Mason believed a governess should be useful as well as educa-
tional, and saw no reason why, on Miss Chantry's half day, she
should not do a little mending for her employer or, better still, take
the children with her on her outings.

What need did a governess, especially one who was
orphaned, after all, have for free time?

Miss Chantry did not agree. So, rain, hail or snow, she
absented herself from the Mason house the moment after the
clock in the hall chimed noon, returning a few minutes before
six to resume her duties.

Having spent most of her life in the country, Abby was loving her forays into this enormous city, discovering all kinds of
wonderful places. Last week she'd found a bookshop where the

owner let her read to her heart's content without pressuring her to buy—only the secondhand books, of course, not the new ones whose pages had not yet been cut. She'd returned there today, and had become so lost in a story—*The Monk*, deliciously bloodcurdling—that now she was running late.

If she returned even one minute after six, Mr. Mason would dock her wages by a full day. It had happened before, and no amount of argument would budge him.

She turned the corner into the Masons' street and glanced up at the nearby clock tower. Oh, Lord, three minutes to go. Abby picked up speed.

"Abby Chantry?" A young woman, a maidservant by her garments, limped toward her with an uneven gait. She'd been waiting opposite the Masons' house.

Abby eyed her warily. "Yes?" Apart from her employers, Abby knew no one in London. And nobody here called her Abby.

"I got a message from your sister." She spoke with a rough London accent.

Her mouth was swollen and a large bruise darkened her cheek.

"My *sister*?" It wasn't possible. Jane was hundreds of miles away. She'd just left the Pillbury Home for the Daughters of Distressed Gentlewomen, near Cheltenham, to take up a position as companion to a vicar's mother in Hereford.

"She told me where to find you. I'm Daisy." The girl took Abby's arm and tugged. "You gotta come with me. Jane's in trouble—bad trouble—and you gotta come now."

Abby hesitated. The girl's bruised and battered face didn't inspire confidence. The newspapers were full of the terrible crimes that took place in London: murders, white slavery, pickpockets and burglars. She'd even read about people hit over the head in a dark alley, stripped and left for dead, just for their clothing.

But Abby wore a dull gray homemade dress that practically shouted "governess." She couldn't imagine anyone wanting to steal it. And she was thin, plain and clever, rather than pretty, which ruled out white slavers. She had no money or valuables and, apart from the Mason family, she knew no one in London, so could hardly inspire murder.

And this girl knew her name, *and* Jane's. And Abby's address. Abby glanced at the clock. A minute to six. But what did the loss of a day's wages matter when her little sister was in London and in trouble? Jane was not yet eighteen.

"All right, I'll come." She gave in to Daisy's tugging and they hurried down the street. "Where is my sister?"

"In a bad place," Daisy said cryptically, stumping rapidly along with an ungainly gait. Crippled or the result of the beating she'd received? Abby wondered. Whichever, it didn't seem to slow her down.

"What kind of bad place?"

Daisy didn't respond. She led Abby through a maze of streets, cutting down back alleys and leading her into an area Abby had never felt tempted to explore.

"What kind of bad place?" Abby repeated.

Daisy glanced at her sideways. "A broffel, miss!"

"A broff—" Abby broke off, horrified. "You mean a *brothel*?"

"That's what I said, miss, a broffel."

Abby stopped dead. "Then it can't be my sister; Jane would never enter a brothel." But even as she said it, she knew the truth. *Her baby sister was in a brothel.*

"Yeah, well, she didn't have no choice in the matter. She come 'ere straight from some orphanage in the country. Drugged, she was. She give me your address and arst me to get a message to you. And we ain't got much time, so hurry."

Numb with shock, and sick at the thought, Abby allowed herself to be led down side streets and alleyways. Jane was supposed to be in a vicarage in Hereford. How could she possibly have ended up in a London brothel? *Drugged, she was.* How?

They turned into a narrow street lined with shabby houses, and slowed.

"That's it." Daisy gestured to a tall house, a good deal smarter than the others, with a freshly painted black door and windows curtained in crimson fabric. The ground-story windows were unbarred, but the higher ones were all barred. To keep people in, rather than out. *She didn't have no choice.*

As she stared up, she saw a movement at one of the highest

windows. A glimpse of golden hair, two palms pressed against the glass framing a young woman the image of Abby's mother.

Abby hadn't seen her sister for six years, but there was no doubt in her heart. *Jane!*

Someone pulled Jane back out of sight and closed the curtains.

Her sister was a prisoner in that house. Abby hurried across the street and started up the front stairs. Daisy grabbed her by the skirt and pulled her backward.

"No, miss!" Her voice held so much urgency it stopped Abby dead. "If you go in there arstin' questions now, it'll only make things worse. You might never see your sister again!"

"Then I'll fetch a constable or a magistrate to sort out this matter."

"Do that and for certain sure you'll never see your sister again. He—Mort—him who owns this place and all the girls in it now"—she jerked her chin toward the upstairs—"he pays blokes to warn him. Before any constable can get here your sister will be long gone."

Abby felt sick. "But what can I do? I must get her out of there."

"I told you, miss—we got a plan." The sound of carriage wheels rattling down the street made Daisy look around. She paled. "Oh, my gawd, that's Mort comin'! Go quick! If he catches me talkin' to anyone outside he'll give me another frashing! I'll meet you in the alley behind the house. Sixth house along. Big spiked gate. Go!" She gave Abby a shove and fled down the side steps to the basement area.

Abby, still in shock—Jane, in a brothel!—hurried away down the street, forcing herself not to look back, even when she heard the carriage draw to a halt outside the house with the black door.

She turned the corner and found the alley Daisy had described running behind the houses. It was narrow, gloomy and strewn with filth of all kinds, the cobbles slimy, the damp stench vile. Abby covered her nose and grimly picked her way along the lane. From time to time something squelched underfoot but she didn't look down. Whatever she'd stepped in, she didn't want to know. All that mattered was getting Jane out of that place.

She counted along the houses and came to the sixth, set behind a tall brick wall, the top of which was studded with shards of broken glass. A solid wooden gate was set into it, topped by a line of iron spikes.

The sinister row of spikes gleamed dully in the faint light. Ice slid slowly through her veins. With her dying breath Mama had made Abby promise to keep Jane safe, to keep them both safe. It hadn't been easy—Jane's beauty had always attracted attention, even when she was a little girl—but Abby had kept that promise.

Until now. Jane was imprisoned *in a brothel*. Abby raised a hand to her mouth and found it was shaking.

Her whole body was trembling.

How long had Jane been there? Abby tried to work it out, to recall what Jane had said in her last letter, but she couldn't. Over and over, the question pounded through her mind: How had Jane come to be in a brothel?

Abby shoved the fruitless question aside. She had to think, to plan what to do to get Jane free. What if Daisy didn't come? Abby would have no option but to fetch a constable.

Do that and for certain sure you'll never see your sister again. Abby shivered. She was entirely dependent on the goodwill— and ability—of a girl she'd never seen till a few minutes ago.

If constables and magistrates couldn't help, how could one small, crippled maidservant make a difference? And where was she?

The minutes crawled by.

Abby was almost ready to give up when she heard something on the other side of the gate. Her heart gave a leap of relief; then it occurred to her it could be anyone. She pressed back into the shadows and waited.

The gate cracked open an inch. "You still here, miss?" came a whisper.

"I'm here."

The girl poked her head out. "I got no time to explain, miss, but come back here in an hour with a warm cloak and some shoes."

"Shoes, but—"

"I was going to try and get your sister out now, but I can't while Mort's here. But he's goin' out again shortly."

She turned to leave, but Abby grabbed her arm. "Why? Why would you do this for us? For Jane and me?" It was obviously dangerous. Why would this girl—a stranger—take such a risk? Was she expecting payment? Abby would gladly give all she had to save her sister, but she didn't have much.

The girl shook her head. "'Cause it's wrong, what Mort's doing. It never used to be like this, stealing girls, keeping them locked up—" She broke off. "Look, I ain't got time to explain, miss, not so's you'd understand. You'll just have to trust me. Just be back here in an hour with a warm cloak and some shoes."

"Why?" Some kind of payment for services rendered?

"'Cause she hain't got nothin' to wear outside, of course." She jerked her chin at the filth in the alley. "You want her to walk through that in her bare feet? Now I gotta go." And with that the girl was gone, the gate shut behind her. Abby heard a bolt slide into place.

Numbly, Abby found her way back to the Masons' house.

An hour.

A lot could happen in an hour.

"What time do you call this?"

Abby, her foot on the first stair, turned back. Mr. Mason stood in the hall entry, fob watch in hand, glowering. "You're late!"

"I know, and I'm sorry, Mr. Mason, but I only just learned that—"

"I shall have to deduct the full day from your wages, of course." He puffed his chest up like a particularly pleased toad.

"It was a family emergency—"

He snorted. "You have no family."

"I do, I have a sister, and she has come to London unexpectedly and—"

"No excuses, you know the rules."

"It's not an excuse. It's true, and I'm hoping. . . I was wondering . . ." She swallowed, belatedly realizing she should not have argued with him.

"What were you wondering, Miss Chantry?" Mrs. Mason

swept down the staircase, dressed in a sumptuous puce silk dress, a feathered headdress and a cloak edged with fur. "Have you forgotten, Mr. Mason, we are to attend the opera this evening? I do not wish to be late."

"It's fashionable to be late," her husband responded.

"I realize that, my dear." Mrs. Mason's voice grated with sugarcoated irritation. "But we are going to be more than fashionably late—you don't even have your coat on."

The butler arrived in the hallway, heard the remark and went to fetch Mr. Mason's coat.

Mrs. Mason pulled on one long kid evening glove and glanced at Abby. "Well, what is it, Miss Chantry?"

Abby took a deep breath. The Masons were very strict about visitors of any kind. Abby was allowed none. "My younger sister is in London, ma'am, and I was wondering if she could stay with me, just for the night—"

The woman's well-plucked eyebrows rose. "Here? Don't be ridiculous. Of course not. Now come along, Mr. Mason—"

"But I haven't seen her for years. She's just left the orphanage and she's not quite eighteen. I can't let her stay in London on her own."

"That's not our concern." Mrs. Mason frowned into the looking glass and adjusted her headdress. "A stranger, sleeping in the same house as my precious babies?" She snorted.

"She's not a stranger; she's *my sister.*"

"It's out of the question." Mr. Mason allowed the butler to help him into his coat. "Blake, is the carriage here?"

The butler opened the door and peered outside. "It's just turning out of the mews, sir."

"And this is your last word?" Abby asked.

Mrs. Mason turned on her. "Why are you still loitering about? You heard my husband; the answer is no! Now get upstairs and attend to the children."

There was no point in arguing, so Abby went upstairs. She had no intention of obeying anyway.

She checked on the children, as she did every night. They were all fast asleep, looking like little angels, which they absolutely were not. The two older ones were full of mischief. Abby didn't care. She loved them anyway.

Susan, the toddler, was sleeping on her front with her bottom poking up as usual. Such a little darling. Abby gently turned her on her side and the little girl snuggled down, smiling to herself, still fast asleep. Abby tucked the covers around her.

These children were the joy and also the agony of her job. Abby loved them as if they were her own. She couldn't help herself—she knew it was foolish, and that one day they'd break her heart. She knew they'd be taken away from her, or she'd be sent away from them as if they'd outgrown her like a pair of old shoes.

It was heartbreak waiting to happen, loving other people's children.

She'd learned that hard lesson from the Taylors, her first position. Two years she'd been with them, loving the little ones with all her hungry heart. Not thinking ahead. Never even considering that one day she'd be dismissed and never see the children again.

They lived in Jamaica now.

She would lose the Mason children now too, but she would not—could not—leave her sister alone in a London hotel—not after what she'd been through. Even if she hadn't, if Jane had arrived in London unexpectedly, as she'd told the Masons, they had six years to catch up on; Jane had been a child of twelve when Abby saw her last.

Jane.

She bent and kissed each sleeping child and hurried out to collect the cloak and shoes for her sister, adding a shawl to the bundle, just in case.

Gaslight had not yet reached the more sordid parts of the city. In the evening gloom the alleyway seemed more noisome and full of sinister shadows. Abby trod warily, counting the houses until she reached the high brick wall with the spiked wooden gate.

She stationed herself opposite the gate and waited, watching the windows like a hawk, noting every passing flicker of light, every shadow of movement. Was that Jane? Was that?

The time passed slowly. A distant clock chimed the hour. It

was taking much longer than she'd expected. Had something gone wrong?

Something ran over her foot, a flicker of tiny damp claws and a slithery tail. She jumped, stifling a scream. She loathed rats.

She was concentrating so hard on the windows above that the scrape of the bolt on the gate opposite took her unawares and she jumped in fright.

The gate creaked open. A head peered out. "Abby?" A low whisper.

"Jane?"

A pale wraithlike shape slipped through the gap and then her sister was in her arms, clinging tightly, trembling, weeping and laughing. "Abby, oh, Abby!"

"Janey!" Tears blurred Abby's vision as she hugged her little sister. Not so little anymore, she realized. Jane was as tall as Abby now. She hugged her tighter. "Jane, dearest! Are you all right? How did you come to be in London? I thought Hereford—"

A hard little finger poked her in the ribs. "Oy! We're not out of danger yet, y'know. Escape now, happy reunion later!" It was Daisy. "Now quick, where's them shoes?"

"Of course." Abby released Jane and as she stepped back her jaw dropped. Her sister was naked but for a thin chemise. "Good God, Jane, where are your clothes?" She pulled the cloak out and threw it around her shivering sister.

"It's to stop us leaving," Jane said between chattering teeth. "We can't go into the streets dressed like this."

Abby crouched to slip the shoes on Jane's cold feet, which were filthy from the alley. She wiped them clean as best she could with a handkerchief, her hands shaking with rage and distress. For her sister to be kept in such an indecent state, without even clothes to keep her covered! And in such cold weather!

"Put this on as well." She passed the shawl to Jane.

"No, Damaris can use it."

"Damaris?" Abby glanced up and saw another girl hovering uncertainly outside the gate, shivering, her arms wrapped around herself. She too was scantily clothed, but unlike Jane, this girl looked exactly like a woman out of a brothel.

She wore a thin red-and-gold gauzy wrapper that barely reached past her thighs. Her dark hair was piled high, spiked into place with two sticks. Her face—clearly painted—was a dead white oval. Her lips and cheeks were garishly rouged, her eyelids had been darkened and the line of her eyes was elongated at the corners.

"Damaris is my friend." Jane took Abby's shawl and tucked it around the shivering girl. "She's coming with us."

Abby frowned. Take this painted brothel creature with them?

Jane saw Abby's hesitation and put a protective arm around the other girl's shoulders. "She has to come with us, Abby. She saved me. I owe her everything."

"Come with us? But . . ." It was going to be difficult enough to smuggle Jane into the Mason residence, let alone this . . . this person.

"Damaris is the only reason I wasn't raped," Jane said urgently. "She has to come with us, Abby!"

Shocked, Abby stared at the garishly painted girl. *The only reason Jane wasn't raped?* Suddenly she didn't care what Damaris looked like, how much paint she wore, how scandalous her clothing was, what her past was. Whatever she'd done before this moment, she'd saved Jane from rape.

Daisy shifted restlessly. "Goin' to stand around all night talkin'?"

It jolted Abby to her senses. "No, of course not. Here, Damaris." She unfastened her own cloak and wrapped the shivering girl in it. She tugged the hood up to conceal her face and hair.

Abby glanced down at Damaris's narrow feet, pale against the dark mud of the alley. "I don't have another pair of shoes, but here." She passed Damaris her mittens. "Put them on your feet. It's the best I can do."

"Thank you," Damaris said in a soft voice. "I don't mean to be a burden."

The girl's gratitude made Abby ashamed of her earlier hesitation. "You're not a burden," she lied. "You helped my sister and for that I owe you. Besides, I wouldn't want anyone to return to that horrid place." They would manage. Somehow.

She turned to Daisy. "I cannot thank you enough for what

you've done. I have a little money. It's not much, but . . ." She
proffered a small purse.

"I don't want your money!" Daisy stepped back, offended.

"But you risked so much—"

"I didn't do it for money. Anyway, I got me own money.
Now, are you lot goin' or not?"

Abby stepped forward and hugged her. "Thank you, Daisy."
Jane and Damaris hugged and thanked Daisy too; then, with
whispered good-byes, they hurried down the alley.

Almost immediately Abby heard footsteps behind them.
Had they been discovered? She whirled around. It was Daisy,
carrying a small bundle.

"Are they Jane's belongings?"

Daisy clutched the bundle tightly against her chest. "No, it's
me own bits. I'm getting out too."

"You?" Abby exclaimed. "But why?"

"Mort'll flay me alive when he finds out what I did." She
must have noticed Abby's hastily concealed dismay, because
she added proudly, "Don't worry about me, miss; I can look
after meself. Now hurry! They'll be out lookin' for them girls
any minute now. Valuable property, they are."

Slip-sliding as fast as they could down the alley, the girls
broke into a run as soon as they reached the street. They turned
down the first corner, ran several blocks, turned another corner
and kept running. When they had no more breath, they collapsed, panting, against some railings bordering a quiet garden.

A minute passed . . . two. . . . The only sound was their
labored breathing. They watched the way they'd come, ready
to flee at the first sign of any movement.

But no one came. Nobody was following them. They'd
escaped.

"Right, I'll be off then," Daisy said gruffly when they'd
caught their breath. "Good luck to you."

But Abby couldn't let her go like that.. "Where will you go?
Do you have family in London?"

"Nah, I'm a foundling." She shrugged. "But don't worry;
I'll find somewhere." She went to push past them but Abby
caught her by the sleeve.

"It's my fault you're in this situation—"

"Nah, I was going to leave anyway." Daisy pulled her arm out of Abby's grip.

"Abby!" Jane turned pleading eyes on her sister, but Abby didn't need any prompting. If she could take a painted prostitute under her wing, she certainly wasn't going to let this small heroine stump gallantly off into the night, alone and friendless. And bruised.

She took Daisy's hand in a firm grip. "You're coming with us, Daisy, for tonight at least. No, don't argue. After all you've done for us there's no way in the world I'm going to let you wander off in the dark with nowhere to go. Now come along; let's get Jane and Damaris into the warmth."

Chapter Two

*"A young woman of inferior birth, of no importance in the
world, and wholly unallied to the family!"*

—JANE AUSTEN, PRIDE AND PREJUDICE

"Wait here until I can let you in." Shivering, the girls
waited next to the front entrance of the Mason house
while Abby entered through the servants' entrance down the
side steps.

The other servants had gone to bed; the butler was just lock-
ing up for the night. He gave her a curious look as she came in
but all he said was, "Just in time."

While he was still occupied, Abby sped to open the front
door. The three girls slipped quietly inside and hurried up the
stairs to Abby's bedchamber. When Abby shut the door behind
them there was a moment of complete silence. Then . . .

"We did it!" Jane exclaimed, hugging Damaris, who was
half laughing, half crying in reaction.

"Softly, softly!" Abby cautioned them, hugging, laughing
and weeping a little herself. "We mustn't let anyone hear us."

Jane hugged Abby again, then sat on Abby's bed with a
thump, as if her legs had collapsed. "We're safe, Damaris," she
whispered. "Safe!"

"I know. I can hardly believe it," Damaris whispered back.
"I keep thinking that any minute someone's going to throw
open that door and it'll be Mort come to fetch us back." She
glanced at the door and shivered.

"I told you my sister would help us."

"Yes, without her and Daisy . . . Thank you both," Damaris whispered fervently.

"Oh, Daisy, you were so brave!" Jane leaped up to embrace Daisy again.

Daisy squirmed and protested and wriggled out of the hug as soon as she could.

Abby had a thousand questions, but the girls needed a bath and something to eat. A proper bath wasn't possible, not at this hour, not for a governess, and not without raising a lot of unwelcome curiosity downstairs. But warm water in which to wash—and bathe their chilled and dirty feet—that she could manage.

She fetched towels and a kettle of steaming hot water from the nursery.

"Give 'em here, miss," said Daisy, relieving her of her burden. "A wash is just what the doctor ordered. Them two is frozen."

"No wonder, with the little they had to wear! And, Daisy, please call me Abby."

"Is there anything to eat?" Jane asked. "I'm starving."

Even as Jane spoke, Abby's own stomach rumbled, and realized she hadn't eaten since the apple she'd had for lunch. "I'll see what I can get."

All was quiet downstairs. Abby crept to the kitchen. In the pantry she cut half a dozen slices of bread and a large chunk of Wensleydale cheese—Jane's favorite. She filled a large cup with fresh milk, took a handful of ginger nuts from the biscuit tin and slipped two oranges into her pockets.

A large meat pie, freshly baked, still warm and untouched, sat on a shelf in the larder. She cut a generous slice. There would be hell to pay in the morning, but Abby didn't care. The pastry was light and flaky and the filling oozed out a little, fragrant and delicious. Her stomach rumbled again.

"Is that all?"

Abby whirled around. Blake, the butler, stood there.

"I . . . I'm hungry," Abby said with a defiant air. Servants were not allowed to eat outside mealtimes.

The butler sniffed. "Give it here." He took the knife from

Abby's resistless grasp, sliced a much larger chunk of pie—fully one-third of it—and slid it onto the plate. "Might as well be hanged for a sheep as a lamb."

Abby gave him a puzzled look.

He quirked an eyebrow. "Your sister won't thank you if the two of you have to share that mingy little slice."

"My sis—" Abby gasped. "How did you know?"

He snorted. "I heard the Masons refuse to let her stay. Heard you open the front door after you came in tonight, and put two and two together. How many years is it since you've seen your sister?"

"Six."

"Then it warrants a little celebration." He placed a bottle of wine and two glasses on the tray. "Be careful; the cork is only lightly replaced."

He saw Abby's amazement and winked. "Old skinflint docked your wages a full day, didn't he? So take it in kind."

"It's very good of you, Mr. Blake. Thank you," Abby whispered, a little overwhelmed by the unexpected kindness. She carried the tray upstairs, feeling a little guilty.

What would he think if he knew that as well as her sister, she'd smuggled in two complete strangers? And that all three of them had come directly from a brothel?

By the time she returned, the girls had washed and changed into Abby's warm flannel nightgowns. "You don't mind us borrowing your things, do you, Abby?" Jane asked.

"Of course not, silly. Now, here's supper." She set down the tray in front of the fire and spread the food out on the cloth, like a picnic.

The girls fell on the feast with delight.

"They wouldn't let us eat yesterday or today," Jane explained between mouthfuls of pie.

"Why ever not?"

Jane and Damaris exchanged glances, then laughed. "Damaris made me sick."

"What? Why?" Abby glanced at Damaris. With her face freshly scrubbed and her shiny dark hair hanging loose down her back, Damaris looked as young and innocent as her sister. And perhaps she was. If Jane could be stolen away, drugged . . .

Abby felt ashamed of her earlier prejudice.

"It's how she saved me, Abby. She made this nasty-tasting tea and soon I felt terrible, and when they took me down for the auction I—"

"Auction?"

"Yes, for my first time. Men will pay a lot for a virgin, apparently, so they hold an auction," Jane said matter-of-factly.

Sick outrage filled Abby's throat. "What happened?"

Jane shuddered. "It was horrible—all these men staring, and me with hardly anything on—they just let me have a length of gauze, like some Greek statue—but suddenly the stuff Damaris gave me worked and I threw up—all over the men standing in front." She chuckled. "The starers. I was feeling too sick to notice, really, but they were furious. And so was Mort. He gave Damaris a whipping—"

"It wasn't too bad," Damaris assured her quickly. "He didn't want to mark my skin."

Abby swallowed. She'd so misjudged this girl.

"—and they took me away and put the auction off for another night." Jane started shivering again, but it wasn't the cold.

"Tonight," Daisy said into the silence. "In about an hour."

"So that was why . . . Oh, thank you!" Abby hugged the little maid again. "I cannot thank you enough, Daisy."

Daisy blushed and muttered an embarrassed, "Weren't nuffin'."

"No, you're a heroine!" Abby insisted. "You saved Jane and Damaris at the expense of your own job."

Daisy snorted. "I was leaving anyway. I hate what that place has become. When Mrs. B ran the brothel it was a happy place—nobody doing nothing they didn't want to, and all the girls there of their own free will. Nobody was ever drugged or locked up, and nobody made to whore unless they wanted to. But since Mrs. B retired and her son Mort took over . . ." She shuddered. "He's a bad lot, Mort."

Daisy glanced at Damaris and Jane and added bitterly, "One of the girls told me yesterday that Mort had promised me to one of his gentlemen—one of those as likes to hurt girls. Fancies hisself a little cripple, so he said, and Mort won't take no for an answer." She touched her bruised cheek gingerly. "All those years I worked for Mrs. B, from a little girl, and never once did she try to sell me—and she could've, believe me. She asked me once, and I said no and that was that. But Mort . . . he didn't care."

She cut herself a slice of cheese and said to Abby, "So you don't owe me nothing, miss; I was doing it for meself as much as these two. And you're puttin' me up for the night and fed me, so I reckon we're square."

Abby didn't agree. She owed Daisy much more than that, but right now she wanted to find out about her sister. "Jane, how did you end up there in the first place? You were on your way to Hereford."

"I know, and I have no idea how it happened. I did set out."

"On the stage?"

"No, one of the governors of the Pill—the Pillbury Home for the Daughters of Distressed Gentlewomen," she explained to the others. "That's the place where Abby and I were sent after Mama died. Well, Sir Walter Greevey—he's one of the governors; he's ever so nice—he arranged the placement at the vicarage in Hereford, and he sent a carriage to convey me there. We stopped at an inn to change horses and I had a drink and something to eat and after that . . . I don't remember a thing until I woke up wearing nothing but a chemise—and it wasn't even mine!—and Damaris was in the room with me."

"That's terrible," Abby exclaimed. "What about the coachman—why didn't he stop them? Or was he in on it?"

Jane shook her head. "I don't think so. I think he was drunk. He was drinking from a bottle every time I saw him."

"He deserves to be sacked." Abby turned to Damaris. "Were you kidnapped too?"

She looked away. "My situation was different." She looked uncomfortable.

Abby bit her tongue, annoyed with herself for embarrassing the girl, but Daisy chimed in unexpectedly. "Mort bought her off a ship a couple of days before your sister come in. I saw them bring her in after dark. She was struggling, weren't you, miss?"

"Not that it did me any good," Damaris murmured.

"Mort wasn't too happy with her," Daisy said. "Sickened the day she arrived. He was worried she'd brought some foreign illness in, but you're a sneaky one, aren't you?" Daisy grinned at Damaris. "You made yourself sick, didn't you? With tea, like Jane said?"

Damaris nodded. "But Mort caught me picking more of the weeds in the backyard and put two and two together. He had Jane and me stripped and locked up together, and given no food, only water." She glanced at Abby. "I was due to appear downstairs tonight too. That's why I was all painted up. The golden-haired virgin and the Chinese whore."

"Chinese? You're not Chinese," Abby said.

"No, but I'd just arrived from China," Damaris explained. "My parents were missionaries there. They died," she added, anticipating Abby's next question.

"And you were forced into a brothel? It's . . . it's iniquitous!" Abby said fiercely. "We must inform Bow Street first thing in the morning!"

"No!" Three voices spoke at once.

Abby stared. "Of course we must report it, else these atrocious practices will continue."

"No!" Daisy insisted. Jane and Damaris nodded in urgent agreement. "You can't, Abby; you can't."

"Why not? I don't understand." To Abby it seemed unquestionable that they ought to seek help from the authorities, but the others' fear was palpable.

"I told you before, miss," Daisy said. "If you go telling the law about us, we'll be done for. Mort's got spies everywhere—even Bow Street—and the minute he gets a sniff of any of us, he'll send blokes to fetch us back—and after that it won't be pretty."

Jane shuddered. "It's true, Abby. You don't know what kind of man he is."

"I would rather *die* than go back," Damaris added with quiet intensity.

Abby frowned. "But how could he possibly find you? This Mort fellow doesn't know anything about me, and nobody knows of my connection with any of you—"

Daisy said, "Anyone who reports something to Bow Street has to give their name and address, right?"

Abby nodded. She supposed so. She'd never actually reported a crime before.

"We share the same name," Jane said. "And Chantry isn't a common name."

"And then they'll come after us," Daisy finished.

"Who will?"

Daisy shrugged. "Someone. We won't know who. But they'll get us, and they won't be friendly-like." She shuddered. "Better we just disappear, miss, with no ripples." Jane and Damaris nodded in fervent agreement.

Abby looked at them helplessly. It went very much against the grain to do nothing, but she was ignorant of the criminal world. She hadn't experienced what the girls had. And Daisy had grown up in that environment. Abby would be foolish to ignore her advice.

"Very well. I don't like it, but I won't go to Bow Street," she said reluctantly. "But what if I send an anonymous letter?"

Daisy shrugged. "Won't do no good. Mort'll know about it two minutes after it gets there, and by the time anyone gets to the brothel it'll be sweet as pie. But if writin' a letter makes you feel better . . ."

"It will," Abby said.

Exhausted and emotionally drained, they went to bed soon after they'd eaten. Jane shared Abby's bed, as she had when they were children. Daisy and Damaris slept on a trundle bed brought in from the nursery.

The three girls fell asleep in minutes, but Abby lay there, wide-awake. So much to think about. How had Jane ended up in that frightful place? Why had the coachman not reported her disappearance? Why hadn't the vicar reported Jane's non-arrival at the vicarage? Or Mrs. Bodkin at the Pill—surely she would have been informed, so why hadn't she written to Abby? Over and over her mind turned over possibilities, and yet nothing, no explanation came to her.

And now that she had her sister safe, what to do next? Jane

couldn't stay here; that was certain, and yet, Abby didn't want to send her sister away.

She ought to. Her own meager savings wouldn't support the two of them for long. It would be the sensible thing to send Jane back, either to the Pillbury or to the vicarage in Hereford, to take up her position as a companion.

Jane started up from her sleep, whimpering in fright.

"Hush, love, it's all right," Abby soothed.

Jane turned to her, shivering. "Oh, Abby, you *are* here! Thank God. I thought I'd only dreamed you, and that I was still in that place." She wrapped her arms tightly around Abby. "I've missed you so much, big sister."

"I've missed you too, little sister." Her eyes blind with tears, Abby kissed the crown of Jane's head. "You're safe now, love, so go back to sleep." She stroked her sister's hair as she had when Jane was a little girl, until Jane's breathing slowed and she was asleep.

One thing was settled, Abby thought as she finally drifted off to sleep in the wee small hours of the morning: There was no question of sending Jane anywhere; they'd stay together as a family. Somehow, Abby would manage it.

"My sister and her companion and maid were set upon and robbed." Abby stood in the morning room, explaining to Mr. and Mrs. Mason why three strange women had been discovered in her bedchamber. Mrs. Mason had come to Abby's room to demand something and found them.

Jane and Damaris, dressed in Abby's clothes, waited with Daisy in the hallway.

Abby continued. "They'd just arrived in London and with no money, no baggage and nowhere to go; what was I to do?"

"You had no right to bring them into my home," Mr. Mason said. "You know my policy on staff visitors."

"It was an emergency," Abby said calmly. She was skating on thin ice, and her position was on the line, but she refused to apologize. "I will also need to take some time off this morning to see my sister settled. She is not yet eighteen and a stranger to London."

"No, you've just had a half day—and returned from it late," Mr. Mason said in a bored voice, and returned to reading his newspaper.

"Yes, but this situation is both unexpected and urgent. I need at least half a day to make arrangem—"

"No," said Mr. Mason from behind his newspaper. His wife nodded in self-righteous approval.

"I would ask you to reconsider," Abby said quietly. "I've worked for you for four years and have never once asked for anything extra. You must understand this is a family obligation." Abby's time here was over; she knew it, and she wouldn't give them the satisfaction of begging.

But the thought of being jobless and having to support four people on her meager savings terrified her.

"The only family you have any obligation to is mine," Mr. Mason said.

"That is your last word?"

"It is."

"Then I hereby tender my resignation, to take effect immediately."

"What?" Mrs. Mason gasped.

Mr. Mason lowered his paper. "You cannot."

"You've left me no choice," Abby said, amazed at how calm she sounded. "I will leave this morning, as soon as I have packed my things."

"Leave? But what about the children? Who will take care of them?" Mrs. Mason demanded.

"They're your children. You look after them—you might even get to know them, poor little things." Abby turned on her heel and marched from the room.

Behind her Mrs. Mason squawked, "Don't you dare turn your back on me—I'm not finished with you, young woman! Do something, Edwin! I've never in my life been treated to such insolence! Come back here, Miss Chantry!"

Abby kept walking. She would miss the children desperately, but she had no choice.

* * *

"What are we going to do?" The four girls had gathered in the small bedroom they'd rented in a respectable lodging house. It was their first evening as independent women.

"Find a job," Daisy said. "Find a place to live. I can't afford to stay here."

"I think we should stay together," Abby said. She'd given it a lot of thought during the night.

Daisy said in a cautious tone, "What, all of us? Me included?"

"Yes, all of us," Abby said firmly. "Mama used to say, 'A woman without family is so vulnerable,' and she was right. Alone each of us is vulnerable, but together we can be stronger, like a family."

"Four orphans: one family," Damaris said. "I like the sound of that."

"I like it too." Jane held out her hands. "Let us take hands then, and make a vow to become as sisters to one another."

"Sisters? I can't be your sister," Daisy objected.

"Why not?"

"'Cause you're all quality born and I'm just a foundling from the gutters." She hesitated, then added, "I can't even read."

"I'll teach you," Abby and Damaris said at the same time, and laughed.

"Yeah, but—"

"Daisy, darling, if it weren't for you, we wouldn't even be here," Jane pointed out. "So come along and swear."

So, with the heady air of freedom firing their blood like a sweet and potent wine, they vowed to be as sisters to one another, to become a family. They toasted their pact with weak tea and then returned to the question of what they were going to do.

The answer was the same for each of them—get a job, earn a living. The question was how?

Eventually Abby said, "What if you could have whatever you want?"

"Ooh, yes." Jane, who was drooping over the edge of the bed, sat up eagerly. "Abby and I used to play that game when we were children—what we'd want if we could have things exactly as we'd wish," she explained.

Abby smiled. "It doesn't hurt to dream." Dreams had long been Abby's friend.

Jane clasped her hands and thought for a moment. "I want to have a come-out like Mama did—remember the stories, Abby? She'd go to dances and balls and picnics and plays and concerts and . . . and everything. I want that. I want to go to balls and wear pretty dresses and dance with handsome men. And one of them—he'll be tall and handsome and rich, of course—will make it his business to attend all the same balls that I go to, and he'll ask me for the supper dance and the last dance of the evening. . . . And then he'll ask for my hand."

Abby's eyes were misty. "Just like Papa did with Mama," she said softly.

Jane nodded. "Except Papa wasn't rich. I know it's not possible, of course, but that's what I want, Abby—what Mama had. And what do you want?"

Abby smiled. "That's what I want for you too, Jane." And she swore her sister would have it, one way or another.

"No, I mean for you—what do you want? Don't you want the same?"

"Of course I do," Abby said lightly. To not be lonely ever again, to feel loved and wanted . . . To have someone to talk over her worries with, and maybe even to lift the burden of care from her shoulders . . . who wouldn't want that?

And children . . . She ached for children of her own, children she could love as much as she wanted to, children nobody could take from her.

But these days, Abby had few illusions about her marriageability. Laurence had seen to that. She turned to Damaris. "What do you want?"

Damaris didn't even pause to think about it. "I want a home of my own, a place where I belong, truly belong. A small cottage, a cat, a dog, some chickens."

"Don't you want to get married?" Jane asked.

"No man would want me now."

"You don't know that," Jane said. "And anyway, how would

he know? You don't have to tell him. You don't have to tell anyone. It wasn't your fault."

Abby frowned. Damaris was acting as if . . . "I thought you hadn't been . . ."

"No, not at the brothel. But . . ." A blush rose to her cheeks and she looked away and said in a hard little voice, "I'm not a virgin."

Her face in the candlelight glowed, framed by her long dark hair falling straight as rain to her waist. "If I ever gave myself to a man again—and I doubt I ever would—I'd wish to give myself wholly, without reservation, with nothing between us, not even secrets. But that won't happen, so . . ." She shrugged.

There was a long silence. Then Jane turned to Daisy. "And you, Daisy, what's your dream?"

"Me?" Daisy swallowed. "Girls like me don't have no dreams." But a blush slowly rose on her face.

"Yes, you do, Daisy. Go on," Abby prompted her.

"Yes, tell us, Daisy."

"Nah, you'll think it's stupid."

"No, we won't."

Daisy's pale freckled face was almost beet red by now. "Promise you won't laugh?"

"We promise."

Daisy looked down and picked at her fingers, seemingly debating whether to say anything or not. After a moment she climbed off the bed and collected the bundle she'd brought with her from the brothel. "It's why I brought me bits."

She unknotted the outer cloth and onto the bed spilled a tangled glory of ribbons, braids, old lace, sequins, strings of buttons, offcuts of satin and velvet, taffeta and other fabrics—even a few strips of fur.

In a gruff little voice she mumbled, "I want to make dresses, real pretty ones, to me own design. I want to own me own shop, a place where the quality come to buy their clothes." She darted them a quick glance and scowled at her boots. "See, I told you it was stupid."

"It's not stupid at all," Abby said quietly.

Jane nodded. "Yes, it's a lovely dream, Daisy. And those pieces are beautiful."

"Daisy is a talented seamstress," Damaris told them. Daisy looked up in surprise. Damaris went on. "I saw some of the garments she made for the girls in the brothel, and she has an eye for style and something of an original flair." She looked at Daisy. "I'd be happy to work with you to help your dream come true."

"Would you, miss?" Daisy gasped.

"We all will," Jane said warmly. "Won't we, Abby? Abby?"

Abby blinked. "Sorry, I was woolgathering. I was thinking of something," she said slowly. "About our various dreams . . ."

"Tell us," Jane said. She turned to the others. "Abby always has wonderful ideas."

Abby grimaced. "I don't know about wonderful, but I was thinking . . . It's going to be hard to meet handsome gentlemen— of the respectable sort—in London."

In a city the size of London, respectable society, let alone the genteel society that her and Jane's birth should have entitled them to, was far out of their reach. They could promenade at the fashionable hour in the park, and that was about it.

And if any offers from gentlemen were forthcoming, they wouldn't be the respectable type at all.

"What if we went to Bath?" She let the thought sink in a moment. "Anyone can visit the Pump Room—"

"And all sorts of people, from dance instructors to duchesses, go to take the waters there," Jane said.

"And any respectable person with the price of admission can attend the public assemblies," Abby finished. In Bath, among the old and infirm, Jane's youthful beauty and innate sweetness would stand out; she had a much better chance of meeting respectable gentlemen, and receiving a respectable offer.

She looked at Daisy. "But if we are to dazzle handsome gentlemen, we'll need beautiful clothes. And how better to make a splash in Bath society than to have these two beautiful young ladies"—she waved a graceful hand at Jane and Damaris, who bowed graciously back—"dressed by a most exclusive, exquisite and original dressmaker."

"I love it!" Jane exclaimed.

"I can make the clothes, miss; I promise I can," Daisy said breathlessly.

Damaris nodded. "But we'll need money."

"I know," Abby said. "We'll need to work until we earn enough to hire rooms in a fashionable part of Bath. And it'll be easier to find work in London." Besides, Bath society would shun them roundly if Jane or her sister were known to have had anything so vulgar as a job.

"So it's a plan?" she asked.

The others nodded. "We oughta drink to it," Daisy said, and lifted her cup of weak black tea.

They all clinked cups. "To the plan."

Before she went to bed, Abby wrote some letters: to the vicar in Hereford; to Mrs. Bodkin, the matron in charge of the Pill; and to Sir Walter Greevey, whose driver had been so drunk and careless as to allow his passenger to be kidnapped.

Abby didn't mention the brothel—she didn't want any whiff of scandal to attach itself to her sister's name—so she simply wrote to say Jane would be living with her sister in London from now on.

She also asked Mrs. Bodkin for a character reference. The Masons had refused to give one to Abby. It was a devastating blow, for without one, no respectable employer would take her. And with four people to support, Abby's savings would disappear in no time. She gave her return address as the post office at Charing Cross. Their current lodgings were so expensive, they would have to move shortly.

Finally she wrote an anonymous letter to Bow Street, to report the brothel for kidnapping girls and holding them prisoner. Daisy might be right—the letter might do no good—but you never could tell, and Abby had to do *something*.

Chapter Three

*"Her mind was all disorder. The past, present,
future, everything was terrible."*

—JANE AUSTEN, MANSFIELD PARK

Six weeks later

"You can't—it's too risky," Damaris hissed. "What if you're
caught?"

"I don't have a choice," Abby whispered back. "We haven't
a penny, and the doctor won't see her otherwise." She glanced
across to where her sister now tossed and turned on a straw
pallet on the floor of their attic room, her normally bright
golden hair dull in the pale moonlight. Jane lay oblivious. She
was muttering, delirious. On the edge of death.

On another pallet beside her, Daisy slept—it was her turn.
The two girls and Abby had been tending Jane for two days
now, taking it in turns to sleep.

All their bright dreams lay shattered. Work had been harder
to get than they'd thought, food more expensive, rent dearer.
Only Damaris had regular work, painting plates in a pottery.
She'd be paid at the end of the week, but Jane was sick now. . . .

Abby looked out across the rooftops of London, her gaze
returning again and again, like a tongue probing a sore tooth, to
the window on the second floor of the grand house behind them.

The window was open, as it had been every day and night
since they'd moved there.

A seventeenth-century mansion on the Strand. What might it contain? A few small valuable items nobody would miss?

Nobody was in residence—only a skeleton staff. At night, no lights shone in the main part of the house, only in the domestic quarters where the servants were.

That open window was temptation, a taunt, an open invitation.

All evening, ever since the idea had come to her, Abby had found herself mentally plotting the course she could take—down the drainpipe, along the top of the wall, up to the second floor with the aid of another drainpipe, and then it was just a stretch to the open window.

Was it breaking and entering if a window was already open?

She shook her head. Semantics. Whatever she called it, the punishment—if she were caught—was transportation. Or worse.

But if she did nothing . . . She glanced across the room.

"Oh, Papa, forgive me," she whispered. All those years of anger she'd felt toward him for getting himself killed, for leaving it to twelve-year-old Abby to somehow hold the family together, Mama fading before their eyes with some dreadful, wasting illness, and little Jane only six years old.

Now Jane twisted on her pallet, muttering with fever, hovering on the edge of death, and Abby understood now what had driven Papa to do what he did. Desperation.

Because if the risk paid off . . .

She turned back to the window. The first dry night in a week. Clouds scudded by, riding the light breeze. The moon cast shifting shadows. Perfect conditions. Fate beckoning.

Fate twisted on such frighteningly slender threads.

She pulled on the breeches she'd borrowed earlier in the day. It was just a matter of screwing her courage to the sticking place. . . .

"So you're really going to do it?" Damaris whispered.

Abby nodded. "I'll be back soon. Take care of her."

"Good luck, Abby." Damaris returned to Jane's bedside.

With damp palms Abby raised the sloping attic window and climbed out onto the roof. She paused, her gaze sweeping the horizon. Chimney pots, a few still smoking gently, and the sharp angles of rooftops as far as the eye could see. Between the houses she could see the silver gleam of the river, could smell it on the breeze.

How many years since she'd climbed a tree? Surely one didn't forget. She carefully inched along the sloping slate roof until she reached the drainpipe. It was old, and rusty in places. Pray that it would hold.

Clinging to the pipe, she climbed down to the next level, then edged her way along until she reached the place where the back of the building met the side wall. It was just a matter of stepping between the shards of glass embedded in the wall. Lucky her feet were narrow and her balance good.

She had rehearsed this in her mind. She could do it.

Taking a deep breath, she set out across the back wall. The brisk night wind sliced through her thin garments. It was supposed to be summer, but it was cold, so cold. She ignored it. *Steady, stay steady. One foot after the other. Watch out for the glass. Don't look down.*

Pounding heart. Shallow breaths. *Don't think about the height, the broken glass.* Balance was all. It was no different from walking on a line drawn in chalk. Nearly there. Three more steps . . . two . . . and then she was on the other side. Just one small jump to reach the other house now. She jumped, teetered and clung to the wall, her fingernails scrabbling at the stone in desperation. *Steady now. Deep breaths. See, it was easy.* Now one last climb, the pipe that ran up right beside the open window on the second floor.

The sash window was stiff, but she managed to push it up some more. She leaned in, listened, checked. Not a sound. A bedchamber. She could see the heavy hangings of the bed, an ornate wardrobe, a dressing table. No sign of life.

She swung one leg over the sill, heaved and she was in. She crouched a moment in the darkness, waiting for her eyes to adjust to the gloom, breathing deeply until her racing heart slowed.

Now to seek what she had come for. She crept toward the dressing table.

"Have you come to kill me?" The hoarse whisper coming out of the darkness almost stopped Abby's heart. She swung around, scanning the room, braced to flee. Nothing moved, only shadows lit by the faint shimmer of moonlight from the windows where she'd pulled back the curtains. No sign of anyone.

"I said, have you come to kill me?" It came from the bed. Sounding more irritated than frightened.

"No, of course not!" Abby whispered back. She tiptoed closer to the bed, straining her eyes in the darkness. What she'd taken for a bundle of clothes piled on the bed was an old woman lying awkwardly, fallen between her pillows, her bedclothes rumpled in a twist.

"You're a gel. Wearing breeches, but I can still tell you're a gel."

"Yes." Abby waited. If the woman screamed or tried to raise the alarm she'd dive out of the window. It was risky, but better than being hanged or transported.

"You're not here to kill me?"

"No."

"Pity."

Abby blinked. *"Pity?"*

"A dog in my state would be put out of its misery with a bullet." There was a pause. "You don't have a bullet, do you?" Said with an edge of hopefulness.

"No, and even if I did, I wouldn't shoot you." She wouldn't—couldn't shoot anyone.

The old lady sighed. "So you're just here to steal?"

"Y—er—" Abby bit her lip. The bald truth of it made her uncomfortable.

"I doubt there's anything left to make it worth your while."

By now, Abby's eyes had adjusted to the gloom. The old woman was right. The room contained a lot of heavy furniture, thick with dust, and not very much else. No polished silver bibelots or small, valuable ornaments, no strings of jewelry, and just one painting on the wall, a watercolor, fairly amateurish, of a young boy. Nothing that a desperate young woman could slip into a pocket and steal away with. Not even a valuable rug on the floor. No rug at all, only dust.

From the outside this house had looked quite grand, if rather old.

But the place reeked of neglect. Abby wrinkled her nose.

That wasn't all it reeked of. The old woman stank. Clearly she'd been bedridden for some time, and whoever was taking care of her—well, if anyone ought to be shot—

"Could I have some water?"

"Of course." Abby filled a glass from a jug on a side table. The old lady reached for it, a trembling claw of a hand.

"Here, let me help you." Abby slid an arm beneath the old woman's shoulders, raising her so she could drink, holding the glass to her lips. She was all bones and skin, as light and frail as a bird.

She drank thirstily, the whole glassful. "Thank you," she said with a gasp, and subsided weakly. "I needed that."

Abby smoothed the pillows and tugged the bedclothes into a more comfortable arrangement. The old lady watched her from huge sunken eyes that glittered in the faint light.

"Odd sort of burglar you are. Breeches aside."

Abby didn't reply. She refilled the glass and set it on the table next to the bed, moving a tea tray out of the way.

"Beginner, are you?"

Abby said nothing. For an old, sick woman she was very acute.

The tray contained a spoon, a cup and a bowl of something that looked like wallpaper paste, dried and crusted around the rim. She picked it up and sniffed cautiously.

"Gruel." The old woman pulled a face. "Disgusting muck."

It certainly looked and smelled unappetizing. And old.

"How long has it been here?" Abby asked.

"Since this morning. They'll bring more up tomorrow." She sniffed. "I won't eat that either."

No wonder she was so thin and frail. "Who brings the food—your family?"

The old lady gave a snort of mirthless laughter. "Servants. Got to keep me alive, don't they? Otherwise they won't get paid."

"You have servants?" Abby wasn't sure she believed her. What kind of servants would leave their employer in this state?

She tiptoed to the door, opened it and peered out into the corridor. The chill night air hung still and silent, no sign of life. The floor was thick with dust here too. She crept down the corridor and looked into the next room. It smelled musty and unused. The furniture sat shrouded in dusty holland covers.

She checked every room along the corridor until she came to the stairs. All were the same: neglected, dusty, unused.

There couldn't be servants. Nobody had cleaned here in months.

She returned to the old woman's bedchamber. "Is there anything else I can get you before I leave, Mrs. . . ?"

The old lady held out her hand in a courtly gesture. "Davenham, Lady Beatrice Davenham, my dear. How do you do?"

Abby took the old lady's hand, started to introduce herself, "Miss—" and just in time recalled her circumstances. "How do you do. I'm sorry, Lady Beatrice, but I can't tell you my name."

"Perfectly understandable, given your current profession. So, what are you going to do?"

"Do?" For a moment Abby couldn't think what she meant.

"Well, you didn't climb in my window just to bring me a glass of water, did you, Miss Burglar?"

"Oh, that. I don't know." Despair filled her throat. What was she going to do? Jane . . .

"You weren't born to this life. You've the accent of a lady."

Abby bit her lip.

"So why take such a risk? You must be desperate."

Abby shrugged. She wasn't going to admit or explain anything. Lady Beatrice might be physically incapacitated, but she was very sharp. And Abby, even though she hadn't yet stolen a thing, had committed a serious crime.

All for nothing. There was nothing here to take. Sick dread washed over her. If she couldn't get the money for the doctor . . . She had to get back to Jane.

"Lady Beatrice, I have to go now," she whispered, for all the world as if she were taking leave after paying a morning call.

A three a.m. morning call.

She hesitated. "Is there anyone I could contact for you? The doctor, perhaps? How long since he was here?" A doctor would surely come for a titled old lady, even if she had no money. Surely?

Lady Beatrice shrugged thin shoulders. "Weeks? Months? Don't remember."

"What about family? Is there someone I could contact on your behalf?"

"No family left. Just my nephew, Max, in India or the spice islands or some such foreign place."

"I could write to him if you had an address."

She dismissed Max with a wave of her hand. "It wouldn't make any difference. He's been gone for years. He hasn't even written in . . . I don't know how long."

"Friends, then? You must have friends you could call on for help."

Lady Beatrice snorted. "I haven't had a caller in . . . I don't remember . . . months? Everyone's forgotten me." A sliver of pale moonlight caught the gleam of a tear as it slid slowly down the withered cheek. She scrubbed it fiercely away. "But I don't need anyone. I'm all right as I am."

Abby didn't bother to contradict her. It was obvious to both of them that Lady Beatrice was far from all right, but a person's pride was to be respected. "Surely there's someone I could write to."

"There's no one. I'll die soon enough and then I'll be no trouble to anyone." A sigh wheezed out of her. "I'm sorry your visit was in vain, Miss Burglar." She lifted a wizened claw, held it up against the faint light from outside and looked at her fingers as if puzzled. "Don't know where my rings went. You would have been welcome to them."

"Thank you," Abby whispered, patting the old lady's hand. "Now I really must leave. Good-bye, Lady Beatrice, take care."

"Good-bye, my dear, thank you for calling on me." As gracious as if Abby had indeed made a morning call.

Morning. It was almost dawn. Birds were waking, chittering noisily in the half dark. They said people often died just before the dawn. Mama had.

Her throat tight with dread, Abby rapidly made her way down the drainpipe and back across the wall. She raised the attic window and wriggled back inside.

Damaris, wrapped in a shawl against the chill, crouched beside Jane's pallet. Jane was no longer tossing or muttering.

She lay on her pallet, still and silent. As Abby dropped to the floor the other girl rose and turned toward her. Her face was wet with tears.

A fist closed around Abby's heart. "Oh, no . . . Oh, Jane . . ."

"Her fever's broken," Damaris whispered. "She's sleeping. She's going to be all right."

The illness that had come on so rapidly went almost as fast, and by the end of the next day, Jane had woken from a long, healing sleep and was able to sit up and talk and drink a little soup.

Unfortunately Damaris had let slip to Jane and Daisy what Abby had done. Jane was shocked. "Abby! You didn't! You went out to *steal*?"

Abby glanced at Damaris, who mouthed a silent apology. Abby shrugged. "You were so ill, I had to do something."

"You climbed across all them rooftops? Over that wall? In the dark?" Daisy shook her head, half in admiration, half disapproving. "I never would've believed it, miss. I thought you was respectable to the backbone."

Abby flushed. She'd thought so too, until recently. "Respectability is a lot easier when you have money."

"But what if you were caught?" Jane said.

"We had no money, Jane. I had to do *something*."

"Have you forgotten what happened to Papa? What if you'd been *shot*? And all for nothing." She dashed a tear away.

Abby bit her lip. There was no way to explain how desperate she'd felt. Jane had only a hazy memory of her illness, and now, even for Abby, with her sister's eyes bright and clear instead of clouded with fever, that desperation felt almost like a bad dream.

"Promise me you'll never do such a risky thing again," Jane said. "Thank goodness nobody saw you."

Abby dropped her gaze, but not quickly enough.

Jane gasped. "Abby, no! Someone saw you? Who?"

"An old lady—Lady Beatrice Davenham—but it's all right; she won't tell."

"How do you know?" Jane demanded.

"Did she see you climb back in here?" Damaris asked.

"She'll report you," Daisy said. "We'll have to leave this place."

"No, no, truly she won't tell a soul," Abby assured them. "She even offered me her rings, only she didn't have any."

"So she's barmy?" Daisy said hopefully.

"No, quite the opposite, at least she seemed so to me at the time, but the more I think about it, the more I wonder if she might be deluded after all."

She told them about Lady Beatrice. "And I can't tell whether she's living in that big old house alone, ill and poverty-stricken, or whether she really has got servants who are neglecting her dreadfully. Someone gives her gruel, but it's awful and she doesn't eat it. Nobody cleans her room—it's thick with dust—and they certainly don't wash her; she stinks. And if there are servants, they leave her in the dark from dusk until dawn, and her water jug was not even on the bedside table, within reach."

There was a short silence; then Damaris said, "You liked this old lady, didn't you?"

Abby nodded. "There's—I don't know—something gallant about her. You should have seen the way she introduced herself." She glanced at her sister. "It could have been the queen's drawing room, Jane, she was so elegant and assured. But she's desperately unhappy. She asked me to shoot her, to put her out of her misery."

The girls fell silent.

Daisy frowned. "You're not thinking of doin' something stupid again, are you, Miss Abby? I mean, we can't even help ourselves at the moment."

Abby sighed. "I know. Things are desperate enough for us without taking on anyone else's troubles. But I can't stop thinking about her. At least we all have one another; she's alone and ill and bedridden and in desperate trouble."

"You can't go back there," Jane said quickly.

"I can't leave her like that, Jane," Abby said. "I just can't. If you'd seen her, you'd feel the same."

Jane gave her a troubled look. "But what can you do?"

"I don't know yet. I'm going to call on her tomorrow and see what I can find out. Then I'll think of something."

"Nothing illegal?" Daisy warned.

Abby smiled. For a girl with such a shady background, Daisy was remarkably straitlaced. "No, I promise." Once had been nerve-racking enough.

"And what are we going to do?" Damaris said quietly. "It's obvious the plan to go to Bath won't work. We're worse off now than we were six weeks ago."

They fell silent.

Damaris said, "I have no claim on any of you. If I leave—"

"And me," Daisy added. "I'm nothing to any of you either, just—"

"No!" Abby cut her off. "The two of you gave me my sister back in the first place. And since Jane's illness I'm even more determined we must stay together. I don't know what I would have done without you. What if it had been you who caught the fever, Damaris? Or Daisy? And you'd been alone?"

Each girl's face showed she knew what that would have meant.

Abby linked her arms through theirs. "I know things are about as bad as they can be, but please, no matter what, let us stay as a family, as sisters?"

They glanced at one another and nodded. "Sisters."

"But not if you reckon on doing anything against the law," Daisy said firmly. "I ain't never been a thief and I ain't starting now. I don't want to get transported to the other side of the world."

Abby laughed. "Don't worry; there's no danger of that."

Chapter Four

*"What one means one day, you know, one may not mean
the next. Circumstances change, opinions alter."*

—JANE AUSTEN, *NORTHANGER ABBEY*

Malacca, formerly in the Dutch East Indies

"Glaring at it won't make it any more legible." Patrick Flynn sipped his rum punch and added, "Though mebbe you're trying to make it burst into flames, in which case . . ." He gave his friend a sardonic look.

Max, Lord Davenham, took no notice. He scowled at the letter. He threw it down, glared at it again, then snatched it up and held it to the light, trying for the dozenth time to make out the words that had been washed away when some damned fool had let the letter fall into seawater, somewhere on the journey from London. Only half had been dunked, which meant that half the letter was legible and the other half had the words washed away, leaving only blurs of faint lilac, water stains and traces of salt. And because the letter had been folded, the legibility came in strips, with every third sentence petering out into a lilac wash for several lines before commencing again, usually on some new subject.

"It's the first letter I've had in months, dammit! And I can't read a blasted thing."

"If it's business—"

"It isn't."

"Ah." Flynn leaned forward and pushed his friend's glass, so far untouched, toward him.

"Damn, but it's sticky today." The third in the partnership of Flynn & Co. Oriental Trading, Blake Ashton, flopped loosely into a comfortable cane chair, turned it for better access to the sea breeze and signaled a servant to bring him a drink. "Roll on, wet season."

His drink arrived. He drained the glass, ordered another and glanced at the pile of letters in front of Max. "Anything interesting?"

Max growled something unintelligible, picked up the water-stained letter again, held it to the light again and scowled at it for a long moment—again.

Blake Ashton glanced at Flynn and raised an eyebrow.

"From London," Flynn said. "From a *lady*. But someone dropped it in water, and though it's dry now, all the interesting bits have been washed away. Or so I gather." He jerked his head at Max. "He hasn't shared."

Blake's brows rose further. "A lady, eh? You dark horse, Max."

Max tossed the letter on the table with an exclamation of disgust. "Don't be ridiculous. It's not that sort of letter."

"How can you tell?" Flynn murmured provocatively. "Since you can't read most of it." He turned to Blake. "Definitely a lady's hand, and in a *beautiful* shade of lilac."

Blake chuckled. Max slanted Flynn a black look. "She's not that sort of lady."

Flynn's green eyes glinted. He swirled his rum punch. "How do you know? You haven't been home in years. She might be a widow now, and longing for the handsome youth who first captured her heart, or a young lady who's been nursing a *tendre* for you since she was a tender wee thing in pigtails."

"There's nobody like that," Max said brusquely.

Blake gave him a sharp look. "But I thought—"

Max cut him off. He'd let something slip once and Blake had probed about it ever since. But in nine years Max had told nobody the full tale of his devil's bargain, and he didn't intend to start now. "It's from an *old* lady. Some friend of my aunt's."

"Oh." Flynn immediately lost interest. He leaned forward

and pushed the pile of business correspondence toward Max. "So, are we ready to start?"

Max nodded, though his mind was far from easy about that letter. Particularly the line, *I fear they are taking shameless advantage of your . . .*

Your *who*? His aunt? He couldn't tell; it was all blurred. But he could read enough of it to recognize that it was from Lady Beddington, a longtime crony of his aunt's, and who else would Lady Beddington be writing to him about, if not his aunt?

So who was taking shameless advantage of his aunt? And how?

He struggled through the water-stained missive. Other phrases stood out among the blurs: *deeply concerned . . . withdrawn from all society . . .*

Whatever the problem, it had worried Lady Beddington sufficiently to write to Max on the other side of the world.

"Max?" The others were waiting.

Max turned his mind to the business at hand. "First up is the report from our China office."

Twice a year the three of them met in a prearranged location that only they three knew. Shifting the meeting place was a good way to keep an eye on their various bases of operation, scattered throughout East Asia. As always, Max chaired the meetings.

Flynn sprawled in his chair, his green eyes half closed, staring out to sea as if his thoughts were miles away, but Max wasn't deceived. Patrick Flynn had a brain like a razor. It had taken him from the gutters of Dublin to being the owner of his first ship by the time he was twenty-three, but Flynn was no hand with paperwork.

Blake made notes. They were all good with figures—you had to be to succeed in trade—but Blake was something special. Max watched his friend calculate percentages and odds and profit and loss without so much as pausing in the discussion. Amazing.

He'd been at school with Blake, and yet never suspected he had this skill. Of course, Blake had been wilder then. A gambler, even at school, and wildly successful at it too . . . for a time. Everyone thought it was luck. Nobody then had any idea that Blake Ashton had a gift for numbers.

Not until his luck had run out and, in the aftermath, Blake had come out east . . . where Max had found him, sobered him up and put him to work.

And Max? What did he contribute to the partnership? Nothing very special. Mainly connections to people back home with money to invest. And a habit of seeing the bigger picture, taking a long-term strategic view of things. You couldn't help but develop that kind of attitude when your uncle and father had frittered away a fortune that generations of forebears had built.

And of course, Max had brought the three of them together—the four, if you counted their silent partner back in London. It was a winning combination.

In a little over four hours they completed their immediate business and Flynn yawned, stretched and said, "So, Ash, lad, what's the current state of the company?"

Blake made a few notes, checked, then read out a figure that made them all blink. He grinned. "I triple-checked it. It's correct. We've had a good year."

"A bloody good year," Flynn murmured thoughtfully.

They packed away the documents, and Max gave the signal for lunch to be brought out. Servants scurried around setting out platters of fresh, juicy prawns and crab—plain boiled with tangy dip for Blake and Flynn, grilled in their shells and fiery with chili for Max. As well there were skewers of spiced, nutty chicken, dumplings of various kinds, slivers of melt-in-your-mouth duck, a tangy salad of green mango and herbs, golden noodles in a luscious sauce and mounds of fragrant rice.

And champagne, because Max had expected a good result—though not such a spectacular one. And possibly a life-changing one.

They ate on the terrace overlooking the bay. Ignoring the view of the brilliant blue sea and the ships dancing at anchor, they ate more or less in silence, dividing their attention between the food and the extraordinary result of the meeting.

The company was more solidly grounded than ever, and there was profit to spare. Huge profit. Last year he'd paid off the last of the debts. All that was left to pay was the interest. And the pound of flesh.

He'd been given ten years. He'd done it in nine.

Time for major decisions.

But though he was elated at the company report, and was enjoying the food and champagne, Max's mind kept drifting back to that letter and what it had said about his aunt. Or what he thought it might have said.

Deeply concerned . . .

She was his only close relative—he didn't count the mother he hadn't seen since he was ten. She was dead now anyway. His aunt had more or less brought him up, and she was getting on now. What was she? Seventy? Older? She never would tell him her age.

He could almost hear her say it: "If men have the impertinence to ask, serves them right if they get lies in return."

Max had been gone a long time. Years. And if his only relative was his aunt, all his aunt had was Max.

And Lady Beddington was worried enough about her to write to him.

His aunt had had a fall last . . . Good Lord, was it almost a year ago already? She'd broken her wrist, and since then her letters had been dictated to a servant. That hadn't worried him at the time. Accidents happened.

Recently, though . . . Her last few letters had been odd. A bit repetitious. More formal than usual. Nothing he could put his finger on. But now . . .

"Ah, that was a grand meal," Flynn said, pushing away his plate. He burped and gave a sigh of contentment. "Too many of those little dumpling thingummies."

Suddenly Max realized what had disturbed him about his aunt's last few letters. They were too bland, too polite. His aunt was *never* polite. Not the burp-after-a-meal kind of impoliteness—her conversation was pithy and irreverent, full of entertaining gossip and scathing commentary.

Her last letter was so bland as to be dull, and she'd even finished with advice for him to take care of himself and to "wrap up warmly."

Wrap up warmly? She never fussed like that. Even when he was a scrubby schoolboy.

The aunt he knew would die before writing that kind of drivel.

Deeply concerned . . .

"So," Flynn said, "where do we go from here?"

He meant we-the-company, but, "I'm going to London," Max said abruptly. It was a full year before he'd promised to return—a year less of the freedom he'd cherished in the last nine years—but it couldn't be helped.

Flynn's eyes gleamed with interest, but he said nothing.

"London," Blake exclaimed. "Whatever for?"

"I'm worried about my aunt."

"Why, what's the matter?"

"Her letters are too polite." Max scanned the ships in the bay. Five of the eight currently at anchor belonged to them. "Any of them bound for London?"

Blake nodded. "*Devon Lass* is. And *Dublin Lass* too, but she's slower."

"A grand little lady all the same," Flynn said. *Dublin Lass* was his first ship and he was very fond of her.

"*Devon Lass* it is, then," Max said. "Sailing on tonight's tide?"

Blake nodded, his expression bemused. "Yes, but . . . you're sailing t*onight*? Because your aunt's letter is *too polite*?" He glanced at the empty bottle of champagne. "Are you sure that wine isn't tainted?" Blake hadn't touched alcohol in years.

Max gave him a dry look. "You've met my aunt, Blake. Would you describe her as polite?"

"Hardly." He glanced at Flynn. "Full of piss and vinegar, Lady Beatrice. Burn your ears with some of the things she comes out with. Marvelous old bird."

Max said, "So, her last letter was full of polite nothings and ended with the advice to wrap up warm! *Wrap up warm?*"

Blake frowned. "Don't she realize it's the tropics?"

"She didn't dictate that letter. Something's wrong! So I'm going to London to find out what it is. And fix it."

"I'm of a mind to come with you," Flynn said.

"You?" Max stared at him in amazement. "Good God, why?"

"I've been thinking for some time that once the company was doing all right, I'd like to settle down before I was thirty." He spread his hands. "The company is doing grand. And I'll be thirty next July."

Blake's mouth dropped open. "You mean *marriage*?"

Flynn gave him a tranquil smile. "I do."

Max asked casually, "To an English girl?"

Flynn gave him a sidelong glance. "And why not?"

Max shrugged. "I just thought . . . you being Irish . . ."

"There's nothing in Ireland for me any longer," Flynn said softly. His whole family had been wiped out by cholera when he was eleven, the others knew. "An English lady will do fine for me. A proper fine lady."

"You might find it difficult," Max said bluntly. "A lot of English aren't fond of the Irish."

"Well, I'll not be marrying any of them, then," Flynn said, unperturbed. "I've got where I am by always goin' for the finest available, and I don't see why I should change my ways in finding a bride. I want the finest lady available. An English lass. A blue blood. With a title—or a daddy with a title."

He glanced at the others. "You don't think I can afford it? Didn't young Ashton just tell us all we're rich?"

Max shrugged. "You have the blunt, I know. But English aristocrats don't take kindly to rich men of no particular background sniffing around their delicately raised daughters—let alone rich Irishmen."

"You don't think I'm good enough, is that what you're saying?" An edge of belligerence entered the conversation.

Max snorted. "Don't be stupid. If I had a sister I'd give her to you gladly. You'd make any woman—any lady—a fine husband, I know. But *I* know what kind of man you are. Nobody in England does. How do you imagine you're going to meet any fine ladies?"

Flynn chuckled. "I'm thinking I'd get my good friend Lord Davenham to introduce me around. And then there's our silent partner—what's his name?—the Honorable Freddy Hyphen-Hyphen?"

"Monkton-Coombes." Another friend of Max's from school.

"Aye, a fine gentleman of ancient family, you said. So that's two of you. Of course, you might need to give me the odd tip on how to go on like a gentleman—dress and such."

Max regarded his friend with what he hoped was a grave expression. Flynn was a quite good-looking fellow when he was cleaned up. Currently, however, he looked more like a pirate than a gentleman, even down to the gold ring in his ear. His thick black hair hung down over his eyes, and black bristles covered his chin, making his admittedly good teeth gleam when he smiled, a crooked slash of white.

Flynn's dress would never be described as restrained elegance; he favored the flamboyant over . . . well, over anything, Max reflected. Today Flynn wore tight black breeches, a red muslin shirt with flowing sleeves and an emerald green waistcoat embroidered with striking red-and-black designs. Somewhere in his sea trunk Flynn even kept a purple coat, which he produced for special occasions.

"Freddy will be delighted to introduce you to his tailor, I'm sure," Max agreed smoothly.

Blake choked, and tried to turn it into a cough. Blake had gone to school with Freddy too.

"Excellent." Flynn turned to Blake. "And what about you, Ash? Want to make a threesome of it? Come to England with us, find out why Max's aunt has turned all polite on him—apparently 'tis a terrible affliction, politeness in aunts—and help find me a fine lady bride?"

"Thank you, but I won't ever return to England," Ash said, turning abruptly away. "There's nothing for me there."

Max frowned. "But your mother and sist—"

Blake cut him off with a freezing look. "There's *nothing* for me in England."

Flynn said, as if changing the subject, "Right, then, all we need to do now is decide where we're meeting next and when. So since you and I will be in England, Max, not to mention our fourth partner, the Honorable Hyphen-Hyphen, let's make it London in October."

"Dammit, I just said—"

Max cut Blake off. "The motion on the table is that we meet in London next October. All in favor?"

"Aye," Flynn said.

"Aye," Max said. He glanced at Blake, who hadn't voted. "Carried by a majority of two. London in October it is."

"Daisy, do you have a veil I could borrow?" Abby asked later the next afternoon. She'd worked all morning at a nearby tavern, scrubbing in the scullery, and was due back again in the evening, but in the meantime she had an hour or two to herself.

Daisy picked through her collection and pulled out a length of charcoal gray gauze from her bundle of bits. "Will this do?"

"Perfect. It's even better than black, for it matches my dress." Abby had changed out of the clothes she wore at the tavern and donned a simple gray woolen dress with a three-quarter-length darker gray coat. It was very plain and governessy, but it was the best she had.

She swathed the gray gauze lightly around her hat, allowing it to drape down at the front, and, once she was satisfied, pinned it in place. She put the hat on and turned to Daisy. "Does it look all right?"

Daisy nodded. "Where you going?"

"I'm going to pay a call on that old lady I met the other night."

Daisy gave her a narrow look. "Going in through the front door, I hope."

Abby laughed. "Yes, all perfectly respectable, I promise." She picked up a note she'd written earlier and tucked it into her reticule.

On her way back from the tavern she'd detoured to stroll past Lady Beatrice's house. She'd bent down beside the railings separating the property from the footpath, near the steps leading down to the servants' region, and fiddled with her shoe as if something were wrong with it.

She couldn't quite see into the house, but it was a pleasant day and a window had been opened to let in fresh air. She heard people talking—a burst of laughter—and there was something cooking, something delicious—roast beef, if she wasn't mistaken. She blissfully inhaled the aroma. How long since she'd eaten roast beef? Any kind of beef. Her stomach rumbled. Too long.

Footsteps sounded behind her and Abby walked on. The old lady wasn't alone in that house; there were servants—at least three from the voices she'd heard—and if they were cooking roast beef in the middle of a weekday, they weren't short of money.

Now, dressed in her respectable best, and veiled like a widow in mourning, Abby made a second reconnaissance.

She marched up the front steps of Lady Beatrice's house and rang the doorbell. She could hear it jangling in the hall. A moment later the door opened.

A butler scrutinized her with languid indifference. His formal black coat strained across a well-rounded stomach. Flesh bulged over his tight, slightly grubby white collar. His hair was oily and combed over a thinning scalp. His face was flushed, his eyes were red rimmed and his large-pored nose glowed.

A drinker, Abby thought, and going steadily to seed. She lifted her chin and waited.

"Yes, madam? How can I help you?" He addressed a point above her head and slightly to the right, giving Abby the impression that she was perhaps three levels above a cockroach in importance.

"I am here to see Lady Beatrice," she announced crisply.

Her accent was better than her clothes. His beady, bloodshot eyes tried to pierce the veil. He bowed halfheartedly. "Lady Beatrice is not available."

"Please check with Lady Beatrice before you make such a statement. She will want to see me."

"Lady Beatrice is not at home." He made to shut the door.

Abby put her foot in the doorway. "Then when she returns will you please give her this note?" The butler made no move to take it. He smelled of unwashed linen. And unwashed butler.

Abby changed her approach, adding in a confiding manner, "I am an old friend, in London for only a day or two, and I would so like to catch up with her. She hasn't written in ages, and I'm sorry to say, after my late husband fell ill, I didn't do as much as I should have in keeping in touch with all my friends. But Lady Beatrice will be glad to know I am thinking of her." She handed him the note.

He took it disdainfully between a gloved thumb and finger,

a soiled glove that had once been white. "When her ladyship returns, I shall see that she gets it. Though I cannot say when that might be." He bowed again, then shut the door.

"I'm going back to that house over the back," Abby said, donning the breeches she'd worn two nights before.

"No! You mustn't! It's too dangerous!" Jane exclaimed.

"I have to, Jane. I'm sure that old lady is in desperate trouble." Abby explained how she'd tried to pay a call on Lady Beatrice but the butler had denied she was home. "And she might not want callers while she's ill, that's true, but I cannot feel easy about it. There are three or four servants there, possibly more, eating their heads off at her expense and leaving her in the most dreadful state."

"But what can you do about it?"

"I left a note with the butler to give her."

"Why?"

"Just to see if she gets it. She told me all her friends had forgotten her, and that nobody calls, but after the way that horrid butler behaved, I don't believe nobody calls. I think he sends everyone away. So I'm going over there now to check whether she received my note." Abby picked up a jar. "And since there is some of Damaris's delicious soup left over, I thought I'd take some. Even cold, it has to be better than that horrid gruel."

"I'll heat it," Damaris said quietly. Thanks to her ingenuity, the girls had a small fire, quite illegal in the run-down tenement house. It was just an old ceramic plant pot, cracked and discarded, that she'd brought home one day. As the others watched, she'd built a tiny fire in it, using a few chips of wood and some paper. It was a tiny, portable fireplace, and the way Damaris cooked—rapidly, in one pot with everything shredded—it was enough to keep them fed, if not warm.

Jane clutched Abby's arm with worried fingers. "What if you get caught this time?"

"There's no danger, truly. I did it the other night without any problem, and the second time will be easier." Abby squeezed her sister's hand. "Don't be angry, Jane, dear. If you'd only seen what a desperate plight Lady Beatrice is in . . ."

"But what can you do about it?" Daisy said. "You can't go carrying soup over the rooftops every night."

"I know," Abby agreed. "But once I'm certain of the situation, I can report—"

"No!" Daisy, Damaris and Jane exclaimed in unison. "Not Bow Street!"

"No, not Bow Street, I already promised you I wouldn't go there." She took the jar of newly warmed soup that Damaris handed her. "But I have to do something, so I'll take her this soup tonight and see whether she received my note or not."

"And if she didn't? What can you do about it?"

Abby shrugged. "I don't know, but there must be someone— some friend or distant relative we can contact on her behalf. She says she has a nephew in India or somewhere, but there must be someone less distant and more useful."

Jane gave her an unhappy look.

Abby shrugged. "Do you have any better idea?"

"No, but you will take care, Abby, won't you?"

"Of course I will." She gave Jane a quick hug. "And I'll be back in a trice."

"Back again, Miss Burglar, are you?" the voice rasped from the dusty shadows of the bed. "Bring a bullet for me this time?"

"No, soup," Abby said.

"Soup?"

"I thought it might make a nice change from gruel."

Lady Beatrice snorted. "Wouldn't be hard."

The supper tray sat in the same place on the dresser. The bowl of gruel, as before, was untouched, congealed and unappetizing. Its surface was crusted and dry. A spoon and cup sat beside the bowl of gruel, unused.

Did nobody care whether the old lady ate or not?

Abby unwrapped the jar of soup and set it on the bedside table. "It's not very hot, I'm afraid, but it's quite tasty. We had it for supper."

"We? Who are 'we'?"

"My sisters and I."

"Sisters? Tell me about them."

"Let me help you to sit up." Abby slid an arm under the old lady's shoulders and slipped a couple of pillows behind her back. "There, that's better."

"Matter of opinion," Lady Beatrice grumbled.

"How long have you been here—in bed, I mean?"

"Weeks. Months. I don't know; what does it matter?" the old lady said pettishly.

Abby unstoppered the jar and poured some soup into the cup. Lady Beatrice looked at it with suspicion. "What's in it?"

"Vegetables, mainly." They couldn't afford meat. "Damaris made it. It's delicious and nourishing and it will do you good."

"Damaris? Is she your cook?" The old lady's hand was shaking violently.

"No, my sister." Abby held the cup to the woman's mouth. "She's a friend really, but we've sworn to be sisters."

"I don't like vegetables." Lady Beatrice pressed her lips together like a child.

Abby drew the cup back thoughtfully. "Perhaps Jane was right."

"Jane? Jane who?"

"My sister—my real sister. She said I shouldn't risk my neck to bring soup to a stranger."

"Stranger? I'm not a stranger—we were introduced last night. At least I was," the old lady added pointedly. "And I'm not the one who has pretend sisters."

"Then drink the soup and I'll tell you my name—my real name—and how Damaris became Jane's and my sister." Not for nothing had Abby been a governess for the last six years.

The old lady gave her a sour look and, with every evidence of reluctance, took a mouthful. She rolled it cautiously around in her mouth, then swallowed. "Hmph. Not bad for vegetables. Now, your name, miss?"

"It's Abigail Chantry." Abby fed the old lady another mouthful.

"Of the Hertfordshire Chantrys?"

"I don't know much about Papa's side of the family," Abby said evasively, and continued feeding the old lady.

"Where is your father? Does he know his daughter gads about in men's breeches at night and breaks into houses?"

"Papa's dead. He died when I was twelve. Mama died the following year," she added, anticipating the next question. "Jane and I are alone in the world."

"Except for this Damaris person who makes soup. The pretend sister."

"Yes, except for Damaris and Daisy, who are both our sisters now. They are orphans too."

As she fed the old lady the soup, Abby answered her questions, telling her a little bit about each of them—though not how they all met. "There, that's the last of the soup. Don't you feel better for it?"

"I do, thank you, my dear, but the company was as much a tonic as the soup. I like the sound of those gels. Wouldn't mind meetin' them."

"That brings me to the other reason for my visit. Did you have any callers this afternoon?"

Lady Beatrice said wearily, "I told you: Nobody comes to call anymore."

"Did you not even receive a note?"

"A note? No, of course not. Who would send me a note?"

"I would," Abby said. "I did."

The old lady frowned. "When?"

"This afternoon. I gave it to your butler."

The old lady stared. "To Caudle? My butler, Caudle?"

"Large, self-important fellow with a glowing red nose?"

Lady Beatrice gave a choke of rusty laughter. "That's Caudle." The laughter died from her eyes. "But he didn't give me anything, didn't even mention anyone had called. No one ever calls."

"Does he have instructions to refuse all callers?"

"No, of course not." Lady Beatrice glanced down at herself, seeming to take in the grubby nightgown, the rumpled bedclothes. "I couldn't receive callers in this condition—but with a little warning, I could make myself presentable. . . . And as for a note, I could always accept a note."

"I thought as much," Abby murmured. "That's why I made the call this afternoon, to check. Your butler is the reason you haven't had any visitors. He turns them all away, says you are not at home. And he doesn't deliver your mail to you."

"But why would he do such a thing?"

Abby didn't know why; nor did she care. As far as she was concerned, all of Lady Beatrice's servants gave atrocious service, and it clearly started with the butler. A butler set the tone for a house.

"Who supervises your servants while you are ill?"

Lady Beatrice shook her head.

"Who pays them?"

"Man of affairs. Forgotten his name." She gave a vague wave of her hand. "Little fat fellow with pince-nez. It used to be his father, but his father died."

"Think," Abby urged her. "I cannot keep coming to visit you at night, and you cannot go on much longer as you are."

"Why can't you come back?"

"Because it's dangerous. And because the place we are living in—the house over the back from you—is going to be demolished in a few weeks and we have to move. So think—there must be *someone* I can contact to let them know that your servants are neglectful and you need better care."

There was a long silence.

"Why do you care?"

"I just do, that's all. So think. An address is all I need. Can you remember where he lives, this man of affairs?"

Lady Beatrice prodded her gently. "Seems to me you have plenty to be worried about on your own account without fretting about a stranger."

"You're not a stranger," Abby corrected her with a smile. "We've been introduced, remember?"

Lady Beatrice gave another rusty laugh. "Minx."

"Your man of affairs, the fat fellow with the pince-nez," Abby prompted after another long silence. "Have you thought of his name yet? Or where his office is?"

"No." The old lady gave her a long, thoughtful look. "You could always come and live with me—you and your sister and those two others. Plenty of rooms here."

Abby blinked. "Live with you?" She struggled to take it in.

Lady Beatrice nodded. "Why not? This house is empty."

"But . . ."

Lady Beatrice waved a bony hand. "Pish-tush to your buts,

silly gel. Demmed good idea. You need a home. I've always
wanted daughters." She sighed. "Never was blessed with
children . . ."

"But you don't know anything about us."

The old lady snorted. "Aiming to take advantage of me, are
you?"

Abby gave the old lady a troubled look. "Well, yes, if we
are to come and live here, it would indeed be taking advantage."

Lady Beatrice snorted. "Aiming to do me harm, I should
have said."

"No, of course not." Abby gave the dirty room a scornful
glance. "We'd take a lot better care of you than those servants,
for a start."

"I know it. And this arrangement will suit both our needs.
So will you come?"

"Do you really mean it?" It was the answer to all her prayers.

"Never say anything I don't mean," said Lady Beatrice.

Abby took a deep breath and closed her eyes. She wrestled
with her conscience for a moment, but it was no good; she
couldn't possibly accept this miraculous offer under false pre-
tenses. She sat back down on the bed. "I can't accept your
offer—"

"Nonsense!"

"—without explaining exactly how I met Damaris and
Daisy—and where they and Jane were before I was reunited
with my sister."

"Pshaw! D'you think it makes any difference to me where
they were?"

"I think it will," Abby said.

Lady Beatrice regarded her thoughtfully. "Then if you must,
Miss Burglar, go ahead. Tell me your tale."

The old lady listened carefully as Abby told her the whole
story, from her mother's death onward. Abby left nothing out:
Pillbury Home for the Daughters of Distressed Gentlewomen,
becoming a governess, meeting Daisy in the street, the escape
from the brothel, the plan to go to Bath, the struggle to make
ends meet, and Jane's illness, which had prompted her desperate attempt at burglary.

The old lady peppered her with questions as she went, and

at the end said, "So you and your sister don't have a penny between you, but even so, you took in the cooking girl with the outlandish name—"

"Damaris."

"—and a servant from a brothel?"

"Yes, of course, for without them, Jane would have been lost forever. And we help one another as a real family would. But you see, we're not quite as respectable as you might have imagined—"

Lady Beatrice threw back her head and laughed. "Good gad, how respectable do you think I imagined a gel who climbed in my window to rob me was?" She chuckled again. "Never had much time for respectability anyway. I don't blame you for your situation, and it seems to me you've shown a great deal of courage and loyalty in the face of adversity, and that's far more important to me than any notion of respectability. I'm more than ever convinced you should come and live with me. All of you."

Such generosity. Abby's throat filled with emotion. "Are you sure?"

"Very sure. Now, off you go, Miss Burglar. I'm tired. Come tomorrow. And come as a proper young lady. Don't wear breeches. Use the front door. Bring your sister and those other two gels."

"But your butler—"

Lady Beatrice gave a sleepy chuckle. "If you can't deal with Caudle, you're not the resourceful young lady I think you are."

Chapter Five

*"It isn't what we say or think that
defines us, but what we do."*

—JANE AUSTEN, *SENSE AND SENSIBILITY*

"The carriage will be here at two."

"Carriage? Three shillings to take us around the block? We've only just been paid and you want to spend it on carriages? Squandering money, if you ask me—we could walk there in five minutes," Daisy grumbled. "Not to mention the waste of hiring trunks and bandboxes when we've got nothin' to put in them."

"We need to arrive in style, and being well-connected young ladies, we must have luggage," Abby explained. "And we're not coming from five minutes away; we will have traveled all the way from Cheltenham."

"Cheltenham?" Daisy sniffed. "I've never been out of London in me life."

She'd been carping and grumbling ever since Abby had explained the plan to everyone that morning. It wasn't like Daisy.

"Whatever is the matter with you, Daisy?" said Abby, deciding to take the bull by the horns. "Aren't you happy about this plan? I promise you, Lady Beatrice did invite us. It's not illegal, what we're doing. I know it's not completely honest, but it's only her servants we'll deceive, not Lady Beatrice. And it will give us the chance for a new life, and you know how much we need that."

Daisy hunched a shoulder and went on tacking the sleeve

into the spencer she was sewing for Jane. "It's all right for some, I suppose."

"What's that supposed to mean?"

Daisy glared up at her. "I said I wasn't never going to go back into service, that's what!"

Abby didn't see what she was getting at. "I know."

"So you said before we'd—no, *you'd* have to have a servant in attendance when you arrive at Lady Beatrice's, being proper young ladies and all. Because proper young ladies don't travel without servants."

"Yes. And . . . ?"

"So no guesses at who gets to be the servant!" Daisy snapped. "And how long's that going to last? Forever, that's what! And here am I with no savin's left and havin' spent weeks making all these clothes for you *young ladies*, and now I've got to be a servant again!"

Abby put her arms around the girl. "Oh, Daisy, why didn't you say something sooner?"

Daisy shrugged her off. "I said it now, didn't I?"

"You're not going to be a servant. We vowed to be as sisters, and I meant it."

Daisy gave Abby a skeptical look. "Then who's going to be the servant? One o' you toffs, who can't speak cockney to save your lives?" She snorted.

Abby smiled. "No, Mr. Featherby."

Daisy stared. "Mr. Featherby? Hewitt Featherby? The poncey old bloke who lives on the second floor? Lives with his friend the boxer?"

Abby nodded. "That's the one. He used to be in service—as a butler, I think—so this morning I talked to him and he's agreed to do it."

"Be the servant?"

"Yes. He's a very dignified man and will lend us exactly the air of respectability we need." Mr. Featherby too had worried about what they were doing. Abby had assured him it wasn't illegal, since Lady Beatrice had invited them, but had admitted it would involve a certain level of deception, and that she feared Lady Beatrice's butler would deny them entrance. Mr. Featherby had seemed to think that amusing.

Daisy considered that for a moment. "Then what do I do?"

Abby gave her a puzzled look. "The same as the rest of us, of course. Be one of Lady Beatrice's nieces."

Daisy's brows shot up. "Me? Be the niece of a proper titled lady? I can't do that!"

"Of course you can."

Daisy shook her head. "No one will believe we're sisters, miss."

"They won't if you keep calling me *miss*," Abby told her. "Now stop worrying and finish Jane's sleeve. Lady Beatrice's niece cannot arrive from Cheltenham wearing a spencer with only one sleeve."

Daisy shrugged and returned to her sewing, but Abby could hear her humming a popular tune as she sewed: "We're Bound for Botany Bay." A song about convicts being transported . . .

At quarter to two, just as Abby had finished ticking off the list of things that had to be done, there was a knock on the door. It was Mr. Featherby.

"I've brought my friend William to help," he said. "I presume there is luggage to be carried."

"Oh, thank you, Mr. Featherb—"

"Just call me Featherby, Miss Abby," he said firmly. "Servants are not granted honorifics. And call William, William."

William nodded at Abby. "I'm comin' too," he said, effortlessly hefting the trunk onto his broad shoulders. "For luggage and in case of trouble."

"Oh, there won't—"

"—be any trouble, naturally not," Featherby assured her smoothly. "But for some reason William's mere presence seems to bring out people's cooperative tendencies."

Abby could well believe it. Featherby was a man of medium height, smooth, dapper and smartly dressed if you didn't look too closely at the not-quite-frayed cuffs and the suit, beautifully pressed, but worn and shiny from use. William, a former boxer, was huge, with shoulders as wide as an ax handle, and a thuggish-looking face shaped by years of being battered in the ring, but he had a sweet smile. The two men had helped the girls out several times, and Abby had no hesitation in trusting them.

William winked at her. "No trouble, miss. Them days is

behind me now." He glanced at Featherby. "Did you tell her, Hewitt?"

"Tell me what?"

"There was someone asking about you last night," Featherby said.

Abby frowned. "Asking about me?"

William nodded. "Asked for you by name, he did. Asked me if a Miss Chantry lived here. And did she have a blond sister with her."

Ice trickled down Abby's spine. "And what did you say?"

"I told him, no, of course," William said. "I hope that was right, Miss Abby."

Abby breathed again. "Perfect, thank you, William."

"But I dunno who else he might've asked, miss—not everyone is discreet. And he was offerin' an incentive." And William rubbed his thumb and fingers together, making the universal sign for money.

Abby took a shaky breath. "Well, we'll be gone in a few minutes, and I hope you won't tell anyone where we've gone."

"We wouldn't dream of it," Featherby assured her with a slight bow. The other girls arrived, carrying their things. "Now, Miss Jane, may I relieve you of this? You're still looking a trifle pale and wan. And this, Miss Damaris?" He lifted the covered basket from Jane's arm, took a bandbox from Damaris and followed William downstairs.

"Thank you," Abby said, blinking. Featherby had taken charge, just like a real butler.

Below, the wheels of the carriage sounded on the cobbles.

"Ready?" she said to the others. They nodded. "Then let's go." She could do this; she could.

"What if it goes wrong, Abby?" Jane sat in the corner seat of the chaise, hugging her basket nervously. She'd recovered rapidly from the fever, but still tired very easily, and when she was tired, she tended to become a little emotional.

Abby hugged her and said soothingly, "It won't. Just follow my lead." All day Abby had maintained an outward air of calm and confidence, but now the butterflies in her stomach felt like

birds trying to escape. The news that there was someone looking for them hadn't helped. Could it be that man Mort? And if
so, how had he traced them here?

Jane's basket emitted a long, unhappy yowl. Followed by a
series of mews.

"Oh, Jane, you didn't bring that wretched stray and her kittens, did you? I told you—"

Jane clutched the basket tighter. "I couldn't leave them
behind, Abby! They'll pull down this building any day now,
and what will happen to Puss and the kittens? The kittens are
not yet big enough to fend for themselves."

Damaris added, "And from the situation you described at
Lady Beatrice's, there's bound to be mice in the house, Abby."

Abby sighed. Even as a toddler, Jane had brought home stray
animals. "Very well. The mother cat will probably run off anyway. Cats never do what they're told. Just keep them in that
basket until we find out whether Lady Beatrice likes cats or not."

The chaise turned the corner and rumbled to a halt at the
front of Davenham House. William jumped down from the
back of the chaise and let down the steps; then Featherby
alighted and, with immense dignity, handed Abby and the three
girls down.

Abby took a deep breath and rang the doorbell. After a
moment or two the door opened and the butler stood there. His
chin was greasy, and a spot of gravy quivered on his waistcoat
as if he'd been interrupted in the middle of a meal.

"I wish to see Lady Beatrice Davenham," she said crisply.
Thank goodness she'd worn a veil last time.

He glanced at her, at the girls standing behind her and at
Featherby standing impassively by her side. "And you would
be . . . ?"

"Miss Abigail Chant—Chance," she amended, deciding on
the spot that another name would be safer. Someone was looking for a Miss Chantry and her sister. "I am Lady Beatrice's
niece, and these are my sisters, Miss Jane Chance, Miss Damaris Chance and Miss Daisy Chance." She stepped forward,
removing her gloves, hoping he didn't notice how her hands
were shaking, acting as if being granted entry were a matter
of course.

The butler stood squat and large in the entrance and bowed in an oily manner. "Lady Beatrice is not at home."

"Nonsense! She's expecting us. Now step aside—Caudle, is it not?"

He looked rather taken aback that she knew his name.

"We've come all the way from Cheltenham, and my sisters and I are in need of rest and refreshment."

Caudle swelled up like a toad. "Lady Beatrice made no mention of this to me."

"I cannot help that. The arrangements were made some time ago. No doubt it slipped her mind. She has not been well, I believe." Abby gave him a penetrating look—it was an expression she'd perfected in the schoolroom. "I intend to see to her care myself. Now, if you would be so good as to—"

"Stand aside, please!" Featherby declared, pulling Abby to one side just as William, bearing the trunk on his shoulders, came barreling up the front steps. He headed straight for the butler like a runaway coach at full speed.

Caudle yelped and leaped aside just in time. Before the butler could recover his wits, Featherby had whisked them all into the entry hall of the house.

Shoving a valise, a bandbox and a yowling basket into Caudle's nerveless grasp, Featherby whipped off Damaris's cloak, draped it over the flustered butler's arm and bowed to Abby in a smooth movement. "Miss Abby."

Abby wanted to hug him; instead she seized the moment. "Thank you, Featherby." She hurried toward the stairs, saying over her shoulder, "Caudle, please arrange for the stowing of our luggage and see to some refreshments—my sisters and I are parched. I'll just pop upstairs and let L—Aunt Beatrice know we have arrived."

"Stop!" A large woman in a stained white dress stepped in front of her, arms akimbo. "You can't go up there." Her hair straggled down from beneath a grubby cap in lank, ratty curls.

Sighing inwardly, Abby tried to stare the large woman down. "And who might you be?"

"Mrs. Caudle," the woman replied in a belligerent tone. "Cook and housekeeper of Davenham House. And you can't go up there."

"Why not?"

"Lady Beatrice can't be disturbed. She's ill."

"Then as a dutiful niece, I must go to her at once." Abby tried to dart around the woman.

The cook moved sideways in a swift blocking movement. "She don't want to be seen when she's not at her best."

"Nonsense, I'm her niece, not a guest. I warn you, I don't mean to be denied, so stand aside and let me pass."

"I'm under orders not to let—Ow!" The cook, hopping on one leg, bent to rub her ankle. She glared at Daisy, who had kicked her hard on the ankle.

"Waste of time arguing with her kind," Daisy told Abby. She jerked her head upward. "Go on, then."

Abby raced up the stairs. She hurried to Lady Beatrice's bedchamber, knocked and entered.

The old lady was lying in the bed, almost exactly as Abby had left her the previous night. She struggled to sit up, and Abby helped her.

"So you came after all, Miss Burglar. I wasn't sure you would."

"Yes. I've come. And I hope when you invited me you meant it," Abby said, moving to the window to draw back the curtains and let in some light. "Because I've brought my sister and my friends and have claimed we're all your nieces—even Daisy, who's now terrified of you—and Jane has brought a cat and her three newborn kittens, and I've had an argument with your butler and your cook because they didn't want to let us in or let me come up here, only Daisy kicked your cook, and so here we are."

She dusted off her hands—the curtains were filthy—turned and faced the bed. Lady Beatrice was smiling. "Nieces, you said? That's good, because the whole world knows I have no daughters, but nieces, now, they can spring from all sorts of places."

"I suppose you have plenty of nieces already," Abby said hopefully.

"No, I never had any brothers or sisters, and my husband's only brother had just one son, Max."

"Oh, dear."

Lady Beatrice waved an imperious hand. "Don't worry about it. If I want nieces I'll have 'em."

"And I told the butler our name was Chance."

"Why?"

"Someone came looking for us yesterday. Someone bad, we think, meaning harm to my sister," she said. "I thought a false name might be better just for a while, until we know what's happening, and when I was introducing myself to Caudle, I started to say Chantry, and out popped Chance. I'll tell you all about it—I promise, I did not mean to deceive you, and if you're unhappy, of course we'll leave—but since we've already arrived, shall we sort things out here first?"

"Yes, yes, of course. But why Chance?" Lady Beatrice asked, apparently more interested in her choice of name than that her unknown guests were using a false name.

"It was the only name I could think of that started with the same letters as Chantry. And the instant Chance came to me, I thought, well, we'd been talking about this being our chance to make something of our lives, and also we were taking a chance, so it seemed as if it were meant to be. But if you don't like it—"

"No, I like it. I like it very much. The Chance sisters. My chance for a better life too. Perhaps I should change my name to Chance, as well."

Abby opened her mouth to try to convince Lady Beatrice that it was a bad idea, then noticed the old lady's eyes twinkling. "Oh, you're funning me," she said in relief.

"Do you mind, my dear? It's been so long since I've been so entertained."

"I don't mind at all," Abby said warmly. She glanced around the room. It really was a disgrace. A tray with a bowl of gruel stood in the same place as it had last night. Abby paused and looked again more closely. It was in exactly the same place.

She examined the contents. Gruel, even more dried up than before, and a cup . . . with a film of dried soup in the bottom. Those evil creatures! It was afternoon, but nobody had tended to their mistress since the day before. She clenched her fists. Any faint thought she might have had of working with these servants suddenly went up in flames.

"Lady Beatrice—"

"Aunt Beatrice. You're my niece, remember?"

"I'm afraid I'm going to have to sack your servants. They're not only slovenly, dishonest and neglectful, which I knew already, but they're also mean!"

"I know. Go ahead and sack them, by all means, my dear."

"You don't mind? You're very trusting of a complete stranger who climbed in your window one dark night."

The old lady gave her a shrewd look. "I like you. Besides, I could hardly be any worse off than I was, can I?"

"No, indeed, in fact you'll be a great deal better off!" Abby vowed. "I'll take the very best care of you, as if you were indeed my beloved aunt. We all will."

"I believe you, child. You've already done me a power of good."

Abby was puzzled. "In what way?"

"I was so *bored* before you came along! Now I have gels in breeches climbing through my window at all hours of the night, bringing me soup and conversation and plotting to sack my butler. And gels kicking my cook—I want to meet this Daisy who's terrified of me and yet can kick my cook! She's a sizable grim wench, Mrs. Caudle!—and gels bringing me cats and kittens, and who knows what else? For the first time in . . . oh, forever, I want to see what the next day brings."

Abby looked at her in astonishment, then found herself grinning. "It's going to be an adventure for all of us, isn't it?"

"It is, dear gel, it is," Lady Beatrice said. "And I can't wait. Now fetch me a cap and a shawl so I can look halfway respectable. And my lorgnette, which is in that drawer there. And fix these pillows, so I can sit up straight. I want to meet these new Chance nieces of mine."

"Lady—I mean, Aunt Beatrice wants to m—see you," Abby said when she returned to the entrance hall.

"All of us?" Daisy asked nervously. "Only . . . I could mind the cats."

"All of us, you included, Daisy. The cats can stay down here for the moment." She smiled at Jane. "Yes, I told her. Apparently she likes cats."

She looked over to where the butler and his wife had been joined by a footman and a slatternly-looking maid. They stood in a sullen, hostile huddle, glaring at her balefully. Abby thought of that untouched tray upstairs. "Are there any more servants in this house?"

"No."

"Then I will speak to all of you in half an hour, after my sisters and I have, er, been reunited with our aunt. I have to say, I'm disgusted with the state she's in, and her quarters are filthy!"

"As is this whole house, from what I can see," Damaris interjected. "There are dead leaves on the floor in the hallway, Abby, and cobwebs in every corner!" She pointed.

"There's not enough staff here; that's the prob—" Mrs. Caudle began.

Abby turned on her in a rage. "How *dare* you try to justify yourself to me! I have seen with my own eyes your appalling neglect of your mistress! You've taken advantage of her illness in the most iniquitous way, and you ought to be—" Her gaze took in all four of them. "You all ought to be *flogged* for the way you've treated her. I have no doubt you've cheated her out of money, as well as care, and I'm going to see that you get what you deserve!" She took a deep breath and tried to calm herself. "But first, my sisters are wanted upstairs."

Featherby and William stood quietly to one side of the hall, observing the procedures. "*Mr.* Featherby," Abby said, stressing the honorific deliberately, "may I leave you in charge here?"

He bowed. "Of course, Miss Chance."

"Come, girls," she said, and stalked upstairs.

They followed in shocked silence. When they were out of sight of those below in the hall, Jane whispered, "Abby, I've never seen you so angry."

Abby took a shaky breath and gave Jane a rueful smile. "Wait until you've met Lady Beatrice. You'll understand why."

She knocked again and entered.

"So these are my nieces." Lady Beatrice scrutinized the

girls lined up at the end of her bed. "This is Jane, the one you said was a beauty. Been ill, have you, young lady?" She glanced at Abby. "I thought you might be exaggeratin', but you're right; she is a beauty, even if she's still a mite peaky from the sickness." To Jane, she said, "We'll have all the gentlemen making cakes of themselves over you, missy. Will you enjoy that, eh? Will you?"

"Yes, Lady Beatrice," Jane answered promptly. "It sounds delightful."

The old lady chuckled and turned her attention to Damaris. "And you're the maker of that soup, eh? You're not exactly plain yourself, my gel. The two of you together, one so fair and the other with such lovely dusky locks—oh, the gentlemen'll be making cakes of themselves to be sure! They'll be hard-pressed to choose between you."

"I'm not looking for a husband, ma'am," Damaris said quietly.

Lady Beatrice regarded her thoughtfully. "Don't want to get married?"

Damaris blushed and shook her head.

"P'raps what you need is a good lover; then you might change your mind."

Damaris blushed deeper and Lady Beatrice chuckled. "Oh, this is going to be entertaining. Now, gel." She leveled her lorgnette at Daisy. "You must be Daisy, who kicked my cook. Is that true, young woman—you kicked my cook?"

Daisy's chin came up at that. "Yes, I did," she said defiantly. "And I'd do it again if I had to. That woman's a nasty, greasy old cow!" And then she suddenly recalled she was talking to a titled lady. "Er, your ladyship," she added in a mumble, and curtsied.

Lady Beatrice watched the curtsy with a critical eye. "I'll teach you how to do that properly later. There's a trick to it if you have a bad leg. So, Miss Daisy, do I understand from Abby here that you made these clothes you're all wearing?"

"Yes'm," Daisy muttered.

"Jane, come over here and turn around so I can get a good look," she ordered. Jane did a slow pirouette. Lady Beatrice scrutinized her outfit through her lorgnette.

"Now Damaris." Damaris did the same.

"And Daisy." Daisy, a sullen look on her face, turned in a reluctant circle.

"Hmmm." Lady Beatrice was silent for a moment. Then she said, "The sleeve of that spencer is coming unpicked." She pointed to Jane.

Daisy made an irritated exclamation and hurried over. "I told you it was only tacked in place and to be careful of how you moved," she said, tugging Jane's sleeve straight.

"Sorry, Daisy, dear, I forgot," Jane said.

Daisy looked at Lady Beatrice. "My fault. I didn't have time to finish it."

"Well, if you made all these clothes, my dear, all I can say is, you have talent. You have an eye for style and for what suits a woman." She gave Daisy a narrow look. "And you, missy, have my permission to kick my cook as often as you want. My butler too, if you feel like it." She winked.

Daisy gasped, then grinned sheepishly.

"Would you make something pretty for me?" Lady Beatrice hugged the shawl around her, but it failed to hide her worn and dirty nightclothes. "It's been a long time since I've worn anything half so pretty as those dresses."

"I'd be honored to, your ladyship," Daisy said. She eyed the old lady thoughtfully. "Something with a bit of pink, I reckon."

"But first, I think, a bath," Abby said.

"And a good cleanout of this room as well," Jane added. "Make it all nice for you."

"And I'll make you something tasty to eat," Damaris said. "What about a soft-boiled egg with soldiers?"

"A soft-boiled egg with soldiers?" the old lady repeated in a whisper. "I haven't had that since—" She broke off, her mouth wobbling. Her face crumpled and she scrubbed at her brimming eyes. "Blast the dratted dust in here. It's got into my eyes again."

Chapter Six

"Varnish and gilding hide many stains."

—JANE AUSTEN, MANSFIELD PARK

"Oh, Abby, I see what you mean," Jane exclaimed as they walked downstairs again. "That poor old lady. It's wicked, the condition she's in."

"You were right; she stinks!" Damaris said. "How could anyone let her get into such a state? Especially when they're being paid to look after her. No wonder you said they ought to be flogged."

"They deserve it and worse," muttered Daisy. "You know, even though she stinks like the worst beggar down the docks, you can tell she's still a real lady. And she even swears. I never thought a titled lady would be . . . like that."

"She's nice, isn't she? And funny." Jane hugged Abby. "Oh, you were right about coming here, Abby. I have the best feeling about it."

"I hope there are eggs in that kitchen," Damaris said. "If not, I'm going to the market. Did you see her face when I suggested a boiled egg with soldiers? If that woman tries to stop me getting into the kitchen . . ."

"Don't worry; I'm going to sack her," Abby said. "Lady Beatrice said I could. I'm going to sack them all." She'd never had to sack anyone before, and though she was more than justified, she was not looking forward to it.

But when she got downstairs, there was no sign of the servants.

"They're gone," Featherby said. "I, er, intimated that you'd be calling in the law shortly, and . . ." He swept his hand toward the door. "Gone in an instant. I hope you don't mind, Miss Abby. I thought it best they be gone without fuss."

"No, it's a relief. I confess I was dreading another battle." She tilted her head and looked at him. "Jane mentioned you'd been in service before. What, er—"

"I was a butler to a gentleman," Featherby said with dignity. "But I'm ashamed to say I lost my position because of an addiction to spirituous liquors."

"He don't drink no more," William interjected anxiously. "We both took the pledge more'n a year ago. Not a drop have either of us touched."

Abby took a deep breath. Surely if she had the power to fire servants, she could also hire them. "Mr. Featherby, would you consider—"

"I'd be delighted," he said swiftly. "As long as William can come with me."

Abby beamed up at him. "William would be most welcome. A big strong footman is exactly what this house needs."

"And an army of maidservants," said Jane from behind.

"Would you like me to arrange for the hire of some domestics, Miss Abby?"

Abby hesitated. She would love to have help cleaning this filthy old mansion, but . . . "How can we afford it, Mr. Featherby?"

He snorted. "Those servants weren't short of money, stuffing their faces on roast beef like that, and I'll wager they weren't spending their own brass. There's money here, Miss Abby; trust me—not a lot, perhaps, but enough to hire some girls to get this place cleaned up. My guess is the old lady has some fellow somewhere administering her accounts—somebody paid their wages, and if he can pay them, he can pay us. And some domestics."

"Well, if you think so, that would be wonderful. We'll make a start on things. We're going to give Lady Beatrice a bath first—"

"And clean up her bedchamber," Daisy added.

"Yes," Jane agreed, "we can't wait to hire anyone—she mustn't spend another night like that. It's horrid."

"But before we do anything," Abby said, "it's occurred to me that since she's ill, before we move her or anything, we ought to have her examined by a physician. Only how are we to pay?"

"Oh, nobody expects the aristocracy to pay on the spot," Featherby said. "They send a bill. We won't need to find the money until the end of the month, at the very least. I'll see to a doctor at once."

But when they found Lady Beatrice's former physician, his very superior assistant informed them that the doctor would not be able to come, not until tomorrow at the very soonest. Or perhaps the day after that. He was, he informed them loftily, one of the most sought-after physicians in the land.

Luckily Featherby knew of another physician, a Scotsman who lived not very far away, a man with an excellent reputation who operated a clinic for the poor.

Dr. Findlay came immediately, and when he first clapped eyes on Lady Beatrice, he was inclined to report Abby and her sisters to the authorities. However, once they'd assured him they were as outraged as he at the old lady's condition, that they'd arrived at her home only today, that those responsible had fled and that from now on Abby and her sisters would ensure the best of care for Lady Beatrice, he calmed down.

He pronounced Lady Beatrice extremely run-down and enfeebled due to prolonged and unnecessary bed rest and poor nutrition. Whatever illness had originally laid her low was no longer in evidence, but, Dr. Findlay confided to Abby, it looked as though her ladyship had gone into a decline afterward. She needed building up.

He recommended a nourishing diet, sunshine and, as for her needing quiet and rest—what nonsense! She should, he said firmly, have as much activity and excitement as she could bear.

"Not such a fool as most quacks," Lady Beatrice said when he was gone. She sipped some beef tea that Damaris had made.

"Never heard of a doctor prescribing excitement before. Where'd you find him?"

"Featherby knew of him," Abby explained. "Featherby is your new butler."

"I've got a new butler, have I? That was quick."

"Was that all right? Do you want to interview him?" Abby said, wondering whether she'd overstepped the bounds.

She wearily waved the notion away. "No, no, I have no interest in butlers."

"Well, you should," Abby told her. "Look what a mess you got into because of a bad butler."

Lady Beatrice sniffed. "I didn't hire him. My man of affairs did. Perkins."

"So you remembered his name at last? Good. I shall make a note of it and inform him of the staff changes. Now, drink your tea. We're going to give you a bath."

The old lady sighed. "I'm tired."

"I know," Abby said softly, laying a hand on the old lady's hand. "A great deal has happened today, and you must be feeling exhausted. But you'll feel a lot better after a nice hot bath, I promise you."

Just then there was a knock on the door and Featherby entered, carrying a large hip bath. He was followed by William carrying two large cans of steaming water.

Abby introduced them. They put down their burdens, bowed and waited for their new employer to speak. Featherby's expression was wooden. William looked like an anxious bull mastiff.

Despite her expressed disinterest in butlers, Lady Beatrice gave both men a long, leisurely scrutiny. Abby felt certain the old lady missed nothing about them: not Featherby's beautifully pressed but slightly shiny suit, not the cuffs that were worn, but not quite at the point of being frayed. Nor did she miss the restrained anxiety in both men's posture. Abby hoped she also noticed the immaculate linen, the clean fingernails and the highly polished shoes.

She and the other girls were not the only ones desperately needing a second chance.

"So, you're my new butler, are you?" she said at long last.

Featherby bowed again.

There was a long silence; then she sniffed. "Well, go on then; I suppose that's my bath. Don't want the water getting cold."

William let out the breath he'd been holding. A quiver of emotion passed so swiftly across Featherby's face that if Abby hadn't been looking for it, she would have missed it. He picked up the bath, hesitated, then said in a low, heartfelt voice, "Thank you, Lady Beatrice, you won't regret it; I promise you."

They set up the bath in the small dressing room that adjoined the old lady's bedchamber. William hurried off to fetch more hot water and returned with Daisy, bearing a sponge and towels. "And I found this soap and some bath salts. Smell lovely, they do," she told Lady Beatrice cheerily.

Abby looked at her in surprise. Was Daisy actually volunteering to act the maid?

Daisy must have read her thoughts. "Thought you might need me help," she said in a low voice. "It's going to take two of us to get her in that bath. I don't reckon she can walk without help, do you? Besides," she added with a wink, "I reckon I've seen more naked bodies than you've had hot dinners."

Lady Beatrice could barely stand unaided. She'd been too long bedridden, the doctor had told them, but there was nothing physically wrong with her limbs. They struggled to hold her upright, until, "Here, let me," William said, and gently scooped up the surprised old lady and carried her into the dressing room. Before she could utter a word, he'd set her carefully on a chair and left the room.

"While you're taking your bath, we'll tidy up out here, m'lady, make it nice and comfortable for you," Featherby said, and shut the dressing room door.

Almost immediately thumps and bumping sounds started coming from the other side of the door.

"Whatever are they doing out there?" the old lady muttered.

"Just tidying up," Abby murmured soothingly, as she undid the grimy gray nightgown. She'd been dreading this procedure. It was necessary, but . . . Thank goodness for Daisy, so matter-of-fact and unembarrassed.

They peeled the old lady's soiled garments off her and gently lowered her into the warm water. She was like a shriveled, plucked chicken, so thin and frail Abby was shocked anew.

"This is going to make you feel so good," Daisy murmured, soaping up the sponge. "I'll give you a good scrub from this end and Abby will wash your back and shampoo your hair."

From outside came more bumping noises.

"What the deuce is that? Tidying up? More like a herd of elephants stampedin' around out there," the old lady said irritably, but under Abby's gentle pressure she leaned back in the hot water, closed her eyes and gave herself up to their ministrations.

Abby tried to untangle the strings of long, iron gray hair. It was horribly matted. She glanced at Daisy with dismay.

"Lady Beatrice, I think we're going to have to cut your hair," Abby said.

The eyes flew open. "Cut my hair? I've never cut my hair in my life!"

"Time you tried something new." Daisy was up to her elbows in water, scrubbing unmentionable old-lady parts without turning a hair.

Abby tried to soften the blow. "Short hair is very fashionable at the moment. And it will be so much easier to look after."

"Most ladies can't carry it off," Daisy declared. "Short hair only suits women with good bone structure." She squinted critically at Lady Beatrice. "You got good bones."

Lady Beatrice gave her a shrewd look. "Don't try to butter me up, young woman. I never trust the word of people with their hands on my privates. Just do what you have to do."

Abby fetched some scissors. "I'll just trim it, and later on Jane will cut it properly for you. She's very good at cutting hair."

She snipped and snipped. Matted clumps of wet, gray hair fell to the floor. Lady Beatrice observed them sadly. "I used to have beautiful hair. Russet, like autumn leaves at sunset. My crowning glory as a gel."

"Red, eh? You could go red again if you wanted," said Daisy, scrubbing energetically.

"You mean dye—Ouch! Must you scrub so vigorously,

young woman? I'm not a horse, you know! You mean dye my hair?"

"Dye? Nah. I mean restore your natural color."

Abby grinned to herself. Daisy was showing signs of a born saleswoman. A useful skill in a budding modiste.

"The girls in the . . ." She glanced at Abby. "Some girls I used to know used this stuff; henna, it's called—you can get it down the docks—and it dy—er, brings out the natural red highlights in your hair. Stinks like a sailor's armpit, but the smell don't stay and the color comes up lovely and it makes your hair real soft and shiny. Now, there you are, m'lady, all done now. Just a rinse off and you'll be lovely and clean and smellin' like a rose."

They helped the old lady to stand, and Abby poured the last of the clean water over her. Then they wrapped her in bath towels and sat her on the chair while they dried her and dressed her in a clean nightgown.

Abby combed out her wet hair, fluffed it dry with a towel and then trimmed it a little more, just to neaten it; then she and Daisy trimmed her nails.

"You got nice feet," Daisy commented. "Most old ladies don't. You oughta paint your toenails."

"What am I, a whore?" muttered Lady Beatrice.

Daisy shrugged. "Who'd see?"

Lady Beatrice snorted, but peered critically down, watching Daisy's ministrations.

Finally they were finished. "There, now, don't you feel better?" Abby said.

"I feel tired," Lady Beatrice grumbled, but she patted Abby's hand. "You're good girls, both of you. Not many would have done that for a stranger."

"Stranger?" Daisy had been tidying up the towels. "Who are you calling a stranger? I've had me hands on your privates, remember?"

Lady Beatrice choked, then laughed until the tears ran down her cheeks. "Now, that," she gasped when the laughter had run out, "has done me a power of good. But now I need my bed."

Hoping everything was ready, Abby opened the dressing

room door, peered out and beckoned to William. *Perfect*, she thought, as she glanced around the room.

William came in, carefully picked up Lady Beatrice and carried her to her bed.

Her new butler held the bedclothes ready for her to be put into her bed, and when she was comfortable, he and William stepped back. Featherby's face was properly expressionless, as a butler should be, but William was grinning. Jane and Damaris hovered with expectant smiles. Damaris stood by, holding a covered tray.

The old lady gazed around her, openmouthed. Her bedchamber—her gloomy, grubby prison for the last who-knew-how-many months—had been transformed.

The floor was swept and mopped, the furniture gleamed with beeswax and the bed had been moved into a different part of the room, closer to the window. It was made up with fresh bedclothes, a bright scarlet coverlet and . . . She poked the bed beneath her. "Is this a new mattress?"

"Almost, m'lady," Featherby said. "We found it in an unused bedchamber. The old one will be burned."

Lady Beatrice nodded, too overwhelmed to speak. On her bedside table sat a jug of water, a crystal glass and a blue Chinese vase containing wallflowers and sprays of leaves picked from the overgrown garden. The room smelled of beeswax, fresh linen and the scent of flowers.

The dusty old curtains were gone and replaced with a temporary covering, a pink swathe of fabric pinned across the window. And everywhere, all around the room—on the mantel, on the dressing table, on every available surface—there were candles banishing the coming night, banishing the dark thoughts and bathing the room in a soft, golden glow.

The old lady's face crumpled and her eyes filled. She couldn't speak. All she could do was hold out her hands to Abby, grip her fingers tightly and nod to the others in silent appreciation.

Abby squeezed her hands. "I'm glad you like it," she said softly.

Lady Beatrice nodded helplessly.

"And here's your supper." Damaris came forward, set the tray down and removed the cloth. "Soft-boiled egg and toast soldiers."

Three weeks later . . .

Max Davenham sailed into London on the *Devon Lass* just after dawn. Flynn would be about a month behind him, traveling on the *Dublin Lass*. It was their policy never to have two partners travel on one ship, in case of disaster.

Max made a hearty breakfast at a dockside eating house— eggs, good English bacon, toast, marmalade and coffee, not quite as strong as he preferred, but good enough. He enjoyed most foreign food, but there was something about coming home to a sizzling plateful of good English bacon. For breakfast, nothing else came close.

It was still too early to call on his aunt, but he had no qualms about calling on Perkins, the man of affairs he'd appointed to oversee his aunt's affairs. Perkins's residence was above his office, and the man, dressed in a garishly colored dressing gown, was at his breakfast. His eyes almost popped when Max arrived.

Max didn't know this Perkins. In the past he'd always dealt with Perkins senior, who, he learned, had passed away some five years before.

Max made his condolences, but before he could broach the subject of his aunt, Perkins poured out a torrent of accusation about some woman who'd apparently wormed her way into Lady Beatrice's house and taken control of everything.

Taken advantage, just as the letter had intimated.

"You say she sacked the entire staff?"

"Every last one of them, my lord, from the butler down. Sent them all packing."

"A woman you've never seen before?"

"Yes, my lord."

"Without so much as consulting you?"

"She did, ahem, speak to me about it. But it was *after* the event. She had already sacked the staff." Perkins bristled with indignation. "And when I queried the propriety of her doing that, the lady expressed some, er, rather strong opinions about the quality of staff I'd hired in the first place, and I assure you, my lord, they had the *finest* references."

"Blistered your ears, did she? A harpy, I take it," Max said in an indifferent tone. This Perkins wasn't half the man his father had been. Old Perkins would never have let a woman get the better of him.

"Indeed, my lord, you have the right of it. No woman has ever spoken to me in such a manner. She informed me in the boldest way that she had employed all new staff—"

Max's brows rose. "At her own expense?"

Perkins gave an apologetic wince. "No, she came here to ensure they were paid from the same source as the previous staff, out of Lady Beatrice's allowance. She also made arrangements for payment for herself and her sisters."

"Oh, she did, did she? How much?"

Perkins named a sum that made Max narrow his eyes. "Is that all?" It was quite a modest stipend. He would have expected three, even four times the sum. "What's her game?"

"I cannot say, my lord." Perkins gave a longing look at his plate of congealing eggs.

Max saw the look. He wanted to rub the man's fat face in his blasted eggs. "You say she claims to be some kind of relative of my aunt?"

"Lady Beatrice's niece, yes."

Max snorted. "My aunt has no nieces. I'm her only relative."

"I know that, sir." The man's eager fawning set Max's teeth on edge.

"Yet you did nothing to prevent this impostor from taking over my aunt's home, sacking her staff and replacing them with who knows what kind of servants?"

Perkins swallowed. "She bore a note from Lady Beatrice."

"Show me this note."

Perkins hurried out and returned with the note in a moment or two. Max scrutinized it. It was not the same writing as those other letters—the overly polite ones. This note did look like his aunt's hand, though a little spidery and uncertain. Max had never known his aunt to be uncertain about anything.

"Did you ascertain from my aunt that she wrote this note? And that all was well with her?" Max said with an edge of steel.

Perkins fiddled with his cutlery. "I confess when I called three weeks ago, I was unable to gain entry to the house. That . . . that so-called butler she appointed had the cheek to tell me Lady Beatrice was indisposed and not receiving visitors when I called, and he was supported by a veritable Goliath of a footman. Well, naturally I had no intention of starting a vulgar brangle on her ladyship's doorstep. . . ."

"And this was what—three weeks ago? And you haven't called since?" Max inquired coldly.

Perkins twitched and began to mumble some feeble excuse.

Max cut him off. "So you left my elderly and possibly ill aunt in the hands of what you are certain is an impostor and her hired minions?"

Perkins shifted uncomfortably. "Well, what could I do? I have not the authori—"

"The authority? Damn it, man, in my absence you had *complete* authority over the staff of Davenham House!" Max thumped the table with his fist, making the crockery—and Perkins—jump. "The arrangement I made with this firm was that your father would assist my aunt in all financial and other matters, including the supervision of household matters on her behalf. And since your father's death, his responsibility devolves to you. So how the devil have you let some blasted female impostor march in and assume command of my aunt's affairs?"

"She's a very difficult woman." Perkins gave a helpless shrug that made Max want to thump more than the table.

"I'll just bet she is!" The man was a fool; whether or not he was a rogue was yet to be seen. "Bring me the account books."

Perkins scurried to fetch them. Max tucked them under his arm and rose to leave.

Perkins eyed him with dismay. "But, my lord, I shall need those—"

"Not anymore, you won't," Max said crisply. "My arrangement with this firm is hereby terminated. I shall send my own man around to make all the arrangements. After he's gone over the books in detail."

Ignoring Perkins's babbled pleas and excuses, Max left the house and hailed a cab. He dropped the account books off at the London office of Flynn & Co. Oriental Trading, with a note to Bartlett, the head man there, that he'd be back later.

So much for waiting for a decent hour. He would call on his aunt this very minute. And her so-called niece.

Difficult woman indeed!

Max knew exactly how to handle women—difficult or otherwise. A firm hand, that was all that was needed.

Abby had just left Lady Beatrice's room and was coming down the stairs when she heard the front doorbell jangling in the hall below. A visitor? At this early hour?

She heard Featherby answer.

A deep voice said, "I wish to see Lady Beatrice Davenham." Abby peered over the balcony, but she couldn't make out more than a tall, dark shape in the doorway.

Featherby said something—presumably a denial; it really was too ridiculously early for a morning call—but then the visitor snapped, "No, I don't care to return at a more convenient hour, dammit."

There was the sound of a scuffle, and she ran down the last few steps to the landing in time to see Featherby fall to the floor and a tall, dark-haired stranger push past him and enter the house. Before she could gather her wits, he'd crossed the hallway and was racing up the stairs toward her, taking them two at a time on long, powerful legs.

"Stop!" Abby braced herself, flinging her hands out to bar his way. "You can't come up here."

She fully expected him to shove her roughly aside, as he'd shoved Featherby, but amazingly, he stopped.

She had an impression of a hard, chiseled jaw, a bold nose, a firm, compressed mouth. And he was tall; even standing three steps below her, he was taller than she. Her heart was pounding. What sort of a man would shove his way into a lady's house with so little ceremony? At this hour of the morning?

He was casually dressed in a loose dark blue coat, a white shirt, buff breeches and high black boots. His cravat was carelessly knotted around a strong, tanned throat. Despite the almost civilized clothing, he looked like . . . like some kind of marauder. His jaw was unshaven, rough with dark bristles; his thick, dark hair was unfashionably long and caught back carelessly with a strip of leather. Gray eyes glittered in a tanned face.

A dark Viking—surely no Englishman would have skin that dark, burnished by years under a foreign sun.

"Who's going to stop me?" He moved up one step.

She didn't move. "I am."

The angle of his high, hint-of-Viking cheekbones was underscored by a thin scar on his left cheek. It gleamed pale against his tan. His eyes drifted over her in a leisurely masculine examination that scorched her to her skin even though she was wearing one of her thick gray governess gowns that morning.

A shiver ran down her spine.

He looked like a man who knew exactly who he was, who knew what he wanted and took it, without apology.

"Really? You?" He seemed amused. He moved up another step. A step closer. A step taller.

"Y-yes. Me." Just one step remained between them. Abby braced herself. She was shaking; she refused to let him see how intimidating she found him. She would not retreat. Lady Beatrice was counting on her. William would be here soon—Featherby would have gone to fetch him.

She thought she could see a lurking smile in the gray eyes, as if he were amused that she thought she could stop him. There was brazen masculine challenge there as well as he took another step. Now they were almost touching.

In an instinctive reaction she put her hands on the broad, deep chest to push him back. Her palms tingled. Beneath the fine linen of his shirt, he felt warm and hard and powerful.

The lurking amusement deepened. Pure male arrogance, counting her as no threat at all. He was so close she could see each individual bristle on his unshaven chin. He smelled of the sea, of something dark and masculine.

She pushed. He didn't budge.

"Who *are* you?" she said. She couldn't imagine. What would

such a dangerous-looking—and acting—bandit want with Lady Beatrice?

"Who are *you*?" His voice was deep and smoky dark. It shivered through her.

The contact between them was too unsettling. Abby took a step back to break it. Marshaling her defenses, she said, "How dare you come bursting into my house like—"

"*Your* house?" The gray eyes hardened. "I was under the impression this house belonged to Lady Beatrice Davenham." He took another step. It was like being stalked by a big, dark panther.

Abby held her ground. "I speak for Lady Beatrice. What do you want with her?" Who could he possibly be?

"That's my business." His gray eyes narrowed to a slash of ice in his tanned face. Two slashes. They glittered with hostility.

Abby put up her chin. "No, it's mine." Viking or not, she would not be intimidated.

"Out. Of. My. Way. Madam." Spoken with each word bitten off like an Englishman in a rage, the Viking leashed tight . . . for the moment.

He made to push past her on the stairs, but Abby stepped in front of him again and shoved hard against his chest to keep him back. "I said, stop!"

His gray eyes smoldered down at her. Black brows forked in a frown.

"I demand to know—Eek! What do you think you're—" Powerful hands seized her by the waist. In the same instant William and Featherby emerged from the domestic region. "William! Help!" she shrieked, and heard William start thundering up the stairs.

The Viking's grip tightened. Without warning he lifted her as if she weighed nothing at all, turned and thrust her into the oncoming William's arms.

William caught her and staggered back down a few steps to recover his balance, and in the seconds it took for Abby to untangle herself, the intruder had mounted the remaining stairs and was striding down the passage toward Lady Beatrice's bedchamber.

Abby flew after him.

She reached him just as he threw open the door to Lady Beatrice's bedchamber, entered and stopped stock-still.

Jane and Damaris leaped to their feet and arranged themselves on either side of Lady Beatrice's bed. Daisy, in the act of painting Lady Beatrice's toenails, froze, staring up at the stranger, her mouth agape.

Abby pushed past and placed herself between him and Lady Beatrice. Over her shoulder she said, "I'm sorry, Lady Beatrice; I don't know who—He just burst in—"

William arrived at the door, followed by Featherby, panting.

"Max, my dear, dear boy." Lady Beatrice, beaming, held out her hands to the Viking, just as William and Featherby were about to seize him. "You're home at last."

William and Featherby froze.

"Max?" Abby looked from Lady Beatrice back at the Viking. "Your nephew, Max?" She glanced at the watercolor painting. That sensitive-looking young boy had turned into this big, brutal Viking?

Ignoring her, the Viking bent down, took Lady Beatrice's hands and kissed her gently on the cheek. "Aunt Bea. How are you, my dear?" He spoke quietly, with rough, deep-voiced affection. Abby felt a lump in her throat. The way he spoke to his aunt was quite touching. At the same time she wanted to smash a vase over his head for the fright he'd given her.

Lady Beatrice patted his jaw. "Left your razor in India, dear boy?" Half caress, half reproof.

He straightened and gave her a crooked smile, an oddly appealing slash of white against the darkness of his face, and said without a trace of apology, "My ship just docked and I was anxious to see you."

"Why on earth didn't you simply say you were Lady Beatrice's nephew, Max?" Abby said.

He turned and gave her a hard look, all charm wiped from his face. "Lord Davenham to you. And now leave us. I wish to speak with my aunt—alone."

"But, Max, darling, you haven't been introduced to these lovely girls yet. This is—"

"Later, Aunt Bea," he said curtly.

"Left your manners behind with your razor, Max, dear?" Lady Beatrice said.

"He certainly has; he burst in like a . . . a *Viking*, and gave us all a fright." Abby turned to Lord Davenham. "How was poor Featherby to know who you were when you didn't even give your name? And did you really need to push him down?"

"He tripped," the Viking said, not even bothering to feign regret.

"A *gentleman* would have offered him a card and waited," Abby retorted.

One dark, winged brow rose in a sardonic arch. "Had a lot of experience with gentlemen, have you?"

Abby bared her teeth at him in a smile. "Not as much as I'd like." As he absorbed the implications of that, she added sweetly, "And none at *all* in London so far."

"Vixen," Max said under his breath.

Aunt Beatrice watched the exchange with interest. "Now, now, children, behave. Max, Abby is quite right; you should have given your card to dear Featherby."

Max could have sworn the butler didn't move a muscle: Still he managed to convey to Max a look of deep reproach. With a faint suggestion of smugness.

Impudence. Her servants were in need of a firm hand too.

His aunt snapped her fingers. "Max, pay attention. I want to introduce you to these charmin' gels. This is Miss Abigail Chance—"

He knew who she was, with her wide, innocent eyes and bold, pretty mouth. The woman who'd taken advantage of his aunt.

She was younger than he'd expected from the description Perkins had given. Prettier too, but then harpies came in all shapes and sizes.

Slender as a willow, but stubborn, from the jutting of that chin. Well, he knew that from the way she'd confronted him on the stairs. Stood up to him in a manner that had amused, even charmed him at first. Until he'd realized who she was. In that drab gown he'd taken her for a maidservant or companion, not the manipulative little baggage he knew her to be.

"Miss Chance." Max gave the woman a curt bow. He wanted

to throttle her. She knew it too, for those speaking gray-green eyes sparked with bright challenge as they met his.

One glimpse at Aunt Bea had told him that for all the seeming luxury of her bedchamber, she'd suffered badly. And not for a short time. She'd aged shockingly. Her face was thin and drawn and bore an echo of suffering and malnourishment that he'd seen before, in the beggars of Asia. *The beggars of Asia!* His magnificent, arrogant, beloved aunt! She was a ghost of her former self.

And this pretty, composed young woman with her creamy, smooth skin and her clear gray-green eyes was the cause of it. Miss Chance? Mischance, more like it.

She made him a curtsy, a study in insolence and indifference.

"Her sister, Miss Jane Chance."

A girl just out of the schoolroom, a pretty blonde who blushed and smiled as she curtsied and said her how-do-you-do. Max made her a curt bow. He had no interest in schoolgirls.

"Miss Damaris Chance, another sister."

Max bowed. Miss Damaris curtsied and murmured a greeting but did not meet his gaze. An oval face, dark eyes and long sable hair. A secretive expression. Full sister to the blue-eyed blonde? He doubted it.

"And Miss Daisy Chance." The little one painting his aunt's toenails gold. She had an angular heart-shaped face and the kind of pale skin that had never seen country air.

She bobbed a crooked curtsy and said in a broad Cockney accent, "Pleased to meetcha, m'lord."

Max didn't bother to hide his skepticism. The idea that this girl was a sister to the others was laughable. They at least sounded like ladies, even if they were harpies in disguise. He quirked a brow. *"Sister?"*

"Wrong side of the blanket." Daisy gave him a cheeky look that dared him to deny it.

Mischance put an arm around the girl's shoulders. "But she's still our sister." The blonde and the brunette stepped up too, glaring at him in a united front.

"My nieces, Max," said Aunt Beatrice with a smile that had

a lot in common with the look the little cockney had given him. Lying through her teeth and daring him to deny it.

But why? "Damn it, Aunt Bea—"

"Later, Max," she said airily. "Thank you, girls. My nephew and I have much to catch up on. Featherby, perhaps a cup of tea in half an hour."

Max waited with folded arms as the girls bustled about gathering things—magazines and bits of lace and fur and fabric lay scattered all over the counterpane—and examining him surreptitiously from beneath lowered eyelashes.

No sidelong glances from Mischance. She met his gaze full-on, with brazen confidence. Butter wouldn't melt in that soft little mouth.

She'd be out on her ear by the end of the day, he vowed.

She passed the tray that had been resting on his aunt's knees to the butler. The remains of her breakfast: sweet pastries and hot chocolate. His aunt's usual breakfast. Something that hadn't changed. Some small comfort in that.

Guilt lashed at him. Aunt Bea looked so worn and old. Why hadn't he listened to those twinges of concern earlier?

The butler passed the tray to the footman, who was like no footman Max had ever seen. He looked more like an aging prizefighter—not a successful one either, by the damage done to his face. The kind of hoodlum you wouldn't want to meet down a dark alley. Now working as a lady's footman—his aunt's footman—thanks to Mischance.

A motley crew indeed. What hold did they have over his aunt?

He glanced again at Mischance. No sign now of the little virago who'd challenged him on the stairs. With his aunt she was all soft, pretty words from a soft, pretty mouth. Gentle, ladylike manners hiding a heart as hard as nails.

If he didn't already know she was the kind of woman who'd take advantage of an old lady when she was ill and helpless . . .

Why the hell had his aunt claimed them as her nieces? Was it some kind of blackmail? Or threat?

The women were still fussing over the bits of fabric, sorting them in a manner calculated to annoy him.

"That will do," Max snapped. "Collect it later." He moved to sit on his aunt's bed.

As he did so, five women and a butler shrieked.

"What the—"

Lady Beatrice snatched up a tiny white kitten from the spot where Max had been about to sit and cradled it to her bosom. "Max, you could have killed her."

"Well, how was I to know you'd taken to keeping cats? I thought it was a bit of fur."

"It is—attached to a kitten. This is Snowflake, and over there is his brother, Marmaduke." A small tortoiseshell kitten emerged from under a magazine, regarded Max and yawned extravagantly. "Say how do you do, Max."

Max stared at her. He was not about to talk to a kitten in front of a gaggle of giggling girls. Not that they were giggling yet, but he could tell from their expressions that they weren't far off. He reached out to pat the white ball of fluff, and a small black missile flew out and attached itself to the fabric of his sleeve. It clung determinedly, growling.

"What the—" Max picked his assailant off his sleeve. Black as soot, black as sin, the tiny piece of fluff sat on his palm and stared back at him, undaunted, then clamped needle-sharp teeth down on his thumb.

"Ouch!"

"This is Max," his aunt said. And then, bewilderingly, "Stop it, Max! That's a very bad habit."

Max frowned at her. "I beg your pardon?"

Mischance, repressing—not very successfully—a smile, came forward and removed the kitten from his grasp. "Yes, Max," she said sternly addressing the kitten, face-to-face. "A very bad habit." The kitten gave her nose a few exploratory pats.

"You named that kitten *Max*?" Max said.

"Yes." His aunt beamed up at him.

"Why?" He looked at the small, scruffy kitten, now resting against the soft bosom of a deceitful woman. The creature was too young to know the dangers of that.

"Because he is bold and dashing and handsome, of course," said his aunt.

"Because he is always off adventuring and never where he ought to be," said Miss Abigail Chance at the same time. With a pointed look, damn her cheek. What did she know of his business?

She held the small black kitten against her bosom, caressing it behind the ears. Max the kitten purred blissfully, like a rusty little coffee grinder.

Max the man glowered.

Chapter Seven

"Angry people are not always wise."

—JANE AUSTEN, *PRIDE AND PREJUDICE*

"So that's Lady Beatrice's *dear Max*," Jane said as the girls went downstairs. "I'd imagined someone quite different, from the way she talked about him. He's frightfully grim, isn't he? And quite rough-looking."

"And he don't like us being here, not one little bit, nor yet that Lady Bea called us her nieces," Daisy said. She glanced at Abby. "He's going to be trouble, Abby."

"Oh, I think he was just worried about his aunt," Jane said.

Abby nodded. The way he'd burst into the house was as if he were coming to save his aunt from being murdered. He'd glared at her with unconcealed hostility ever since. Blaming Abby for his aunt's condition.

A bit late for that. He'd stayed away how many years, and now he came marching in, throwing black looks and wordless threats around?

Damaris said, "He's very attractive, don't you think, Abby?"

"Attractive?" Jane laughed. "How can you say that? Did you see that long hair, and he hadn't even bothered to shave. And apart from being amazingly grim, he's quite old!"

"Old?" Abby turned to Jane. "Don't be ridiculous! He's barely thirty."

Jane shrugged. "Thirty seems old to me."

Abby supposed thirty might seem old to a girl not yet eighteen. Whereas to a woman of twenty-four . . . And she didn't mind the long hair and the rough, masculine jaw at all. . . . And she did appreciate a man with broad shoulders and long, strong thighs. . . .

Not that she thought of Max Davenham in that way.

"He couldn't take his eyes off Abby," Damaris said.

"Only because he wanted to murder me," Abby said dryly. That moment on the stairs when the faint humor in his eyes had faded and cold hostility took its place still had the power to send a shiver down her back. What had she said? That she spoke for Lady Beatrice? Was that what had infuriated him?

Jane gave a shocked laugh. "You must be mistaken, Abby. Why on earth would he wish you harm?"

"I don't know," said Abby. "But from the way he burst in today I suspect he thought we meant ill by his aunt. That she was in danger from us." He'd conducted himself like a stiffly growling watchdog.

"Well, he must know now that that's nonsense. So perhaps the next time we see him he'll be positively charming, like the 'my dearest Max' Lady Beatrice talks of," Jane said.

"Perhaps," Abby said. But she wouldn't bet on it.

"Who the devil are they?" Max said when the door was finally shut.

"I told you, my nieces."

"Nonsense, you don't have any nieces. Who are they really?"

She shrugged in a manner he recognized of old. "If I say they're my nieces, they are."

"You forget who you're talking to, Aunt Bea. I'll take an oath those girls aren't even related to one another, let alone you."

She gave him a warm smile. "Dear boy, so lovely to have you home again. Now, tell me what you've been up to. What's brought you back to England after all this time? Going to settle down with a nice gel and make me a great-aunt, are you?"

"Don't change the subject."

She smacked his hand. "Don't be dreary, Max. I've told you

they're my nieces and that's all you need to know. They're here as my guests."

"Guests don't take money from their hostess."

She made a sound of annoyance. "The wretched Perkins boy told you that, I suppose."

"It's his job to keep me informed."

She snorted. "He's a lazy little pipsqueak."

"I know. I've sacked him." He put up his hand to halt the objections that came spilling out. "I know, I know; I've over-reached myself again."

She pulled a face. "Much you care about that."

He smiled. "Quite right. I didn't mind leaving you in the hands of Perkins senior, but his son is quite another matter. I have removed the account books and handed them to my own man, Bartlett. He, I know, will take excellent care of you."

"Well, make sure he pays Abby and her sisters a handsome allowance."

He was silent for a moment. "Is she blackmailing you?" He couldn't imagine what his aunt could possibly have done that could allow for blackmail, but everyone had secrets.

His aunt gave a spurt of laughter. "Don't be silly; of course she's not!"

"They why would you pay her?"

"Because she hasn't a penny—none of them have."

"That's no reason. London is full of beggars, but you don't take them in."

"You have no idea what they've done for me, Max, no idea. The little they accept from me is nothing to what I owe them. Oh, stop looking at me like that! I haven't entered my dotage, if that's what you're thinking. But what's between Abby and her sisters and me is our business, not yours."

"They're not who they purport to be, Aunt Bea."

"I know that, but the gels are entitled to their secrets. I know who they are, and if I'm not worried, you have no cause to be concerned."

He didn't respond. He just looked at her and waited. And waited. Not taking his eyes off her. It was a trick he'd learned at school and honed abroad, and it rarely failed. Under his cool, unwavering regard, eventually most people talked.

She made an exasperated sound. "Oh, for heaven's sake. Well—I didn't want to tell you this, for it's demmed embarrassin', but I let a pack of worthless, lazy servants get the better of me." She waved her hand irritably. "You don't need to know the details, but it was Miss Abby and her sisters who helped me out of that situation—and no, don't look at me like that, for I won't explain the depths I had sunk to, but suffice it to say—and it's no exaggeration—those girls saved me, saved my life. And if it pleases me to make them a small allowance—well, as a matter of fact, it would please me a great deal more if she would accept a larger one, but she won't, and she's nearly as stubborn as you, Max, so don't think I haven't tried."

What Max thought was that Miss Chance was even more cunning than he'd imagined. Oh, he could just imagine her prettily objecting to an allowance, all the while fanning the flames of his aunt's gratitude, but he could see there was no point trying to convince Aunt Bea.

He'd speak with the woman himself. He was well able to deal with the likes of Miss Abigail Chance.

"She claimed she spoke for you, dammit. In my whole life-time nobody—not even my uncle, God rest his soul—has ever spoken for you." It flayed him to see the forceful Tartar aunt he remembered having become this . . . this helpless, *grateful* victim.

She shrugged. "I've been ill, Max. Things change when you've been ill. It gives you a new perspective on life."

"I can see you've been unwell, Aunt Bea. Are you quite recovered now?" He gently squeezed her thin little hands. Dammit, she was so frail. Guilt lashed at him.

"Better than I was, certainly. And the sickness that laid me low has passed, according to the doctor. But I can't walk any-more, Max."

"What?" His gaze shot to the shape of her legs under the coverlet. "What do you mean, you can't walk? Did you have an accident? Break a—"

"No, no, nothing like that. It's just that I've been sick and in bed for so long—now, don't look like that, dear boy; it's not your fault. I'm slowly regaining my strength, and the girls are helping me. They make me exercise several times a day, following the doctor's instructions to the letter, curse them—it's not at all amusing. And William carries me wherever I need to go."

Suddenly the reason for the powerful, thuggish-looking footman became less sinister.

Max said slowly, "Why didn't you let me know?"

She gave him a puzzled look. "That I'd been ill? But I did."

He shook his head. "I haven't had a letter from you in nearly a year—not directly from you, only the letters your maid has written for you since you broke your wrist. All formal and polite nothings. And not one mentioned the kind of illness that would keep you in your bed."

She gave him a puzzled look. "I never broke my wrist, or hurt it in any way. And I never dictated any letters to you. I wrote 'em all myself." She snorted. "Catch me letting a maidservant read my private correspondence?"

"Are you saying you wrote me letters yourself? And they never got mailed?"

She made a helpless gesture. "I don't know what happened, but I haven't had a letter from you in ages either. Of course I know ships go down and mail doesn't always arrive. . . ."

"I wrote to you every month, the same as I did at school." It was the habit of a lifetime. He said thoughtfully, "So somebody has been misappropriating our letters. I should have realized sooner. Yours didn't sound like you, but it took me a while before I really started to worry. It wasn't until I received this letter that I seriously got the wind up that something was wrong." He pulled the water-stained letter from his pocket and showed it to his aunt.

Using her lorgnette she examined the letter closely. "Why, that's my old friend Clara Beddington's writing. I haven't seen her for years. She always did love purple ink. A dear creature, but with the most appalling taste. Fancy her writing to you." She groped for her lorgnette and tilted the letter to the light, squinting. "I can't make it out. What does it say?"

He was about to explain that the letter said she'd been taken advantage of—and he knew by whom, now—but he changed his mind. His aunt was oddly defensive about these girls. No need to ruffle her feathers further. He'd get to the bottom of the matter—and fix it—without upsetting or involving her.

Dammit, *she couldn't walk*. He should have come home much sooner. He'd put it off because of . . . No point dwelling on that.

But he'd put his own freedom before his aunt's welfare, and he wouldn't forgive himself until he'd fixed it.

He took the letter back and tucked it in his pocket. "The details aren't important. As you saw, much of the writing was washed away when I got it, but there was enough in it to make me worried about you. And so I came."

"Well, I'm delighted to have you home again, dear boy." She patted his hand. "Luckily dear Abby was there before you and she sorted everything out."

Max would just bet she did. Nothing easier than to take over the home of a sick, lonely, bedridden old lady.

"So how did you say you met her?" he asked casually.

"I didn't." His aunt smiled. "She just flew in at the window one night, like a good fairy." Her eyes twinkled. He wasn't going to get any sense out of her, he could see.

"Oh, don't look so grim, dear boy." She laughed and patted his hand. "Be a good nephew and don't make a fuss. We all have our little secrets, and there's nothing there for you to be concerned about. Just accept it from me that Abby and her sisters are dear, good-hearted girls and leave it at that."

He didn't like it, but he knew there was no point arguing. He'd find out about Miss Abby and her sisters his own way. In the meantime: "I'll talk to your doctor—"

She waved a hand—a ringless hand, he noted grimly. "No need, dear Abby handles all that."

"Nevertheless, as your only blood relation, and the head of your family—"

His aunt laughed. "Dragging out the head-of-the-family card so soon, dear boy? It never worked for your grandfather or your uncle, so I can't imagine why you think it will work for you. But go ahead, if it makes you feel better."

"I'll call on Bentinck today." Bentinck was his aunt's usual physician, with a practice made up of half the *ton*.

She snorted. "That old woman. Abby found me a much better man. Shows more sense than any doctor I've ever met. Prescribed me excitement; can you imagine?"

Max could. The man was obviously a quack. He'd get the fellow's address from that butler fellow. There was no need to involve *dear Abby*.

"And what are your plans, dear boy? Is this a flying visit? Are you heading off to sail the seven seas again, now that you've seen for yourself I'm in good hands, or have you decided to settle down at last?"

"I'm back for good," he told her. He might make an occasional voyage, but it would no longer be the main focus of his life. And she was not in good hands. Far from it.

She cocked her head. "Marriage?"

"Yes."

She sat up, her eyes sparkling. "We'll give a ball. It will give you a chance to become acquainted with all the young, eligible gels and—"

"No need," Max cut her off. "You know who I'm going to marry."

His aunt made a disgusted noise. "Oh, you're not still on about that Parsley gel!"

"Parsloe. Miss Henrietta Parsloe, as you very well know."

"A cit's daughter. I thought you would have grown out of that nonsense."

"Aunt Bea, you know very well I gave my word."

"Yes, but it was nine years ago! Surely it doesn't count? You were just a boy of eighteen, not even old enough to be legally held to your word."

"Legality has nothing to do with it. My word is my bond," he reminded her gently. "And I have no intention of breaking it."

She sat back against her pillows with a huff of irritation. "Have you even seen the gel in the last nine years?"

"No."

"Written to her? Exchanged letters?"

"Occasionally."

"How do you even know she's waited for you? Nine years is a long time for a young gel to wait."

"She'll have waited."

She sniffed. "She wants the title."

"You don't think I'm worth waiting for?" Max asked, unruffled. He knew very well what his aunt thought.

She gave him a severe look. "Not for nine years. It's not reasonable. And if you'd loved the gel, she wouldn't have *had* to wait." She wagged a finger at him. "If I'd loved a man I wouldn't have let him spend nine years gadding about the globe."

Max didn't doubt it. His situation, however, was different. "I wasn't gadding," he pointed out. "I was repairing the family fortunes."

She flapped an impatient hand. "The question is, do you love this gel? Does she love you? If you haven't seen her for nine years you can't possibly know if you still want to marry her."

Want had nothing to do with it. "Love is not the only basis for marriage."

"You mean it's for money?" she demanded. "I thought you'd repaired the family fortune."

"I have."

"Then if it's not love or money, what other reason is there to marry a cit's daughter?"

"I gave my word." Max stood up. "Now, I have business to attend to, but we'll talk more later." He kissed his aunt on the cheek and promised to look in on her again before dinner. He left her room in a thoughtful frame of mind.

There was more here to be done than he'd expected. He made a swift examination of the other rooms on his aunt's floor and found faded wallpaper, worn and shabby carpets, cracks in the plaster and some evidence of rising damp in one corner. Not to mention the faded squares, like the ghosts of missing paintings.

Of course, the really valuable paintings had been sold nine years before; still, he was sure the house had not been quite so denuded.

He hadn't noticed it before. When he'd first arrived, he'd been concentrating on getting to his aunt, and while he was in her bedroom there was no sign of the shabby, run-down state of the rest of the house.

The state of the place had been disguised, he realized, with beeswax polish and flowers and foliage arrangements scattered about, and bright fabrics pinned to the wall in lieu of paintings.

The house needed serious work. It galled him to think of

his aunt living here, in what almost amounted to squalor. He should have insisted on an upkeep clause, he realized. Had he been here, he would have— No, no point in regretting the past. Max had long ago learned the futility of that. All regrets did was drain you of energy to make the future.

Ah, well, the responsibility for the house wouldn't be his for much longer. His aunt was all he cared about, and now that he was home again, it was time for a change—past time. The neighborhood was in a state of flux.

In the sixteenth century, when his ancestor had built Davenham House, the Strand was a fashionable address, filled with palaces and mansions of the wealthy. But several centuries later, most of those old palaces had been demolished to make way for new buildings, and those that were still standing had deteriorated badly, some into slums.

The process had started before he'd left, but when he'd arrived today he'd seen very few well-dressed people or smart carriages, and quite a lot of riffraff.

Aunt Bea's bedchamber was a bright, comfortable, self-contained world created especially for a bedridden woman. When he'd first clapped eyes on her she'd reminded him of an Indian maharani, richly dressed, sitting against a pile of sumptuous cushions, surrounded by exotic fabrics and pretty young attendants, in a room filled with flowers and who knew what else. Cats.

Miss Chance's work, he had no doubt, designed to keep his bedridden aunt comfortable and compliant. But this was no place for Aunt Bea, not anymore.

Most of the *ton* had long ago shifted their town residences to Mayfair and places like that. He'd wanted to move Aunt Bea after his uncle died, back when he was eighteen and preparing to leave England. But once he'd discovered the state in which his uncle had left things, there was no question of Aunt Bea moving. It had been all Max could do to ensure she had a roof over her head and an allowance to keep her in the style to which she was accustomed.

The price of that arrangement still had to be paid.

Max had never let his aunt know about the mess his uncle had left behind, the crippling debts. He'd thought he was doing the right thing, leaving her in the home she'd lived in all her married life.

Instead he'd left her in a situation that only added to her isolation and loneliness, her vulnerability. Leaving her open to chance. Miss Chance. Mischance.

He'd like to wring Miss Abigail Chance's neck for taking advantage of a sick and dependent old lady, binding her with ties formed by gratitude and loneliness, illness and vulnerability. But he'd discover her game. He was an entirely different proposition from his aunt.

Nine years sailing the seven seas, doing business in the darkest, most cutthroat reaches of the world . . . These days nobody took advantage of Max Davenham. Not even sweet-faced, two-faced young women.

But first, to deal with this quack and get his aunt some proper medical attention.

Abby was in the entry hall, heading for the front door, when Lord Davenham appeared on the landing. Unfortunately she'd advanced just far enough into the hall to make retreat impossible, not without appearing craven.

It wasn't cowardice, she told herself; she simply had no desire for private conversation with his still-hostile lordship, not while he was spoiling for a fight, which he so obviously was.

The question was, How much did he know? Would he know Abby had climbed in his aunt's window, intending to steal? And what about the brothel?

Lady Beatrice had assured Abby she would keep it a secret, but was an assurance the same as a promise? And now that her nephew was here, asking questions, demanding answers, would she still maintain her silence? Abby wasn't sure.

From the corner of her eye she spotted the moment Lord Davenham spied her. He took the last half dozen stairs in a couple of strides and headed toward her.

He must have spent almost two hours with his aunt. It spoke well of him, she reluctantly admitted. Most men would have made a brief visit to an elderly aunt and then hurried off, citing some important business to attend to.

She lifted her chin and quickened her pace, making for the front door, hoping to appear oblivious of him, though how anyone could reasonably be oblivious of a tall, dark Viking prowling purposefully toward her with a gleam in his eyes that spelled trouble was more than she could imagine.

Still, a girl could only try.

"Miss Chance."

Abby affected a start of surprise and turned. "Oh, Lord Davenham, I thought you'd left already."

The gleam in his eye turned faintly sardonic. She'd fooled no one.

"I'm told my aunt is now attended by a new physician. You deemed the most popular doctor of the *ton* unsuitable?" It was an accusation rather than a question. Typical man, she thought: arrives on the scene after years of absence and immediately starts criticizing.

"Not unsuitable, merely unavailable the first time we sent for him, and since Featherby had heard excellent reports of Dr. Findlay . . ." She shrugged. "Your aunt has flourished under Dr. Findlay's care, and she is well satisfied with the change."

"I'm sure she is," he said, making it clear who was satisfied and who was not. "He prescribes *excitement*, I believe." There was a world of cynicism in his voice.

"Yes. *He's* not hidebound by convention." Had he noted her emphasis? Hard to tell when you were talking to a graven image. "Featherby has the doctor's card, should you wish to speak to him yourself," she said, and swept resolutely toward the door. "I have errands to run."

The black brows snapped together. "You're going out? By yourself?"

"Being well beyond the age of needing a chaperone, I am," she told him. "Good-bye, Lord Davenham."

A fine, light drizzle was drifting down outside, but Abby was ready for it, having snatched an umbrella from the hall stand as she passed.

However, in her haste, she'd taken the one with the stiff catch. She stood on the front steps, wrestling with the wretched thing, cursing it under her breath. Of course, just when she wished most to disappear down the street while Lord Davenham was delayed getting the doctor's address from Featherby . . .

"Having difficulty?" A large, tanned hand closed over hers where she held the umbrella. His hand was bare and brawny, nicked with old scars, a hand used to hard work. Or fighting. Or both. She could feel the warmth of him even through her gloves.

He removed the umbrella from her grasp.

"Please do not concern yourself. The catch is broken. I will get the other one from the hall sta—"

The umbrella popped open. She wanted to thrust the infuriating thing into the nearest bin. Instead, she thanked Lord Davenham politely and reached for the handle.

"Allow me." He loomed over her, holding the umbrella above her head. Other than wresting the umbrella from him, she had no choice but to accept his assistance. His arm half circled her, keeping her close and dry. He smelled of the sea and that dark, masculine scent. She recognized it now: scent of arrogant male.

Holding the second umbrella, Featherby darted past them and out into the street. He produced a small silver whistle, blew into it and waved.

"I told him to find me a hackney cab." The deep voice rumbled just above Abby's ear. "I will give you a lift, Miss Chance. Save you from the damp." It was neither question nor invitation. Lord Davenham ordered.

Abby had no illusions about his concern for her dampness. "Thank you, but I'm perfectly all r—"

"Nonsense. There's no need for you to become drenched. A little patience is all that's required. The hackney will not take long." His big fist remained firmly closed around the handle of the umbrella.

Abby mentally added umbrellas to her shopping list. A dozen.

The drizzle intensified. He wasn't even touching her, but she could feel the warmth of his body even through her best gray cloak. It felt almost . . . intimate.

The hackney arrived and Lord Davenham shepherded her to the curb, taking care she didn't slip on the wet cobblestones and holding the umbrella above her. Abby, feeling absurdly like his prisoner being escorted to the gallows, allowed herself to be helped in.

He climbed in after her, and suddenly the small carriage felt a good deal smaller. His shoulders touched hers, and she was certain she could feel the warmth of his thighs even through her cloak and skirt. Though that was impossible. But it was suddenly quite warm inside the carriage.

"Where are you going?" he asked.

"Charing Cross," she said. She wanted to visit the post office, see whether there was a letter yet containing a character reference. And to post some letters. "It's but a step, so there really is no need—"

"Charing Cross, driver," he told the jarvey, and the hackney jerked into motion.

They sat for a moment in silence, Abby pressed against the side of the carriage, staring out the window to avoid his gaze. She could feel him watching her the way a cat watched a mouse. A big relaxed cat, certain of his prey. Playing with it.

She sat up straighter. She was no prey of his. Or any man's.

"Now, Miss Chance, I had another reason for—" he began, but Abby had had enough of dancing to his tune.

She seized the initiative. "I suppose you want to thank me for taking care of your aunt in your absence, but truly, there's no need."

"I have no doubt of that."

What did he mean? That there was no need to thank her? Why? Because he doubted her motives? She took a quick, side-long glance at his profile. Impassive. Severe. Of course he doubted her motives. He was the kind of man who doubted everyone's motives.

He'd learn.

"How did you meet my aunt? And spare me the faradiddle about being her niece, for I know the truth of that one."

Abby eyed him cautiously. She wasn't going to admit a thing she didn't have to. "Didn't Lady Beatrice tell you?"

"Oh, yes," he said, dry as sandpaper. "Apparently you flew in her window like a good fairy."

Abby looked out the window, biting her lip to keep from smiling. "Then I wouldn't dream of contradicting Lady Beatrice."

His eyes narrowed but he didn't challenge her. He tried a different tack. "My aunt's bedchamber looks nothing like it used to."

He was getting at something, but she didn't know what, so she decided to take the comment at face value. "We tried to make it as cheerful as possible for her. When you're an invalid, it's so easy to succumb to dejection. And your aunt enjoys having pretty things around her."

"Your 'sisters,' for instance?"

She inclined her head, acting as if he'd complimented them, even though she was sure he'd intended some subtle insult. "They are pretty, aren't they? And, of course, Jane is a beauty, but then I'm biased. And they do make very good company for your aunt. It's beneficial for a recovering invalid to have youth and high spirits around, and they enjoy her company too."

"You're an expert in the care and constitution of invalids, are you?"

That edge of cynicism was beginning to annoy her. She met his gaze squarely. "Not an expert, but my mother was an invalid for more than a year when I was young, and I took care of her, so I do have a little experience."

"And where is your mother now?"

"She died." Abby stared out the window. She was quite proud of the way that had come out, without a wobble or a quaver to hint of the lump that came to her throat every time she spoke of Mama.

"My condolences," he said stiffly. Outside the close confines of the hackney an argument exploded as the jarvey exchanged insults with the driver of a wagon that blocked the street. The wagon was moved, and as their journey resumed Lord Davenham asked, "And since your mother died? What did you do before you came to live with my aunt?"

But Abby had had enough of his questions. She turned and gave him a long look, then said in a cool voice, "Lady Beatrice knows everything she needs to know about my background."

"Everything?"

"Naturally I have not burdened her with the minutiae of my life story, but I have informed her of the relevant portions." And it looked like Lady Beatrice intended to keep their secrets, for which Abby was immensely grateful.

"Speaking of portions, explain the stipend you and your sisters receive from my aunt's widow's jointure."

She stiffened. "Lady Beatrice insisted on that, but I assure you we earn our keep. You may snort, but I run the household, and though we have since employed a cook, Damaris is the one who most often manages to tempt your aunt's appetite. Recovering invalids often lack app—"

"Yes, we know about your great knowledge of the care of invalids."

She did not respond.

"I apologize," he said. "I did not mean—"

"It doesn't matter," she said in a brittle voice. "You were asking about the stipend. Jane is your aunt's companion—well, we all perform that role, but Jane can happily sit and chat and read novels and magazines all day long if your aunt wishes it. She's a sunny-natured girl and keeps your aunt cheerful and entertained."

"And the little one with the bad leg?"

"Daisy? Oh, Daisy reminds your aunt she is a woman."

"A *what*?"

She gave a half smile at his tone. "A man no doubt cannot imagine how good it feels to a woman to wear pretty clothes, to feel feminine and desirable, especially a woman who's—"

"—an invalid." His lip curled faintly. She could see he put no value on such things as cheerful company, pretty clothes or tempting food, but they were important; she knew it. She refused to be intimidated by that hard gaze.

"I was going to say a woman in the autumn of her years, but yes, an invalid also needs to be reminded she's an attractive woman."

"And how does Daisy create this miraculous effect?"

"She makes clothes, wonderful clothes. You saw the green-and-pink gauze and embroidered satin bed gown your aunt was wearing today?"

"The one designed for a woman half her age? And for a different class of female altogether?"

Abby itched to smack him. "Indeed. Clearly it's wasted on a man like yourself, who cares nothing for his own appearance. Now, if you've finished interrogating me . . ." The carriage was approaching Charing Cross, and she moved to knock on the window to signal the driver to stop.

Max caught her wrist before she could do it. "Not yet! I haven't finished with you." She struggled and tried to pull away, but he held her effortlessly in a light, firm grip. The gloves were off now.

"Let go of me!" she said in a low, furious voice. She raised her other hand, but he caught that too, and then they were almost chest to chest. "I have no interest in what you have to say."

"No, you wouldn't want to know what I think of the kind of harpy who takes advantage of a sick, lonely old woman! The truth is ugly, but hear it you will." His face was bare inches from hers, his eyes slits of icy contempt.

"Harpy?" She tried to pull free. "How dare you impugn my motives! Let me make this quite clear—Lady Beatrice invited my sisters and me to come and live with her, not the other way around. I never asked—but I was very glad to come. I don't deny it. We all were. But I don't have to justify myself to you—"

"You damned well do."

"Then put it this way—I won't. My arrangement was with your aunt, not you."

"She's in no fit state to make decisions—"

"Rubbish! She might not be able to walk at the moment, but there's nothing wrong with her brain."

"You're a very high-handed young woman, aren't you?" He shook her wrists. "Worming your way into my aunt's life, taking over her home, sacking her servants, appointing your own in their place, dismissing the physician who'd attended her for the last twenty years, treating her home and possessions as your own—and don't think I haven't noticed all the things that are missing—even her rings, dammit! You can't pull the wool over my eyes, young woman. I'm not a feeble old lady ripe to be fleeced and hoodwinked!"

He loomed over her, his chest just touching her breasts, his storm-filled eyes dark with some kind of unknowable emotion.

"You're hurting me," she said coldly. It wasn't true, but Abby didn't care. She was in a rage now.

His gaze dropped to her mouth, and for a long, breathless, incredulous moment she thought he was going to kiss her. Which his next utterance proved was ridiculous.

"I'd like to strangle you," he growled, releasing his grip on her and moving back. "You deserve it and more."

She shook herself like an angry cat and rubbed her wrists, her eyes sparking with anger.

"I should haul you and those others off to the nearest magistrate, but that would distress my aunt. But what if I offered you a handsome sum to leave my aunt's home and never return?"

"What, and leave her in your capable hands?" She made a contemptuous noise. "You're the one who hared off to India for nearly ten years, leaving her to rot!"

"Leaving her to *rot*?" The gray eyes were flinty with rage. "I did nothing of the sort. When I left her she was as fit as a flea, a leader of the *ton*, with a dozen servants to take care of her, a man of business to oversee her domestic affairs and a horde of friends."

"Oh, that's all right, then. I'm glad your conscience is clear. It doesn't matter, I suppose, that the servants were appalling, robbing a sick old lady blind, keeping her in the most atrocious conditions and denying her friends admission until they drifted away, leaving her even more helpless. Or that your so-called man of business never came near her from one end of the year to another, allowing the servants even more freedom to abuse her trust. And what about the fashionable doctor who never bothered to inquire after his patient of twenty years, even though she'd been terribly ill the last time he saw her?"

He stared at her, his face unreadable, his eyes chips of ice.

Abby stormed on. "You *all* left her to rot—every single one of you—and *that's* why you can't bear to have me and my sisters there—because *we didn't*. Well, don't think you'll chase me away, Lord Davenham, because I didn't come at your invitation and I won't leave at your command. I'll go when Lady

Beatrice asks me to go, and it won't take a *bribe* to do it. And
don't you *dare* take that as an invitation to hound her until she
does your bidding. She's not nearly as strong yet as she likes
to think."

She dashed a hand across her eyes and said with a voice that
trembled on the edge of tears. Angry tears, she told herself.
Furious tears. "Now, Lord Davenham, if you don't mind, I wish
to get down."

"No, I need to—"

"I don't care what you need. I wish to get down. *Now.*" She
knocked on the window and the cab immediately slowed. "You
will find Dr. Findlay, Lady Beatrice's physician, in the white
building on the corner over there." She opened the door before
the hackney had come to a complete halt, and jumped lightly
down.

Behind her Lord Davenham shouted something, but Abby
ignored him, hurrying away without a backward look. Hateful,
horrible man!

Max watched her thread her way through the traffic with a
straight back and a swish of indignant skirts. She'd left her
umbrella behind.

He twisted the umbrella handle in his hands. Damned if he
knew what to think.

He'd planned to force her to admit to the fraudulent deception of his aunt. Instead she'd ripped into him like a little shrew,
blasting him for his neglect of Aunt Bea. As if she had a right
to, when they both knew she was no more her niece than . . .
than the butler was.

Did she think to bamboozle him with her righteous little
tirade?

He frowned. There had been genuine emotion in that outburst. As if she truly did care about Aunt Bea.

And for a girl without a penny, she hadn't even tried to
discover his terms. The moment he'd hinted at a bribe, she'd
ripped into him, flinging it back in his teeth without a moment's
hesitation.

He'd never had a woman stand up to him in quite that way,
spitting defiance at him without a shred of fear, dressing him

down like a feisty little governess, even when he had her pressed back against the carriage seats, her wrists imprisoned in his hands. He was twice her size, but had she let it intimidate her? Not for a moment.

He found her perplexing. Annoying. Frustrating.

And damnably arousing, curse her.

Chapter Eight

"How hard it is in some cases to be believed!
And how impossible in others!"

—JANE AUSTEN, *PRIDE AND PREJUDICE*

"Of course, when that young woman first conducted me to your aunt's bedchamber, I was of a mind to report her to the nearest magistrate."

A few minutes in Dr. Findlay's presence had convinced Max that the physician wasn't the plausible rogue he'd expected. A snowy-haired, blunt-spoken Scotsman with a degree from one of the finest medical schools in the world, Findlay had made it clear he was a busy man and could spare Lord Davenham ten minutes only. His manner implied he had more interest in treating the poor than pandering to the whims of aristocrats.

"And yet you didn't."

"No, not when I realized they'd only just arrived and found her like that." The doctor shook his head. "The state that puir woman was in!"

Max's gut clenched. "Please elucidate."

"Filthy, emaciated, dehydrated—I've seen street beggars in better condition than your aunt."

Guilt lashed at Max. He should have come home sooner. "How long ago was this?"

"Three weeks."

He frowned. Only three weeks? It didn't add up. "You say the misses Chance had only recently arrived at my aunt's?"

"Aye, but no' recently—they'd arrived that verra day. Their first act was to fetch me to attend her—they wanted to bathe and feed her, but they feared to move her before getting a medical opinion. Quite right too. Verra frail the old lady was."

"And still is."

"Och, she's coming along nicely now. Those nieces of hers are devoted to her care. Your sisters, are they?"

"No." Max was about to deny all relationship, either to himself or Aunt Bea, but prudence won out. "They're not from my side of the family at all."

Again he wondered who they were and where they had come from.

How had they met an ill, bedridden old lady? People didn't simply arrive in a city, find an old lady in need and move in with her.

And if what the doctor said was true—and he had no reason to doubt the man—why had they taken it upon themselves to save her?

What was their connection to his aunt?

What had Miss Chance said? Lazy and neglectful servants? Was that how she'd come to meet Aunt Bea, through some connection with the servants?

But if that were the case, why would she have sacked them? Perkins said she'd sacked the entire staff.

"Aye, your aunt's in verra safe hands with Miss Abigail Chance in charge. She's a young lady who knows exactly what to do and does it without any roundaboutation. Lady Beatrice is flourishing under her care."

It was an uncanny echo of what she'd said about the doctor.

"Your aunt must be verra grateful to have those young ladies with her, as are you, I'm sure."

Max didn't know what he felt. This whole situation was . . . murky. Confusing. But he'd get to the bottom of it.

The doctor continued. "Like a breath of fresh air, they are." He gave a bark of laughter. "Literally. The first time I went there the house was like a dusty mausoleum. Apart from the bedchamber, which—without beating about the bush—stank like the worst slum dwelling."

The doctor's plain speaking was like a punch to Max's gut.

He'd been all wrong about Miss Chance and her sisters. It seemed they truly had rescued Aunt Bea from a dire situation. And he wasn't ungrateful.

There was no denying the pleasure his aunt took in the girls' company. And much as it galled him to admit it, according to this doctor they were taking good care of her.

But how did they get there in the first place? And why? And who were they really? Those questions still bothered him.

"I believe you prescribed excitement for Aunt Beatrice."

"Aye, she's no' ill anymore, simply worn down, weak and mentally dispirited. Aye, I know what you're going to say— she's frail—and that's true. But underneath that, her constitution is as strong as a horse—she'd no' have survived such a long period of neglect otherwise. Physically what she needs is building up, with good food and exercise, and I've given the lassie—forgive me, Miss Chance—a tonic of my own devising that will strengthen her blood. Mentally . . ." He shook his head.

"Mentally?"

"Aye, she was sinking into a decline when I first came on her. Dwelling on morbid thoughts, that kind of thing. Melancholia."

Max stared at him, deeply shocked. Aunt Bea had never suffered from melancholia in her life. He remembered what she'd said: *Things change when you've been ill. It gives you a new perspective on life.*

The doctor eyed him with shrewd blue eyes. "Och, don't look like that, m'lord; she's improved a great deal, but you'll find when she's tired, she might get a bit weepy and despondent. So a bit of young life around her is exactly what she needs. Friends, activity, excitement. Give her a reason to wake up in the morning, something to look forward to each day."

Max left the doctor's in a much chastened mood. There was no question now of getting rid of the girls, even if he could, at least until his aunt had fully recovered.

He didn't know what to think. After all his work, all the time he'd spent in exile on the other side of the world, repairing the family fortunes, reliant on nobody—and now, to be beholden to this snip of a girl, a female he knew to be a liar and an impostor—and a girl, what was more, to whom he found himself attracted at the most inconvenient of moments. It was unbearable. Unacceptable.

He'd find out who she was and what she was up to—and then, dammit, he'd decide whether he was grateful to her or not.

And he was not attracted to her. It was just a . . . an odd moment. A result of being too long at sea. Nothing a bit of self-discipline couldn't cure.

She'd left her umbrella in the hackney with that hateful man, but Abby didn't care. She lifted her face to the sky and let the cool, misty drizzle mingle with the few angry tears that had escaped.

Wretched, suspicious man.

Of course, he had a right to wonder about her motives—she was a stranger, after all. But it was just like the way he'd first arrived—barging in like a . . . a Viking raider, assuming the worst. Couldn't he simply have *asked*, like any civilized man would?

How did you meet my aunt?

Apparently you flew in her window like a good fairy.

She pulled out a handkerchief and wiped her face dry. Perhaps he had a point. But if he hadn't rubbed her the wrong way in the first place . . .

Surely he could see they were taking good care of his aunt. That they sincerely cared about her.

She called in at the post office, but there was still no character reference from Mrs. Bodkin. Nor a response from the vicar in Hereford or Sir Walter Greevey, for that matter, though she wasn't really expecting anything from them; she'd informed them both that although Jane had been kidnapped on the way to Hereford, she was now safe in London with her older sister. Clearly neither of them was interested in investigating how that had happened.

She hadn't mentioned where she'd found Jane. The fewer people who knew that the better.

After the post office, she did her shopping and walked home via the riverbank. She always found it a soothing walk, watching the ripples on the water and the traffic on the Thames. Even when the stench of the river was at its worst, she still found it fascinating. It was another world.

This time, however, she found herself stomping along the pathway, taking little notice of her surroundings. Her mind kept spitting up bits of the conversation—well, you could hardly call it a conversation, more like a tirade.

You wouldn't want to know what I think of the kind of harpy who takes advantage of a sick, lonely old woman. . . . Worming your way into my aunt's life . . . treating her home and possessions as your own . . . I'd like to strangle you. . . . I should haul you and those others off to the nearest magistrate.

Wretched man. Yes, she'd pretended to be his aunt's niece, but only to get admitted to the house that first time. It was Lady Beatrice who'd continued the falsehood. And he knew it to be a falsehood—they all did—so it wasn't truly a deception. Who was harmed by it? Nobody.

She'd cared for his aunt when nobody else did.

She was also using a false name, her conscience reminded her. But *he* didn't know that. And it was for a very good reason—the protection of her sisters.

All right, there might be *some* justification for him to be suspicious of her. But had he bothered to ask about *why* she was living with his aunt? No, he'd just jumped to the worst possible conclusion. And then . . .

That moment when he'd leaned closer in the darkness of the hackney . . . his breath warm on her skin, and she'd thought . . . she'd imagined . . . A shiver rippled through her.

Nonsense. As if he'd kiss her, a man like him. He'd wanted to strangle her.

And then he'd offered her a horrid bribe.

Wait till she told the others about that!

After leaving the doctor's office, Max took a hackney to the London office of Flynn & Co. Oriental Trading to see his man Bartlett.

Max had first appointed Bartlett to manage his personal affairs when Max was eighteen and about to depart for India. He wished now that he'd insisted Bartlett also watch over his aunt, but she'd been loyal to Perkins senior at the time, and refused to change.

Bartlett had proved to be an exemplary man of business, and when Max first became the "& Co." part of Flynn & Co. Oriental Trading, he'd nominated Bartlett as the London representative of the company. Bartlett had handled it so well that after five years they'd made him a minor partner.

Max was shocked when he met Bartlett again. In the nine years since Max had last seen him, Bartlett had gone almost completely bald. He was plump and rosy and looked almost middle-aged. It was a shock.

Bartlett was only a few years older than Max.

But cut from quite different cloth, Max reminded himself. Bartlett was a family man through and through—he'd been married and a father already when Max had first employed him.

Max inquired after Mrs. Bartlett and the children. "How many is it now?"

"Five," said Bartlett proudly. "All girls, but there's another one on the way, and we're hoping for a boy."

Max blinked. The man was barely past thirty. Max tried to imagine himself with five children. Six. He couldn't.

That fate awaited him in the future. The near future. He thrust the thought aside and got down to business.

Once the company business was dealt with—not that there was a lot; it was all in excellent order—Max raised the question of the books he'd confiscated from Perkins.

"I've only had time for a quick glance through," Bartlett said, "but even so, there are a few obvious discrepancies."

"Discrepancies?"

"The servants appointed by Miss Chance, for instance."

Max stiffened. "Yes?"

"There don't seem to be enough."

Max gave him a sharp look. "What do you mean?"

"Well, Perkins was paying a staff of twelve, but Miss Chance—leaving off the allowances for herself and her sisters, and disregarding the temporary help she got in when she first took over—I imagine for a spring clean; women like to put their own stamp on a house—she has only appointed six permanent servants: a butler, footman, cook, two housemaids and a scullery maid." He turned the book in Max's direction and indicated the entries. "Why would she need fewer servants? It's a big house."

"Twelve? She told me she'd sacked four servants—'all four of them,' she said." He recalled her words exactly.

"Aha." Bartlett made a note. "Then it's just a matter of finding out who was pocketing the extra—Perkins or Caudle, the former butler. I shall investigate."

"I plan to call in at Bow Street after this," Max told him. "A number of my aunt's valuables have gone missing. I believe Caudle to be responsible. I shall refer the runner to you, as well. Keep me informed."

"Of course." Bartlett made another note and closed the Perkins accounts.

Max watched him arrange his papers. Very organized was Bartlett. The secret of his success. "Do you know of a good man who can make discreet inquiries?"

"Not related to the Bow Street matters, my lord?"

"No. Personal."

Bartlett considered the matter. "Morton Black might do it."

"Morton Black?"

"A most discreet and efficient man. He's employed by a Mr. Sebastian Reyne, but he occasionally takes on private assignments. If you like I could send a note around and see if he's available."

Max nodded. "Ask him to call on me at Davenham House tomorrow morning."

"Of course. Will half past nine suit, or is that too early?"

Max nodded. He was not yet used to town hours. He was used to being up at dawn. "Half past nine will do nicely."

Bartlett wrote it down in his notebook.

"Next, find me a house," Max said.

"Bachelor quarters, I presume."

"No, a house. Somewhere in Mayfair."

Bartlett's eyes lit up. "Are we anticipating a happy event, my lord?" he asked with a coy smile.

Max stared at him blankly. "A happy what?"

"A wedding, sir." Bartlett beamed at him.

Max had no intention of discussing it, not until he had

finalized his plans. "Davenham House is no longer suitable, so I'm moving my aunt and myself to a more convenient location."

"And the four girls?"

"I haven't made up my mind about them yet, but make allowances just in case." He was damned sure Aunt Bea would kick up if he tried to separate her from those girls. Hard enough to move her in the first place. But he'd do it.

Bartlett chuckled happily. "Petticoat government for you, then, my lord. I know just what that's like, ha, ha."

Max looked at him. *Petticoat government?* Over his dead body. "Just find the house."

The jolliness disappeared from Bartlett's face. "Quite so, my lord. Do you wish to buy or lease?"

"Buy for preference, but if nothing suitable is available, then a lease will do for the moment. I want my aunt out of Davenham House as soon as possible."

"I see. Speed is of the essence." Bartlett made a note. "I take it Lady Beatrice is happy about the move."

Max grimaced. "She doesn't know about it yet. But whether she wants to or not, she's going to move. But first, find me the house. Something modern, spacious and in the first style of elegance. Make a short list and I'll make the final decision."

"Of course, my lord. I shall do my best to find something worthy of her ladyship."

"And do it quickly," Max said as he rose to take his leave. "The sooner the better." He wasn't looking forward to the fuss Aunt Bea would make about leaving Davenham House. But she'd do it, he vowed.

Next, Max made a visit to Bow Street. He gave them the particulars of his aunt's former servants, especially the man Caudle. The fellow didn't seem particularly skilled at covering his tracks; a Bow Street Runner would soon run him to earth.

Max was far from confident that Aunt Bea's stolen possessions would be recovered—most of her jewelry had long been copied in paste before being sold by her spendthrift husband—but he'd never been able to get her to give up her rings; they'd been the genuine article. Still, as long as Caudle was caught and punished to the full extent of the law, he'd be satisfied. He couldn't have the fellow punished for his real crime—his neglect and abuse of Aunt Bea. A trial on those grounds would be too publicly humiliating for her—but theft, embezzlement and fraud would do nicely.

He didn't mention the misses Chance to the Bow Street Runner he briefed. He'd leave Miss Abigail Chance and her sisters to Morton Black to investigate.

Outside Bow Street it took him fifteen minutes before he was able to hail another hackney cab. He was getting fed up with this. He needed his own carriage. A visit to Tattersalls was in order.

But first he'd pay a call on his oldest friend, Freddy Monkton-Coombes.

"He called you a *harpy*? And accused you of taking advantage?" Jane echoed. "How *dare* he?"

The four girls had gathered in Abby's bedchamber. She was telling them about her quarrel with Lord Davenham in the hackney. They were all satisfyingly indignant on her behalf.

"And then he said he'd offer me a handsome sum to leave his aunt's home and never return."

There was a sudden silence.

"How much?" Daisy asked.

Abby blinked at the question. "I don't know. It never occurred to me to ask."

"But you said it was a handsome sum," Jane said.

"Yes, they were his actual words. He didn't give any specific figure." She waited for the outburst of indignation. Didn't they understand the insult? "It was a horrid bribe!" she said.

There was an awkward silence. Abby looked at each of them and understanding slowly dawned. "You think I should have accepted? Taken his bribe? Admit that we have indeed been doing something wrong? Confirm his vile opinion of us?"

The silence stretched, and Abby read the shameful truth in their eyes.

"I know it's not very nice of him, Abby, but . . . we need the money," Jane said. "We're still planning to go to Bath, aren't we?"

Abby stared at her, crushed. They thought she'd done the

wrong thing. They thought she should have swallowed the insult and taken the money. Instead she'd flung it back in his teeth without even considering it. Considering them.

"A handsome sum" might buy a cottage for Damaris, help Daisy begin her business, fund Abby and Jane for a season in Bath.

"After all, Lady Beatrice won't need us now that her nephew is here to look after her," Damaris said. "And if he doesn't want us here . . . It is his house."

"And it's not as if Lady Bea can introduce us to society," Jane added. "Everyone knows she has no nieces."

"And we're using a false name," Daisy reminded them. She'd never approved of the false name, even though she accepted its necessity.

"So we'll probably have to leave soon anyway," Jane finished. "And a handsome sum would have helped. You needn't think of it as a bribe, Abby—why not look at it as a farewell gift, a thank-you for helping Lady Beatrice?"

Because it *was* a bribe, Abby thought, but she didn't say it. Her sisters' disloyalty shattered her. No, not disloyalty, she decided—thoughtlessness. They were young and eager to get on with their lives. Jane, in particular, was desperate to meet young men and fall in love, and Abby couldn't blame her for that in the least—in fact she rejoiced in the knowledge that Jane had emerged from that vile place unscathed.

None of them cared what Lord Davenham thought of them. All they were thinking of was their future. And they'd lived so close to disaster for so long that they were willing to snatch at any chance. Just as she'd risked everything to burgle this house.

"Well, it's too late now," she said. "I rejected it in no uncertain terms." And left him stinging with insult into the bargain. The lowering thought occurred to her that if he tried to bribe her a second time, she'd fling it in his teeth just as hard. Harder.

Regardless of what her sisters wanted.

Because, she realized slowly, she did care what Lord Davenham thought of her.

And that was the most lowering thought of all. She had no reason to care. He was nothing but a rude, insulting, arrogant Viking!

* * *

"Good God, it's a pirate!" Freddy Monkton-Coombes declared by way of greeting. He grinned as he wrung Max's hand hard and thumped him on the back.

Max did a bit of grinning and thumping of his own. "If you think I look like a pirate, you won't know what's hit you when you meet Flynn. He's arriving in London in a month or so, weather permitting."

Freddy snorted. "I care nothing for Flynn. But you!" He eyed Max with a mock-critical expression and shook his head. "You've fallen to pieces in the last ten years."

Max raised his brows and glanced down at himself. "Odd, and here I thought I was quite an impressive specimen."

"Of piratehood, perhaps," Freddy said dismissively. "Don't they carry razors or scissors on ships anymore? And is that a leather thong you've tied that mop back with?" He shuddered.

Max pulled the thong off. His hair fell around his face. He inspected the thong. "Yes, it's leather. Well spotted." He tossed it to Freddy, who caught it deftly, then dropped it disdainfully on the floor.

He eyed the length of Max's hair and said dryly, "Just in time. Any longer and you'd look more like a mermaid than a pirate!"

Max laughed.

"It's no joking matter; you used to look almost elegant," Freddy informed him. "Almost. You never could come up to my standards."

Max stood back and inspected Freddy's attire. "Is that what you're wearing? Standards?"

It being a mere hour or two after the crack of noon, Freddy had only just woken. He was attired for his breakfast in a black silk dressing gown embroidered with scarlet dragons. On his feet were a pair of red leather Turkish slippers.

"I am setting a fashion," said Freddy with an air of great dignity.

Max pulled out a chair and sat down. "You're dining alone where nobody can see you."

"Well, good God, you don't think I'd wear this in public, do you? It was a gift from a lady. Besides, I'm not dining alone. You're here. What will you have? I can recommend the sausages. Pork with a hint of fennel and a touch of hot spice. Made especially for me by an Italian butcher."

"Don't mind if I do," Max said, sitting down in the place hastily set by Freddy's man. A lot had happened since his first breakfast, and he was ravenous. He poured himself an ale from the jug on the table. "Ahh, good English ale, how I've missed it."

"So, are you back in England for good?" Freddy asked as he tucked into his breakfast.

"I am." Max chewed with relish. The sausages were all Freddy had claimed.

"And what brought you back early? You did say when you left you'd be away for ten years, did you not? Or have I misremembered?"

"No, I'm back nearly a year early. My aunt. She hasn't been well."

"I'm sorry to hear it. How is she now?"

"Out of danger and improving." As they ate and drank, Max filled Freddy in on all that had happened.

"So she's being looked after now by this young woman and her sisters? Pretending to be nieces but they're no relation, you say? Odd, that."

"Yes, but I'll get to the bottom of that little mystery."

"Pretty?"

Max looked up. "What?"

"Any of them pretty?"

"What's that got to do with it?"

Freddy shook his head mournfully. "Max, Max, Max! What did they do to you out there in the Wilds of Foreign, apart from making you—both of us—delightfully rich, that you fail to see the importance of whether the girls your aunt has taken in are pretty or not? It's of the first importance."

"Why?"

"Because I might want to meet them."

Max thought about his handsome, charming and elegant friend meeting Miss Chance and decided he didn't want Freddy anywhere near her. Or her sisters. "You don't."

Freddy's face fell. "Dull?"

"Very." It was for Freddy's own good, Max told himself.

"Ugly?"

"Plain as a box of toads," Max said, warming to his theme. "But kindhearted. Sweet natured. Very . . ." He tried to think of something that would quench Freddy's interest once and for all. "Very *earnest*. They read a lot." That was true. From what he could gather, they read lurid novels by the boxful, aloud to his aunt.

Freddy pulled a face. "In that case, they're your problem."

"You don't intend to help me?" Max feigned mild indignation.

"Not with a bunch of muffin-faced bluestockings," Freddy said callously. "I've met the type before. For some reason they always want to reform me. Through marriage." He shuddered. "Horrible thought." He slathered a piece of toast with butter and marmalade, glanced at Max and said, "The mater has started to harp."

"On marriage?"

Freddy nodded. "Wants me to settle down with a nice serious girl. A *serious* one! What would I do with a serious girl, I ask you? I'm frivolous to the bone." He contemplated his toast for a moment, then bit into it. "The mater wants to reform me too. Talks wistfully of heirs, and dandling babies on her lap before she dies. She's barely fifty, not that she'd admit to it."

"You've changed."

"How?"

"Since when have you ever taken a scrap of notice of your mother's desires?"

Again Freddy pulled a face. "I know, but she's gradually wearing me down. Women are good at that. It's exhausting." He took a reviving mouthful of ale. "So, where are you staying?"

"Davenham House, for the moment. With my aunt."

"With a houseful of muffins?" Freddy said, shocked. "You can't! You'll come out of your bedchamber one morning in your smalls and a dressing gown and next minute you'll find one of them shrieking the house down that you've compromised them. And demanding marriage."

Max laughed. "That sounds like the voice of experience."

"It is," Freddy assured him. "House party last year. I'd spent a very pleasant evening in the arms of a lady who shall remain nameless—married, of course, and horribly neglected by her fool of a husband—and was returning to my room in the wee small hours when a dratted muffin saw me—though what the devil a supposedly respectable spinster was doing creeping around the corridors at that hour, I'd like to know." He thought about it and grimaced. "No, I wouldn't. Anyway, she set up such a screeching anyone would think I'd murdered her in her bed."

"And yet you escaped wedded bliss with this, er, muffin?"

Freddy grinned. "Her father was one of those fire-and-brimstone types. Was horrified at the prospect of a notorious rake—did you know? I'm notorious, apparently!—marrying his precious virgin daughter. Gave me a blistering lecture about my morals and told me to begone at once. Well, I didn't need to be told twice, did I? I damned well bewent as fast as my curricle would take me. Had just taken possession of my grays. Beautiful movers they are—and fast! You'll be green with envy. Sixteen miles an hour."

Max threw back his head and laughed. It was so good to see Freddy again. "That reminds me: I'm in need of a carriage and pair. I've no transport. Want to come with me to Tattersalls tomorrow?"

"Delighted to, but if it's a pair you want, Simpson is selling his matched bays—poor fellow is rolled up. Lovely goers, nearly as good as my grays. Certainly better than anything coming up at Tattersalls. I'll take you to see them tomorrow if you like, make a day of it. They're at his place out at Richmond."

"Excellent," Max said.

"So, why aren't you putting up at the club?"

"Can't. Haven't been a member for nearly ten years."

Freddy looked appalled. "Well, you can't stay with your aunt and the muffins. Stay here tonight. You can have the sofa. We'll dine at the club and I'll put you up for membership immediately."

"I can't. I told my aunt I'd be back at dinnertime."

"She's an invalid, ain't she? It'll be soup and toast on a tray in her bedchamber for her, so you won't be dining there unless it's with a pack of muffins. Why not drop in on Lady Beatrice, do the pretty for five minutes and then come out with me?"

Max considered it. It wasn't as if his aunt would be alone. And an evening in Freddy's company, eating good English food at the club, was very appealing. "Good idea."

Freddy jumped up and rang the bell for his manservant. "But before you go anywhere, I'll have my man give you a shave and a decent haircut. I'm not taking a blasted pirate to the club. They'd blackball you in an instant. Where are the rest of your clothes? Still on board the ship? I'll get someone to fetch them. Not that they'll be suitable, I suppose. I'll make you an appointment with my tailor."

Max grinned. "I can't wait for you to meet Flynn."

Chapter Nine

*"A woman especially, if she have the misfortune of knowing
anything, should conceal it as well as she can."*

—JANE AUSTEN, NORTHANGER ABBEY

"Jane tells me you're planning to go to Bath soon. You're not
leaving me, are you, Abby?" Lady Beatrice demanded later
that afternoon. Abby had brought her a cup of tea and some
fresh-baked ratafia biscuits, and when she'd entered the room,
Jane had hurried out with a slightly guilty expression. Now
Abby knew why.

"That's not quite true," Abby began. "Jane is just—"

"Frightful place, Bath. Went there once. People claim the
waters are good for you. Pack of nonsense. Nothing that tastes
so foul can possibly be good for you," the old lady declared.
"Give me good red claret every time. In my youth Bath used
to be all the rage—the influence of Beau Nash, you know, even
though he was dead by then—but these days I hear they let
anybody in."

Abby smiled. "Actually, that's why we thought of going
there in the first place."

Lady Beatrice raised her lorgnette. "To mingle with *riffraff*?"

Abby had to laugh at her outraged expression. "Not quite.
But we did think we'd have a better chance there. Bath society
is limited enough that Jane can meet eligible gentlemen." The
highest Bath sticklers probably would consider Abby and her

sisters, if not precisely riffraff, certainly representative of the "anyone" they let in these days.

"Make a splash, you mean? Get the gel a husband?"

Abby nodded. "But we don't plan to go to Bath for a good while yet."

The old lady snorted. "Don't need to go to Bath for a beautiful gel like that to meet gentlemen."

"No, but I'd prefer her to have respectable offers," Abby said dryly.

Lady Beatrice considered that thoughtfully. After a moment she said, "Don't blame the gel for getting restless, then. Natural for a young gel to want a bit more excitement than sitting with old ladies, reading novels and ladies' papers and sewing."

"Jane enjoys your company—"

"Oh, I know that, my dear, and she's a dear, sweet gel. But it shouldn't be all she does. Not right for pretty young gels to be cooped up all day; they should be out meeting other young things—young men, in particular—going dancing, attending the theater, having fun. I can't bring her out myself, of course, but—"

"I wouldn't dream of asking it of you," Abby assured her. She knew it was out of the question. People sponsored only close relatives into society, and by doing so they vouched not only for the character and virtue of the girl, but the quality and lineage of her family.

They did not sponsor girls they met when they climbed in a window, or girls who used false names, let alone girls with shady pasts and brothel connections.

Lady Beatrice patted her hand. "I know, m'dear, I know. You're a good gel. But I don't see why you need to go to Bath to find the gel a husband—unless you want one with one foot in the grave." She tilted her head in inquiry. "Is that what she wants, a rich old man who'll quickly pop his clogs and leave her a wealthy widow?"

"No, ma'am, not at all." Abby laughed. "Jane's a romantic."

"And what about you, Miss Burglar, are you a romantic like your sister? Do you not dream of a husband and family of your own?"

Abby felt her cheeks warming. "Well, of course I do, but

I'm also practical. Poor, plain and past my first youth—I'm hardly anyone's ideal bride," she said lightly. "Jane, on the other hand—"

"Yes, yes, but I'm not talking about her. She'll do very well for herself. It's you I'm concerned about—I want to see you happy, my dear."

Sudden tears pricked at the back of Abby's eyes. She blinked them away and hugged the old lady. "There's no need to worry about me, dear Lady Beatrice. Once Jane is safely married, I shall be free to look around for some worthy man, a widower, perhaps, with a tribe of children desperately in need of a mother."

"Pfft! We can do better than that for you, I hope. You're not the least bit plain when you smile, you know, and your eyes are quite beautiful. And in those dresses young Daisy has made, you look both elegant and desirable. No, don't screw up your nose like that, Miss Burglar—you're a dear, sweet girl and you have a heart that any man would be lucky to win."

Abby's eyes misted over again. She tamped down on the surge of unexpected emotion, saying, "Oh, you flatterer," as she straightened the old lady's cushions.

There were other reasons, though she'd never told a soul. Laurence had destroyed more than just her dreams.

Why would I marry you?

The old lady's shrewd gaze was on her and Abby managed a laugh. "Very well, once Jane is married, I shall look around me, I promise."

Lady Beatrice gave a brisk nod. "Very well, if that's what you want. We can do better than Bath for her here. Don't need a come-out to meet eligible gentlemen. Dear Max should be able to round up one or two for a start. They generally run in packs, bachelors. I'll mention it to him."

Abby thought of the last exchange she'd had with the old lady's nephew. "Dear Max" was more likely to throw Jane and her sisters in Bridewell Prison than help her to marry one of his friends.

"Your nephew has changed quite a bit since that painting was done." She indicated the watercolor portrait that had hung on the wall of Lady Beatrice's bedchamber ever since Abby had known her.

"Oh, that." Lady Beatrice glanced at it. "It never was much good in the first place. I had that done just before he went away. I would have preferred something in oils and from a better artist, but he was in a rush to leave, so it was the best I could manage in the time available. The artist made a few sketches and Max left the next day. The fellow had to finish it from memory." She sniffed. "As you can see, the chin isn't right. And the eyes are blue, whereas Max has the most beautiful gray eyes."

Beautiful wasn't the word Abby would have used. *Chilling*, *flinty*, even *hard* would suit, but *beautiful*? Hardly. But she didn't say so. Lady Beatrice obviously doted on him. "He looks quite young there."

"Just eighteen. Still a boy, though he wouldn't have admitted it at the time. Too young to go off adventuring." She sighed. "And far too young to become betrothed."

"Betrothed?" For some reason the news came as a shock.

Lady Beatrice shook her head. "Never officially announced—not yet—but Max told me before he left that he had an understanding with the gel and her father." She wrinkled her nose. "He was very scant with the details. He only told me about her at the last minute, I think in case something happened to him."

"I see," Abby said. Eighteen did seem rather young for a man to become betrothed. "But he still went away?"

Lady Beatrice nodded. "You're thinking it's hardly the act of a young man in love, but personally I was delighted to see him putting an ocean between them. And, of course, having a few adventures and sowing a few wild oats. It almost reconciled me to his going away. . . . Almost."

"You didn't approve?" She'd meant about his leaving, but Lady Beatrice misunderstood.

"Max was a schoolboy when the harpy got her hooks into him. As I understand it, her father introduced Max to her when he was just sixteen."

"You don't like her."

"I know nothing about her. I've never met the gel or her

father," Lady Beatrice said in a fair-minded manner that deceived Abby not at all. "Max made me promise not to contact either of them while he was away—unless, of course, the worst happened, which thank God it didn't. I kept that promise, though I confess I've prayed almost daily for news of her. Fatal news. Complete waste of time—apparently the wretched gel continues to thrive." She sighed. "I suppose we'll meet her soon enough now he's returned."

She brooded in silence a moment. "Miss Henrietta Parsley." She pronounced the name as if it put a sour taste in her mouth.

"An unusual name."

The old lady sniffed. "*We* don't know them."

Abby wondered whether she was speaking for herself or for the entire upper ten thousand of the *ton*.

"A northern family, I'm told. Parsley is some kind of cit—a merchant or manufacturer or coal heaver or some such person. Max met him in a *manufactory*!" she said, as if it were some den of iniquity.

"How unusual. Was it something to do with school?" It was an odd place for a sixteen-year-old gently reared boy to be.

Lady Beatrice shrugged. "It was some kind of exhibition, I believe—steam power or some such nonsense. As a boy, Max was always mad for machinery, which is why I was so surprised when he told me he was going away to sea. I never realized he'd harbored a secret passion for travel and adventure until the day he came to tell me he was leaving. So sudden. But far more acceptable than smelly, noisy engines." She shook her head reminiscently. "He used always to be going to this foundry and that, down mines and all sorts of frightful places. He used to talk incessantly about it, saying steam was the future." She shrugged. "Instead he went to sea. But then, a boy's passion never lasts long, does it? Pity he didn't forget about La Parsley as well."

"It seems his interest in the sea stuck," Abby observed.

"Yes, for nine years, can you believe it?"

"Miss Parsley presumably didn't mind him being away so long?"

Lady Beatrice said indifferently, "I don't suppose she had any choice, my dear. Men are a law unto themselves."

"I'm surprised she was willing to wait all this time."

Lady Beatrice raised her lorgnette. "A cit's daughter? Not willing to wait for *my nephew*?"

"Of course, I'm sure she cares for him very much," Abby said soothingly. She'd have to love him, to wait for nine years. Abby felt for poor Miss Parsley, spending her youth waiting.

Lady Beatrice made a rude noise. "Cares for his title more. Oh, I don't know what the wretched gel thinks—nor do I care. For the last nine years I've been praying for her to drown or elope or fall down a mine hole or pit or whatever they call it in the north. But she hasn't, or Max would have mentioned it. But enough of the wretched creature—I don't even want to think about her, or about the fact that Max will no doubt want me to arrange his wedding now he's back."

Abby looked again at the portrait of Lord Davenham. She'd seen it a hundred times before, and wondered about Lady Beatrice's nephew, but he was just a theoretical nephew to her then; now he was very real. Big, arrogant and insulting.

It wasn't a particularly good portrait, she agreed, but there was something about it, some quality about the boy in the painting that wasn't visible in the man. And it wasn't to do with the shape of his chin or the color of his eyes. There was something very . . . alone . . . about the boy in the painting.

"Was he orphaned young?" she found herself asking. "Is that why you brought him up?"

"Oh, I didn't bring him up, my dear. His mother ran off with another man when Max was just six—she died abroad a few years later giving birth to his bastard half brother. I would have taken him in straightaway, but his father would have none of it. Sent the boy off to boarding school, said he was too soft, that school would make a man of him." She pulled a face. "Too soft! Natural for a little boy to miss his mother."

She fell into a silent reverie for a moment, and Abby thought about a small six-year-old boy sent away to school all alone. To be made a man of.

It didn't make her forgive the man for his insulting behavior toward her, but she did soften in her heart toward the little boy he had once been.

"He never stopped waiting for her to come back, you see, which angered his father no end."

"Angered? Why anger?" It was only natural for a child that age to miss his mother. Abby still missed hers, and she'd been twelve when Mama died.

"You had to know Hector. Everything was about him; nobody else mattered. So when Max ran to the landing or the window every time a visitor arrived—thinking it would be his mama come back, as she'd promised him she would!—Hector took it as a personal criticism."

Abby was appalled. "How could a little boy missing his mother be a criticism of the father?"

"Rubbing his nose in his cuckoldry—and no, of course a child of Max's age would know nothing about such things. But the boy's distress was a constant reminder of his humiliation— yes, humiliation is the word. Hector was a cold man and never loved his wife. Never loved anyone, come to think of it, not even his son. Only himself."

"So his father sent a grieving little boy away to school," Abby finished. "He came to you for the holidays, I suppose."

"No, not until after his father died."

Something about Lady Beatrice's expression made Abby ask, "So where did he go for the holidays?"

"Nowhere." Lady Beatrice shook her head sorrowfully. "His father made arrangements several times to have him collected at Christmas, but something always came up and he left the boy at school, waiting. . . ." She looked up. "I didn't know at the time, of course, else I'd have driven up to Middlesex myself and brought him home." She gave a gusty sigh. "He had his first family Christmas with me when he was a gangly young boy, after his father was dead. And of course he came then for every holiday, not just Christmas."

Despite her current resentment of the man, Abby was horrified at the picture the old lady had painted. Poor, lonely little boy, left waiting for parents who never came for him. It was worse than having parents who died, she realized. There was something so cruel about hope endlessly delayed.

No wonder he loved his aunt. And yet, why had he left her for so many years?

"And, of course, all those years of broken promises," Lady Beatrice continued. "It's why he sets such store on keeping his word now. It's one thing you can always depend on my nephew to do—keep his word. Which is why he'll marry that little harpy, curse her!"

She grimaced. "Now, can you ring for that maid of mine, Abby, dear? I want a bath. And ask Daisy if she can spare me a moment. I'm going to go down for dinner this evening and I want to look my best for Max. The dear boy got a bit of a shock when he saw me today."

Abby looked up. "He's coming back tonight?"

"Of course. He said he'd be back before dinner. His first night home, and my first time dining downstairs, so I want to make sure everything's as it should be. Ask Featherby and Cook to step up too, will you? No time to go to a lot of trouble, but I want to make sure we serve some of his favorite dishes."

"I could make the arrangements for you," Abby offered.

"I know, my dear, but this is something I want to do for him myself. For once, you and your sisters can stop fretting about me and this house, and go off and make yourself pretty. I'd like to make this a meal to remember."

Abby went downstairs, a little troubled by what she'd learned. The image of a sad little boy waiting endlessly at the window clashed powerfully with her impression of the unshaven, long-haired Viking who'd stormed up the staircase and lifted Abby right off her feet, stealing the very breath from her body. And then there was the cold, cutting accuser who'd torn her character to shreds in the carriage, and offered to bribe her.

Which one would she see at dinner? If he even came.

"This is fun, isn't it?" Jane commented. "My first proper dinner in company—outside of the Pill, that is." She looked at the others and explained, "The Pillbury Home for the Daughters of Distressed Gentlewomen. It's where Abby and I lived after Mama died."

They were all seated in the drawing room, dressed in their best. Lady Beatrice looked frail but magnificent in a startling purple satin gown that Daisy and her maid, Sutton, had taken in for her.

Daisy sat beside her, clutching her sherry glass in a nervous fist. She'd never dined in formal company either, but unlike Jane, she wasn't at all looking forward to it. Maidservants, let alone maidservants who'd grown up in brothels, were not usually taught the manners expected at the tables of the *ton*. "All you have to do is copy me," Abby had assured her.

Featherby, resplendent in a fine new suit, handed around sherry. He'd been handing around sherry for the last twenty minutes. Abby caught his eye, glanced at Jane and shook her head slightly. Featherby looked at Jane, who was looking a little rosier than the fire warranted, removed her empty sherry glass and replaced it with a glass of lemonade.

The clock struck fifteen minutes past the dinner hour.

"Are you sure Lord Davenham was intending to dine here tonight?" Abby asked.

"Oh, yes, m'dear," Lady Beatrice said serenely. "Max always does what he says he will."

Abby had no such faith. Few men who'd spent nine years abroad, and the last few months on a ship would choose to spend their first evening in London with their elderly aunt. She'd yet to see this much-vaunted word of his kept.

She glanced at the clock for the fourteenth time in the last ten minutes and pressed her lips together. Jane wasn't the only one keyed up. They'd all gone to a lot of trouble for this dinner—throughout the afternoon, Lady Beatrice had been issuing orders right, left and center, and they'd all been flying around trying to make everything perfect. But the one who'd be most disappointed if Lord Davenham didn't show up was Lady Beatrice.

Damaris leaned across and murmured to Abby, "He's not coming, is he?"

Another five minutes elapsed. Abby had had enough. She set down her sherry glass with something of a snap, and rose. "I think it's time we went in. It seems as though Lord Davenham has been delayed—"

A voice, deep and masculine, sounded in the hall outside, followed by brisk, firm footsteps.

The sitting room door opened and there stood Lord Davenham. Abby couldn't help but gasp. All trace of Viking was gone. The long dark hair tied back with a strip of leather had been replaced by a short, almost severe crop, with just a hint of curl surviving at the temples and forehead to soften the hard planes of his face. The haircut known as the Brutus.

That'd be right.

He hadn't plastered it down with pomade, as a lot of men did. It looked clean and soft to the touch, the sort of haircut that made one want to run fingers through it—not that she did, of course.

The stubble was gone too, his chin freshly shaved and smooth, the strong line of his jaw etched cleanly. There was a slight dent in his chin, like a dimple, only not so frivolous.

His dark brown breeches fit snugly to his lithe and powerful form. His boots were high, black and polished to a high gleam. His coat was dark brown also, worn over a white shirt and a subtly striped gray silk waistcoat. His cravat was severely knotted.

He looked magnificent.

Abby thought of the vulnerable small boy in Lady Beatrice's story. Not a hint of vulnerability remained in this man's face or bearing.

She was still smarting from the insults he'd hurled at her. He glanced her way and stopped dead, his hard gray gaze holding hers captive for a long moment. She felt it like a touch, like a wave of heat sweeping over her body, so strong that she stepped back a pace, as if he'd reached for her and held her, instead of just staring.

Feeling suddenly hot and self-conscious, she dragged her gaze away and adjusted the new cream ruffled evening spencer Daisy had made her. Abby loved it. She'd never worn anything so pretty and feminine in her life.

Still Lord Davenham stared.

Why? Was he going to denounce her here and now? She hoped not. Lady Beatrice was so excited to have him home, and had gone to so much trouble to make the dinner special, Abby didn't want anything to spoil it.

He cleared his throat and crossed the room to bow over Lady Beatrice's hand. "Aunt Bea, you're dressed and out of bed! And looking very elegant, may I say."

His aunt beamed up at him. "Of course, dear boy, did you think I wouldn't make the effort for your first dinner at home?"

He looked briefly disconcerted. "At home, but—"

She raised her lorgnette and scanned him with approval. "I see you've found your razor."

He ran his hand absentmindedly across his freshly shaved chin. For the first time he seemed to take in the significance of the emptied sherry glasses, and that they were all dressed for dinner. "You've been waiting. I'm sorry; I didn't realize you expected me."

"You said you'd be back before dinner."

"I know. I apologize for my lateness." He glanced at the door. "I need to step outside—I'll be back in a moment. Freddy Monkton-Coombes is outside in his curricle—"

So he'd made his own plans for dinner, Abby thought.

"Young Monkton-Coombes? I remember him," Lady Beatrice said, giving Abby an arch glance. "Invite him in. Skinny young fellow, as I recall. Could do with a good feed. But eligible, very eligible."

Lord Davenham frowned. "He's already made arrangements to dine at his club—"

But his aunt had taken several glasses of sherry and was in no mind to be dissuaded. "Nonsense, he can go to his club later. We have plenty here. William, set another place. Max, go and bring Freddy in. I haven't seen the boy for years, but I was always very fond of his mother and could do with a good catch-up. Besides, these gels have been pining for some young company, and a well-bred, elegant young fribble is just the ticket, isn't it, gels?"

Lord Davenham looked anything but delighted by that suggestion, Abby thought. His reluctance to introduce his friend to them couldn't be more obvious.

He shrugged. "I'll convey your invitation, Aunt Bea, but I doubt he'll come."

Max went back outside to where Freddy was waiting in the curricle.

Freddy gathered up the reins. "That was quick."

"Sorry, but my aunt is expecting me to dine with her this evening."

"On a tray in her bedchamber?" Freddy pulled a face.

"No, she's made an effort to dress and come downstairs for

my first night home in England, and I won't disappoint her. We'll have to put off that dinner at the club for another time." Max paused, then added, "She asked me to extend the invitation to you—"

"With the muffins?" Freddy inquired darkly.

Max repressed a smile. "With the young ladies, yes."

Freddy shuddered. "Not on your life. You're on your own there."

"Coward."

"To the bone," Freddy agreed. "And if you end up walking down the aisle with one of them, leg-shackled for life to a muffin, don't say I didn't warn you. Stand back." He snapped his reins and the curricle moved off.

Max watched him take the corner in a stylish fashion, and grinned. Freddy was going to kill him when he finally clapped eyes on the girls.

They were all looking particularly fetching tonight, dressed in their finery. The younger ones were set to dazzle, but Miss Chance . . . He swallowed.

Her dress was quite plain—elegance personified, the pale sage color bringing out the green in those extraordinary eyes of hers. But the way it clung subtly to her slender curves had caused his mouth to dry. . . .

As for that short, long-sleeved white thingummy that fastened just above her waist . . . a frothy concoction of ruffles that gently cupped her breasts like a dressing of whipped cream.

The sight wiped his mind blank for a full minute.

Chapter Ten

*"Seldom, very seldom, does complete truth belong to any
human disclosure; seldom can it happen that something
is not a little disguised, or a little mistaken."*

—JANE AUSTEN, *EMMA*

The table was heavy, ornate and outmoded, and even with all its leaves removed, it was still too large for six people, unless they wanted to shout and wave instead of converse—a sign of the more social, more formal past of the house.

The butler had solved the problem by placing them all at one end, with Aunt Bea at the head, Max on her right, and beside him, Miss Jane and Miss Damaris. Miss Chance sat opposite him, on Aunt Bea's left, with Miss Daisy beside her.

"As many of your favorite dishes as we could arrange at such short notice," Aunt Bea told Max as he seated her. She'd insisted on walking the dozen or so steps into the dining room, though she'd had to be supported by Max on one side of her and "dear Abby" on the other. Her frailty still shocked him.

"Roast beef with Yorkshire pudding—I'm sure you never got good English beef while you were away. And steak-and-kidney pie—recall how you used to love that? And potatoes baked in butter and cream, and green beans, oh, and Westphalian ham, you know you enjoy that," she added as the servants placed a giant ham on the table, followed by a dish of chicken in some kind of creamy sauce, a tureen of soup, a bowl of fresh green peas and a jelly.

"It's wonderful, Aunt Bea, thank you." He hadn't actually

noticed the food. Now, as he looked at the array of dishes being set out on the table, he couldn't help but be touched that she'd remembered. These had been his favorite dishes when he was a schoolboy and came to Aunt Bea for the holidays.

His tastes had changed somewhat since then—these days he preferred spicier food—but the dishes before him evoked a nostalgia in him that he couldn't help but enjoy.

"And wait till you see what we have for pudding—bread-and-butter pudding, a lemon tart, another fruit jelly and a syllabub." She turned to the girls. "My nephew always was a sweet tooth."

Max smiled. That hadn't changed all that much.

Aunt Bea turned to Miss Chance, who'd hardly said a word. "I told you, didn't I, Abby, that I knew what would please my nephew best."

"You did indeed." Miss Chance smiled warmly at his aunt, but didn't so much as glance in Max's direction. She was still angry with him for what he'd said in the carriage. Max couldn't entirely blame her.

He didn't know her motives, or why she was posing as Aunt Bea's niece, but he now accepted that she'd intervened in a dreadful situation and saved the old lady, and for that he owed her. And he always paid his debts.

"The dear gel wanted to save me the trouble, but I enjoyed it. Ah, *potage Crécy*," said his aunt as the footman entered with a large soup tureen. "Potatoes, leeks, carrots, celery and cream—I know it's a winter soup, but this ridiculous weather is cold enough to justify it, and you always used to enjoy it."

"Aren't you having any?" Max asked as the footman went to serve him. His aunt should be served first.

"No." She pulled a face as the butler placed a bowl of creamy greenish liquid in front of her. "Apparently *I* have to have *potage crème de compost*."

Max frowned. "*Crème de* what?"

"Compost." She shrugged. "Well, that's what I call it, and it's perfectly apt, I assure you. It's full of weeds—some witch's brew of Damaris's—oh, I grant you she puts in butter and cream and does her best to make the vile stuff palatable, but it's still just weeds."

Max turned to Miss Damaris. *"Weeds?"*

"It's the same as our soup, only with a lot of extra herbs, including nettles and young dandelion leaves," she said, quite composed. "They help cleanse the system, strengthen the blood and stimulate the appetite."

"It's very good for you," Miss Chance said, clearly aiming to draw his fire.

He glanced at his aunt's bowl of soup. "May I try some?"

"Be my guest." She pushed the bowl toward him.

Max tasted it. It wasn't bad. There was a slightly bitter after-taste, but it was perfectly palatable. But if his aunt didn't like it . . .

"Do you have to eat it?"

"Not if she doesn't want to get better," Miss Chance said brightly.

"Oh, well, if I must," Aunt Bea said in a long-suffering tone, and reached for her soup. "Since dear Damaris has made it for me herself. The girl can cook," she told Max. "The very day the gels arrived, she made me my first decent meal in months—boiled egg with toast soldiers. And that's not all—she cooked for the entire household for nearly a week until Featherby found Cook for us."

"Indeed, Miss Damaris, that's an unusual skill for a lady," Max said. Aunt Bea was drinking her soup quite happily, he saw, encouraged by Miss Chance, who broke open a warm bread roll and buttered it for her. She was, he saw, very attentive to his aunt. Almost protective. He just wished he knew why.

Abigail Chance wasn't the person referred to in Lady Beddington's letter. The Scottish doctor had sung her praises, and Max could see she took good care of his aunt. And Aunt Bea was clearly very fond of her and the other girls.

But why someone like Miss Chance should interest herself in the affairs of an aristocratic old lady who Max was sure had no connection to her—and how she'd met his aunt in the first place—was still a source of unease.

Max didn't believe in altruism—in his experience, people usually had secret, less-than-admirable motives.

"My father gave me a very broad-ranging education," Miss Damaris said.

"And, Miss Jane, do you cook too?" Max asked her.

"Heavens, no." The girl laughed. "We never learned anything useful at the Pill, did we, Abby?" Her sister looked daggers at her across the table, but Miss Jane was oblivious.

"The Pill?" Max prompted.

"The Pillbury H——" She gasped and turned to Damaris in surprise—Max guessed it was a sharp elbow to the ribs—then looked at Abby. "Oh." Blushing, she started drinking her soup.

The Pillbury H—House? Home? Whatever it was, Miss Chance didn't want her sister to speak of it, which meant Max was very interested indeed. He turned back to Miss Damaris. "So you two must have had different fathers."

She blushed and mumbled something in the affirmative.

"And yet you are both called Chance." He let that dangle in the silence for a long moment, then added, "How very singular."

"Isn't it just?" Miss Abby said with a glittering affability that fooled no one. "But then, life is singular, isn't it?" Daring him to make something of it.

Max smiled. There was a short silence as the servants cleared away the soup bowls and replaced them with dinner plates.

"I'm afraid Miss Chance is a little cross with me, Aunt Bea," Max said, as the butler served him from a dish of freshly carved roast beef. He was rewarded with a flash of gray-green as Miss Chance darted him a narrow glance. "We had an . . . exchange of views this morning."

"Abby, is that right? You're cross with my nephew?" Apparently this delighted his aunt.

"Not at all. It's not his fault," Miss Chance said smoothly.

It was not forgiveness in any way, shape or form. It was bait. Max waited.

"What isn't his fault?"

Miss Chance finished serving herself from a dish of green beans. "That he's lived in wild and uncivilized parts for so long, he's forgotten how a gentleman should conduct himself."

Her sisters gasped. His aunt gave a startled glance at Max, then let out a crack of laughter. "And what do you say to that, dear boy?"

"Nothing, Aunt Bea. I believe I was twelve when you taught

me that a gentleman never contradicts a lady." He looked at Miss Chance and added, "In public."

Unconcerned, she speared a green bean and ate it.

"And what was your exchange of views about?" Aunt Bea pursued.

Her sisters tensed and watched him covertly. She'd obviously told them everything, but hadn't mentioned it to his aunt. Why not? It would have been to her advantage.

But Miss Chance said nothing. Clearly she didn't intend to disclose their quarrel at all, even when invited to. Instead she ate a second bean. Slowly.

"I do believe," Max said, just as the bean slid between her lips, "that I owe Miss Chance an apology for some of the things I said."

Her eyes widened. She choked.

Max waited until she'd stopped coughing and had drunk the rest of her champagne.

"I said some harsh things, Miss Chance. I was mistaken, and for that I apologize."

"Handsomely said, my boy," his aunt said approvingly. "A credit to your upbringing—that would be me," she added to the girls at the table. "Now, Abby, what do you have to say to that?"

"I accept your apology, Lord Davenham," she said quietly, but made no attempt to apologize for the things she'd said to him. Including the accusation that he'd left his aunt to rot. Which still rankled.

So she was not wholly reconciled. That was fine with Max; he was still suspicious of her motives. And her background.

"I believe you've visited a great many interesting places, Lord Davenham," she said as Featherby removed her plate. "Would you tell us about them?"

"Oh, please, Lord Davenham," Jane chimed in, clearly eager to make up for her earlier faux pas. "I'd love to hear about your adventures; wouldn't you, Damaris?"

"Yes, indeed," Damaris murmured obediently.

He glanced at Daisy and waited for her to express her passionate desire for a traveler's tale, but perhaps nobody had nudged or kicked her, for she continued to concentrate wholly on her dinner. Actually, he saw, she was concentrating on managing her cutlery. Scowling over it, with sideways glances every few minutes to watch how Miss Chance was managing hers.

With elegant assurance and complete lack of self-consciousness, he noted; she'd been well brought up, as had the other two.

The second course was brought out: crumbed sweetbreads, a fish dish and a predominance of sweet dishes that his aunt had promised.

"Well, Max?" his aunt demanded. "Are you going to tell us about your travels?"

So for the rest of the meal Max entertained them with traveler's tales about some of the more interesting and exotic places he'd been and some of the adventures he and his friends had had.

It was all going well until Miss Chance reached for the syllabub, one of his favorites, a dish of sweet, tangy whipped cream. It matched the frothy top she was wearing.

She dipped a spoon into the creamy confection and transferred it to her mouth.

Max swallowed. His narrative faltered.

Her eyes half closed in bliss as her lips closed over the spoon and she let the sweet mixture slide over her tongue and down her throat.

Max forced himself to resume his story. There was nothing at all unusual about the way she was eating; it was all perfectly *comme il faut*. So why could he not take his eyes off her?

She spooned up another mouthful. This time when the spoon was slowly withdrawn a tiny, gleaming morsel of syllabub remained quivering in the corner of her upper lip. Unhurriedly she licked it off.

Max's words dried up along with his throat.

After a moment Miss Chance stopped spooning up the syllabub. Her brows rose. She was looking at him. The entire table was looking at him, waiting for him to continue his story. Hanged if he knew what it was. He cleared his throat.

"You're fond of syllabub, Miss Chance?" Sparkling conversation, indeed.

"Very. And you, Lord Davenham?" She took a third leisurely spoonful. His groin tightened.

"Yes." It came out as a croak. He wrenched his gaze off Miss Chance's delectable mouth and turned to his aunt. He half expected to receive a knowing grin—she could be very acute at times—but instead she looked weary and rather worn, and Max was immediately concerned. "How are you feeling, Aunt Bea? Not too tired?"

"I am, as it happens." She grimaced. "Getting old, I'm afraid."

"Nonsense, it's your first night downstairs and it's been a day full of excitement," Miss Chance said. "No wonder you're tired. You're making wonderful progress, but you must not overtire yourself. Shall I call William to take you upstairs?" She rose to help.

"I'll do it," Max said. He walked around the table and scooped his aunt into his arms—she was shockingly light—and carried her up to her bedchamber. Miss Chance hurried ahead, opening doors and sending for Sutton, Aunt Bea's maid.

"I'll be all right now with Sutton," the old lady said testily as Max placed her gently on the bed. "There's no need for you two to hang around."

Max left. Abby took a few moments more, but Lady Beatrice flapped her hands, shooing her away. "Just because I'm a hopeless crock doesn't mean you young things should have your evening spoiled."

"You didn't spoil anything," Abby assured her. "It was a lovely evening and the dinner was delicious. Anyway, I expect Lord Davenham has another engagement—he'd hardly wish to drink his port in solitary splendor, would he?"

But when she emerged from Lady Beatrice's room, she found Lord Davenham waiting for her in the corridor.

"I meant what I said earlier," he said. "Some of the things I said to you in the carriage were unnecessarily harsh, and for that I apologize."

She could hear the *but* coming, so she said it for him, with an assumption of cool composure. "But?"

"But you and I both know you're no relation to my aunt, let alone her nieces." He took a step closer. "So while I value the care you've taken of my aunt in the sickroom—and I do thank you sincerely for it—I also want to make it clear that it doesn't give you and your so-called sisters the right to impose on her in other ways. And I'm warning you now: I mean to ensure you don't. The minute I see the least hint of imposition, you and those others will be out on your ear—is that understood?"

He stared down at her for a long moment. Abby tried desperately to think of some *devastating* response, but her mind was infuriatingly blank. All she could do was glare. Impotently.

Apparently satisfied with her response—or lack of it—he turned on his heel and strode off. A moment later she heard the front door open, then close as he left the house.

"I can't work out what she's up to," Max told Freddy. He'd tracked him down at the club, accompanied him to another club and finally wandered back to Freddy's lodgings for a quiet drink. "I'm sure she has some scheme in mind, but what the devil is it?"

"Probably marriage—it's what muffins usually want." Freddy had already made impressive inroads on the brandy when Max had arrived.

Max snorted. "How would looking after my aunt lead to marriage? I wasn't even in the country when she started, and nobody, not even you or my aunt, knew I was coming home."

Perplexed, Freddy scratched his stylishly coiffed head. "It's an exceptionally cunning plot, I grant you, but you should never underestimate the tortuous subtleties of a muffin's mind."

"She's not a muffin." Not that Max knew precisely what a muffin—in Freddy's terminology—was, but he was certain Abigail Chance wasn't one. She was too damned attractive, for a start. Too much for his own ease of mind.

Freddy shook his head. "You've been away so long, living the free life of an adventurer, you're out of touch. Trust me, muffins are everywhere." He considered the statement, then added, "Except on ships, which is why you're so ignorant on the subject."

Max thought about that. Freddy was a trifle castaway, but there was some truth in what he said; Max had been out of the company of Englishwomen for the last nine years. In fact, given that he'd been eighteen when he left, and hadn't had much experience with women—Englishwomen, at least—he could be said to be almost completely ignorant of the species.

"So what do you think?"

Freddy swirled the brandy in his glass, observing the candlelight through it. "It's about gratitude."

"Gratitude?"

Freddy nodded wisely. "Knows you're fond of Lady Bea. Thinks if the old lady's fond of her, you'll pop the question."

Max snorted. "That's the stupidest thing I ever heard of. Marry someone because my *aunt* likes her?"

"Not saying it's what you'd do; saying it's what a muffin would think."

"Nonsense. She'd be a fool if she expected marriage for such a reason, and she's no fool. Nor is she a muffin, whatever that is." He walked over to the fire—really, it was ridiculously cold for summer—and stirred up the coals with the poker. "She's getting bed and board from my aunt, and a small allowance—and if that's all it was, I'd understand it, but she takes real trouble with my aunt. Far above and beyond what it would be reasonable to expect any servant or paid companion to do. A stranger seeing them together would imagine them to be mother and daughter. Or grandmother and granddaughter." Aunt and niece, as his aunt ludicrously claimed.

"Maybe that's what she wants, then."

"What? To be a granddaughter?"

"It's how women think," Freddy insisted. "Very family-minded, females."

"But that's ridiculous—she can't. She's not—*they're* not my aunt's family—that's my whole point. You don't just walk up and move into someone's family."

Freddy shook his head. "Max, Max, Max, the trouble with you is for the last nine years—well, most of your life, come to think of it—you've lived in a masculine world; you're used to logic, reason, *sense*. Females don't think like we do; they're *emotional*."

That was true enough. When the mood took her, Aunt Bea was quite impervious to logic. Max poked the fire savagely, sending sparks dancing up the chimney.

"F'r instance, the other day the mater wept at me."

Max blinked. It didn't sound like Freddy's mother. Of course, he hadn't seen her in years, but his impression of her had always been that of a brisk, no-nonsense woman, a noted society hostess who'd managed to fire off all of Freddy's sisters successfully.

"Assure you, she produced actual tears. As if that's going to make me hoof it down the aisle with some suitable female. I ask you—can you see me leg-shackled for life to someone *suitable*?"

"It doesn't exactly spring to mind," Max agreed.

"Not logical, you see. If it was m'father, now, he'd simply issue an order."

"And you'd obey?"

Freddy considered that. "No, I'd probably do exactly what I've always done."

"The opposite?"

"More or less. So in a devious move, he's set the mater onto it. Because you can't reason with females. They don't think logically. And they fight dirty."

Max raised a brow.

"Tears," said Freddy darkly. "The lowest move of all, mark my words."

It was all too frustrating, Abby thought as she prepared for bed. She wasn't used to being in the wrong. She didn't like it one little bit.

She removed her clothing swiftly, folding each garment neatly. The situation—and the man—made her so cross.

It was all very well to tell herself that Lord Davenham's suspicions of her and her sisters were *perfectly* justified. They *were* no relation, they *were* living under a false name and they *had* made the acquaintance of Lady Beatrice in a less-than-honorable manner.

The fact that they intended her only good, that they cared for her, should outweigh those things, but she could understand why, to some—to him—they might not.

All he really knew was that they weren't her nieces, but since Lady Beatrice claimed they were, he could have nothing to say. Should have nothing to say.

She pulled her nightgown on.

The way he prowled around Abby like a big, suspicious guard dog sparked her temper as well as her guilt. She might not be completely lily white and pure in her motives, but she'd rescued Lady Beatrice from a dire situation, whereas he'd left her to rot!

It was probably guilt about that that was making him so overprotective now. Too little, too late.

The minute I see the least hint of imposition, you and those others will be out on your ear—is that understood?

She plumped her pillows up, then punched them down. He didn't *know* what she'd done, so he had *no* justification for threatening her like that. She wanted to fling his accusations and suspicions back in his teeth. It was infuriating that she couldn't.

Even more infuriating that some small part of her still wanted him to think well of her. Of them.

She climbed into bed, enjoying the cool, smooth feel of the sheets against her skin.

How much lower would his opinion sink when he discovered where Jane and Damaris and Daisy had been when she found them? And that Abby had met Lady Beatrice in the middle of the night? On her first attempt to be a thief?

So while I value the care you've taken of my aunt in the sickroom—and I do thank you sincerely for it—it doesn't give you and your so-called sisters the right to impose on her. . . .

Impose on Lady Beatrice? Even as she resented the accusation, guilt pricked at her. Yes, they lived in Lady Beatrice's house, at her expense, and accepted a small allowance from her, but they earned every penny; Abby was very clear in her mind about that.

She wished now she had accepted Lady Bea's more-than-generous offer of payment. Well, no, she didn't—it was an offer made out of loneliness and fear, a kind of bribe to make them want to stay with her. And no matter what his high-and-mighty lordship thought of her, she wouldn't take advantage of a sick, scared old lady.

Abby punched her pillow again. It would have served him right if she had.

She snuggled down under the covers. The trouble was, deep down, in her secret heart of hearts she did hope for more. Not to impose on Lady Beatrice precisely, but certainly to take advantage. Of the situation, not the woman.

If only she could think of a way to do it. There must be a way for Jane to meet eligible men. . . .

The minute I see the least hint of imposition, you and those others will be out on your ear—is that understood?

Lord Davenham could toss them out at any moment. Oh, his aunt would object, but would he take any notice? He was the arrogant, autocratic type. A Viking dressed as a gentleman.

They didn't have enough money—or clothes—for Bath yet. There must be a way to get Jane to meet eligible men. There must. . . .

Most people counted sheep to go to sleep; Abby lay in the big warm bed, counting possibilities. . . .

But once she'd drifted off to sleep, it wasn't dreams for Jane that disturbed her. It was a big, dark Viking with steely gray eyes, hunting her down. . . .

There was nowhere to run, no place to hide. Every way she turned, he was there, stopping her, trapping her, judging her. She woke up sweaty, her pulse pounding, her nightgown twisted around her waist.

She sat up, drank the water in the glass by her bedside and lay down again, with firm instructions to herself that she was not to dream, that she needed a clear head in the morning and that she needed to *think*, not to dream.

Lord Davenham had no part in her dreams. She knew better than that. Yes, he was tall and strong and ridiculously good-looking, and something about him made her heart beat faster, but she didn't even like him. Much.

He certainly didn't like her.

Besides, he was betrothed.

She'd been down that path before, with Laurence, though she had no idea he was betrothed at the time. Shame shimmered through her. She never wanted to experience that again.

Chapter Eleven

*"There is a stubbornness about me that never can bear
to be frightened at the will of others. My courage always
rises at every attempt to intimidate me."*

—JANE AUSTEN, *PRIDE AND PREJUDICE*

Max woke early and in a bad mood. He was randy as hell, having passed a restless night full of erotic dreams, most of which involved him licking syllabub from a pair of delectable little breasts . . . and then progressing downward.

He needed exercise: a good, hard ride.

He rose and dressed in riding clothes. He'd hire a horse from the livery stables around the corner and ride off his frustration that way. Damn the wench.

A couple of hours later he returned, feeling slightly less tense, though not enough to banish the memory of those damned dreams. Consequently he was still irritable. The livery stable hack was a slug; he'd have to buy a decent horse.

He hurried upstairs to wash, shave and change. He could smell bacon and toast cooking. He'd feel better after breakfast. Get the taste of syllabub out of his mouth. His mind.

Morton Black would be here in an hour. He'd get to the bottom of the mystery that was Miss Chance and her sisters. Max lathered up his shaving brush.

It prompted an unfortunately erotic image. Max swore.

* * *

Morton Black was a grave-faced man with a wooden leg, the latter a legacy of Napoleon and his minions, Max assumed. After a few questions about the people Black had worked for before, and the kind of tasks he'd carried out, Max was satisfied that the man was discreet and capable.

"It's a delicate matter," he told Black. "My aunt has taken into her home four young women of unknown background: Miss Abigail Chance, and Misses Jane, Damaris and Daisy Chance. My aunt is claiming, for some peculiar and irrational reason of her own, that they are her nieces, but she has no nieces, no close relatives at all, in fact, other than myself."

"I see," Black murmured, writing down the names.

"I wish to learn who these young women are, where they have come from, what they were doing before they came to my aunt and—of course this would be purely speculative—what they intend."

Black nodded.

"The oldest one, Miss Abigail Chance, is their leader; the others all look to her. If Chance is her surname—and I cannot be sure of that—it is not, I believe, the surname of them all. Miss Damaris let it slip that she had a different father, yet they claim her as a sister, not a cousin, and Miss Daisy proclaims without embarrassment that she was born a bastard; yet she too goes by Chance."

Black made a note. "Any other information, my lord?"

"At dinner last night, Miss Jane Chance let slip that she and Miss Abigail once lived in a place she called 'the Pill,' the Pillbury H-something. She didn't complete the name but it occurred to me it could be some kind of institution. I have no idea if the others lived there as well." He sat back in his chair. "Do you think you can track them down? It's not much to go on, I know."

Morton Black gave a thin smile. "I'll do my best, my lord."

The butler ushered Morton Black to the front door. A few minutes later the man returned bearing a note on a gleaming silver salver.

Max raised his brows. "Silver? And still here?"

"It was very dirty, m'lord, and easily overlooked."

Max opened the note. Excellent. His man Bartlett had found two houses fitting his lordship's requirements. He'd made arrangements for someone to be available to show Lord Davenham the houses, should he be interested.

Lord Davenham was. He glanced at the clock. There was just enough time to inspect the houses before he'd arranged to meet Freddy for the excursion to Richmond.

He scrawled a quick note to Bartlett and handed it to the butler for delivery. "See that it gets there immediately." As the butler turned to leave, Max added, "I'm intending to purchase some horses. I'll hire a groom, of course, possibly two, so I'll need you to make the necessary arrangements for their accommodation."

"Of course, my lord. I believe there are grooms' quarters in the stable building in the mews at the rear of the house. I shall have them prepared. And would you wish me to have the stables swept out and prepared as well?"

"Do we have the staff for that?" He was very well aware that indoor servants would be most affronted to be asked to do a groom's work.

"I shall hire someone for the job, and William will supervise."

"Good man." Max headed upstairs to fetch his coat. His day was improving. With any luck by the end of it he'd have a house and his own transport.

As he passed his aunt's bedchamber, he heard a gurgle of laughter. It was not his aunt. The door was ajar. Max paused to listen.

"Curse you, you dreadful gel!" Aunt Bea sounded most put out. What the devil was going on?

Miss Chance—there was no mistaking that warm, spiced-honey voice of hers—replied, "Please yourself, but you know the consequences."

Aunt Bea made an irritated noise. "You have no heart, young lady."

Again, that soft gurgle of laughter. "I know."

"So, you're determined to torture me, you callous creature?"

"I am."

"What if I tell my nephew that you're bullying me shockingly?"

"Go ahead; see if I care."

That was all Max needed. He shoved open the door. "Aunt Bea?"

His aunt was sitting up in bed dressed in a fetching dressing gown: ruffled, pink and frivolous—quite unsuitable for an elderly woman. On her bedside table sat a tray containing the remains of her breakfast: the shell of a boiled egg, a pot of chocolate, a few flakes of sweet pastry. A couple of kittens—Snowflake and Marmaduke—lay in a sleeping tangle in her lap.

She did not present a picture of a woman being callously tortured.

"Max, there you are!" his aunt exclaimed. "Tell her!"

Max glanced at the "her" in question.

Miss Chance rose from her chair beside the bed, laid a book down on the counterpane and said calmly, "Good morning, Lord Davenham. I trust you slept well?"

Dressed in the simple gray gown of the morning before, she nevertheless managed to look fresh as a spring morning. Her hair was drawn back in a loose knot, with soft tendrils feathering at her temple and nape. She looked nothing like Max's image of a callous torturer.

But looks were often deceptive.

"What's the problem here?" he asked.

"No problem. I've been reading to your aunt, that's all. And now I've finished."

"Hah! Tell him *where* you finished!" Aunt Bea snapped.

Clear gray-green eyes danced with laughter. "Just before the end of the chapter."

"It's outrageous," his aunt grumbled. "Nobody finishes reading *before* the end of a chapter."

Max looked from his aunt to Miss Chance, then back again. He had no idea what they were talking about.

Miss Chance took pity on him. "It's quite an exciting point in the story, and I'll be very happy to finish reading it to your aunt once she's walked to the window and back."

"Walked to the window . . . ?"

"As the doctor said she must, several times a day, if she's to gain the full use of her limbs again."

Ah. Now he understood. "I see, well, in that case—Ow!" He looked down to where a small, disreputable scrap of black fluff had leaped out of nowhere and attached itself to Max's knee. With tiny, very sharp claws. It began to climb him like a tree.

He bent and carefully pried the creature from his leg, unhooking one small claw at a time. He raised the kitten to eye level, narrowed his eyes sternly at it and said, "That is no way to greet your namesake! Or, indeed, anyone. And breeches are *not* for climbing up."

The kitten narrowed its eyes back at him. And started to purr.

Max placed it on the bed with its brother and sister, where it immediately pounced on its brother and started a fight. "Atrocious manners," Max informed it, and turned back to the matter at hand.

His aunt was grinning openly. Miss Chance had her lips well primmed and under control, but her eyes danced with laughter.

Damn. His dignity shot to pieces by a tiny scrap of black fluff. Oddly, catching the warm light in Miss Chance's eyes, he didn't mind. Then she smiled, his breath hitched and for a moment his mind blanked completely.

He was a betrothed man.

"Carry on," he told Miss Chance crisply. "Good morning, Aunt Bea."

"Featherby, you shouldn't be telling me this—you shouldn't eavesdrop on Lord Davenham's private conversations. It could cost you your position."

Featherby looked unconcerned. "A good butler knows everything that goes on in a house, Miss Abby, so don't you fret about me. Besides, William and I owe you everything."

"It's very kind of you, truly, and I appreciate the good intentions, but please don't risk your job on my behalf again."

"Don't you want to know what he wanted Morton Black to do?"

Abby sighed. "You know I do."

He drew her aside.

When he finished relating what he'd overheard, Abby looked at him in dismay. "It won't take Mr. Black long to find the Pillbury Home. And then our names will come out—Jane's and mine, that is."

"Is that such a bad thing?"

She frowned. "Not really, I suppose. It's the rest I worry about . . . the worst. But I doubt Mr. Black can discover that."

"Does the old lady know? About the brothel, I mean?"

Abby stared at Featherby in shock. You knew?"

He smiled. "I told you, a good butler knows everything. William told me about it before we left the other place. One of the girls—young Daisy, I think—let it slip. But don't worry, Miss Abby; wild horses couldn't drag it out of us. But have you told the old lady?"

"Yes, before we moved in here. I couldn't accept her invitation and leave her in ignorance of the worst."

Featherby gave her a benevolent smile. "I wouldn't expect anything else of you, Miss Abby; such a true lady you are. Well, as long as Lady Beatrice knows, you're all right then. It's her house, and she's not going to let Lord Davenham kick you out; you can be sure of that."

Abby swallowed. "I hope not." She paused. "Speaking of our previous residence, have you or William ever been back there?"

"You mean have we heard whether anyone has come looking for a Miss Chantry and her sister again?" Featherby shook his head. "William says not. He keeps his ear to the ground, does William, and nobody's come asking questions since that time I told you about, the day we left."

"Does anyone there know where you and William live?"

"No. William's very discreet. In any case, most of the former tenants have moved; it's mostly vagrants who live there now. The demolition is imminent. Everyone assumed that's why you girls left too. William put it about weeks ago that you'd gone to live with relatives in the country—that traveling chaise was remarked on by a few people."

The tension in Abby unraveled a little. "So nobody is looking for us?"

"Nobody," Featherby assured her. "Only Morton Black."

"What are you doing?" Lady Beatrice interrupted Abby's reading. She raised her lorgnette and peered in the direction of Daisy, Jane and Damaris.

They were seated around the window to get the best light for their task. The return of Lord Davenham had made them all aware of the precariousness of their situation, and the first priority was to sew the dresses to be worn at Jane's season in Bath.

"What do you mean?" Jane asked.

"I thought you gels were sewing, but looks to me like you're unpicking. Seen Abby doing it often enough." Abby was the worst seamstress, which was why she mostly read aloud. "But all three of you? Making a mistake at the same time?"

"Oh, that." Jane laughed. "We're unpicking a dress."

"I can see that, m'gel, but why?"

"To use the material, of course," Daisy said.

Lady Beatrice tilted her head, as if she'd misheard. "To what?"

"It's how we get the fabric for all our clothes," Damaris explained. "We buy—well, it's usually Daisy who does the buying. She knows all the best places and has the best eye for what she can use or not."

"You buy what?"

"Old clothes."

"You mean you make your dresses from *old clothes*?" Lady Beatrice exclaimed.

"We can't afford to buy material new," Daisy said. "The fabric is the most expensive part of any dress. I can get half a dozen old dresses for the price of one length of new material, and depending on what they are, I might get as many as three or four new dresses out of them. Or a dress and a pelisse."

"But you can't wear other people's old clothes!"

"Where do you think I got the material for that?" Daisy pointed to Lady Beatrice's pink-and-green dressing gown and said proudly, "Two dresses I got down Petticoat Lane and some of me bits and pieces."

"*My dressing gown?* Made from *rags cast off by strangers?*" The old lady recoiled, casting a horrified glance down at herself, as if her favorite garment had suddenly turned into a pile of old rags, reeking and crawling with vermin.

Abby laughed at her expression. "Everything is perfectly clean."

"*Rags?* They're not rags," Daisy said, clearly offended by the slur on her shopping abilities. "I only buy the best, me. I'm *very* choosy!"

Unconvinced, the old lady sniffed.

"It's true," Daisy insisted. "Some people get rid of a dress after one or two wears—one, sometimes, if they've spilled something and their maid is too stupid or too lazy to get the stain out."

"Old clothes worn by complete strangers," Lady Beatrice muttered crossly, smoothing her hand over her dressing gown. She was obviously torn.

"No choice, me lady," Daisy said. "Beggars can't be choosers."

Lady Beatrice drew herself up in her bed. "*I,*" she said in the voice of outrage, "am *not* a beggar!" She narrowed her eyes at Daisy. "And neither are you, m'gel. Abby, ring the bell for Featherby. It's time for my luncheon."

Featherby arrived and set out a light luncheon of soup, poached fish, cucumber salad and bread and butter on a table by the fire. It might be summer, but it was still a chilly, gray day.

After their luncheon, Lady Beatrice had a nap and the girls went for a walk by the river. When they returned, a large, elaborately carved wooden trunk was sitting in the middle of the bedchamber. The kittens, Marmaduke and Snowflake, were sniffing cautiously around it. Max the kitten sat on top of it, ready to pounce.

The girls eyed the trunk curiously. "What's in the trunk?" Abby asked, picking up the small black kitten. A small, rusty-sounding purr was her instant reward.

"I believe we have a chapter to finish," Lady Beatrice said austerely.

Abby hid a smile, passed her the kitten, picked up the book and continued from where she'd left off before luncheon. The others eyed the trunk curiously but continued work on their garments.

While she was reading, Featherby and William carried in two more large trunks and placed them with the first. These were leather, well-worn and embossed with the Davenham coat of arms.

"Will that be all, m'lady?" Featherby asked.

"Yes, yes." She waved them off imperiously and gestured to Abby to keep reading. Abby did, but nobody's attention was on the story. What was in the trunks? Lady Beatrice was being very mysterious.

Finally Abby reached the end of the chapter and closed the book firmly. "Time for your exercises."

The old lady eyed her speculatively. "Don't you want to know what's in the trunks?"

She did, of course, but, "After you've done your exercises."

Lady Beatrice snorted. "You're a hard woman, Abigail Chance." But she handed the kittens to Abby, pushed back the bedclothes and swung her legs over the side of the bed. Jane and Damaris put her slippers on, then helped her to stand. She waved them off. "I can do it."

She walked to the window and back three times, a little wobbly, it was true, and the last was more of an exhausted totter to the bed, but her progress was noticeable.

"Getting better, aren't I?"

"You'll be waltzing by Christmas," Abby said warmly.

The girls tucked her back into bed, and when she'd caught her breath the old lady said, "Go on, then. Open them—the carved cedar one first. And put everything on the bed so I can see."

Jane opened the cedar chest. It contained dozens of parcels wrapped in tissue. She unwrapped the first one and gasped in wonderment as a length of brilliant blue-and-silver silk slithered from her fingers.

"Oh, my gawd," Daisy murmured, as she unwrapped another

length, this one of ruby silk as fine and delicate as anything any of them had ever seen.

Damaris said nothing as she unwrapped a length of heavy cream silk, embroidered on the border with fine knots of roses, but her eyes widened. She stroked it with lingering fingers.

"Here." Lady Beatrice passed a parcel to Abby. Opening it, she found a cashmere shawl of scarlet and blue and green and gold.

"Put it on," Lady Beatrice ordered.

Abby swung it around her shoulders. It was so light and soft and fine, it settled around her body like warm snow. "It's the most beautiful thing I've ever seen."

"My nephew sent me all these things when he first went away. Parcels used to arrive on a regular basis, all kinds of strange and beautiful things—he sent the chest too."

"Cedar," Abby said, inhaling the clean fragrance from the shawl. "I'm amazed it wasn't stolen—the chest alone is worth a lot of money, and as for this shawl . . ." Shawls like this sold for a hundred pounds or more.

Lady Beatrice nodded. "These all came before Caudle came to work for me, and before I got sick. I forget why I had the chest placed in the attic in the first place—I didn't even recall it was there, but obviously it's been in some dark corner, gathering dust for years. It was the other trunks I sent Featherby and William up for, and when they brought this down I nearly wept."

She turned to where Daisy was holding up a length of fine shimmery rose fabric. It had an elaborate gold-embroidered border. "Pretty, isn't it? That's a saree or some such thing— from India. The women wrap themselves up in it, and call themselves dressed. And there's jewelry too," she added as Jane unwrapped a jangly silver necklace. "Just trinkets—nothing an English lady would wear except for a masquerade ball—but pretty. Shame I didn't put the good stuff in this box; might have had some jewels left."

"It's very pretty, though." Jane held it up against her throat, and admired it in the looking glass.

"There should be letters, somewhere to go with each item," Lady Beatrice said. "See if they're in there, will you, Abby?"

Abby dug around in the chest and found tucked in at the side a packet of letters tied with a ribbon. It was quite a thick packet, all addressed with the same firm hand.

"Put them here." Lady Beatrice patted the bedside table. "We'll read them later. My nephew was always a good letter writer."

Abby was surprised. Lord Davenham hadn't seemed to her to be the kind of man who'd send his elderly aunt beautiful things, let alone take the trouble to write regularly. She recalled his anger when she'd accused him of leaving his aunt to rot.

But if he cared about her so much, why had he stayed away for nearly ten years?

"So what's in the other trunks?" Jane asked eagerly, after they'd examined and exclaimed over every beautiful item in the cedar chest.

Lady Beatrice smiled. "My youth."

Abby opened the first leather trunk and lifted out the tissue-wrapped gown that lay on the top, a deep rose satin with a faint cream stripe and dozens of tiny embroidered roses. The skirt was very full and gathered to a tiny waist. With it came a bodice that looked as if it would be amazingly tight, almost like wearing a tube.

She shook it out of its folds and held it up, looking from the dress to Lady Beatrice, trying to imagine her wearing it.

"You are wondering about the pink clashing with my red hair, I suppose," Lady Beatrice said, "but recollect, we all wore our hair powdered in those days."

"This is beautiful," Daisy said, shaking out a dress in apple green silk trimmed with white gauze and knots of ribbon.

"Oh, yes, that one." Lady Beatrice gazed at the dress fondly. "I wore that one at a ball given by the Duchess of Salisbury. Ah, what a night that was. I danced until dawn. . . ."

"Who did you dance with?" Jane asked.

"Everyone," she said with satisfaction. "I was no beauty, but I was never a wallflower. I remember . . . Oh, you don't want to listen to an old lady boring on."

"Yes, we do," said Abby, "and it's not the slightest bit boring."

Jane joined in. "Yes, please go on. Our mama used to tell us stories about her come-out, and I loved them."

"Well, if you insist . . ." The girls gathered around. "It became quite warm in the ballroom, and one young man enticed me onto the terrace to cool down. Oh, it was all perfectly respectable at first—there were plenty of others doing the same." She sighed. "But this man had rather a naughty reputation, and we danced on the terrace, and soon we found ourselves alone. . . ." She gave them a mischievous look. "Without my realizing it, he'd danced me off the terrace and down the garden path—in more ways than one." She sighed. "My first kiss. My mother scolded me roundly for disappearing, of course, but oh, it was worth it." She stroked the green dress. "That man kissed like a dream."

She sat up. "And I wore the most divine pair of shoes—green silk with pearls and diamond buckles."

"Diamond?" Daisy gasped.

"They were paste, of course, but the pearls were real. They should be in the trunk too. See if you can find them."

Daisy felt around and came up with several odd-shaped cloth bags. She pulled them open and a pair of shoes fell out. She opened bag after bag and soon nearly a dozen pairs of shoes lay tumbled on the bed. The girls exclaimed over the old-fashioned shoes.

"Look at those heels," Jane exclaimed. "They're so high! However did you manage to dance in them?"

Lady Beatrice laughed. "Try them on and see for yourself."

Jane eagerly pulled off her own low slippers. A scene out of Cinderella ensued, with Jane, Abby and Damaris all trying and failing to fit in the tiny, exquisite shoes. "Your turn, Daisy," Jane said.

"No, no point in me trying," Daisy said, pulling a face. "Look stupid, I would, clumping along all lopsided in them things." But she looked longingly at the pretty shoes.

"Nobody here would think any such thing, young woman," said Lady Beatrice sternly. "And if you don't try them on, you'll always wonder if they would fit. So you have a limp! What does that matter? All women are entitled to pretty shoes. Do not let fear or embarrassment make you less than you are."

Daisy shrugged and pulled off one of the heavy boots she habitually wore. She picked up a pair of dark rose pink embroidered satin shoes with high heels and diamond buckles and slipped one on. And stared.

"A perfect fit," Abby breathed, and handed her the other shoe. Daisy put it on.

"Let me see," the old lady demanded, and Daisy stepped back, raising her skirts to show the shoes.

"Beautiful," Lady Beatrice said, and Abby had to agree.

"Yeah, until I walk," Daisy said.

"Pish-tush! Those shoes weren't made for walking," Lady Beatrice said. "They're for dancing."

"I can't do that neither," Daisy said.

Lady Beatrice gave her a thoughtful look, but all she said was, "Keep the shoes, Daisy girl. Put them on whenever you need to remind yourself that you have beautiful feet." She glanced at the others. "Unlike Cinderella's big-footed stepsisters." She cut off their laughing protests. "Now, let's see what else is in those trunks."

They pulled out gown after gown, and for each one there was an event—a ball, a soiree, a night at the opera, at Ranelagh, at a fireworks display, a picnic—and a story: a stolen kiss, a magical dance, a particular young man. . . .

As Lady Beatrice reminisced, those long-ago nights came to life in their minds, and they pictured the gentlemen in their powdered wigs and the ladies in their full-skirted dresses and high-piled white-powdered hair teetering along on high-heeled shoes.

The clothes were odd—old-fashioned, heavy and, to the girls' eyes, cumbersome, but the fabrics, they all agreed, were beautiful.

Daisy, in particular, eyed them covetously. "Look at all that fabric—there's yards and yards and yards in that dress," she whispered to Abby. "I could make two whole dresses from just that skirt."

"But weren't they uncomfortable to wear?" Jane asked, holding one of the dresses against her and examining her reflection in the cheval looking glass.

"Not with the correct corsetry," Lady Beatrice said. "They should be in there too. The dresses won't fit properly without the corsets. And the petticoats and the panniers and all the rest."

But when they looked, the corsets and panniers were nowhere to be found, and only two particularly fine petticoats were in the chests.

"They'd make beautiful summer dresses for all of us," Daisy whispered to Abby.

"I want to try them on," Jane said, lifting a cerulean blue silk gown trimmed with blond lace from the piles on the bed. "May I, Lady Beatrice?"

"Go ahead, my dear, but they won't look right without the underpinnings."

Jane passed a rose pink gown to Damaris. "Come on." The two girls disappeared behind the Chinese screen in the corner of the room, and soon giggles and rustles came from behind the screen, and a call for Daisy to come and help them.

Abby tried not to feel a small pang at the giggles and murmurs. These days Jane turned more often to Damaris than to her sister. Abby supposed it was natural. For a start, they were closer in age. Abby had left the Pillbury when Jane was only twelve, and in the six years since, Jane had learned to do without her big sister.

And, of course, the recent ordeal that Damaris and Jane and Daisy had shared had forged a strong bond among them—and Abby was glad of it.

Still, it was hard not to feel left out occasionally.

"What were you wearing the night you met your husband?" Abby asked Lady Beatrice while the others were changing. "Did you fall madly in love with him and slip out into the dark velvet night for some stolen kisses?"

"Ta-daaah!" Jane and Damaris stepped out from behind the screen. They posed a moment, then, picking up the skirts—which, unsupported by the "underpinnings" dragged along the floor—they twirled around in a vague kind of old-fashioned dance.

As they turned, Abby saw the dresses had been laced over bare skin. Of course, their modern underclothes would be all wrong for these dresses. How strange, the way ladies' figures had changed over the ages.

"Come on, Abby," Jane called. "Put this apple green one on; it will look lovely with your coloring."

Lady Beatrice, who had been absently stroking a satin bodice with fingers that still remembered, set it aside, frowning thoughtfully. She waved at Abby to go ahead. "Do you know, I can't for the life of me recall what I was wearing the day I met my husband."

"The day? So it wasn't at a ball?" Abby said as Jane pulled her dress off over her head.

"No, my parents introduced him to me at a house party at his country estate. His father had arranged it all with my father, and he was presented to me as a desirable *parti*."

"Eh?" Daisy stuck her head out from behind the screen. "A desirable *party*? He was a lot of fun, then?"

The old lady chuckled. "No, they meant I should marry him. It was all arranged by the fathers."

Jane tugged the gown up around Abby's shoulders. It felt odd, a little uncomfortable. "You didn't fall in love with him?" Abby asked.

"Not really—well, it wasn't the done thing in my day. Love between husband and wife? A trifle vulgar for our class, though for myself, I wouldn't have minded it at all. But my husband and I respected each other, and it was considered an excellent alliance between our two families. It's how they did it then, and still how people do it today, for all this modern talk of love. Marriage is about property and family, not love."

"Our parents married for love," Abby told her.

"And look where it got them," Jane said, as she laced Abby into the gown.

Abby swiveled around to stare at her sister in shock. She'd always thought Jane felt the same as she did about their parents' marriage—that despite all the hardships, the poverty and the pain, their love had made it all worthwhile. But it seemed she was wrong.

"Our parents both had good marriages all but arranged," Jane explained, stepping out from behind the screen. "But they fell in love with each other and eloped instead. It was all very romantic, I suppose, but they died in poverty, and Abby and I ended up in an orphanage. And after that . . ." She shrugged. "Abby became a governess working for the meanest people—"

"The children were lovely."

"But the last lot of parents were horrid—you wrote to me, recollect, so don't defend them; I know," Jane said. "And I was destined to become a companion to a vicar's mother in Hereford." She looked at Abby. "Was that truly what Mama and Papa would have wanted for us? And that was when everything was going well, and before it all went wrong." She turned to Lady Beatrice. "Before we met you, I mean. You're the best thing that's happened to us . . . ever." She suddenly realized how that sounded. "I'm sorry, I didn't mean you're a *thing*, of course; I meant—"

The old lady patted her on the hand. "I know what you meant, my dear, and you gels are the best thing that's happened to me in forever too. So, young Jane, you'd make a practical marriage, would you?"

Jane nodded. "The very best marriage I possibly can."

Lady Beatrice turned to Abby. "So, Abby what kind of marriage do you dream of?"

Abby looked down and smoothed the fabric of the lovely old dress. "As you said before, Lady Beatrice, we don't all get the choi—"

"What on earth . . . ?" a deep masculine voice interrupted. Lord Davenham stood in the open doorway, lord of all he surveyed.

Chapter Twelve

"Where so many hours have been spent in convincing myself that I am right, is there not some reason to fear I may be wrong?"

—JANE AUSTEN, *SENSE AND SENSIBILITY*

Max had had a good day. The second of the two houses Bartlett had found in Mayfair was most suitable, and Max had instructed Bartlett to buy it. The trip to Richmond had been delightful, the road good, the weather chilly but dry and the inn where they'd stopped for lunch excellent. It was everything he'd missed about England.

To top off the day, Freddy's friend was indeed selling up, and Max had purchased a phaeton and a beautiful pair of high steppers that would give Freddy's sixteen-mile-an-hour pair a run for their money, as well as a pair of matched bays that he thought would suit his aunt's barouche very well. They would all arrive tomorrow.

He'd planned to round off the day with dinner at the club with Freddy and some old acquaintances, and had just dropped past to change his clothes and inform his aunt. Her door was open. He glanced in.

"What on earth . . . ?"

The bedchamber was an explosion of color and fabric and garments, a feminine Aladdin's cave. Even more so than usual. "What are you doing?" he asked, eyeing the pile of fabrics cautiously. Presumably there were kittens buried under it somewhere.

"Max, my dear." His aunt's eyes were a little red rimmed, as though she'd been weeping.

In two strides Max reached her. He took her hands in his. "Aunt Bea, what is it? What's the matter?"

"Nothing, nothing. We're going through all my old gowns, and oh, the memories." She waved a crumpled wisp of lace. "A few sentimental tears, that's all, but mostly tears of laughter."

"I see." His gaze roamed over the tumbled mass of clothing.

"No, you don't, dear boy, but never mind. I've had the most delightful time reliving my youth. The gels have had me in stitches." She chuckled. "Stitches, gels, did you hear? I made a pun."

All the girls except Daisy were dressed in old-fashioned clothing, the dresses sagging a little, as if they were children dressing up. But Abby was no child. She was dressed—half dressed, he saw with a leap of his pulse—in an eighteenth-century brocade gown with panniers. She moved slightly, defensively.

Her back was to the freestanding cheval looking glass and he saw at once that the dress was not properly laced. . . .

She was naked from the nape of her neck to just below the small of her back. His breath caught in his chest as his gaze traced the graceful line of her spine.

Unaware of what the looking glass revealed, she faced him calmly, secure in the belief that the gown she held to her chest protected her modesty. Her shoulders and arms, as well as her back, were completely bare. She was wearing no chemise.

If she dropped the gown . . .

A delicate wild-rose color flushed her just-concealed breasts, and slowly spread to her cheeks. She'd noticed him staring.

With an effort he dragged his gaze off her. Off her image in the looking glass.

"These clever gels are going to make new dresses from my old clothes—we're checking to see what is suitable."

"Everything." Daisy sighed. "It's all beautiful."

His aunt's words finally penetrated Max's fogged brain. "From *old* clothes? Good God, why?"

His aunt shrugged. "Exactly what I said myself, but they insist. So I'm giving them all of these." She gestured to the welter of clothing that covered the room.

The girls gasped. Miss Chance gasped too and then had to

hitch her gown higher. As he watched, she stole an arm around behind her. Had she felt a draft? She gasped again and stepped behind a screen, blocking his view of her slender, creamy back and shoulders.

From behind the screen he could hear rustling noises, and in his mind's eye he saw the green silk dress ripple down her body and settle in a puddle at her feet. He imagined her, like a Botticelli Venus, rising naked from a green pool. He swallowed to get rid of the hard lump in his throat, and forced his mind off the image, telling himself the sounds he heard were nothing but that gray woolen dress being dragged over her body.

"Old clothes? For God's sake, I have a silk warehouse, Aunt Bea," Max said irritably. "Anything you need, you can take from there."

That got another series of gasps and a whole lot of excited exclamations, in the midst of which Miss Chance stepped out from behind the screen with heightened color, as he'd expected, thoroughly swaddled in the gray dress. She glanced at him, bent down and picked up the ginger kitten. Max couldn't see her expression.

He decided to drop his bombshell now, while his aunt was in a good mood. "It's no bad thing you're sorting through your old possessions, Aunt Bea. We're moving house."

"Moving *house*?" Aunt Bea repeated. She groped around in the tumble of clothing on her bed and found her lorgnette. She raised it and peered at him with a beady expression. "Not Davenham Hall? Not the *country*? Because I'll tell you now, Max, you won't get me—"

"To Mayfair."

"Mayfair?"

"I purchased a house on Berkeley Square this morning. We move into it next week. So you can start the servants packing, Aunt Bea."

There was a stunned silence. Finally Aunt Bea said, "You bought a house?"

"I did."

"And we're *moving*? And just when did you think to tell me?"

Max smiled. "Just now, and there's no point arguing, Aunt Bea. We move in at the beginning of next week."

His aunt stared at him through her lorgnette. "And what if I say I don't want to move?"

He just looked at her. "As I said, you have to the end of the week. And now, if you'll excuse me, ladies, I have a dinner engagement at the club. I bid you all good evening."

And before anyone could say a word, he left.

There was a short silence. The girls looked at Lady Beatrice, concerned for her feelings.

Lady Beatrice looked back. "Well," she said after a moment. "I do like a masterful man."

"You what?" Jane gasped.

"As long as he does exactly what I want, that is."

"And if not?" Abby asked.

"Oh, then he's impossibly arrogant and interfering."

Abby smiled. "And in this case?"

"In this case I'm delighted, though I won't tell my nephew that, of course. Not for a week, at least," Lady Beatrice confided. "It really doesn't do to let men think they can have their way just like that."

"You really won't mind leaving this house?"

"Not at all. I'm fed up with it, if you want to know the truth. I've lived here since I was a young bride, more years than I care to count. It's been my London home—my only home since my husband died—and I never did like it in the first place. Nor did I like Davenham Hall—that's the country seat of the Davenhams, my dears. I haven't had to go there in years, thank goodness. Max arranged something before he went away, so I wasn't bothered with it. I never could abide the country. So noisy with all those ducks and dogs and whatnot. No, not ducks—peacocks. My late mother-in-law adored the creatures and kept a dozen of them. Have you ever heard the cry of a peacock?" She shuddered. "Disembodied shrieks from the grave—enough to curdle your blood."

Abby laughed. "So you don't mind moving to Mayfair?"

"Not at all, my dear. High time I had a change, and Mayfair is where everyone lives these days. Of course, it's bound to be a little poky—"

"Poky? On Berkeley Square?"

"Exactly, all those modern houses are. I daresay it will have only half a dozen bedrooms. Still, that's to be expected. Nobody in the city builds houses on a decent scale anymore. We'll squeeze in, I suppose."

Abby smiled, but didn't respond. She was too busy wondering whether Lord Davenham's plans included the Chance sisters or not.

"He said he was moving his aunt to Mayfair. And himself. He didn't say anything about us going with them," Damaris said later that evening.

So Abby wasn't the only one who'd noticed the omission. Lady Beatrice had retired for the night, and the girls had gathered in the small, cozy downstairs parlor.

"You think he's going to leave us behind?" Jane said.

"Lady Bea won't let him," Daisy said.

They all looked at Abby. "Daisy's right—Lady Beatrice won't let us go without a fight, but it does change everything."

"I don't see why," Jane said.

"It will be his house, and what he says goes. If he wants us gone . . ."

There was a long silence, broken only by the sound of the fire crackling in the grate.

"Do we have enough saved to go to Bath yet?" Damaris asked.

Abby shook her head.

"With the dresses Lady Bea gave us we'll have enough material for the clothes we need," Daisy said. "But it'll take a lot more than a week to make them."

"Did you hear what he said about the silk warehouse?" Jane said.

"Don't get your hopes up. That was for his aunt, not us," Abby said.

"New silk. I wonder what that'd be like?" Daisy murmured. "I've never made nothing from new. Never cut into anything that hasn't been worn before."

"You'll just have to talk him 'round, Abby," Jane said.

"Me? What makes you think he'd listen to me?"

"He likes you."

"Nonsense."

Jane shrugged. "You don't see the way he looks at you when he thinks you're not looking."

"It's true, Abby," Damaris said. "I believe he desires you."

"Desire is even better. When a man desires you, you have him on a string."

"Jane! Where did you pick up such notions?" As if she didn't know.

Jane gave her a knowing look. "You don't need to look at me like that—I knew that much even back at the Pillbury."

"Well, I wouldn't have the first idea how to influence Lord Davenham, even if he did desire me, which I very much doubt. He is betrothed, recall." And if he did desire her, well, Abby knew where that path led. It was playing with fire, she knew to her cost.

For all Jane's worldly talk of desire and leading men about on strings, she was still basically innocent and heart-whole. Jane hadn't a clue of the dangers involved, of the pain that could result.

Abby might be attracted to Lord Davenham, but she'd never act on it. A man's desire was not anything Abby wanted to evoke again. She'd been badly burned once, and never wanted to feel such pain again.

But talk, reason, argument—that she could do. "I'll talk to him tomorrow," she promised.

Later, as they were preparing for bed, Abby sought her sister out. She was still a little disturbed about what Jane had revealed when they'd been discussing marriage earlier. "I thought you remembered Mama and Papa being happy together."

"Well, I *think* I do, but mainly I remember you telling me how happy they were."

"Because they were happy. And they loved us both very much."

Jane nodded. "I know."

"Then why wouldn't you want that for yourself?"

Jane gave her a rueful look. "Because they're just stories, Abby. All I really remember about Papa is being lifted up by him, and feeling so safe and tall in his arms. And his smile. But I remember Mama's stories about her come-out and the balls and everything, because you used to tell them to me when we were in the Pill. What I mainly remember of Mama is her being sick and coughing all the time."

Abby looked at her in dismay. "Don't you remember anything else about them? Anything good?"

Jane shrugged. "Mainly I remember being cold, Abby, and being hungry and frightened, and a couple of times having to sneak out of our lodgings in the middle of the night because Papa couldn't pay the rent. And I remember Mama worrying endlessly and trying not to let Papa see, and Papa doing the same, and you worrying most of all."

"Me?"

"Oh, Abby, you spent your entire childhood worrying about all of us, and you do it still. And I thought, if that's what marrying for love means, I'm never going to do it. I don't want my children to go through what we did."

"I never thought . . . I didn't realize you were so aware of all the bad things. You were so small." Only six when Mama had died.

"At the time I didn't understand, but I remembered a lot. And I think when you're small you remember bad things more easily than good ones. After you left the Pill, I had plenty of time to think about it and realize in retrospect what it all meant. I decided then that I was never going to go hungry, or be cold or frightened again."

"Oh, Jane." Abby hugged her sister. "And then you were kidnapped."

Jane gave her a determined look. "Yes, and it has to mean something that I escaped from the brothel—unscathed—against all the odds. And in that attic room, I could have died of that fever but I didn't. That's when I made up my mind once and for all—we've got one chance in life, Abby, and I mean to seize what I can to make mine better."

She grasped Abby's hands in hers. "Mama was given a pretty face and she wasted it. I'm not going to waste the only gift I've been given. Somehow I'm going to marry well and get myself a better life. And, big sister, I'm going to take you with me."

Abby hugged Jane tightly. She didn't agree with her—loving

Papa was the right thing for Mama, no matter what the cost. To believe otherwise was a betrayal of them and their love; it was the one certain thing in her childhood—and if she didn't believe in that, well, she couldn't believe in anything.

Abby hadn't forgotten the bad things either, but she remembered more than Jane, and the most important thing she remembered was that the love between her parents and their love for their children made the bad times better.

But in another way her little sister was right: They had a chance, here with Lady Beatrice, to make a better life, and she should seize it with both hands.

Seduction was out of the question. Even if she were the kind of woman who could seduce men to her will—which she wasn't—it was too risky, too painful. The woman always paid the price.

Still, Abby could try to talk to Lord Davenham. You never knew; he might listen, though she doubted it.

She might not be the seductive type, but she did have brains. If only she could think of a plan.

Lady Beatrice spent the morning after Lord Davenham's surprise announcement writing notes to all her old friends, informing them that she'd been ill but was now well on the way to full recovery, and from the following week onward would be in residence at her new home in Berkeley Square, where she would welcome callers. The last two words were heavily underlined, and thus would carry, Abby suspected, almost as much weight as a royal decree.

The first batch of notes had barely been delivered when, late that afternoon, the front doorbell rang. A few moments later Featherby carried in a calling card on a silver salver. Lady Beatrice inspected it through her lorgnette.

"Clara Beddington!" she exclaimed with delight. "One of my oldest friends. Show her in, Featherby." To the girls she said, "Good thing I decided to dress and come down this afternoon. Wouldn't do to have Clara see me lolling about in bed—terrible gossip, Clara." She tidied her hair, straightened her beautiful cashmere shawl and sat up straight.

Featherby announced the visitor. "Lady Beddington, m'lady."

A small, plump woman trailing several shawls and a sumptuous fur entered excitedly. She hurried across the room and the two women embraced. "My dear Bea, when I received your note I simply couldn't wait. Do you know, I cannot recall how many times I called on you in the last year, only to be told by that horrid butler that you weren't at home—not even to *moi*! I'm so glad you got rid of him, the disagreeable creature—this new fellow is so much better!" She bestowed a gracious smile, two shawls and a frilled purple oiled-silk parasol on Featherby, who received them all with unruffled composure. "Do you know, I was so worried about you that I wrote to your nephew. And I can see you've been ill—not surprising, given the truly appalling weather we've been having—can you believe this is supposed to be summer? *Summer?* It's absolutely freezing!" She retrieved one of the shawls from Featherby and flung it around her neck in a dramatic movement that caused Max the kitten to pounce on the tempting fringe.

"Good God, is that a kitten? How amusing. I dislike cats. This illness of yours, it's nothing infectious, is it? I should have asked that first, shouldn't I? Never mind, I'm sure you wouldn't pass it on. And how are you, my dear?"

"I'm well, Clara, thank you, and you're looking the same as ever. It's nothing anyone can catch, and thanks to these dear gels—my nieces, you know—I'm getting stronger every day." She introduced the four girls to Lady Beddington and then said, "Now, I know it's atrociously ill-mannered of me, but would you mind terribly, Clara, if we let Abby finish the chapter she was reading me when you arrived? She's only just started chapter two and it's at a very interesting point. It won't take more than about ten minutes." She glanced at Featherby and added, "And in the meantime my butler can bring us tea and cakes."

"You're reading *books* now, Bea? Good heavens! Well, of course I don't mind, if that's what you want." But though she allowed herself to be seated in a comfortable chair by the fire, it was clear she thought the request a peculiar one.

However, as Abby read on, Lady Beddington edged forward in her chair, twisting her shawl into a rope, listening eagerly, until by the end of the chapter she was perched right on the edge of her chair, hanging on every word.

When Abby finished the chapter Lady Beddington fell back in her chair, exclaiming, "Bless my soul, I never knew a book could be so entertaining."

"I *know*," Lady Beatrice said. "Before these gels came to live with me, I can't remember when I last read a book. All the books I'd ever been made to read were dreary, *improving* things, full of morals and lessons and homilies or facts—and that's when I could understand the dratted things. But Abby and the gels always find the most thrilling tales, and the only thing that's *improved* when we're finished is my mood."

"I wish I'd read the start of that one," Lady Beddington said.

Abby held out the book to show her the title. "You could always buy a copy, or borrow it from the circulating library."

Lady Beddington squinted at the cover, then shook her head, dislodging her shawl. "No point, my dear. I can't read much of anything these days. Eyesight ain't what it was."

"I know," Lady Beatrice agreed. "Which is why these gels are a godsend."

"And you read so well, Miss Chance. As entertaining as a night at the theater, I do assure you."

Featherby arrived with the tea and cakes, and Abby and the girls retreated to leave the two old friends to catch up.

A couple of hours later Abby was summoned to return.

"Lady Beddington is going to stay for dinner, Abby, dear."

Abby smiled at their visitor. It was clear her visit had done Lady Beatrice a lot of good. "How delightful. Do you wish me to speak to Cook and—"

"No, no, Featherby can see to that. Lady Beddington has a special request for you—go on, Clara."

Lady Beddington hesitated, fiddled with the fringe of her shawl and then said, "My dear Miss Chance, would you mind very much reading me the first chapter of that delicious book?"

Abby stared at her in silence for a long moment. An idea had popped into her mind, a crazy, possibly ludicrous idea. . . . If she could bring it about . . . it might just be the solution to all their problems.

"Abby?" Lady Beatrice prompted.

Abby gave a start and picked up the book. "I'm so sorry; I was woolgathering. Of course, I'd be delighted to read it to you, Lady Beddington." She looked at Lady Beatrice and said, "It's just that I had . . . an idea."

Lady Beatrice was sharp as a razor. "About what we discussed the other day? Your sister and society?" Abby nodded.

"Then tell us, my dear. Clara won't mind."

Abby explained her idea.

"A *literary society*?" Lady Beatrice exclaimed, screwing her nose up. "Where they discuss books nobody wants to read, and everyone pretends they're all very learned and compete to say the most intelligent things?" She grimaced. Her old friend nodded in agreement.

Abby leaned forward eagerly. "Ah, but this won't be that sort of literary society. It will be fun."

"Fun?" Lady Beatrice asked doubtfully.

"It'll be much the same as we already do—one of us will read a chapter at a time, aloud, and then we'll have conversation, tea and cakes, just as we usually do."

Lady Beatrice's eyes narrowed. "No clever remarks? No looking for metaphors and themes and hidden dratted meanings?"

"Not if you don't want them," Abby said. "It will be your literary society, after all, and you will make the rules." Lady Beatrice clearly liked the sound of that.

"Just for the story, then, and the company?" Lady Beddington asked.

Abby nodded. "What do you think?" It wouldn't exactly introduce Jane to eligible men, but at least they'd have made some connections with their mothers and aunts.

"A literary society for people who don't want to be improved," Lady Beatrice said thoughtfully. "Just a good story, with wine and cakes . . . I like it." She looked at Abby and added, "The kind of thing an eligible young man could be prevailed on to escort his mother to."

Abby grinned at her optimism. "I'm not so sure of that. It's not really a young man's cup of tea—"

"Nonsense, we only need to get them here the first time. Once they meet those pretty gels, they'll be fighting to come back."

Abby laughed. "I like your optimism."

"So when do we start? Officially, I mean," Lady Beatrice said. "I'll send out invitations, to start with—"

"And I'll spread the word," Lady Beddington said. "Oh, this will be fun, Bea."

Lady Beatrice rubbed her hands. "It will, indeed. I think it's a splendid idea, Abby. And, Clara, I don't think we should mention this to my nephew. He has a tendency to fret, and is sure to say it will be too much for me, which, of course, it isn't." She winked at Abby. "Now, my dear, Clara's waiting for you to read her that first chapter and then it'll be time for dinner."

"Well, well, well, it's been a delightful evening altogether," Lady Beddington declared as the dinner was drawing to a close. "I can see what you mean about these gels enlivening the house. I wish I had nieces who came up with delicious schemes, but I don't have any—" She stopped, thought for a moment, then turned a perplexed face to Lady Beatrice. "Thought you were an only child, Bea. Or are the girls your late husband's nieces?"

Abby waited for Lady Beatrice to reply. A courtesy aunt was how she and the others had decided to deal with Lady Beatrice's continuing assertion that they were her nieces—the kind of aunt who was a dear friend of the family, and called "aunt" for affection, not blood.

Abby glanced at Lord Davenham. He leaned back in his chair and regarded his aunt with a sardonic, let's-see-you-explain-this expression.

"No, of course not," Lady Beatrice said. "They're no relation at all to Davenham—or to dear Max."

Lady Beddington looked confused. "Then—"

"They're my half sisters' gels, of course—Griselda's."

"Griselda?" Lady Beddington blinked.

Griselda? Abby and Jane exchanged glances.

Griselda? Max frowned.

"My mother's child by her second marriage," Lady Beatrice said smoothly.

"Aunt Beatrice, will you have some of this delicious asparagus?" Max interrupted. What the devil was she playing at?

"Thank you, no, I detest asparagus."

Lady Beddington persisted. "I never knew your mother married again."

"She didn't." Max fixed his aunt with a stern look.

"No, not immediately," she agreed placidly. "Though you shouldn't be airing our dirty linen, dear boy. Still, we are among friends, are we not? And in the end, they did marry just in time for Griselda to be born. It was very romantic—and perfectly respectable." She beamed at Miss Chance.

Lady Beddington shook her head. "Well, well, well. I had no idea. I always thought she died shortly after you married Davenham."

"She did." Max leaned forward. "Have you attended the opera recently, Lady Beddington? I believe the current Mozart is held to be very good." He had no idea what was playing at Covent Garden. He didn't care, as long as the subject was changed.

"No, Max, dear, it's no use trying to conceal the facts any longer. Mama ran off with an Austrian count," his irrepressible aunt responded, carefully spearing a single green pea. "My father divorced her, of course, and had it all hushed up. Papa gave it out that she'd died."

She *had* died. Max had seen the grave. He frowned at Aunt Bea. This was getting out of hand.

She smiled at him sweetly and ate the pea with an air of triumph. "It was soooo romantic. The count was terribly handsome, of course—one of those tall, golden-haired Austrians with eyes of ice blue. He was utterly mad about my mother. Griselda took after him. Jane has her hair and eyes."

Jane choked.

"Is that so, Miss Chance?" Lady Beddington said.

Miss Chance hesitated, glanced at Max, her expression a mixture of amusement and helplessness, and said to Lady Beddington, "Jane *is* the very image of our mother."

Aunt Bea's glance drifted to Damaris's dark hair, and Max leaned forward and tried to catch her eye, hoping to head off the next outrageous lie. But she had the bit between her teeth and was running with it.

"Griselda married a Venetian, a marchese—that's Italian for marquess, my dear," she explained to Daisy. "Tall, dark and divinely good-looking too—the women in my family have always been lucky that way, marrying the handsomest of men. Dear Damaris has her father's features and coloring."

"What was this Italian marchese's name?" Max asked sardonically. He glanced at "dear Damaris," who had developed a sudden fascination with the weave of the damask tablecloth. Her face was hidden; her shoulders were shaking.

"*Venetian*, dear boy, not Italian. They don't like it when you get them mixed up. Venice is the place with the canals," his aunt explained kindly.

"And his name, this divine Venetian?"

There was a short silence. His aunt's gaze went momentarily blank as she tried to think of a suitable name. Then, "Angelo," she said airily.

"I meant his surname," Max said with silky satisfaction.

She arched her brows. "Why, Chance, of course."

"Very Italian-sounding name, Chance," Max said dryly.

His shameless relative didn't bat an eyelid. "Well, naturally in Venice it's pronounced 'Chancealotto' "—at this point Miss Abby choked—"but here, we Anglicize it to Chance, those Italian names being quite hard to pronounce."

"Venetian."

"Quite so, dear boy, I'm glad you're paying attention."

"Oh, believe me, I'm fascinated. It's like something out of a novel." Max noted that Miss Abigail too was now enthralled with the tablecloth. As was her sister, Miss Jane. Miss Daisy was watching the whole thing with jaw agape. As well she might, he thought grimly.

"Isn't it just? Wonderful things, novels—as Clara has just discovered. Have some more asparagus, dear boy. You look a little liverish."

"Well, I'm amazed," Lady Beddington said. "And to think I've known you all these years, Bea, and I'd never even *heard* of your half sister, Griselda."

"Not surprising, since—"

"Since Papa didn't like us to speak of her. Of course, poor Max was raised believing Papa's lies." His aunt added in a forgiving tone, "He still finds it hard to accept the truth, poor boy."

Max's lips twitched despite himself. She was outrageous. "That's enough, Aunt Bea," he warned her.

"How wonderful that you have her daughters with you now." Lady Beddington smiled at the girls. "You always wanted daughters, I know, Bea. Will you be bringing them out this season? How exciting."

"No," Max said firmly. This was one piece of nonsense he was going to quash once and for all. "There are no plans of that sort. Whatsoever."

"We'll see," Aunt Bea said sweetly.

"No, we won't." Max had had enough. He hadn't wanted to embarrass Aunt Bea in front of her old friend, but she'd pushed things to the limit. "Lady Beddington, I must apologize for my aunt. She's been playing a joke on us all, funning, with her made-up nonsense, but I think we've all had enough. Her mother never did remarry—she died, as you thought, and was buried in England. And there never was any half sister Griselda, nor any Venetian marchese or Austrian count."

"Oh." Lady Beddington looked uncertainly at Aunt Bea.

Aunt Bea rolled her eyes and shrugged as if to say, *Don't believe a word*.

"I assure you it's the truth," Max said. "These young ladies are my aunt's guests, but they are no relation to her. Or to me."

He looked at Miss Chance, a silent order for her to confirm his version of events, but to his annoyance she and the others all still seemed inordinately interested in the blasted tablecloth.

"And she will *not* be bringing them out next season. Or any other season," Max added as his aunt opened her mouth.

He rose. "Now, Lady Beddington, it's been a delightful evening, but my aunt is still under the care of her physician, and needs her sleep. May I escort you to your carriage?"

Lady Beddington took her leave of them all, vowing to return the following day for the next reading of the book. She added with a mischievous glance at Abby, "And I might bring a friend."

While Lord Davenham was putting Lady Beddington into her carriage, Lady Beatrice called for William to be fetched quickly so he could carry her upstairs, Abby assumed to escape her nephew's wrath. The old lady could walk short distances now without assistance, but she still couldn't manage stairs.

But before William could lift her, Lord Davenham marched in and scooped her up without warning, saying grimly, "I'll take her, William. I need a word with this aunt of mine."

She laughed and patted his smooth-shaven cheek. "So delightfully masterful you are, dear boy, but all this masculinity is wasted on an aunt. You should be carrying a pretty young thing up to bed, not an old woman."

"I should strangle you," he told her.

She laughed again. "Wasn't it fun? You should have seen your face when I told Clara my mother wasn't in her grave after all. And Griselda and her Italian marchese."

"*Venetian*," he growled. "Venice is the place with the canals, remember?"

Abby and the girls could hear her merry laughter as nephew and aunt disappeared up the stairs.

"He's not going to hurt her, is he?" Daisy asked worriedly. Daisy's experience of men wasn't exactly conducive of trust.

"No," Abby said softly. "He loves her."

"You can see she's not worried one little bit," Damaris pointed out.

Daisy shook her head. "I never woulda thought that a proper lady like that would tell such barefaced whoppers in company!"

"Yes, I must say he took it very well," Jane said. "Don't you think?"

"Very well," Abby agreed, her voice trembling a little. She met Jane's gaze. "But really—*Chancealotto*?" She started laughing.

Jane giggled. "*You* can talk! You said I was the living image of Griselda."

"I did not; I said you take after our mother, and *that's* perfectly true."

"Yes, our mother, Griselda Chancealotto."

"Our mother, Griselda, the Marchesa Chancealotto," Damaris corrected her, and then the three of them were laughing.

"I don't see what's so funny," Daisy said. "It's just more lies; that's what it is. Diggin' us into a deeper hole."

"Don't worry, Daisy," Abby told her. "Only Lady Beddington believed it at the time, and she knows now it's not true."

"And if everyone knows it's not true, it's not really a lie, is it?—Signorina Chancealotto," said Jane, and that set them off again.

Daisy scowled and shook her head gloomily. "I still don't like it."

As she undressed that night for bed, Abby smiled to herself about the old lady's fantastical fabrications. She climbed into bed, thinking about the literary society and hoping some eligible young men might be prevailed on to attend.

Even if they didn't, at least if Jane had met the mothers, aunts and sisters of eligible young men, they might introduce her to them at the park or somewhere.

But as she blew out her candle and snuggled down in her bed, she thought of Lord Davenham carrying his aunt upstairs, still able to maintain his humor and his patience despite her outrageous behavior.

She thought of the story Lady Beatrice had told her, of that little boy waiting loyally, grieving silently and alone—she could not rid herself of that image either.

Her heart had gone out to that child, and now she saw echoes of the boy in the man—his obvious love of his aunt, his care for her, his protectiveness.

Even the hostility he'd directed at Abby and her sisters was born of the need to protect his aunt. It was a powerfully attractive quality in a man.

Miss Parsley was a lucky woman.

Chapter Thirteen

"Facts are such horrid things!"

—JANE AUSTEN, *LADY SUSAN*

When Max went down to breakfast the next morning he found three of the misses Chance waiting for him. Of course they were pretending to eat breakfast, but they'd long since finished, he saw. They faced him with apprehensive faces.

"I presume Miss Chance is with my aunt," he said after they'd exchanged polite good mornings.

"It wasn't her fault," Miss Jane said as soon as Featherby had served Max some bacon and eggs. "Abby's, I mean."

"I know." Max addressed himself to his breakfast. As he ate, he felt a mild kinship with the beasts in the Royal Exchange, his every mouthful observed by nervous spectators who any moment expected an attack.

"We didn't tell your aunt any of that tale," Miss Damaris assured him. "Or ask her to pretend we were her nieces."

Max knew that. He looked at Miss Daisy to see whether she wanted to add anything. "It was all a lie," she said, "but we never asked your aunt to tell it, I promise. You mustn't blame Abby."

"I don't," he said, and buttered a slice of toast.

"And Lady Bea didn't mean nothing bad by it," Daisy persisted. "She was just . . . just . . ."

"Having fun," Max said. "I know. Now, where is Miss Chance? I'd like to speak with her."

The girls exchanged worried glances. They really were very young.

"I said speak with, not strangle," he said dryly.

"She's gone out," Jane said after a moment. "To the post office, I think."

"Thank you. Featherby, have my phaeton brought around to the front, if you please."

After a few moments of indecision and an exchange of silent grimaces and head jerking that they imagined he hadn't noticed, the girls excused themselves and hurried from the breakfast room.

Max finished his coffee and headed for the front door. The letter he'd left on the hall table the previous evening had gone, presumably posted. Good. When he'd first arrived in England, he'd written to inform Henry Parsloe he'd returned and would call on him at his home in Manchester at his earliest convenience.

Last night he'd written a quick note to Parsloe to postpone his visit. With the situation with Aunt Bea and the Chance sisters, he'd have to delay his trip north, at least until after Aunt Bea was settled in the new house. Whether or not the Chance sisters would be coming with them, he still hadn't decided.

That Aunt Bea doted on the girls and wanted them with her was undeniable. She was, he suspected, a little unbalanced about them—witness the ridiculous Griselda fabrication last night. Thank goodness he'd been there to scotch that piece of nonsense.

That the Chance sisters sincerely cared for Aunt Bea was also quite apparent to him now—and that was a problem. It seemed they had not a penny between them, other than the allowance from his aunt; they were as dependent on her as she was, in a different way, on them. Impostors or not, he couldn't just throw them out.

Whether it was wise to allow them to continue living in her house—in Max's house—was far from clear.

As for how they would all react when Max married Miss Parsloe . . . that was anyone's guess. But marry her he would, so the sooner he got Aunt Bea happily settled into the new house, the better for everyone.

And to that end, he needed the assistance of Miss Abigail Chance.

At Charing Cross, Max was about to hand the reins to his groom and cross the road to check whether she was still in the post office when he saw her come out of the building. "Wait here," he told the groom. He was about to cross the road when he noticed something odd.

A man had followed her out of the post office. Max saw the fellow turn to a group of wastrels loitering nearby and jerk his head in Miss Chance's direction. A shabby-looking man casually detached himself from the group and set out after her. What the devil?

Max had a finely honed instinct for trouble, and he didn't hesitate; he crossed the road—cursing as the traffic slowed him down—and followed.

Miss Chance turned left down a side street. Her follower did the same. Max quickened his pace.

What was the fellow's purpose? Miss Chance wasn't an obvious target for robbery; dressed in that simple gray cloak and plain bonnet, she looked more like a governess than a woman worth robbing. She didn't even wear jewelry—not so much as a gold or silver chain.

Oblivious of her follower, Miss Chance turned down a narrow alleyway—presumably a shortcut to the market. The man turned down too. Max got there a split second later. *Damn!* Apart from them, the lane was deserted.

And in those few seconds the swine had almost closed the gap between himself and Miss Chance.

The shabby man tensed and rose on the balls of his feet. Max didn't wait to see what would happen next. With a shout, he flung himself forward and grabbed the man's coat. Miss Chance whirled.

"Hey—" The man swung around, a knife in his hand, and slashed out at Max without warning. Max tried to dodge it but felt a glancing blow.

"Run," he shouted at Abby. He didn't see her go; he couldn't take his eyes off the man with the knife.

The man had a pasty, ratlike face. "Stay out of it, ya bastard," he snarled. "'S nothing to do with you." The knife glittered in his hand. It was a long, wicked-looking blade with a carved bone handle.

"The woman is with me," Max growled.

Rat Face gave a grunt and a philosophical shrug. "Fair enough, gov'nor." He held up his hands pacifically and seemed about to back away; then abruptly he lunged at Max again, going for his throat.

But Max was ready for it. As the knife flashed toward him, he dodged and at the same time chopped down on the man's wrist hard. The blade clattered to the cobblestones. Max followed through with a swift punch to the gut and another to the throat and, while the fellow was still gasping for breath, shoved him hard against a wall.

"Why are you following her?"

The man struggled and spat an obscenity. Max punched him again.

"Look out!" Miss Chance screamed. Blast it, what was she still doing here? But he had no time to think. Another man threw himself at Max.

Max whirled, dragging Rat Face with him and thrusting him into the onrush of the second attacker, a thickset brute in a cloth cap. They crashed. Rat Face tripped and went sprawling on the cobbles. The second man came on, swinging a cosh at Max's head. He ducked it.

The second man closed in. He and Max wrestled. From the corner of Max's eye he saw Rat Face struggle to his feet and head again at Max.

Max braced himself for the attack, but to his astonishment Miss Chance jumped on Rat Face from behind, screaming like a vengeful banshee, battering him around the head with her reticule. She wrapped her arms around the man's neck, clinging like a monkey, trying to drag him down or choke him. He reeled and swore, trying to fend her off.

Max, wrestling with the second attacker, didn't see what happened next, but he turned just in time to catch the glitter of a blade as Rat Face stabbed behind him at Abby. The blade was buried in a swirl of fabric. Rat Face had to pull hard to get it free.

Abby's grip around the man's neck slackened. Rat Face twisted and flung her violently to the ground. There was a sudden, shocking silence as her scream was abruptly cut off. She lay sprawled on the wet cobbles, unmoving.

"Abby!" Max hurled himself across the gap, grabbed Rat Face by the scruff of the neck and slammed him hard against the wall. Again he dropped the knife. This time Max snatched it up and placed himself between Abby and the villains. "Now let's see what you're made of."

Rat Face and his accomplice exchanged glances, muttered something and fled.

The moment he was sure they really had gone, Max flung himself onto his knees beside Miss Chance's prone body. "Miss Chance! Abby!" She wasn't moving.

"Abby!" Heart in his mouth, he gently turned her over, and saw to his relief she was gasping like a fish, soundlessly, helplessly. Her eyes were wide and panicked, her face contorted as she fought to breathe—and couldn't. But there was no sign of any blood.

Relief poured through him. She was winded, not wounded, thank God.

"You're all right; you've had your breath knocked out of you, that's all," he told her. The first time you had your breath knocked out of you was terrifying, he remembered. Those first few moments where your lungs simply did not work.

He lifted her off the cold, muddy cobbles and pulled her across his knees, supporting her against his chest as he rubbed her back in a soothing rhythmic movement, rocking her gently, murmuring, "There, now, you're safe; you'll be all right in a minute. Just relax and your breath will come."

Her fingers clutched at his lapels; her gaze locked with his in agonized entreaty as she struggled fruitlessly to breathe. The effort seemed to last forever, but at last a great, sobbing gasp sounded and her body shuddered against him as she gulped in her first blessed lungful of air. Again and again she dragged in great breaths of air, until the panicked reaction began to fade.

Max held her close, not ceasing the rhythmic rubbing of her back, though whom exactly he was soothing he wasn't sure. That moment when he saw the knife go in . . . the still, small figure sprawled on the cobbles . . .

His arms tightened around her. He needed to feel her warm, living body against him.

She rested quietly, trustfully against him, her eyes closed, catching her breath, fighting to calm the shivers that racked her body.

"They've gone," he told her. "You're safe. I have you now." He looked down at her. She looked white and shaken, her small, sweet face pinched in a way that put an ache in his chest.

She'd lost her bonnet in the affray. He carefully smoothed the hair back from her forehead. A bruise was darkening just above her eyebrow. There was a raw-looking scrape on her chin.

But there was no blood. He'd checked as thoroughly as he could, but could find no sign of a wound. It was a puzzle: He was sure he'd seen the blade go in, and Rat Face had definitely had to pull to get it out. But somehow, by some miracle, he'd missed her. Thank God.

Abby knew she should make an effort to move. She should; she really should. She could breathe again now, and the trembling had subsided to a manageable level, and her heartbeat . . . oh, her heartbeat . . .

There was no controlling that.

He'd saved her. Fought two men for her, stood over her with a knife, facing them, her Viking protector. And now, the way he held her . . .

She didn't move; she couldn't—couldn't even make herself want to move. Like a child who squeezed her eyes tighter shut, not wanting to wake from a dream, believing as children did that the dream could be made real if only she kept her eyes closed and just . . . didn't . . . move.

The rhythmic soothing of the jangled nerves of her spine: tangible warmth, tangible reassurance. The deep murmuring voice, a bedrock of security.

She pressed her cheek against his chest. It was so broad and strong, she wanted to climb right inside it and stay there forever, stay like this forever, in his arms, breathing in the scent of his body—damp wool, a hint of cedar, fresh linen and the dark, entrancing scent of man, the warm breath of him stirring against her skin.

"How are you feeling now?" he asked, and she wanted to weep, wanted to laugh, to cling to him in undignified desperation, to prolong the moment, the dream, the illusion.

"Miss Chance?" He leaned back to look at her, his arms loosening their hold on her. The cold drafts of self-awareness slipped between them, chilling her body, and she was once more the spinster governess.

"Your forehead is bruised, and you have"—cupping her jaw in one hand, he gently tilted her face—"a scrape on your chin. But is that all?"

A pulse throbbed in his cheek. It drew her gaze like a magnet. She couldn't look at him, not yet.

"Abby?"

"You saved me," she whispered. And glanced up. And found herself drowning in the smoky mystery of his gaze.

His eyes darkened; he seemed to hesitate; then slowly, agonizingly, almost as if it were against his will, he lowered his mouth to hers.

Their lips brushed. It was just the faintest breath of a touch, barely a caress, but she felt it clear to her toes. A deep shiver passed through her.

He drew back with an arrested expression. He muttered something under his breath that she didn't catch, and then he was kissing her deeply, ravenously, pulling her hard against him, cradling her head in his hands, tilting her face the better to . . . sear her soul.

His mouth was hot, the taste of him dark and intense. Addictive.

She clung to his shoulders, kissing him back with everything in her, years of aching loneliness burning away under the assault of his passion, savoring the taste, the feel, the power of him. The hunger in him to match the hunger in her.

His kisses were rough and tender at the same time, deep, as if he were taking her inside him the way she'd gulped in air a few moments before, as vital and necessary as life.

She speared her fingers into the thick, cool darkness of his hair, still damp from the rain. She was afire, heat shimmering across her skin, coiling in hot shudders deep within her.

Then, with no warning, it was over. He wrenched his mouth from hers, a stricken look in his eyes. "I apologize. That shouldn't have happened."

Abby stared at him in dazed disbelief. For a moment all was still, silent, no sound except for two people breathing hard. And the thud of her hammering heart.

She felt raw, new-hatched, her skin so sensitive it was as if the moist, cool afternoon air could pass right through her.

And then suddenly they were sitting on the damp cobbles of a laneway in the middle of London. The sounds of traffic, of wheels rumbling over cobbles, of hawkers crying out—of reality—rolled over them like a wave. Gulls screamed overhead, following the river, fighting over scraps.

"This . . . it can't happen," he said. His chest was heaving. He was panting, his lips still slick from her kisses. He pushed her away just a little, enough to put a few inches between them, but it might as well have been a mile; the shuttered flatness of his gray gaze told her that.

"I'm betrothed," he said tightly.

Shame scalded her. Shaking, clumsy, she scrambled to her feet, brushing herself down, picking up her bonnet, her reticule, tidying herself with shaking hands, looking at the walls, at the cobblestones, at the gulls wheeling and screaming to the sky. Anywhere but at Max, Lord Davenham.

The neediness in her, the way she'd clung to him. What must he think?

It was just a kiss, she told herself. It meant nothing. She was lonely; that was all. She was unsettled by the attack; she'd overreacted. And he . . . well, men were like that, taking what was offered. Even if you didn't mean to . . .

"You're hurt."

"No, no, of course I'm not. It was just a kiss; I know," she managed to say with a fair attempt at worldliness.

"No, I mean . . ." He gestured. "There's blood on your back."

She tried to look, found a smear or two of blood on her skirt at the back. But she didn't feel injured. Not unless mortification drew blood.

"Let me see." He twisted her around. "There's blood on your back, but I can't see any wound."

"I can." She carefully lifted his sleeve. "You're the one who's wounded, not me."

"Me? Nonsense!" And then he saw it, the slash in his sleeve, the blood soaking it, dripping slowly onto the cobblestones now that they were standing up.

"Well, I'll be damned." It was the hand he'd rubbed her back with. He'd bled all over her back and hadn't even noticed.

"Didn't you feel it? Doesn't it hurt?"

He shook his head. "It didn't before, but now . . . yes, I can feel it now."

She began to unbutton his coat.

He fended her off. "What do you think you're—"

"I'm going to check your wound. I can't see it with the coat on."

"It's nothing, a mere scratch."

"You're *bleeding*." She started to tug at his coat, trying to ease it from his shoulder. She felt better now she had something practical to concentrate on.

"Stop that." One-handed, he pulled his coat back into position.

"Don't be silly. How can I help you if I can't see your injury?"

He dragged a handkerchief from his pocket and gave it to her. "Tie that tightly around the cut—from the outside. I'll get the wound seen to later."

It was pure male stubbornness, but Abby didn't argue. She shook out his handkerchief, folded it diagonally, pleated it to form a bandage and tied it around his arm, over his coat. "There," she said, pulling it tight enough to make him gasp. "That should slow the bleeding enough until we get home."

Chapter Fourteen

"I may have lost my heart, but not my self-control."

—JANE AUSTEN, EMMA

Max's phaeton and groom were still waiting around the corner. In silence Max helped Abby—he couldn't think of her as Miss Chance anymore—into the vehicle, climbed up beside her and picked up the reins.

"Are you sure you should drive with that injured arm?" she asked.

"I'm fine." He signaled to the groom to release the horses, flicked the reins and, as the groom jumped on at the back, the horses moved off.

Two questions worried Max. Why had she been attacked? And why had he kissed her in that . . . unbridled manner? And though the first question was the more important, it was the kiss he couldn't get out of his mind.

Why the devil had he kissed her at all? He had no idea. It had been a purely instinctive response—but to what? The danger? The woman in his arms?

Or had he simply meant to comfort her? What a noble fellow he was, his conscience mocked him.

No, it wasn't comfort, though that was part of it. It was just . . . she'd looked up at him with that expression in her eyes . . . and he hadn't been able to resist.

Just a taste, he'd reasoned.

He snorted. Reason had nothing to do with it. He'd known he shouldn't touch her, but the temptation was irresistible.

And then he'd just touched his mouth to hers . . . the barest brush of lips against lips, and . . . *wildfire* . . . leaping up between them. A sizzle of recognition deep in his being.

He remembered staring down at her, shocked at the power of such a brief exchange. He remembered telling himself he shouldn't, that he was betrothed, that this young woman was a mystery, an enigma, embroiled in dangerous matters . . . but all the arguments he could muster were as the chattering of birds, and he couldn't stop himself from bending once more to take her mouth with his.

Instant conflagration; he'd never felt anything like it. The taste of her: pure intoxication. A shudder passed through him now, as he remembered.

He slipped her a sideways glance. Had she noticed? Was she too remembering? Had she too felt the conflagration?

She sat bolt upright on the seat beside him, looking ahead, her face pale and still, her reticule clutched firmly in her lap.

His hands tightened on the reins. He had no business remembering, no business kissing her in the first place.

He was a betrothed man, and he took his promises seriously. Not once in his life—not even as a boy—had he ever gone back on his word. And he wasn't going to start now.

It was just a kiss. Only a kiss.

He had to put it from his mind, focus on the danger she'd just escaped. Why the devil had that fellow attacked her? He was no simple cutpurse, Max was sure. He glanced at her reticule. Then glanced again.

"That's one mystery solved," he said.

She started, as if her thoughts had been miles away, and turned to him. "What do you mean?"

He nodded toward the reticule. "I was sure I saw that knife go into you. The villain had to tug to retrieve it. But it was that."

She looked down and made a small exclamation. "It's been cut." She opened the reticule, examined the contents and took out a small, leather-bound book. She held it up so he could see it. "My book was stabbed!"

He gave a curt nod. That book had saved her life.

He glanced at her to see whether she understood. She did; he could tell from her expression. She sat in silence for a long moment, her thumb rubbing back and forth over the cut in the leather, as if the action would somehow heal it. Her lips trembled. She looked close to tears.

Max ached to take her into his arms again. Instead he said, "And they say an addiction to novels is bad for you."

It surprised a shaky laugh out of her. "I've always found books a great comfort, but never quite like this." With trembling hands she stuffed the damaged book back in her reticule and said in a more normal voice, "How is your arm?"

"It's nothing." Max focused on the road ahead. His path was clear.

"It's just a scratch. No need to make a fuss." Max tried again to rise. They were in the kitchen of Davenham House. There was no sign of the cook or scullery maid. The moment they'd arrived home, Abby had ordered the footman to go for the doctor, but Max had vetoed that.

He'd felt a little dizzy getting down from the phaeton, but it was nothing a brandy wouldn't fix, he was sure. His head and shoulder ached a little from his connections with the cosh, but it was just a bit of bruising, nothing serious. As for the cut, it was a long gash, but not too deep. Blood still oozed from it sluggishly.

She pushed him back onto the chair—and it was a sign of his light-headedness that she could. "If anyone is making a fuss, it's you. You've lost a lot of blood."

She tossed a fistful of salt into a basin, poured water from the steaming kettle into it and stirred fiercely to dissolve the salt. "Don't argue; I'm going to wash and bandage that wound. Cuts can fester, and salt water is good for healing. And besides, the blood is unsightly and upsets Featherby."

And shame on Max for bleeding everywhere, and upsetting her precious butler, her tone implied.

The butler had taken one look at Max's injury, turned an interesting shade of green and tottered out of the room. The footman, William, had helped to strip Max of his coat and shirt.

He peered at the wound with professional interest. "Nasty cut, m'lord, but I don't reckon it'll need stitches. Best let Miss Abby tend to it."

It wasn't what Max wanted to hear. He didn't want her tending him. She was still damp and muddy from where she'd been knocked flat to the ground. And still shaken from the attack. She needed someone fussing over her, dammit. Where were those blasted sisters of hers? Where were the female servants?

But when he said as much, she simply said, "Oh, hush! I'm perfectly all right. You're the one who's bleeding."

He watched her closely. She wasn't perfectly all right at all. Unless he missed his guess, she was experiencing a delayed reaction to the attack. She was trying to cover it with feminine bluster, but her hands were trembling, and so were her lips.

To distract her, Max said brusquely, "Look, I have a great deal to do today; I don't have time for this." He looked around, seeking some masculine support, but the butler was nowhere to be seen and the footman had borne away Max's bloody shirt and coat.

"There's no need to look at me like that," she said. "I'm sure I don't care if you prefer to bleed to death on the floor. I'm only doing this because for some reason your aunt is fond of you."

"You're upset, I know—"

"Oh, whatever gave you that idea? I *enjoy* knife-wielding thugs coming after me! And having a man nearly killed in my defense is positively *delightful*—"

She broke off, pressing trembling fingers against her lips, and more than anything Max wanted to take her into his arms, to hold her slender body against him.

For comfort. Because he hated to see women in distress.

Only he couldn't. He'd already done enough damage. He wasn't free to put his arms around her. It wasn't only the attack that had upset her, he knew; it was the kiss.

It still hung in the room between them.

"I'm sorr—"

She threw up her hands. "Will you *stop* saying that? You've made it very clear—more than clear—that it was a mistake."

"It's not that I didn't want—"

She glared at him and went back to stirring salt. Furiously.

He tried again. "It's just . . . I'm betrothed."

"I *know*! The kiss meant nothing—less than nothing."

For some reason that annoyed Max. "Do you often kiss men?"

"Only after I'm attacked in the street by men with knives!" she flashed. "Does your fiancée know you kiss other women?"

There was no answer to that. Max glowered. She swished around the room, fetching scissors, ripping a piece of clean linen into lengths for a bandage, setting a pot of salve and a length of gauze on the table beside him.

She poured the hot salt water into a bowl, then paused, sighed, eyed him ruefully and said, "I'm sorry. That was unforgivable. I'm very much aware that I owe you my life, and I'm very grateful."

Max gave a gruff nod. "And I owe you mine, so we're quits."

"I didn't do much—"

He cut her off. "You were very brave. I don't know any woman who would have tried to stop a knife-wielding villain, so don't argue." His words came out more harshly than he'd intended, so he added in a milder tone, "Are you sure you're not hurt?"

"A couple of bruises, nothing more," she assured him. Her gaze dropped fleetingly to his naked chest. He felt it like a soft, warm caress.

"And you're right," she added softly. "It would have been better if the kiss hadn't happened, but it wasn't your fault."

"It wasn't anybody's fault." Though he'd apologized for it half a dozen times, in his heart of hearts Max couldn't find it in him to regret the kiss. Not for a moment.

His eyes dropped to her lips, her soft, pink mouth, and the hunger rose again in him to taste her just one more time. It had to stop. He dragged his gaze off her.

"I'll make you some willow bark tea. It will help with the headache." She fetched a jar of willow chips and poured boiling water over them.

He was just being gallant, Abby thought. She knew how greedily she'd responded to his kiss, how eagerly she'd pressed herself against him, run her fingers through his hair, let her tongue tangle and dance with his. And gloried in it.

All the time knowing he was betrothed to another woman, a woman who'd waited for him for nine years. Nine years!

She knew whose fault it was. She'd given him an opening and he'd taken it, as men were wont to do. How long would it take her to learn that it was for the woman to keep her head, for the woman to set the boundaries, for the woman to remember who was the plain spinster and who was the handsome lord?

It was Laurence all over again.

Only worse. She'd never felt with Laurence what she'd felt with Lord Davenham in that alleyway.

The bitter lesson her . . . whatever-it-was with Laurence all those years ago had taught her—the lesson she'd thought she'd never forget, never be able to forget—had just dissolved at the first touch of Lord Davenham's mouth.

Because of the attack? They said danger heightened desire. If so, the danger was past now, and so hopefully would be the desire, though it didn't feel like it, with him sitting there, his shirt off and those somber gray eyes watching her as she moved about the kitchen.

Every dark glance sent shivers of awareness skittering across her skin.

It was all she could do not to stare, not to feast her eyes on that big, broad, beautiful, naked chest, not to run her hands over it, feeling the strength and power beneath her fingertips. He didn't even seem to notice how naked he was. Or did he?

Living temptation.

The salt water had cooled enough, so she dipped a clean cloth into it and knelt down beside him. "This won't hurt," she assured him. "Perhaps a little stinging—the salt, you know."

He gave her a dark look. "I'm not a child."

"I know." Her gaze flickered—again—to his bare chest, and she felt her cheeks warm. No, he wasn't a child; he was all man. She didn't look up.

The wound was shallow, a slice rather than a deep cut, but even a tiny cut could fester. Abby bathed it thoroughly, first with one lot of salt water and then with a second, just to be sure. She owed this man her life. No one had ever risked himself to protect her.

"Who was that fellow?"

She glanced up, her thoughts far away. "What fellow?"

"The one with the knife."

She shook her head. "Some thief, I expect. Taking advantage of my momentary isolation. They cut people's reticule strings to rob them, don't they?"

He shook his head. "It wasn't random. He'd been following you since the post office."

Surprised, she sat back on her heels and looked at him. "Since the post office? Are you sure? How do you know?"

"I saw it. A man came out of the post office after you, gave that fellow the nod and he followed you. So who is it who wishes you harm?"

His assumption that she would know who attacked her, that somehow she might deserve to be attacked, flicked her on the raw. "I have no idea."

"What did you collect at the post office?"

She shook her head. "Nothing valuable. Only a letter." She hadn't recognized the writing. She thought it might be from the vicar in Hereford.

"What sort of letter?"

She made an impatient gesture. "It's nothing. Just an ordinary letter." She hadn't actually had time to read it yet.

"Show me."

She gave him an indignant look. "It's my letter." She didn't want him to see it was addressed to her real name.

He said in a hard voice, "That fellow wasn't carrying a knife to slit the strings of your reticule. He had violence on his mind from the start, and a partner to back him up. So show me the letter, now." He held out his good hand, a masterful command.

Abby gave a huff of annoyance, but fetched the letter from her reticule and handed it to him. He glanced at the address. "Your real name, I presume."

What could she say? The postal clerk had given her the wrong letter by mistake? No, better to admit the truth. She nodded.

"Any relation to the Hertfordshire Chantrys?" It was what his aunt had asked too.

"I have no relations except my sisters." It wasn't quite true, but there was truth in what she said. The Hertfordshire Chantrys had never acknowledged Abby's and Jane's existence, not when they were born and Papa wrote to his parents, not when Papa died and Mama wrote to them, nor when Mama died and twelve-year-old Abby wrote to tell them she and her little sister were now orphaned and alone. The Hertfordshire Chantrys had shown no interest.

And since the Hertfordshire Chantrys didn't acknowledge them, Abby would not acknowledge the Hertfordshire Chantrys.

To her relief he didn't pursue the matter of her name or her possible relations. He broke open the seal, glanced at the letter and gave her an odd look. "There's nothing in it." He passed it back to her.

"I told you so—" She broke off and stared at it, puzzled. The letter was blank inside. No writing at all, apart from the address.

"You must have some idea of who sent it."

"Well, I don't. It's most peculiar." Abby turned it over and over in her hands, trying to think who would have sent her such a thing. Somebody absentminded, perhaps, who'd written the address and forgotten to write the letter? But who? She shrugged and put it down. "But if there's nothing in the letter, I can't see how it could possibly have anything to do with the attack."

"It was bait." He sounded completely certain.

"Bait?" She gave him a puzzled look.

"A way of identifying you to the attacker. Or his confederate. Whoever collected that letter from the post office was the target."

She bit her lip as she considered that, then shook her head. "I don't see how it can be. It's addressed to me, and I cannot think of anyone whom I've hurt or offended or who would want to hurt me. And I certainly have nothing anyone could want to steal."

"You've upset nobody?"

She thought for a moment, then said, with a hint of laughter, "Only you."

His eyes gleamed and Abby instantly regretted her small joke. He was so much harder to resist when he was amused and trying not to show it. And more than ever, she had to resist him. Avoiding his gaze, she bent over his injury.

Carefully she spread salve on the wound, laid a pad of gauze over it and began to bandage it with a clean, freshly ironed cloth.

A thought suddenly occurred to her. Could he possibly be right? Might it really be something to do with her? Something about the brothel, the man Mort? Even as the idea occurred to her, she dismissed it. How could Mort know anything about her?

"Tell me," he said quietly.

She gave him a startled look. "Tell you what?"

"What's worrying you. You know—or at least suspect, don't you?—who's behind the attack. I can help, if you tell me."

"But I *don't* know. Truly, I have no idea." It was the truth, but she felt her cheeks heating anyway. She finished bandaging him, and packed the medical detritus into a basket.

"You're not—" he began, but before he could finish, the kitchen was inundated—Abby's sisters bursting it at one door, and the cook and scullery maid, carrying shopping baskets, coming in at the other. They surrounded Abby and Lord Davenham, exclaiming over the blood, the bandage, and the bruise on Abby's face, asking questions, and all talking at once.

Through the noise and bluster, Abby's gaze met Lord Davenham's. He wasn't finished, she saw. He was certain she knew more than she did.

A moment later Featherby and William arrived, bearing clean clothes for Lord Davenham. Featherby took one horrified look at Max's indecently naked chest—"Not in front of the young ladies, m'lord"—and urged him from the kitchen.

Max went gladly. With all the females loudly exclaiming and carrying on, it was like being in the middle of a flock of distressed parrots.

He caught her eye as he left. The olive branch had been offered. It was now up to her.

Truth to tell, he was glad to leave, to have some time alone. He needed to—what was it army men called it?—regroup.

Barriers had dissolved. A bond had sprung up between them, an intimacy. . . .

He knew her scent now, her taste, how her body felt curled

against him and how her hands felt on his bare skin. How she kissed, with an eager generosity that he would not easily put from his mind . . .

But it would not do. He was betrothed. And he'd never broken a commitment in his life.

As Max was heading upstairs to change, he said to Featherby, "I want you to hire two more footmen—strong ones."

The butler and footman exchanged concerned glances. "Do I understand you're not satisfied with William's work, m'lord?"

"Not at all," Max said. "I want two extra footmen."

Featherby frowned. "For any particular purpose, m'lord?"

"To accompany the young ladies whenever any of them venture outdoors. And at other times make themselves generally useful."

"You fear another attack?"

"I don't know. Miss Chance seems to think it was a random occurrence."

"You disagree, m'lord?"

Max flexed his bandaged arm thoughtfully. "She was targeted."

The butler looked concerned. "Targeted?"

"She was followed from the post office. Do you know anything? A reason why a man with a knife might come after Miss Chance?"

The butler gave him a troubled look. "I can't think of any reason at all, m'lord."

Max didn't quite believe him. There was something the butler wasn't saying. "Loyalty is all very well, Featherby, but those girls could be in danger."

Featherby sighed. "If I knew anything that would help, m'lord, I would share it with you. I am immensely fond—" He caught himself up. It was not for butlers to express fondness. "I owe everything to Miss Chance, and be assured, m'lord, William and I would die to protect her and the other young ladies."

It was not a satisfactory answer, but Max knew enough about men to know he wouldn't get any more out of Featherby. The man knew something, but whatever it was—something to the young ladies' discredit, perhaps—he wasn't prepared to share.

Presumably it was not useful in the matter of their protection. He didn't doubt the sincerity of the man's devotion to Abby.

Miss Chance, he corrected himself. Barriers.

"Can I leave the hiring of the footmen to you, or shall I get Bartlett to see to it?"

Featherby bowed slightly. "I will see to it, m'lord. William has acquaintances who, er, can handle themselves if there is trouble."

"No roughnecks," Max warned.

Featherby looked shocked. "Of course not, m'lord. They shall be all that is proper; I guarantee it."

"Dress 'em in livery. I want to send a clear message that Miss Chance and the young ladies are under my protection."

"Very good, m'lord."

"It must have been a cutpurse," Abby concluded. It was the only answer she could think of for the attack. "I don't see how it could have been one of Mort's men."

The four girls were drinking tea in the back parlor. Lady Beatrice was upstairs, taking a nap. She didn't yet know about the incident with the knife. If her nephew wanted her to know, he could tell her, Abby decided. She didn't want to distress the old lady unnecessarily.

"If he followed you from the post office, "Damaris suggested, "it does argue a deliberate targeting of you, rather than a random attempt at theft. What do you think, Daisy? Could it be Mort?"

Daisy wrinkled her nose thoughtfully. "Mort don't like anyone to get the better of him—especially females—so I wouldn't be surprised if he sent a blade after us; he's a nasty piece of work. But why would he send anyone after *Abby*? How could Mort even *know* about Abby? The rest of us, maybe, but not Abby."

They exchanged glances. There was a long silence. Nobody had an answer.

Damaris glanced at Abby. "The letter was addressed to you as Abigail Chantry?"

"Yes."

Jane leaned forward. "What did Lord Davenham have to say about that?"

Abby shook her head. "Not a thing."

"So he didn't notice?" Jane suggested hopefully.

Abby grimaced. "He noticed, all right. And I had to admit it was my real name."

"What did he say to that?"

"Nothing." And that disturbed her. He'd accepted it a little too easily. Why hadn't he asked why she was living with his aunt under a false name? Did he know it already? How? From Lady Beatrice? Unlikely. So did he not care, or did he have some other plan in mind?

Damaris continued. "And the letter was blank inside?"

Abby nodded. "Lord Davenham called it bait, a way of identifying me, though why anyone should want to identify—let alone harm—me is more than I can fathom."

"So who knows you use that particular post office for your mail?" Damaris asked. "Someone knew you'd collect that blank letter."

"Nobody," Abby said. She'd been wondering about that herself. "Only Mrs. Bodkin, and the vicar in Hereford, and Sir Walter Greevey." All eminently respectable people.

Jane said, "Who else did you write to, Abby? You have that look on your face."

Abby grimaced, knowing the others wouldn't like what she was about to admit. "I might have written some letters to Bow Street and one or two local magistrates, reporting that brothel for—"

She didn't get to finish her sentence; there was a chorus of objection from the others.

"You *what*? But we agreed that you wouldn't—"

"It'll bring Mort down on us for sure!"

"We *told* you reporting it would cause trouble!"

"I wrote anonymously," Abby defended herself. "You said I couldn't report it in person, so I didn't. And you need not look at me like that—I *had* to report it. It is *iniquitous* what that dreadful Mort person did—and no doubt still does—and will keep doing unless someone tries to stop him."

There was a short silence.

"Well, I don't reckon you ought to write any more letters," Daisy said. "Not if blokes with knives are going to follow you home from the post office."

Abby sighed. Daisy had a point. Abby still thought her attacker had to be a random cutpurse, because it made no sense to kill her, but if she was wrong, if it was somehow connected to Mort and the brothel and the letters she'd been writing, she was gladder than ever that she'd changed their name to Chance.

She wondered again what she should do in response to Lord Davenham's offer to help. The interruption to their conversation had been timely; it gave her more time to think.

She couldn't imagine how telling him would help. She had no idea who'd sent that man with the knife—if anyone had—but one thing she was sure of: The moment Lord Davenham learned that three of the four girls his aunt had taken under her wing had come from a brothel, all four of them would surely be out on their ears.

Worse, Jane's reputation would be ruined forever. She'd never be able to make a respectable marriage.

Abby couldn't risk that.

Abby snuffed out the candle. It had been a long, eventful day, and she was so glad finally to slide down into the comfort of her bed. It wasn't every day a girl was attacked by a man with a knife, then rescued by a man she'd assumed up till now was her enemy. And then kissed almost senseless by that same man . . .

She and the other girls had decided not to tell Lady Beatrice about the attack. If her nephew wanted to tell her, he could; they would not distress the old lady.

As the day wore on, the aches and pains of Abby's bruises had made themselves more strongly felt, and by the afternoon she was thinking of asking Featherby to draw her a bath when Lady Beddington arrived with a friend, Mrs. Murrell, in tow, eager to hear the next installment of the novel—which of course was what Abby had hoped for, but still . . . Lady Beddington had been insistent that Abby must read.

It was all Abby could do to focus on reading the story, but

she managed. Now that she'd had her bath and was ready to draw a veil over the events of the day . . .

But as the darkness surrounded her, she found herself reliving in her mind the moment when she'd found herself held tight in his arms. . . .

If she closed her eyes hard enough and lay very still, she could almost feel the corded muscles of his arms, the jagged breathing and the thud of his heart in the broad, deep chest. Her cheek pressed against that chest. . . . Safe . . . protected.

A haven against the world.

And that moment when she'd turned her face to him and— No, not *him*—Lord Davenham, she told herself, refusing to allow herself even the intimacy of thinking of him simply as *him* . . . as if there were no other.

For Abby there was no *him*.

It was fear and reaction and loneliness speaking. She knew that. And to let herself dream that it was anything more was not just foolish; it was dangerous.

She'd been down that road before, with Laurence. And at the end there'd been only heartbreak and humiliation.

It was her own fault, she'd realized; she had a great capacity for self-deception. She'd learned that at nineteen. And if she let herself dream foolish dreams of Lord Davenham, it was her own fault if she was hurt again. If?

When.

And if she read anything into that kiss . . . anything except reaction to danger, and masculine opportunism . . . it would serve her right. Had Laurence taught her nothing?

At nineteen she'd at least had the excuse of youth and innocence. Ignorance. She'd been eighteen months out of the Pillbury, away from her sister and all her friends of the last six years.

As a governess she had no friends. She was neither servant nor member of the family. If the Taylor family had lived in a city, she might have made friends of other governesses, but they lived in the country, outside of a village. The only adults she saw, apart from the household, were the people at church, and even so, she was in charge of the children and had no time to talk.

She ached with loneliness. Oh, she had the children, and they were all that made her life bearable; she'd poured all her love into caring for them, teaching them. But it wasn't enough. She'd craved adult conversation, friendship, intimacy.

And then Laurence had come, Mr. Taylor's son by his first marriage, twenty-four years old and fresh down from his work in the city. She'd heard him mentioned, of course, the oldest son, Mr. Taylor's heir, but somehow she hadn't expected him to be a man. Mr. Taylor's children by his second wife were all under ten.

Laurence had come up to the nursery that first afternoon—to visit the children, he'd said, but his eyes were all for her from the very first.

He'd made her laugh that first day, and had entertained her with tales of his life in the city.

She'd been absurdly flattered; he seemed so sophisticated, so worldly.

On the second afternoon, he'd coaxed her into taking the children for a walk and, once they were away from the house, had tucked her arm through his, like a gentleman did with a lady. Not the governess. Strolling and chatting, telling her about his life, his dreams.

Like a ripe plum she'd fallen, head over heels.

On the third evening he'd come up to wish the children good night, to see them tucked up safe in bed, and he'd sat with her as she read them a story and watched till they drifted off to sleep.

He'd kissed her then, in the hallway outside the children's rooms. Her first kiss. And if it wasn't quite as she'd dreamed a kiss would be, the second and the third were better. He'd placed his hand on her breast that night, and she'd pushed him away, shyly, virtuously, a little alarmed by the speed with which the courtship was proceeding.

Courtship. It was what she thought, of course.

Over the next few days they'd walked and talked, and at every opportunity Laurence had stolen kisses and secret caresses. Abby had tried her best to keep him in bounds, but he adored her, he said, and had no control where she was concerned, and when they were married . . . ah, when they were married . . .

One night, just as she was drifting off to sleep, her bedroom door had opened and Laurence slipped inside, dressed only in his nightshirt.

What are you doing?

What do you think?

No, no, we mustn't . . . you mustn't. . . .

Oh, yes, my dear, we must. You've kept me waiting long enough. . . .

And he'd lain on top of her and started kissing her, pulling her nightgown up, ignoring her objections. . . . Touching her where nobody had ever touched . . .

She'd struggled and tried to stop him, but only halfheartedly, because she loved him, after all, and he wanted her so desperately, needed her—loved her. He told her so repeatedly as his hands groped and thrust.

She must have cried out, for a moment later her bedroom door slammed open and his father stood there, shouting, pulling Laurence off her, shoving him out into the corridor in his bare feet, calling Abby a slut and a whore; she was finished here.

The next morning as Abby was packing her few meager possessions, Mrs. Taylor came to see her. Laurence was betrothed, she'd explained, but young men had needs. The same thing had happened with the last governess too.

Mrs. Taylor was embarrassed, apologetic. The family would be moving to Jamaica soon; she would give Abby a reference and give the move as a reason for her dismissal. It was the best she could do. If Abby found herself with child, the family would deny it.

At least it hadn't come to that, Abby thought. She'd escaped with her virginity intact. Just.

Abby had seen Laurence just once more before she left. *You said we were to be married.*

Why would I marry you? You're poor, you're plain, and all I ever wanted from you was what I nearly got last night. But you had to go and screech, didn't you?

As those hateful words scalded her for the thousandth time, Abby buried her hot face in the pillow. She'd been such a fool. Stupid, naive and gullible. Hadn't they been warned at the Pill that male employers and their sons could sometimes behave in a predatory manner, that a girl needed to wear her virtue like a shield?

But Abby had taken Laurence at his word and opened her lonely, eager heart to him.

Just as she was in danger of doing with Lord Davenham. If the son of a country merchant thought she was too plain and poor to be of interest, what chance would she have with a handsome London lord? Even if he weren't betrothed.

Even if his kisses did make her foolish heart dream . . . They meant nothing, she told herself firmly. *Nothing.*

He'd told her so himself. There was no excuse for thinking otherwise.

Chapter Fifteen

*"A lady, without a family, was the very best
preserver of furniture in the world."*

—JANE AUSTEN, *PERSUASION*

"May I ask you something?"

Max looked up, lowered his newspaper and stood. Abby—Miss Chance, he corrected himself—stood in the doorway of the small sitting room. His gaze went straight to her mouth. He dragged it away.

She looked completely recovered from her ordeal of the day before. For once she wasn't in one of those drab gray gowns. She wore a dress of dusky pink satin with thin cream stripes and dozens of tiny embroidered roses that echoed the roses in her cheeks. The deep rose hue exactly matched the color of her lips.

He glanced again at her mouth. Instantly the sensation of holding her in his arms swirled through him, as immediate and visceral as if the kiss were only a minute ago, instead of a full day. And a night.

"I'm sorry; I didn't mean to disturb you."

He realized he'd been staring. "No, no, come in."

She entered the room. Her dress looked oddly familiar, though he was sure she'd never worn it before. He would surely have noticed; along the scooped, though perfectly decorous neckline rode a narrow line of knotted silk roses that drew his gaze to a tantalizing hint of the creamy bosom beneath.

She looked fresh, pretty and altogether edible.

But she was not for him.

He realized his fists were clenched, crushing the paper, and deliberately forced his fingers to relax. "Please sit down."

When she was seated he sat too and asked, "Are you quite recovered from your ordeal yesterday?"

"Thank you, yes. A good night's sleep was all I needed. And your injury?"

He shook his head. "Perfectly all right, thank you." It ached a little, but that was normal. He folded the paper and set it aside. "So, what did you want to speak to me about?"

She hesitated, smoothing the fabric of her dress with nervous fingers, and for a moment Max wondered whether she was going to confess that she knew the villain after all. He leaned forward.

"Jane said yesterday at breakfast you were asking where I was. And then you followed me to the post office. So did you want me for some reason?" She glanced up, tilting her head. "Or was your being there when that man came after me just a coincidence?"

"No, it wasn't. Have you had any thoughts about who he might be?"

She shook her head and said with a slight edge to her voice, "I told you yesterday, I have no idea. I didn't come here to talk about that; I just wondered what was so urgent that you must follow me to the post office."

"Oh." He sat back. "It wasn't urgent. I was on my way to the new house and wanted to talk to you about it."

"Oh." An anxious pucker formed between her brows and she leaned forward. "What about it?"

"The furniture."

She blinked. "Furniture?"

"There's more furniture in this house than can fit in the new one. Someone must inspect the new house and decide which pieces go and which will remain. Obviously my aunt cannot do it."

There was a short silence. "You want *me* to decide what furnishings are to go into your new house?"

He was a little perplexed at her surprise. "Couldn't you do it?"

"I could, of course. But would it not more properly be a task for Miss Parsley?"

He stiffened. "Miss *Parsley*?"

"Yes, is that not right? Your aunt told me you were betrothed to a Miss Parsley of Manchester."

His aunt. He might have known. "Her name is Miss Pars*loe*. My aunt will make her little pleasantries. And the betrothal has not yet been formally announced." Now why had he told her that?

She did her best to look contrite, but he could see she was struggling not to smile. "I'm sorry. Miss Pars*loe*. But most new brides would enjoy such a task, wishing to make their home their own."

"Miss Parsloe is in Manchester and hardly in a position to make such decisions."

"Can't you decide, then? It will be your home, after all."

He made an impatient gesture. "If the task is distasteful to you, just say so and I'll put that butler fellow in charge. I merely thought that since women are generally held to enjoy such things, you might like to be of service to my aunt but if you don't—"

"No, no. Of course I'll do it."

"Thank you." There was a short silence. Her direct gaze was unsettling.

She seemed to be waiting for him to say something. The reminder of his betrothal should have made things easier between them, clarified the boundaries, but instead Max felt more uncomfortable than ever.

He wanted to explain what had been in his mind when he'd kissed her—a betrothed man kissing a woman he had no right to—but he couldn't find any reason, certainly not anything she could accept.

She kept looking at him with those big wide eyes. Silently asking him questions he could not answer.

He stood. "So, can you be—"

"And what of me and my sisters?" she said in a rush, rising

from her chair. Her fists were clutched in knots at her sides. "Do we move to Berkeley Square next week? Or must we leave?"

He frowned. For himself, he didn't give the snap of his fingers whether her sisters stayed or left—for him, she was the issue. He couldn't let her stay, not permanently, but equally he didn't want her to leave.

It wasn't like him to be so indecisive.

His aunt would create a grand fuss if he tried to throw them out at the end of the week. To be honest, he couldn't care less if the sisters stayed indefinitely. They made the old lady happy and kept her entertained while she was so limited in her movements.

It was only Miss Chance who disturbed his peace of mind.

And there was his bride to consider. It had already occurred to him that she might not be particularly happy at sharing a house with his aunt. He would stand firm on that, of course; his aunt was in no condition to live on her own any longer.

But would any new bride welcome into her home four pretty and vivacious young women who were no relation to the groom or his aunt? Max didn't even have to ask the question.

"I do value the service you have done for my aunt," he said carefully. "And, of course, for the time being you and your sisters are welcome to continue your visit"—he stressed the word, with all its temporary implications—"at Berkeley Square."

"But?" she prompted.

"The visit must come to an end before my marriage. After that date, my bride will take on the care of my aunt."

A glimmer of humor lit her eyes. "I'm sure Lady Beatrice will enjoy that." Before he could respond, she added, "And when is your marriage to be?"

"It's not yet been decided," Max told her. "As soon as the move to Berkeley Square is accomplished, I'll go to Manchester and finalize the arrangements." He glanced at her and added, "Spring, I expect—isn't that when most brides like to get married?" He was not looking forward to it at all.

"I see." That anxious pucker was back, marring the smooth line of her forehead. Of course she'd be worried about her future; she and her sisters seemed to be wholly dependent on the stipend from his aunt.

When they left, he'd bestow on them a handsome sum—not a bribe, as he'd offered her that first day, but a reward for the care of his aunt. He didn't like to think of her—them—struggling, or worrying about money. Perhaps a cottage, as well as a sum of money . . .

Would she accept such a gift from him? He remembered her anger the last time he'd suggested such a thing. No, she was prickly with pride. When the time came, he'd make sure it would look like a gift from his aunt. In the meantime he could ease the worst of her anxieties. "Naturally you will be paid for your trouble in helping with the matter of the furniture."

"There's no need for that," Abby began.

"There's every need," he said in a clipped voice. "You are an employee of my aunt and this is outside of your usual duties."

"But I am not—"

"You accept a wage from her, do you not?" It wasn't a question. Lord Davenham was underlining her status as an employee. A servant.

Any warm feelings Abby might have had for the man dissolved. She was not an employee. But there was no word for what she was. Friends didn't accept a stipend for their friendship. Neither did guests. Abby did what she did for Lady Beatrice because she cared about her, and wanted to help—not for money. If she'd had any choice, she wouldn't have accepted any payment at all.

But she had no choice. It was horrid being so poor. You couldn't even afford pride.

"You're quite right," Abby said crisply, hoping her chagrin did not show. "If you wish to pay me for the service I won't argue." Though it would choke her to accept it.

"You don't know what I'm offering yet."

"I don't *care* what you're offering," she flashed.

He tilted his head. "You don't intend to haggle?"

Was he deliberately provoking her? Abby wondered. There was a gleam in the hard gray eyes that she found a little disconcerting. "Do you wish me to inspect the house or not?"

"I do." He picked up his leather driving gloves and rose. "Immediately, if it suits you. We'll take my carriage."

She hesitated. "Can you drive with that arm?"

He said brusquely, "Yes, of course. Shall we say in ten minutes? Is that enough time for you to get ready?"

"Of course." She hurried away to fetch her pelisse and hat. And to regain her temper. She would not allow him to provoke her again.

Eight minutes later Abby hurried back toward the stairs, pulling on her gloves. As she passed the sitting room, Lady Beddington and her friend Mrs. Murrell waved and called a greeting.

"Are you going out, Miss Chance? But I thought . . ."

"Yes, but don't worry, Lady Beddington: Damaris will read you the next chapter, and I think you'll find she's very good." Damaris's father had been a missionary of the fire-and-brimstone variety, and Damaris had been his assistant. She knew the value of storytelling and could infuse any text with drama.

Abby smiled to herself as she ran lightly down the stairs. The ladies really were enjoying the novel. It was a good omen.

When she reached the entry hall, it was to find three more ladies arriving. Two were much the same age as Lady Beddington, and one was a young lady about Jane's age. They handed coats and shawls to Featherby while they chatted with animation to a harried-looking Lord Davenham. They were here, they said, for the book reading.

Abby hugged a small knot of hope to her breast. Her plan was starting to work.

The trouble was, there was no telling how long they had. Miss Parsloe might not want to wait till spring. After all, she'd waited nine years already.

Still, she had to try. Lord Davenham was leaving for Manchester immediately after they moved to Berkeley Square. The day after that would be the first official meeting of Lady Beatrice's literary society.

Abby hastened to join him. The ladies gave her several curious looks. Abby smiled at them, but Lord Davenham made no effort to introduce her, so she said nothing.

"Well, we must get on. Clara said the reading starts at two," the oldest lady, a hawk-faced dowager, declared. "Delightful to see you again after all these years, Davenham." She glanced at Abby again and gave her a brisk, not unfriendly nod.

As the ladies followed Featherby up the stairs, the hawk-faced dowager's voice drifted back to them. "That'll be one of Griselda's gels. Seems Clara was quite right—Davenham don't acknowledge them. All hushed up at the time and the boy never knew the truth."

Lord Davenham's head snapped around, but the ladies had disappeared from sight.

Abby stifled the urge to giggle. "Don't look at me," she said as he turned toward her. "I didn't say a word."

In grim silence he handed her down the front steps to where his phaeton waited. He helped her into the carriage, his hand strong and warm even through his gloves.

He climbed in after her, picked up the reins and gave her a sideways glance. "One of these days I'll strangle Aunt Bea."

Abby laughed. "You won't. You know perfectly well she means no harm."

He snorted.

"You have to admit life with her isn't the least bit dull."

He snorted again, but his mouth quirked in rueful acknowledgment. He loved the old lady, she knew, and it seemed he'd even tolerate the eccentric invention of a half sister and a handful of faux nieces—not that he had much choice.

But what, Abby wondered as the carriage moved off, would the unknown Miss Parsloe make of Lady Beatrice and her eccentricities?

The carriage threaded its way through the busy London streets at quite a smart pace. For all his years away in foreign places, Lord Davenham was a skilled driver.

The phaeton was very elegant, of course, but it wasn't terribly large. She could feel the warmth of his body all the way down her side. An awkward silence fell.

Or maybe it was just she who felt awkward; no doubt he was concentrating on the traffic. How he managed, with horses, vehicles, barrow boys and pedestrians going in all directions, was beyond her.

A dog shot out into the road, and a boy after it. "Look out!" The carriage stopped with a jerk, catching Abby unprepared and throwing her forward. She might have fallen, except that Lord Davenham caught her with his left hand, pulling her hard against him, while with his right hand—his injured arm—he kept his startled horses under control.

"Are you all right?" He glanced at her.

"Y-yes, thank you."

The carriage moved on. He didn't release her. He could drive one-handed, it seemed. His arm was warm and heavy around her shoulders. He'd probably forgotten he was holding her; he must be concentrating on the traffic again.

Abby knew she should move away, make some sign to him that he should release her. It was almost an embrace, and in public, so not at all seemly. But she couldn't bring herself to speak or even move.

It was like the day before, when he'd held her after she'd been attacked. She wanted to close her eyes and lean into his solidity, breathe in the scent of him. Instead she held herself rigidly erect. And tried not to remember the way he'd kissed her. And the way she'd responded.

Piccadilly Circus thronged with carriages. The phaeton slowed, and finally he lifted his arm from around her to better negotiate his way through the traffic. Or perhaps he'd realized the impropriety of their position.

Or was his arm aching? Her own bruises had certainly made themselves felt this morning, and his injuries were much more severe—but he showed no sign of it.

He'd held her only a moment or two, she realized in retrospect; it just felt longer.

After a few minutes they turned down a side street into a much quieter neighborhood. He cleared his throat. "About yesterday," he began. "I'm s—"

"Please! If you tell me you're sorry for kissing me one more time, I—I'll scream!" There was a short silence. She turned her head for a quick glance at him. He seemed to be trying not to smile.

"Actually, what I was going to say was that I'm certain you and your sisters are in some kind of trouble, and if you could only bring yourself to trust me, I'm sure I could help."

"Oh." Abby felt herself blushing. Of course he hadn't intended to apologize for the kiss. He probably hadn't even given it a thought.

"And while we're setting stories straight, I'm not sorry for kissing you at all."

"What?" She whipped her head around to stare at him. "But you said—"

"I apologized, yes. But I'm not sorry."

Was he flirting? Teasing? Serious? Or was he perhaps thinking she might be willing to become his mistress? She couldn't read a thing from his expression. Nor could she think of a single thing to say, and when she finally thought of a response—the merest commonplace, but better than stunned silence—it was too late. "Ah, here we are, Berkeley Square," he said.

They pulled up outside an elegant white house. The groom hurried to lower the steps for them to alight, but Lord Davenham leaped lightly down, and before Abby knew what he was about, he'd put his hands around her waist and swiftly lifted her down. Just as he'd done that first day on the stairs. Leaving her breathless.

"It's raining again," he said, when she gave him a surprised look. "Quick, inside before you get wet."

The house on Berkeley Square might have been small by comparison to the mansion on the Strand, but Abby had never seen such an elegant abode. With a Grecian-style pediment over an entry supported by Corinthian columns, the house rose to four stories, not counting the servants' quarters in the attic or the kitchen quarters in the basement. Inside it was both grand and spacious. A staircase rose from the handsome entry hall in a graceful sweep rising through several floors before culminating in an elegant domed ceiling.

"Well?" Lord Davenham's deep, rather hard voice startled her out of her reverie. "What do you think?" Quite as if he hadn't just knocked her composure endways by the admission that he didn't regret their kiss. What did he mean by it?

And what was she supposed to think? He'd told her himself he was betrothed. Or was he perhaps thinking she might be willing to become his mistress? Surely not.

Two could play at "let's pretend it never happened," she decided. "It's beautiful. I've never seen such a beautiful house. I think Lady Beatrice will enjoy living here very much. And Miss Parsloe, of course."

He nodded, looking satisfied.

Abby was a little overwhelmed, if the truth be told. Throughout her childhood, she and Jane had played house, furnishing boxes with tiny pieces of homemade furniture for their dolls, and imagining how one day they'd arrange a house of their own. And now she had this to arrange, this grand, elegant house.

Though it would not be her home.

Abby took a small notebook and pencil from her reticule. She wandered from room to room, Lord Davenham following. Their footsteps echoed in the empty house. On the ground floor she found a large drawing room, several smaller salons, a dining room and a ballroom that opened onto a terraced back garden.

Abby had never been to a ball, but that didn't stop her imagining all the details—the scent of flowers and perfume, and music, perhaps one of those marvelous new Viennese waltzes, and people twirling around the dance floor, the ladies in beautiful gowns and the gentlemen so elegant in their crisp black and white. It would be a warm evening and the French doors would be open onto the terrace. . . .

If Lord Davenham and his wife entertained . . .

"How formal do you want the house to be?" she asked him.

"Formal?"

She nodded. "I presume, having bought a house with a ballroom, you plan to entertain a great deal."

He frowned.

"Does Miss Parsloe like to entertain?"

"I have no idea."

She moved on. Lord Davenham prowled silently along behind her. She made notes, trying to imagine the furniture from Davenham House in this fine new setting. From time to time she asked him about Miss Parsloe's preferences—did he think, for instance, that Miss Parsloe would prefer to sleep at the back of the house, or the front? The front bedroom was grander, and looked out over the square, but the back would be quieter.

But he seemed to know nothing of her tastes. Worse, he didn't seem to care.

"I have no idea of her preferences," he would say indifferently. Or, "It doesn't matter." And once, "If she doesn't like it when she gets here, she can change it."

"But in the meantime I need to know what you want," she told him, annoyed with his lack of guidance.

"What do I want?" He paused. They were in a sitting room overlooking the street. He stalked across the room and gazed out of the window across the gray street to the lush green park at the center of Berkeley Square. Abby wondered what he was looking at. All she could see were the leaves of the plane trees just starting to turn. Autumn was coming. By spring he would be married.

Finally he spoke. "Featherby told me the previous servants had left my aunt's house in a disgraceful state and that you supervised the cleaning and rearrangement of the rooms. And do so still."

"That's true." Why would he bring that up? He couldn't want her to clean this house. It was already immaculate, not so much as a speck of dust on the glowing parquetry floors or the marble mantelpieces.

"That house was never homelike. In my uncle's day it was always formal and chilly and . . . unwelcoming. At least, to a boy it was. Now, despite its shabby condition, the house is more attractive and welcoming than I've ever seen it."

Abby felt the beginnings of a glow of pleasure—and then she realized: He hadn't brought her here to talk about furniture; he wanted a home, wanted her to make him a home.

His next words confirmed it. "I don't know how the effect was achieved, but I'd like the same to be done for this place. For my aunt." He turned to face her and added stiffly, "And for Miss Parsloe, of course."

Abby didn't know whether to laugh or to cry. Did he know

what he was asking her to do? To make a home for him to share with Miss Parsloe?

Right after his confession—if confession it was. *I'm not sorry.*

Did he have no idea? Homes were made *by* the people who lived in them, *for* the people who lived in them.

Houses were filled with furniture, but homes were made with love.

She looked into his unreadable gray eyes as he waited for her response. No, he had no idea. Somewhere inside this tall, grave man was the lonely small boy who'd waited . . . who'd been abandoned by his parents and left to grow up at school. And had then gone abroad from the age of eighteen.

Like Abby, he hadn't ever really had a home to call his own.

"Yes, of course, Lord Davenham," she said softly, "I'll try to make it as homelike and welcoming as I can. For Lady Beatrice." And for him.

And for herself. She'd probably never get the chance to make a home for anyone again, so she might as well enjoy this, even if it was only for a few weeks. And creating a homelike atmosphere in this gorgeous house was a lot better than playing with dolls and old boxes.

But she wasn't going to do it with him watching her every move. She couldn't think straight. "Now, I'm better able to do this on my own, and I'm sure you have much more important things to attend to," she told him briskly. "Could you pick me up in, say, an hour?"

H e'd been dismissed, and Max was glad to go.
It was hard enough imagining himself married to Henrietta Parsloe—it was so long since he'd seen her—but planning the arrangement of his house with Miss Abigail Chance was proving rather unsettling.

And what the devil had caused him to say he didn't regret their kiss? He didn't, but telling her had been a fool's act. It changed nothing. He was promised and that was that, and the sooner he got himself married the better. That would put an end to these . . . feelings.

He'd travel to Manchester the minute the move was accomplished. To that end, he decided to call on Freddy. He had a favor to ask.

"I'm going to Manchester," he told Freddy a short time later.

"Good God, why?"

Max hesitated, but he supposed he couldn't keep it secret for much longer. "I'm betrothed."

Freddy's jaw dropped; then a grim expression settled over his face. "Blasted muffins—they'll get a man every time. Never mind. It's not over till the parson sounds. Manchester's an excellent notion! Scotland would be better. The continent, better still. What about Paris? Italy?"

Max stared at him. "What the devil are you talking about?"

"You need to get out of London fast. Let it all blow over. Believe me, I understand."

Max gave a short laugh. "You don't, you know. I'm not going to Manchester to escape a betrothal."

Freddy blinked. "Why else would you go there?"

"Because that's where my fiancée lives."

There was a short, astounded silence; then Freddy shook his head. He took a bottle from the sideboard, poured himself a brandy, downed it in one long swallow, shuddered, shook himself like a dog, then returned to Max. "Let me get this straight— you're betrothed?"

"Yes."

"To a girl in Manchester?"

"Yes."

"And you don't want my help to escape to Scotland or the Continent."

"No."

Freddy said slowly, disbelievingly, "So you *want* this betrothal?"

Max hesitated. "I'm betrothed," he repeated firmly.

"Ah." Freddy gave him a piercing look. "She's a muffin, isn't she?"

"No, of course n—at least, I don't know what she's like. I haven't seen her for nine years."

"*Nine years*? Good God!" Freddy returned to the brandy bottle and poured out two glasses. He handed one to Max.

Max shook his head. "I don't want one. Nor do I want to explain anything. Or escape anything. I came here to tell you I was going to Manchester for a short visit and to ask if, while I'm away, you'll keep an eye on my aunt and the misses Chance."

"The muffins?" Freddy eyed him balefully through the fumes emanating from the brandy glass. "Not a chance. Bad enough one of us has been caught in a parson's mousetrap."

"Miss Chance was attacked in the street yesterday by a villain with a knife."

"Good God! Is she all right?"

"Yes, though rather bruised and shaken. But the only reason she wasn't badly hurt—or worse—is because I was there and stopped the fellow." He held up his arm. "The swine cut me. So while I'm away, I need someone to keep an eye on them."

Freddy considered the request briefly, then shook his head. "Sorry, but you can hire someone to look after them. It'll be less dangerous."

Max frowned. "Dangerous for whom?"

"For me."

"No one's going to attack you; it's—"

"I'm not talking about getting attacked," Freddy scoffed. "Knives and assassins don't worry me. I can look after myself."

"Then what danger are you talking about?"

"Muffins."

Max rolled his eyes, but he could see no amount of argument would get Freddy to change his mind.

But there was more than one way to lead a horse to water.

"Going to Barney McPhee's card party tonight?" Max asked him.

"Definitely," Freddy agreed.

"What's the best way to get to Barney's?" Max asked. "I'm not familiar with the address."

"Don't worry; I'll pick you up in the curricle," Freddy said. "At seven?"

"Perfect."

An hour later Max collected Miss Chance from Berkeley Square. They drove home in relative silence.

When they arrived home, however, Featherby drew him aside. "Two footmen have been hired, m'lord—Turner and Hatch, very reliable men—they start today. And Mr. Morton Black is waiting for you in the small sitting room."

Chapter Sixteen

"This is an evening of wonders, indeed!"

—JANE AUSTEN, *PRIDE AND PREJUDICE*

"I found the place," Morton Black told Max. "The Pillbury Home for the Daughters of Distressed Gentlewomen, in Cheltenham. Mrs. Bodkin, the woman in charge, knows no one by the name of Chance, but she's very well acquainted with sisters Abigail and Jane Chantry—spoke very highly of them both, in fact, particularly of Miss Abigail Chantry.

"According to her, Miss Chantry has worked as a governess for the past six years, ever since she left the Pillbury—for two different families. The first family terminated her employment because they were moving to Jamaica. The second was a London post. She left their employment quite suddenly, Mrs. Bodkin said."

"Why?" Max asked.

Morton Black shook his head. "Mrs. Bodkin said Miss Jane Chantry left the orphanage to take up a position as a lady's companion in Hereford, but for some reason joined her sister in London instead."

A governess and a lady's companion—it all seemed quite respectable and aboveboard. Not at all the kind of thing that would get someone coming after them with a knife.

"What of the other two girls?"

Morton Black shook his head. "She has no idea of anyone

with the first name Damaris, and though she knows several girls called Daisy, none of them has one leg shorter than the other, or speaks with a cockney accent." Morton Black's mouth quirked with dry humor. "She made it very clear they only took in the daughters of distressed *ladies*."

Max nodded. It was as he thought. "So the two misses Chance—Chantry, rather—have no other relatives."

"As to that, my lord, they do, though not Miss Damaris or Miss Daisy."

"Go on."

"Mrs. Bodkin told me Miss Abigail and Miss Jane's story. Apparently the girl's mother and father were set to marry other people, but instead they eloped with each other, which caused somewhat of a scandal. Both families cast them out in disgrace."

Max leaned forward. "So there are living relatives who could take the girls in now?"

Morton Black grimaced. "Unlikely, my lord. When the two girls were first brought to the Pillbury—Miss Abigail was just twelve years old and her sister was six—Mrs. Bodkin made inquiries and wrote to the head of each family, the Chantrys and the Dalrymples." He handed over a piece of paper on which was written the names and addresses. "Both families made it clear that they wanted nothing to do with the girls."

The Chantrys and the Dalrymples. He knew both families by reputation. Both in the upper ten thousand, wealthy and more than capable of taking in two little girls and giving them the kind of upbringing their birth warranted. And yet they hadn't.

Max clenched his fist around the sheet of paper. "Does Ab— I mean, do the girls know that?"

Morton Black shook his head. "Mrs. Bodkin never told them, didn't want to raise false hopes."

"Why would anyone reject two little girls born in wedlock?" Max hadn't realized he'd spoken aloud until Morton Black answered.

"Scandal."

"But that was years before."

Morton Black shook his head ruefully. "Not the elopement.

The girls' father was shot and killed while attempting to rob a coach on the Great North Road."

"Good God."

"My inquiries revealed it was the first time he'd taken to the High Toby—word was he was desperate because his wife was desperately ill and he had no money for medicines. Still, some people don't care for the reason behind a crime; the crime itself—and the scandal—is all they care about."

"So if the father was killed and the mother was ill, who looked after Abby and her sister? She was just a child."

"From everything I can discover, Miss Abigail cared for her family alone."

"How?" It came out as a croak.

"Not what you're worried about," Morton Black assured him. "It was honest hard work. She helped out in a bakery in return for bread and a place for them to sleep. Worked all hours of the day, like a little demon, until her mother died and they took her away to that orphanage." Morton Black looked at Max. "Twelve years old and looked after her mother, herself and her little sister."

And she was still doing that now, Max thought: looking after people. "I see. Did you discover anything about the other two girls?"

"No, my lord. I tried every avenue I could think of. It's a mystery where they sprang from, though when Miss Abigail left the Mason home it was with three other young women. The housemaid I spoke to knew nothing of who they were or where they'd come from, only that one of them was Miss Abigail's sister."

Only one, Max thought. "So somewhere between Jane leaving the orphanage and Abby leaving the Mason house, they acquired the other two. But how?"

"Do you wish me to keep trying?"

"Something else has arisen. Miss Chance was attacked in the street the other day by a man with a knife. Can you think of any reason why?"

Morton Black shook his head. "Everyone I spoke to only had good to say about her. Of course, the Masons, her most recent employers, were annoyed about the way she'd left so suddenly, but otherwise I would have said she has no enemies to speak of."

"Nothing at all odd or fishy?"

Morton Black thought for a moment. "It was odd that Miss Jane set out in a coach for Hereford and ended up in London, without a word to Mrs. Bodkin or, from the sounds of it, her sister." He added, "Her unexpected arrival at the Mason home led to Miss Abigail being sacked. And from the sounds of it, the other two girls were with her then."

Max shook his head. "It seems an unlikely cause for hostility to me, but keep on it, Black. Dig as deep as you need to, no expense spared. I want to know who has it in for Miss Abigail. That fellow with the knife meant business." Max had the aching arm to prove it.

L ord Davenham came downstairs that evening dressed to go out and looking, in Abby's private opinion, quietly magnificent. He glanced into the sitting room, where Lady Beatrice and the girls were taking sherry before dinner, and to Abby's surprise he came in, accepted a sherry and sat down beside his aunt.

"I'm delighted to see you up and about again, Aunt Bea."

"Rather more up than about," she grumbled. "But I'm getting stronger every day." She released her nephew's arm and gave him a critical inspection. "Looking very dashing, my boy. Dining out again, I suppose."

"Yes, ma'am." He returned the inspection with a grave air. Abby and the others hid their smiles as he said, "You're looking rather dashing yourself, Aunt Bea. Your hair in particular looks quite—"

"Natural," she said firmly.

He inclined his head. "I was going to say vivid."

"It's titian, as it's always been." Daisy and Lady Beatrice's maid had spent most of the afternoon giving her iron gray hair what Daisy called "a restorative treatment." Lady Beatrice's hair was now gleaming with life—and bright red henna.

"Thanks to these gels, my health is improving and my natural color is growing back." She eyed him beadily, daring him to contradict her.

His lips twitched. "I'm delighted to see you've made such a leap in health since this morning. I'm sure all your visitors helped," he said, but the gaze that rested on his aunt was fond, rather than sardonic, Abby saw.

"Do you like my very modern crop? The girls insisted I leave off my cap." Nobody had insisted on anything of the sort. She patted the short red curls self-consciously. "I'm told I have the kind of bone structure that can carry it off." She gave Lord Davenham an approving glance. "You do too, Max."

Lord Davenham, in the act of sipping his sherry, choked.

Just then the front door knocker sounded. Lord Davenham put down his sherry glass. "That'll be Freddy. I'll mention your invitation to dinner, but whether he'll come or not . . ."

"Stay here!" Lady Beatrice caught Max by the sleeve. "I can see you haven't the slightest intention of getting young Monkton-Coombes to come in. Featherby, step outside and find a fair-haired young dandy in a dangerous-looking equipage. Present him with Lady Beatrice Davenham's compliments and say he is expected for dinner. And if he hesitates, tell him I'd *particularly* like to inquire after his mother." Lady Beatrice winked at Abby. "That should do the trick."

Abby glanced at Lord Davenham, expecting him to be annoyed at his aunt's high-handed manner. He didn't look at all concerned.

What was he up to? Abby wondered. He'd made no attempt to leave; he hadn't even stood up. And now he sat back with an air of lazy anticipation, almost as if he were amused.

Quick footsteps sounded in the hallway. A tall, elegantly dressed young gentleman entered the room, hat and gloves in hand. He didn't even glance at the other occupants of the room, but made a beeline for Lady Beatrice, saying, "Lady Beatrice, I cannot apologize enough—so delightful to see you again. My mother sends her regards, of course. I'm so pleased you've recovered from your illness—you have recovered, have you not? You're looking wonderful, I must say. Very, ah, up-to-the-minute." He hadn't batted an eye at the vivid head of curls.

The honorable Frederick Monkton-Coombes was quite the specimen of the handsome man-about-town, Abby thought. His face was long, but very good-looking, his eyes were a brilliant blue and his hair was thick and golden, arranged in careful, windswept locks. Jane had gasped audibly and sat up straighter. Damaris too had stiffened and was staring, and Daisy positively gaped.

Without apparently pausing for breath, Mr. Monkton-Coombes continued. "I'm extremely grateful for your charmingly impromptu invitation, but I'm afraid I have an unbreakable appointment—tragic, I know, but there it is. I can think of nothing more delightful than dinner with you and your charming companio—" He glanced sideways and broke off suddenly. He blinked. Slowly a glazed, stunned expression crossed his face.

Wordlessly he stared at Jane and Damaris, sitting side by side on the sofa. They were looking very pretty, Jane in a pale amber dress that highlighted the gold of her hair, and Damaris cool and serene-looking in a soft lilac print. They looked, to Abby's admittedly biased eye, like the sun and the moon, sitting side by side.

Mr. Monkton-Coombes stared. His eyes bulged and his jaw dropped open. He seemed to be having trouble breathing.

Abby wondered whether he was about to choke. She rose, thinking he might need a drink of water.

At her movement, he jumped as if she'd poked him and closed his mouth with an audible snap. He looked at Abby, a most peculiar expression on his face. He glanced at Daisy, who was looking very pretty in a ruffled blue gown, swallowed and then turned to Lord Davenham and in a low, indignant voice that Abby thought only Lord Davenham was supposed to hear, said, *"Muffins?"*

Abby, who was close enough to hear it too, blinked. Muffins? What was he talking about?

Lord Davenham gave a half smile and shrugged. His gray eyes were dancing, Abby saw. It softened his austere face wonderfully.

Mr. Monkton-Coombes gave him a narrow I'll-deal-with-you-later kind of look and turned back to Lady Beatrice. "On second thought, my engagement is not of such an urgent nature," he said smoothly.

"Oh, are you sure?" Lady Beatrice purred, delighted with the success of her little scheme. "I'd hate you to miss your appointment."

"Oh, that's all right. It was with a sad, rubbishy fellow, given to telling the most shockin' untruths," Mr. Monkton-Coombes confided. "The kind of dog-in-the-manger fellow who doesn't deserve my company, let alone dinner at the club."

Lady Beatrice gave a satisfied smile. "You show excellent judgment, dear boy. The girls and I will be delighted to dine with two such handsome gentlemen. Featherby, lay another place at the table, and instruct Mr. Monkton-Coombes's groom to return for him at nine o'clock." Featherby bowed and glided from the room.

"Freddy, dear boy, you haven't yet met my nieces, so let me introduce them."

Max watched sardonically as Freddy bowed gracefully over the hand of each of the misses Chance. He didn't know who was more pleased to become acquainted, Freddy or the girls. Freddy was practically twitching like a hound on a hot scent.

Freddy was built like a greyhound, lanky more than muscular, yet women always clustered around him like bees around a honeypot. Max had no idea why. Freddy claimed it was his blue eyes and fatal charm, but Max thought it was more that Freddy was always up to the mark with the latest fashionable thing. Women liked that.

And, of course, there was the nonsense he talked. Freddy had an endless supply of nonsense and all the latest gossip, and women seemed to love it. Even Aunt Bea was laughing. While there were women to charm, Max wouldn't get a single word of sense out of Freddy tonight.

Well, perhaps one. Max grinned to himself. *Muffins.*

Serve him right. Max would have no trouble now getting Freddy to keep an eye on the Chance girls while he was away in Manchester.

The butler appeared at the door and Aunt Bea held out her hands to Max. "Max, dear boy, your arm, if you please." She picked up a silver-topped ebony stick and gave him a look that told him she was not prepared to appear as an invalid in front of guests.

"Max will take me in to dinner," she announced to the room in general. "Freddy, my dear, will you accompany Abby, and you other girls, I'm sorry—next time we'll arrange it better so that we have more gentlemen and a properly balanced table."

Max helped her to rise, took her hand in his and allowed her to lean heavily on his good arm. His bad one was aching, and so was his shoulder, but he'd had worse pain in his life.

He watched as Freddy tucked Miss Abigail's hand into the crook of his arm in a damned familiar manner. He said something to her in a low voice—Max couldn't hear what—and she laughed, a low, intimate chuckle, like water tumbling over rocks in a mountain stream.

"Max, support is one thing, but if you squeeze my hand any tighter, you'll break it," Aunt Bea said testily.

Between Max and her stick, Aunt Bea managed to walk into the dining room without so much as a wobble. Max seated her at the head of the table, then turned to seat Miss Abigail. Freddy was before him, however, so Max seated Jane and Damaris while Freddy seated Daisy.

As Freddy passed Max to take his seat on the other side of the table, he thumped Max lightly between the shoulder blades and muttered, "Muffins indeed!"

"Muffins?" Aunt Bea had overheard. "Did you say muffins?"

Freddy blinked, for once lost for words. To Max's great pleasure, Freddy started to blush. He didn't think Freddy had blushed since he was about thirteen.

"Yes, Aunt Bea, Freddy has recently developed a . . . well, it's almost an obsession for muffins. Alas, poor Freddy, no muffins here for you tonight."

"So I see," Freddy muttered with a darkling look at Max.

"We don't know that," declared Aunt Bea. "Featherby, ask Cook if we have any muffins. Mr. Monkton-Coombes would like some."

"No, no, it's quite al—" Freddy began. But Featherby, like the excellent butler he was, had already swept out on a Quest for Muffins.

* * *

Freddy climbed into the curricle after Max, picked up the reins and gave him a hard thump on the shoulder. Max grinned, even though it was his sore arm. "What was that for?" He knew perfectly well what the thump was for, but he recognized a conversational opener when he felt it.

"You said they were muffins." The groom released the horses' heads and jumped up behind as the curricle moved off at a brisk pace.

"No, you said that," Max responded. "I merely said they read a lot."

Freddy shot him an indignant look and thumped him again. "Dull and earnest, you said. *Dull and earnest?* Those girls in there are full of fizz. Delightful company."

"Well, I don't even know what a muffin is, exactly."

"Then you shouldn't go around blackening the reputations of charmin' girls. A muffin is dull, earnest, generally plain—though occasionally you'll find one lurking behind a pretty face—and is bent on marrying a fellow and making his life a misery. Reforming him. Forcing him to do Good Works and attend Improving Talks." He shuddered.

"Oh. Then they're not muffins."

"No, they're not." Recalling something else, Freddy added in an aggrieved voice, "Damned if I shouldn't punch you on the nose on their behalf—you also told me they were as plain as a box of toads! A box of *toads*?"

"I saw some absolutely beautiful toads on my travels—" Max began, then broke into laughter and held up his hands in mock surrender. "All right, I take that one back. And apologize. Humbly and abjectly," he said without the slightest humility or abjectness.

Freddy sniffed. The horses trotted on through the night streets.

Max chuckled. "If you'd seen your face . . ." There was a short silence. "And when Aunt Bea sent to the kitchen for muffins . . ."

"One more word and I'll shove you out of this vehicle," Freddy said with dignity.

They drove for some time in silence; then Max said, "So you'll keep an eye on them while I'm in Manchester?"

"They're really in danger?"

"I think so."

"Then of course I will." Neither man said anything for some time; then Freddy added as they approached Barney McPhee's house, "You know I would have even if they had been muffins."

"I know." Max added with a grin, "But you'd have brought along a chaperone to protect you."

"Dammed right I would have," Freddy said fervently.

At the end of the week the move to the new house in Berkeley Square was accomplished. Max, Abby and Featherby had supervised a small army of busy servants—Abby working hardest of all. She so wanted to make the house as perfect a welcoming home as she could. For Lady Beatrice, she told herself. And for him.

To keep the old lady from fussing, Freddy took Lady Beatrice, Jane, Damaris and Daisy for a drive in the park, followed by an ice at Gunter's. After that, the three girls and a footman walked across the square to the new house, while Freddy took Lady Beatrice to take tea with his mother. By the time she returned, everything was in order and the household was ready to greet her.

She was tired, Abby thought, seeing her leaning heavily on her nephew's arm as he escorted her into the house, but there was no mistaking the bright gleam of satisfaction in the old lady's eyes as she looked around her.

All her favorite pieces of furniture, glowing with beeswax, and flowers in every room—no mean feat, given the unseasonal summer they'd had. That the flowers were Lord Davenham's doing was another surprise. Abby had mentioned that flowers would be nice, and he'd ordered them by the armful, apparently.

Lady Beatrice wandered from room to room, her shrewd old eyes taking in everything. "Excitingly new and different," she said, "and yet all my favorite things are here. I feel completely at home." She plopped down in her favorite chair and smiled at Abby. "I detect your fine touch, Miss Burg—"

"Everyone helped," Abby interrupted hurriedly. She hoped Lord Davenham hadn't noticed. Lady Beatrice must be very tired to have slipped like that. "Do you like it?"

The old lady looked around again and nodded. "I'm going to be happy here; I can feel it in my bones. Featherby, I think such an event calls for some—"

"Champagne, my lady?" said the perfect butler, and produced the bottle and glasses with a flourish.

Max left for Manchester the next day. Before he departed, he spoke to his aunt, who was just finishing breakfast in her bedchamber. "While I'm gone, Freddy has agreed to keep an eye on things here."

She waved the idea away. "I don't need an elegant young fribble to look after me. He can take the gels out and about— they've seen nothing of London so far."

"No, I've told him they're to stay close to home for the moment. They can walk in the park, as long as they have Freddy or a footman with them. Nothing else." A high-pitched mewing caught his ears. Max looked around. He could see no sign of anything.

"Close to home? Walk in the park?" She narrowed her eyes at him. "Is this about me wanting to bring those gels out in society? Because if it is, Max Davenham, if you think I'm going to keep those gels hidden away just because you don't know who their people are—"

"It's not that." The mew sounded again, louder and more anxious.

"What is it then?"

Damn. To spare his aunt anxiety, Max had told her nothing of the attack on Abby. He sought refuge in autocracy. "Just do as I bid you, Aunt Bea. I know you want to take those girls out and about in society, but trust me, it will not do." He held up his hand. "Don't argue. My mind is made up." He leaned forward and kissed her cheek. "Take care of yourself. I'll be back in a week or ten days."

She pouted. "The Parsleys, I suppose."

He inclined his head. "The Parsloes, yes."

"I do hope when you get there you won't find dear Miss Parsley fallen down a pit."

Max ignored that. "While I'm gone, you can call on Freddy for anything you need. I hope to see you fitter than ever when I return." He spotted the source of the sound.

She snorted. "Fitter than ever? Stuck in the house all the time? I'm supposed to have excitement! The doctor said so."

Max stood up. "Until I return, you'll just have to get your excitement from those novels you love so much. And from this little demon." He reached up and carefully detached Max the kitten from the top of the curtains. "Badly behaved kittens frequently end up as cat-skin waistcoats," Max informed it severely.

"Oh, the novels, yes, I'd almost forgotten," his aunt said with such a change of tone, his suspicions were immediately aroused.

Max put the kitten down. "What had you forgotten?"

"That the only excitement I ever get these days is from books. And the gels too, it seems. Oh, well, we'll just have to manage, won't we? Good-bye, Max, dear. Travel safely."

Her expression was entirely too saintly for his comfort, but he'd left strict orders with Freddy, Featherby and Abby, and he had a long journey ahead of him. "Good-bye, Aunt Bea."

"Don't speak to me of my nephew," Lady Beatrice said. "He's utterly infuriating."

"I know," Abby soothed. She had a fair idea of what Lord Davenham had done to annoy his aunt before he left. Much the same as had annoyed Abby.

"He's ordered me—ordered, mind you—that you and the gels are not to go out into society! When we've just moved here to be closer to society!" She snorted. "He's become completely autocratic—he has the notion that men rule the world. Well, so they might, but they don't rule *me*!"

"No, of course they don't," Abby agreed.

"He thinks all he has to do is utter an instruction and I'll obey him."

"Surely not." Abby hid a smile. Lord Davenham could surely not be so deluded.

"He does. Thinks just because he's moved me into this place he can dictate terms."

Abby made another soothing sound, and Lady Beatrice turned on her. "And why are you mm-hmming at me in that irritating manner? I'm not a wet hen to be calmed! You can't possibly believe my nephew is right. Why aren't you joining in the criticism?"

"I don't think it's right to criticize a man behind his back when I'm living under his roof." She'd already had—and lost— the argument with Lord Davenham.

Lady Beatrice snorted. "Ridiculous notion. I can."

"Yes, but you're his aunt."

Lady Beatrice raised her lorgnette and stared at Abby. "So you don't find him annoying?"

"I find him stubborn, suspicious and autocratic." And kind and . . . too attractive for her peace of mind.

Lady Beatrice leaned back against her pillows. "And they're not criticisms?"

Abby smiled. "No, ma'am, merely . . . observations." Their eyes met and they both laughed. "Very well," Abby admitted, "he does drive me to distraction at times, but he has good cause. We might not be the adventuresses he thinks us, but we *are* adventuresses. We're not who we say we are, and he wants to protect you from us."

"Nonsense, you're all dear, good gels, and deep down Max knows it, else he would never have allowed you to move into his house. But like all the Davenham men he wants to have his own way in all things. Take it from me, my dear, flouting him is good for his character."

"I'll keep it in mind."

Chapter Seventeen

"It is very difficult for the prosperous to be humble."

—JANE AUSTEN, EMMA

The house seemed unwontedly quiet without Lord Davenham. Or perhaps, Abby thought, it was because the girls went out more often, now that they lived so close to all the fashionable shops in Oxford Street—not shopping, for they had little money to spend, but gleaning inspiration for the outfits Daisy was designing for them all. Or being taken for drives in the park by Mr. Monkton-Coombes.

Lord Davenham's restrictions had not gone down well with the other girls either. Of course, they loved being escorted by Mr. Monkton-Coombes—who could object to such a handsome, entertaining and fashionable escort?—but the girls soon started to object to being shadowed everywhere by the new footmen, Turner and Hatch, dressed in livery.

"It's silly," Jane said, when Abby discovered her and Damaris returning home yet again with no escort. "We don't need an escort."

"It's for your own safety," Abby said, although privately she thought it was a little overprotective.

"Yes, but you were attacked, not me or Damaris or Daisy, and you said yourself he must be a cutpurse, so why must we be shadowed every step? It's like being in prison!"

"In prison you can't go anywhere," Abby pointed out dryly.

"Now stop complaining; you know perfectly well we promised Lord Davenham we wouldn't go anywhere without an escort, and since it's his house we live in, he makes the rules."

"I didn't promise."

"No, but I did for all of us," Abby said firmly. "So please don't do it again."

"We only went across the park to get an ice," Damaris said soothingly. The location of Gunter's just across the park was a constant temptation. "We were visible all the time from the house."

"Oh, and Abby," Jane exclaimed, diverted. "You'll never guess who we saw outside Gunter's—at least, I saw, because Damaris doesn't know him." She didn't wait for Abby to guess. "Sir Walter Greevey."

Abby had to think for a moment. "Oh, the man who found you that job in Hereford? Did you speak to him?"

"No, for he was getting into his carriage and had his wife with him—at least, I think it was his wife—she was quite old. I waved at him but I don't think he recognized me, because he drove off without a sign. I wish he had, because he's ever so nice. He would have bought Damaris and me an ice, I'm sure— he always used to bring the girls little treats at the Pill."

"Well, hurry along; the ladies for the literary society will be arriving shortly."

The literary society was going very well. Lady Beddington had put the word out among her friends and acquaintances, and each day more people came. No young men yet—apart from Freddy Monkton-Coombes, who'd attended the last one, but Lady Beatrice had hopes.

The society met three afternoons a week; there was little on in London at this time of year, so those members of society who disdained country living were delighted to have an afternoon entertainment, something refreshingly different from the usual round of morning calls.

Abby had chosen a very popular and quite fashionable book to start with, and though most of the members of the society knew of it and could discuss it in vague terms, it was surprising how many of them hadn't actually read it. For some it was simply that the print was too small and gave them a headache, but as many confided to Abby later, they hadn't bothered because they never found books entertaining.

It was very gratifying to find the large drawing room filling up for each meeting—they'd even had to send out for more chairs. And each time more people brought a friend or relative, and soon, Lady Beatrice and Abby hoped, they would bring young men.

"My nephew will be so cross," Lady Beatrice had declared gleefully, "but he cannot object, because I'm not *taking you gels out and about in society*—which he strictly forbade—society is calling on *me*."

A few days later, society of a different kind came calling. Abby and Lady Beatrice were sitting quietly in the cozy back sitting room, enjoying a welcome patch of late-morning sunshine, when Featherby appeared in the doorway and cleared his throat.

Lady Beatrice looked up from her game of patience. "Yes, Featherby, what is it?"

"Excuse me, m'lady, but there is a . . . a *person* at the door, asking to see Lord Davenham."

"He's gone to Manchester, as you very well know," Lady Beatrice responded.

Featherby did not move.

Lady Beatrice picked up her lorgnette and eyed him. "A *person*, you said?"

"Yes, m'lady."

"You know I don't receive *persons*, only ladies and gentlemen. Send the fellow away."

Featherby stayed where he was.

Lady Beatrice eyed him narrowly. "You're suggesting I see this person?"

"I am, m'lady." Featherby presented Lady Beatrice with the silver salver, in the center of which lay a lavishly embossed visiting card.

She picked up the card between thumb and finger, scrutinized it, turned it over, then dropped it back on the silver tray. "You've informed him that Lord Davenham has gone to Manchester?"

"I have, m'lady. He seemed to find it highly amusing."

Lady Beatrice exchanged a long look with Featherby, then sighed. "Then I suppose we must admit the wretched man. Send him in then, and bring us some tea. And take this, will you?" She passed him a kitten, which he received with aplomb.

Abby folded her sewing. "Would you like me to leave?"

"Good gad, no—stay where you are. The dratted Parsleys have come to town."

A moment later Featherby announced the visitors. A chunkily built middle-aged man entered the room, looking around him with what Abby felt was the eye of an auctioneer, calculating the value of everything he saw. Some of the furniture, she could tell, did not meet with his approval.

He was dressed in a coat of green tweed, a plainly tied neck cloth, a checked waistcoat and brown breeches—not a fashionable outfit, but clearly expensive. The materials were of the finest quality, as was the heavy gold chain of his fob watch.

A man who knew his own worth, Abby thought, and felt no need to trumpet it. Nor to pander to fashion.

The young woman with him, on the other hand, might have stepped straight from the pages of *La Belle Assemblée*. Pretty as a doll, with eyes of bright china blue, she was dressed in a white muslin dress over which she wore a deep-pink-and-white-striped redingote. Over a cluster of fair ringlets she wore a fetching straw bonnet trimmed with dark pink ribbons and pale pink artificial roses. She smoothed her pink kid gloves nervously and stared at Lady Beatrice with much the same expression as she might regard a viper.

Lady Beatrice held out a gracious hand. "Please forgive me for not rising. I have been unwell."

Mr. Parsloe took the proffered hand, shook it and said, "An honor to meet you, my lady. My daughter, Miss Parsloe."

The young lady curtsied and murmured a polite greeting.

Lady Beatrice eyed her coolly, and indicated Abby. "My niece, Miss Chance."

Abby curtsied. "How do you do, Mr. Parsloe, Miss Parsloe."

Featherby brought in the tea tray, and Abby occupied herself pouring tea.

"And where is your other daughter, Mr. Parsloe?" Lady Beatrice inquired when they had been served.

He looked puzzled. "Other daughter?" He spoke with a broad northern accent.

"I meant Miss Henrietta Parsloe."

He gave her a puzzled look. "This is Henrietta. I have only one daughter, my lady."

Lady Beatrice's brows snapped together. She was silent a long moment, then exchanged a speaking glance with Abby.

Abby had no difficulty reading her mind; she was just as shocked. How could Lord Davenham have been betrothed to this young girl for nine years? She looked barely eighteen.

They drank their tea in silence, the only sounds in the room an awkward clinking of china and silver. Lady Beatrice made no effort to put the Parsloes at their ease; she was very much playing *la grande dame*. Abby hadn't seen this side of her before.

Mr. Parsloe seemed to notice nothing amiss. "To think Lord Davenham has gone up to Manchester to call on us and we're down here, trying to call on him." He chuckled. "We might have passed him on the road, but we didn't see him, did we, puss?"

"No, Papa."

"He wrote to tell us to expect him any day, then wrote again to say he'd been delayed because you had visitors, my lady." It almost sounded like an accusation, Abby thought.

"Indeed?" Lady Beatrice said in arctic tones.

"Aye, he did." Mr. Parsloe seemed unaware it was a snub. He gave Abby a critical inspection. "I suppose you would be one of those visitors, Miss Chance."

"Yes, myself and my sisters."

"Younger or older sisters?" he asked, not seeming to realize it wasn't polite to ask. Or perhaps he didn't care.

"Younger."

He pursed his lips, seeming displeased. "Ah, well, Henrietta's here now."

There was another long, uncomfortable silence broken only by the clatter of tea things.

"I see your London weather is no better than what we've been getting up in Manchester."

Lady Beatrice gave a bored sigh.

"Really?" Abby murmured, to keep the conversation going. It was a bit of a shock to see Lady Beatrice behaving in such a cutting manner; she was normally so kind.

Not that Mr. Parsloe seemed to notice. "Nay, we've not had anything that could be called summer. My girl here has had to bring her winter clothes, haven't you, puss?"

"Yes, Papa," Miss Parsloe murmured, twisting her pink kid gloves restlessly. She saw Abby noticing and immediately smoothed the gloves out.

There was another long silence. "Aye, feels more like a mild winter than summer," said Mr. Parsloe. "Mark my words, we're going to pay for this."

"Indeed?" Lady Beatrice said again.

"Oh, aye, with weather like this the crops will fail, and there'll be shortages all 'round." He rubbed his hands, though whether it was a response to the chilly atmosphere in the room or at the prospect of the shortages, Abby couldn't tell. "A shrewd man would be well advised to buy up whatever grain he can—the price is going to soar once the shortages start to be felt. And so I'll be advising your nephew."

"Profiting off human misery?" Lady Beatrice said icily.

Mr. Parsloe was unoffended. "Bless you, my lady, it's how business works, but there, I should know better than to discuss such matters with softhearted ladies. Members of your sex simply don't have a head for business, but that's how we men like it; isn't that so, Henrietta?"

"Yes, Papa," Henrietta murmured. Abby couldn't make her out. In one way Henrietta seemed quite composed, looking around her with an air of disinterest, but then there was the way she was treating those gloves.

He chuckled, then, as silence fell again, glanced around him in search of another topic. "Now, this is more like it. I took a look at Davenham House before we came—I've been wanting to see inside that house for nine years."

Lady Beatrice stiffened.

"A grand old house in its day, I daresay, but sadly shabby now."

"Indeed," Lady Beatrice said in a freezing tone.

Mr. Parsloe nodded, seemingly unaware of the offensiveness of his comments. He was apparently of the school of men who prided themselves on their blunt speaking. "You won't have noticed it, my lady, having lived there all your life, but young people expect things to be bang up to the knocker, don't you, puss?"

"Yes, Papa," Henrietta said. Those gloves would be ruined, Abby thought, watching her.

Was she normally nervous in society, or was she responding to Lady Beatrice's chilly politeness that barely concealed hostility? Henrietta seemed a great deal more sensitive than her father. It was as though a bull had fathered a doe.

Abby felt sorry for the girl. One's first visit to one's prospective in-laws—one's all-but-official aunt-by-law—would be nerve-racking enough without there being an obvious class difference. And then there was the matter of the disparity in age—and the nine-year engagement, starting from when Henrietta was a child.

It was all most peculiar.

Mr. Parsloe chuckled again. "Likes everything that's new and bright, does my lass. Chip off the old block." He glanced around. "No doubt the minute she becomes mistress of the house, she'll be after her papa to buy her some fashionable new furniture."

Lady Beatrice swelled and seemed about to explode, so Abby said quickly, "Much of this furniture has been in the family for years. They're valuable antiques."

"Valuable?" Mr. Parsloe pursed his lips dubiously. "Ah, well, if you say so. My lass has her heart set on making a splash in London society once she's Lady Davenham, and a fashionable London house on Berkeley Square is just the ticket. You'll like living here, won't you, puss?"

"Yes, Papa."

She didn't sound too excited, Abby thought, but no doubt the poor girl was mortified by her father's crassness.

"Have you been to London before, Miss Parsloe?" Abby asked her, as much because she felt sorry for the girl, as from wanting to distract the company from Mr. Parsloe's disastrous conversational attempts.

"No, it's my first visit."

Abby smiled. "I know when I first came to London, I was so excited, I made a list of all the things I wanted to do and see. Have you made a list?"

"She doesn't need one," Mr. Parsloe said firmly. "Lord Davenham will show her everything she needs to—"

"Abby, we're going out. Do you want— Oh," Jane exclaimed as she came to an abrupt halt in the doorway. "I'm so sorry, Lady Beatrice; I didn't realize you had visitors."

"My sister, Miss Jane Chance," Abby said, and introduced the Parsloes.

"I'm sorry to have burst in on you like that," Jane said with a smile. "But since it's the first bit of sunshine we've seen in days, we're going for a walk and thought Abby might like to come."

"Thank you, but I think I should stay here," Abby said, knowing she could not possibly leave Lady Beatrice alone with Mr. Parsloe.

Lady Beatrice slumped elegantly back in her chair. "Oh, dear, I'm exhausted," she declared, closing her eyes. "Abby, ring for Featherby to show these people out. Good day to you, Parsloe, Miss Parsloe," she said without opening her eyes.

It was very rude, but effective. Mr. Parsloe immediately said he understood, with my lady having been ill and all, and got up to leave, bidding Henrietta to say her good-byes.

Neither Abby nor Lady Beatrice said a word until the front door was shut firmly behind them. Lady Beatrice sat up, all signs of exhaustion gone.

"Promised at the age of *nine*, damn him! I detect the ambitious hand of Papa Parsloe—though how the devil he managed it . . . The only way Max would have agreed to something so outrageous was if Parsloe had him in a trap, some sense of obligation. So what was it? Why would Max throw his future away on the nine-year-old daughter of a cit—good God, he was just eighteen himself at the time." She wagged her finger at

Abby. "You can't tell me an eighteen-year-old boy just out of school is thinking of marriage—let alone with a child of nine!"

"You had no idea?"

"No, and if I had I'd have stopped it. All these years I've been thinking of Miss Parsloe as an older woman, the kind of woman who'd take advantage of a young boy's calf love to trap him into a promise of marriage. And all the time she was just a *child*! So why? *Why?*"

Abby had no answer.

Lady Beatrice was silent for a long time, staring out the window with a brooding expression.

"Can you think of anything that happened to your nephew around that time?" Abby asked. "Something that may have prompted him to . . . I don't know . . . get into some kind of trouble? Gambling, perhaps? A young boy might—"

"No, Max was never interested in that kind of thing," Lady Beatrice said. "He preferred horses. And machines. He was mad for machinery."

Abby couldn't see how machinery would get an eighteen-year-old into trouble. "So you can think of nothing nine years ago that might have prompted him to this . . . agreement?"

"Nine years ago? No, there was nothing, only my husband dying and Max inher—" She broke off, an arrested look on her face. "Good God!" she half whispered. "Of course!" She slumped back in the chair, looking suddenly old and gray and crumpled. "I've been such a fool. . . ."

Abby waited, but Lady Beatrice didn't explain. After several moments of silence she opened her eyes and hauled herself wearily upright.

She sent for Featherby and ordered a brandy, and when it came, she drank it straight down, shuddering. Slowly her color returned. At last she sighed, and said, "We need to fix this, Abby. I won't have that boy making such a sacrifice."

"Sacrifice?" Abby asked, but Lady Beatrice wasn't listening. Or didn't choose to answer.

"Although how we are to prevent it—short of drowning the wretched gel—is more than I can imagine, for Max has given his word, and when he gives his word, wild horses, flocks of elephants and the angel Gabriel himself cannot make the boy break it, curse him!"

"Have they tried?"

But Lady Beatrice was in no mood for a touch of gentle levity. "You know what I mean. Max would rather die than break a promise." She shook her head. "Men and their cursed sense of honor."

"Would you have him any different?" Abby asked softly.

The old lady sighed. "No, of course not. I just don't want his future happiness ruined."

"They might be happy," Abby suggested. "One cannot tell in advance how a marriage will turn out."

Lady Beatrice made a scornful noise. "With that man for his father-in-law? Interfering in everything—because a blind beggar could see he's the meddling type. Did you see the way he turned his nose up at my furniture? And wanting to pull down Davenham House and build some ghastly modern monstrosity in its place? Wretched *cit*!"

"Mr. Parsloe is a forceful man, used to having his own way, I admit, but I don't believe he'll be able to bully Lord Davenham. I don't know what he was like as a boy, but the man I know is more than a match for the Parsloes of this world. Or anyone, really."

Lady Beatrice gave a halfhearted shrug, which might have indicated agreement.

"And Henrietta is pretty and seems very sweet and biddable, and she's young and will soon learn how to please—"

Lady Beatrice cut her off. "You think my nephew could be happy married to a spineless little ninny with no conversation? A cit's daughter who can only bleat, 'Yes, Papa, no, Papa, three bags full, Papa'?"

Abby didn't think that. Or rather, she didn't want to think it. But in her admittedly limited experience men did generally like women who were sweet and pretty and who agreed with everything they said.

Abby was plain and she tended to argue back.

"Well, when all's said and done, it's not up to us, is it?" she said. "Lord Davenham will do what Lord Davenham wants."

Lady Beatrice sighed and said in a defeated voice, "No, Lord

Davenham will do what he believes is *right*—there's a difference. Now, Miss Burglar, ring for William and my maid. I'm tired and I need to lie down."

J ust over a week later, Max returned to London. He'd had a thoroughly wasted trip. It was early afternoon as he threaded his way through the busy streets, but when he turned into Berkeley Square, he was surprised to find a line of carriages lined up along one side of the square. Somebody holding some kind of event, he presumed. Odd for the time of year; London in summer was usually thin of company. Then again, it wasn't exactly a typical summer.

Impatient with the slow-moving traffic, he jumped lightly down from the carriage and cut across the square to his house. He was eager to get home. *Home?* The thought startled him.

He'd slept only a night in the house; why would he think of this place as home? His aunt, he supposed.

But it wasn't the prospect of seeing his aunt again that had put the spring in his step. And it had to stop, he told himself firmly.

The housekeeper at the Parsloe residence in Manchester had told him that Mr. and Miss Parsloe, having heard of his arrival in England, had posted down to London to prepare for the wedding. They'd set their hearts on the most fashionable kind of wedding—St. George's in Hanover Square—and Miss Parsloe was intent on ordering her bride clothes from the most fashionable London modistes.

The arrangement stood, then, firm and unalterable. He'd given his word; he was a betrothed man and he should not—could not—look at any other woman.

To do so would compromise his honor—and hers.

As he crossed the park in the center of the square, he saw two fashionable ladies being admitted to his house. A moment later another two stepped down from their carriage and mounted the steps of his new house. They too were admitted.

Morning callers for Aunt Bea. Excellent. It was as he'd hoped: This location would make her much less isolated.

Max quickened his pace. By the time he reached the house,

two more carriages had disgorged their occupants, and fully
half a dozen more people had entered Max's house. What the
devil was going on?

Bemused, Max mounted the steps.

"Lord Davenham, is it not?" a voice hailed him from behind.

Max turned. An old friend of his aunt's stood there beaming,
a small, fussily dressed white-haired old gentleman. What was
his name again? Sir something.

"Don't suppose you remember me, do you, Max, m'boy?"
the old gentleman said. "You were a mere striplin' the last time
we met."

"Of course I remember you, sir, how do you do?" Max
pumped the old gentleman's hand, hoping the name would
come to him. Sir Edward? Sir Oliver?

The door opened, and they entered. "Ah, Sir Oswald," Featherby greeted him as they entered. Sir Oswald Merridew, Max
thought. Of course.

Sir Oswald turned to Max. "Your aunt's literary society is
provin' a great success."

"A literary society?" Max repeated blankly. He'd been gone
not quite ten days. How had his aunt established a literary
society in that time? Besides, a *literary* society? Aunt *Bea*?

The old gentleman beamed. "Indeed, and not like the usual
sort of literary society—all allusions and metaphorical whats-
its and epigrammatic thingummies—frightful bore, that kind
of thing, too clever for me by half. But this one . . ." He rubbed
his hands. "Somethin' to look forward to each visit—as good
as going to the theater. Those pretty nieces of hers—Griselda's
gels—they do a splendid job of readin', simply splendid."

"Gris—They aren't Griselda's girls. Griselda is just some
nonsense my aunt made up. The young ladies are simply guests
of my aunt, no relation at all."

Two ladies who had just entered exchanged speaking looks
as they passed them in the hall. "I *told* you," one said to the
other. She gave Max a pitying look. The second lady *tsk*ed
reproachfully at him.

Sir Oswald drew Max aside and said in a confidential tone,
"Don't mind me sayin' this, m'boy, but I've known you since
you were breeched, and take it from one who knew both your

father and your uncle—it's time you accepted the truth about those gels. It's the manly thing to do."

"But—"

"To be sure, it's a scandal—no family likes divorce—and one that was well hushed up at the time; I knew nothin' about it, and I'm usually beforehand with the latest *on dits*—"

Max gritted his teeth. "There was nothing to know—"

"A shame you were raised in ignorance, when as the heir you should have been informed, but you do yourself—and your aunt—no good to deny those gels now they're here. Why, society has taken those sweet young ladies to its bosom, and it's clear your dear aunt is very fond of them, and they of her." He patted Max on the arm in a fatherly manner. "So, best you just accept the gels for who they are, eh? Now, I'd best get along. I don't want to be late. Might miss somethin' excitin'." He hurried along to the large drawing room, leaving Max in the hallway, shaking his head.

"I trust your trip to Manchester was pleasant, my lord." Featherby hovered at his elbow.

"Complete waste of time," Max said.

"Indeed, m'lord, so we suspected when Mr. and Miss Parsloe called here not two days after you'd left. May I fetch you some refreshment?"

"They called? Here?"

"Indeed they did, m'lord. And Mr. Parsloe had a nice long chat with your aunt."

"Damn."

"Are you sure you won't take some refreshment, m'lord?"

"No, I want to see what's happening. A literary society? Founded by a woman who's never read a book in her life? What the devil is going on, Featherby?"

"It's not for a simple butler to say, m'lord." Featherby bowed and glided away. Looking smug.

Simple butler indeed. Max gritted his teeth and marched toward the large drawing room.

Chapter Eighteen

*"It is not every man's fate to marry the
woman who loves him best."*

—JANE AUSTEN, EMMA

The din was deafening. At least thirty people—all talking—were seated inside the room on chairs arranged in a semi-circle. A good many were of his aunt's vintage—ladies and a few gentlemen—but Max was surprised to see dotted among the throng a number of young ladies and, still more surprising, almost a dozen gentlemen of about his own age or younger. And not the sort of gentlemen who usually attended literary affairs.

Facing the semicircle of visitors sat three of the Chance sisters. His heart leaped at the sight of Abby. She wore a dress in sprig muslin with a green velvet spencer that brought out the color of her eyes, and she'd done something different with her hair. He forced his gaze off her.

His aunt, in an afternoon gown of claret satin that clashed superbly with her titian hair, sat to one side in her favorite chair. She was talking to someone and didn't notice him enter. Daisy sat beside her.

And there was Freddy, he was astonished to see, also to the side, but as near to the front as possible, wearing an expression strongly reminiscent of a dog guarding a bone. Max's lips twitched. He'd swear Freddy had never so much as touched a book since he left school.

His gaze returned to Abby. As if she knew he was there, she looked up, straight at him. Their eyes met. And held.

Her sister nudged her. Abby blushed and hurriedly lifted a small, blue-bound book. "Chapter fifteen." Her voice was low and clear and carried to all corners of the room. A ripple of pleasurable anticipation passed through the audience.

A hush fell as she started to read: " 'Mr. Collins was not a sensible man, and the deficiency of nature had been little assisted by education or society. . . . '"

Good God, it really was some kind of a literary society.

There was a spare chair at the back. Max sat down to observe.

Abby read and everyone listened—he'd not heard such a hush except in church; even in theaters, people tended to talk. It wasn't any hardship to listen; her voice was beautiful, and she read so well it was almost like having the story unroll in front of you.

It was an entertaining story too, he had to concede; it even surprised a smile out of him once or twice.

When she finished the chapter there was an audible sigh from the audience, and then the din broke out again as every person there seemed compelled to talk to his or her neighbor about the story. Cakes and wine were handed around, and it all seemed to be finished. Max stood, about to go over to greet Aunt Bea, when a clear young voice announced, "Chapter sixteen" and the hush fell again.

This time Jane read, and though she was not as skilled a reader as her sister, the audience paid her rapt attention. Particularly the young men, he noticed. Aunt Bea was beaming. He didn't think she'd spotted him yet. She waggled her brows at Abby with a quick triumphant expression.

So that was what this was about.

He glanced at Abby and found her watching him. She blushed and looked away. Ah, Aunt Bea had noticed him now. A series of expressions crossed her face—surprise, a kind of gleeful defiance, which made him smile—but then the glee faded and the expression that was left puzzled him; it almost looked like . . . a mixture of reproach and guilt and . . . grief?

* * *

"It's all your uncle's fault, I know. Tell me the worst." The literary society meeting had finished and his aunt had retired to her bed, supposedly for a nap. Instead she'd summoned Max to interrogate him in private. "What was the extent of his debts? What did you have to do?"

Max had no intention of telling his aunt anything. He'd spent the last nine years protecting her from the mess his uncle had left, so there was no reason to hash over the past. It would only upset her. "It's not important now."

"Pshaw! Of course it's important. It's the reason you're marrying that dreary Parsley child, isn't it? The arrangement was made nine years ago—Papa Parsley said as much—and I can put two and two together. Besides, it's as much my responsibility as yours."

"Nonsense. I was the heir."

"You were *eighteen years old.*"

"Nevertheless, I managed." Damn Parsloe for presenting himself to her without Max in attendance. She'd obviously done a great deal of thinking about the situation since then; she'd always been acute.

"I know the other properties were sold off." She waved a careless hand at him. "Oh, don't look at me like that; word gets out. I'm assuming Parsley lent you the money you needed to save the family estate?"

Max had no intention of telling her, but apparently his aunt could read his mind. She frowned. "Why didn't you take a mortgage out on the London house?"

"Because I didn't choose to." No need for her to know how close to homeless she'd come.

She made an exasperated noise. "Why not come to me, then? I have plenty invested in the funds. My father placed my fortune in a trust, safe from Gilbert's greedy hands."

Max rose and strolled to the window as if bored. "There is no point discussing any of this; it's all done and—"

"Oh, my God, he did it, didn't he? Broke the trust?" She didn't wait for his confirmation. "He always was determined to find some way to do it. Was there anything left? Stupid question, of course there wasn't—Gil never did things by halves. If there was a shilling to spend, he'd spend a guinea and promise you the rest. Good gad!" She slumped back against her pillows and was silent for a long moment.

"And of course no reputable source would lend you the funds, not with everything mortgaged to the hilt, and Gil's reputation. It's all clear now. You poor boy, faced with such a horrendous mess. Why did you never tell me?" She didn't wait for his response. "And so you went to Parsley, who I expect was only too delighted to ensnare a green boy."

"He did not ensnare me. The interest was very reasonable."

"The interest." She snorted. "You can't tell me that a promise to marry his daughter isn't akin to a pound of flesh—and more. And a title into the bargain."

She had another thought and sat up again. "Just a minute—where did my allowance come from, if Gil had already broken the trust? And don't lie to me, because I know my husband—he would have cleaned it out and not left me a penny."

Max didn't say anything.

"Parsloe!" She hissed it. "And *that's* why he was so dratted familiar about Davenham House. Said he'd wanted to get a look inside it for nine years—the cheek of him! Holds the mortgage on it, does he?"

"He owns it," Max admitted. No point keeping it a secret any longer. Aunt Bea was too shrewd for words. "On the condition you could live in it as long as you wanted."

"And that's why you moved me here."

"You're better off here anyway. It's a better location. You don't miss Davenham House, do you?"

She shook her head. "You can afford it?"

Max nodded. "I can now. The trading company has been very profitable."

"Parsley spoke of pulling Davenham House down."

Max shrugged. "He probably will. Will you mind?"

"Not at all. I was never particularly happy there until those gels came to live with me. This place is much more fun. So, have you paid Parsley back his money?"

Max nodded.

"And the interest?"

Again, Max nodded.

"Good, then that's the end of it. Send the fellow about his business and tell him you won't marry that little chit."

"I'll do nothing of the sort. I made the man a promise and I intend to keep it."

She rolled her eyes. "Why? A promise like that, extracted from an eighteen-year-old boy? You hadn't attained your majority, and can't be held to such an agreement by law."

"It's not a matter of law; it's a matter of honor."

"Honor!" His aunt made a rude noise. "It's money, not honor that fellow cares about. And having a titled son-in-law to impress his cit friends."

"Perhaps, but it's my honor we're talking about, and I care about that."

"Oh, pish-tush, a lot of masculine nonsense! One little broken promise, and an unfair one at that. Who will care?"

He groped for a way to make her understand. "Aunt Bea, a gentleman's word of honor is the invisible fabric on which the very foundation of our civilization rests. It's not a matter of law, or . . ." She wasn't listening, so he tried another tack. "Men from London to China, India and beyond know that my word is my bond. It took years for these men—who did not understand the code of an English gentleman—to learn to trust me at my word, but now they do. That trust was hard-won."

"So it's about *business*?" she said incredulously.

"No." Max gritted his teeth. "It's a matter of respect. More than that, it's self-respect."

"And that's your final word, is it?"

"It is."

"You're determined to marry this chit and make everyone except Papa Parsley unhappy."

"You'll get over it," Max told her. "And if you don't want to live with her I'll buy another house for us to live in."

She glared at him. "I'm not talking about me! I'm not unhappy; I'm *furious*—there's a difference. You can't tell me you'll be happy with that chit."

"You cannot know that," he began.

"And though I care nothing for the gel, she's barely out of the schoolroom and doesn't deserve to be made unhappy for the ambitions of her papa."

"You don't know she'll be unhappy."

She snorted. "What female can be happy knowing her papa forced her husband into marrying her? And that since she was nine years old she had no choice in the matter of her own husband? Mind you, if she had any kind of spine, she would have rebelled."

He said stiffly, "Arrangements like that are not uncommon."

"Among our class, not hers. Cits are used to marrying for love. *We* are not always given the choice—or we weren't, in my day. But times are changing, and *you* could have it if you weren't so stubborn."

"I'll treat her well."

She made an impatient gesture. "I know that, you stupid boy. But shopkeepers treat you *well*; people treat horses and dogs *well*. I'm talking about happiness, joy, *love*!" She shook her head. "And it's *you* I care about, not that dreary child. You've *never* had the happiness you deserve in life, dear boy, and now, for once, you have it in your grasp. Yet for the sake of this senseless masculine sense of obligation—"

"Honor."

"Stubbornness! Fine words and noble sentiments about the invisible fabric of civilization are all very well, but mule-headed masculine stubbornness is what this is. And for the sake of it you'll shackle yourself for the rest of your life to a dreary little stick who can only bleat commonplace nothings at you and will, no doubt, prove in time to be as vulgar as her papa."

"It's not just fine words," Max snapped. "It's who I am. When I had nothing, when I discovered my uncle had left us with nothing—less than nothing—that *cit*, as you call him, vulgar as he is, saved us—my skin and yours—with a loan secured by nothing more than a promise—*my* promise. And I will not go back on it."

"No matter that it was an unreasonable requirement, and you were a green boy, well out of your depth?"

"No."

She shrew up her hands in exasperation. "Then more fool you to keep it and make the three of you miserable!"

"Three?"

She gave him a dry look. "Are you really so blind, my boy?"

No, he wasn't. But he was by no means sure that there were three in the equation. It wasn't something he would discuss with his aunt.

Besides, there was no point.

The more Max thought about what his aunt had said about the arrangement not being fair to Henrietta, the more it made sense to him. He hadn't actually ever considered her point of view—well, he hadn't seen her since she was nine, after all, and she hadn't made any impression on him at the time. But when he'd spoken to the Parsloes' housekeeper in Manchester she'd informed him that Miss Parsloe had gone to London to order her bridal clothes. Naturally he'd assumed she was looking forward to her wedding.

But what if she wasn't?

Mr. Parsloe could be extremely persuasive, as Max very well knew.

If Henrietta didn't want to marry him he couldn't, in all conscience, allow her to be forced, or even bullied.

His aunt had called her spineless. If she were being bullied . . .

Making three people miserable . . . could that possibly be true?

He couldn't let himself hope. Not yet. But he ought to discover Henrietta's true feelings without delay.

He bathed, shaved and changed his clothes and headed for the Pulteney Hotel in Piccadilly. He hadn't been informed where the Parsloes were staying, but the Pulteney was the favored choice of royalty, which would greatly add to the appeal of the place for Mr. Parsloe, so he'd try there first.

His instinct was correct; on his arrival a message was sent up to the Parsloes' suite, and shortly afterward Max was ushered upstairs.

"Max, my dear boy!" Henry Parsloe came toward him

with his hand outstretched, then withdrew it abruptly. "Ah, but I mustn't call you that now, must I, Lord Davenham?" He bowed.

"It's been Max since I was sixteen, so I see no reason to change it now, Parsloe." Max held out his hand and the two men shook.

"You were a boy then, and now you're a man," Parsloe said. "And here's my little Henrietta. Make your bow to his lordship, puss."

Henrietta curtsied. She was a pretty young girl, the kind of pretty young thing that Max usually found a dead bore. He hoped he was wrong.

"Now sit down, do, my lord, and tell me—tell us—all about what you've been doing in the last nine years. You must have had some adventures, eh? I must say, you've grown into a fine-looking man, don't you think, puss?"

"Yes, Papa," she said, more in obedience than agreement, Max thought. Hoped.

"Life at sea must have suited you."

"It did." Eventually.

"And from all I've heard, you've done very well in business, very well indeed. I'm proud of you, my b—my lord, I should say." He proceeded to question Max about his financial and business dealings in a manner that would normally have caused Max to poker up and give the questioner a blistering set-down, but behind the vulgarity and intrusiveness was a sincere pride in what Parsloe obviously saw as his protégé's achievements.

In the nine years that had passed since Max had seen him, he'd forgotten that he was actually quite fond of the man. When they'd first met, at a steam power exhibition, the successful manufacturer had been very kind to a sixteen-year-old shy schoolboy, and had given generously of his time and advice, using his connections to get Max into demonstrations of the latest mechanical marvels that weren't open to the general public.

Max's own father had shown no interest in anything Max did; nor did his uncle. Henry Parsloe's willingness to listen was why Max had turned to him when he was first confronted by the extent of the financial disaster he'd inherited.

So Max was not going to snub this bluff, kindhearted

business shark by refusing to tell him what he dearly wanted to know.

He owed him, after all. Had Henry Parsloe not lent him the money and sent him off to sea to become a trader—showing an enormous amount of faith in an untried, green boy of eighteen—Max and Aunt Bea would be in a very different situation today.

Besides, the man was entitled to make inquiries about Max's financial standing—he was going to be Max's father-in-law.

Unless . . .

Max glanced at Henrietta, who had sat through the conversation without saying a word. Was she even listening? It was hard to tell. Her face was smooth, blank and impenetrable.

When the conversation reached a natural hiatus, Max said, "Would you mind, sir, if I talked with Henrietta in private?"

Parsloe chuckled. "The eager bridegroom, aren't you, my lord? I'm not surprised. My little girl has grown up into a very pretty young lady, haven't you, puss?"

Henrietta smiled briefly but said nothing.

"But I'm not sure about leaving you two alone together, ha, ha. She's been very strictly raised, my Henrietta, and has never been alone with a man." He wasn't joking, Max saw.

Max rose. "We'll sit in the next room, where we will be under your eye and can still have speech in private." He held his hand out to Henrietta. "Henrietta?"

"My lord."

When they were seated in the next room, Henry Parsloe watching curiously from a distance, Max said, "Miss Parsloe—Henrietta, do you wish for this marriage?"

She blinked. "Yes, my lord." No hesitation at all. Damn.

"Is it because your father wishes it?"

"Yes, my lord." She was quite composed.

"But if left to your own choice, and nothing to do with your papa—if you had complete free will, would you still wish to marry me?"

She gave him a puzzled look. "Are we not betrothed?"

"Yes, yes, but I want to know whether this match is repugnant to you in any way. Am I not too old, for instance?"

"No, my lord." The chains closed around him. He gave it one last try.

"Tell me honestly—and do not fear to tell the truth; I promise I will fix it with your father—is this betrothal your own choice, as well as your father's?"

"It is, my lord."

"Right. Good." He inclined his head stiffly. "I just wanted to be sure you weren't being constrained to marry me."

"Constrain me, my lord?" She gave a little smile. "Papa could never do that."

"Very well." He tried to think of what else to say. "So, er, I gather you want a spring wedding?"

"It is the most fashionable season, is it not, my lord?"

"Yes. And the ceremony—St George's, Hanover Square?"

"It is the most fashionable place, is it not, my lord?"

"Yes," he said heavily.

They sat in silence for several more minutes. "And is there anything you wish to ask me?" he said at last.

"No, my lord."

So that was it. No way out. And fair enough, he told himself. Parsloe had not only loaned him the money he'd needed—albeit at a commercial, though reasonable, rate of interest—but he also had freely offered the kind of solid, shrewd advice that had enabled Max to make sense of the mess, to slowly but surely pull himself out of the financial mire.

Of course, Henry Parsloe hadn't lost by it; Max had repaid the loan with interest—all but the marriage. Parsloe made no bones about the condition: "In business all men are opponents, so make sure you always get something extra for yourself."

In this case the something extra was Max as a son-in-law. It wasn't just the title itself the man valued—though he did love the idea of a titled son-in-law. It was Max himself he wanted: a son to pass the business on to, who was as interested in mechanical innovation as he was, who was excited by the possibilities of steam power and who had proved, now, that he could succeed in business.

Any way Max looked at it, he owed it to Henry Parsloe to

keep his promise. *Dammit*. And Henrietta Parsloe was willing—more than willing.

He'd made his bed and now he'd have to lie in it. With Henrietta.

At least she wouldn't chatter brightly at breakfast, he thought gloomily.

Max stood. "Thank you," he said—although for what, he had no idea—and took his leave of the Parsloes.

Chapter Nineteen

*"Do not give way to useless alarm; though it is
right to be prepared for the worst, there is no
occasion to look on it as certain."*

—JANE AUSTEN, *PRIDE AND PREJUDICE*

Max arrived home to a chaotic scene; half his household seemed to be standing in the entry hall talking animatedly with three complete strangers. In the middle stood a knot of upset females.

"What's going on?" he demanded.

Abby emerged from the clump of women. "Someone just tried to abduct Jane." The knot parted to reveal Jane, pale, disheveled and a little red eyed.

"Who was it?"

A babble of explanation rose from half a dozen throats. Max held up his hand. "One at a time. Miss Chance?"

"We don't know," Abby said. "Two men jumped out of a carriage and tried to force her in."

"Where was this?"

"Outside, in Berkeley Square," Jane said in a shaky voice.

Abby added, "Damaris jumped on one of the abductors from behind and hit him about the head while screaming at the top of her lungs."

"And then I got my mouth free—he'd stuffed a horrid rag in my mouth—"

"And then these three gentlemen ran to help, which drove

the villains off," Abby finished, indicating the strangers, three nattily attired young sprigs of fashion.

The young men bowed, looking modestly heroic. "We heard the screaming," the first one said. "Utter disgrace, something like this happening to a lady—and in Berkeley Square."

"The fight you put up, ladies, dashed if I've ever seen such heroines."

"The least we could do," said the third. "Just sorry we didn't apprehend the villains."

Max clenched his fists. How the devil had such a thing happened after the precautions he'd taken to protect them? But he couldn't give vent to his feelings in front of strangers. They stood there making goo-goo eyes at the girls.

"Thank you for you assistance," he said curtly. "I'm very grateful. We won't delay you any longer." He nodded at Featherby, who immediately opened the front door.

The three young men were clearly reluctant to leave. "Er, should we not wait and ensure that the ladies are quite recovered?" one of them began.

Max wanted to take him by his highly starched shirt points and toss him out into the street, but it was not the way to repay someone for what he had to acknowledge was a signal service. It wasn't the young idiots' fault Max was furious.

"My butler will show you out," he grated.

"It's such a comfort to know that chivalry isn't dead, gentlemen." Aunt Bea came forward, leaning on her stick. "Thank you, a thousand thanks, you wonderful, wonderful boys, for saving my dear nieces." They preened at the praise. "But now I must insist—the gels need to rest after their frightful ordeal—"

"Oh, but—" Jane showed a desire to remain the center of attention.

"Your frrrrightful ordeal," Aunt Bea repeated firmly. "We cannot hold these wonderful gentlemen up any longer; they've been much too kind as it is." As she spoke she moved forward, making gentle shooing motions toward the open door.

"Thank you," Max growled, and they stepped hastily over the threshold.

The moment the front door closed Max turned on Abby. "Were you involved in this fracas?"

"No, I was inside."

Thank God. He took a deep breath. "Good." He turned to Turner and Hatch. "And where the devil were you two when this happened?"

"I . . . We didn't know. . . ."

"It wasn't their fault," Abby jumped in. "Jane and Damaris slipped out without telling anyone."

"It was just across the par—"

Abby turned to her sister. "Don't try to justify it, Jane—you know the rules, and now look what almost happened. And I'm not just talking about the . . . the abduction; you almost got Turner and Hatch sacked."

Jane hung her head. "I'm sorry."

Abby put her arm around her sister. "I know, but you must learn to think before you act."

Aunt Bea said, "Best get the gels upstairs. Discuss it when everyone is calmer." She gave Max a pointed look, but Max was damned if he was going to wait. He'd caught a look exchanged between the sisters and his suspicions were raised.

"Take them upstairs, by all means, but not you—I want to speak to you." He took Abby by the arm, towed her into the small drawing room and closed the door.

"You know who was behind this, don't you?"

"Of course I don't." But there was a troubled pucker between her brows that told him she knew more than she was saying.

It fanned the flames of his already sorely tried temper. Dammit, it could have been Abby who was abducted. He wanted to shake her for her stubborn refusal to trust him with the truth, yet he'd just come from a meeting with his future wife and father-in-law, and he had no right to demand anything from Abby.

The knowledge only lashed his temper more. He caught her by the elbows. "What were you girls up to before you came to live with my aunt?"

"*Up to?* I resent your tone." She tugged to make him release her, but he didn't let go. She glared at him, but he could see she was trying to think of what to say.

"Don't lie to me, Abby. Something's seriously amiss. You girls are in hiding from someone or something—don't bother to deny it, Miss *Chantry*." She bit her lip.

He let her arm slide through his fingers until he was holding her by the hands, gripping them tightly. "Abby, it's clear someone—someone dangerous from your past—is pursuing you. If you don't tell me who it is—"

"I don't know!"

"But you suspect." He knew by her miserable expression that he was right.

"I can't tell you."

"Why? It cannot be so dreadful—"

The door opened and Jane and Damaris stood there. Obviously they'd been eavesdropping. "Leave Abby alone," Jane said. "It's not her fault. And you might as well know, because it's going to come out anyway—we were in a brothel!"

"A brothel?" Max looked at Abby and his face drained of color.

Abby could not bear to see the expression in his eyes. She looked away.

"Not Abby," Jane said. "Damaris and me and Daisy. Abby got us out—"

"Daisy got you out," Abby corrected her.

"—and we all got her sacked. And now Mort is after us," Jane finished, and burst into tears. Damaris put her arms around her and led her, sobbing, from the room.

Max turned on Abby. "You little fool, why didn't you tell me this before?"

"I couldn't; I couldn't. How could I know how you'd . . ."

There was a short silence. "You didn't trust me." His voice was flat, hard.

She swallowed. "No."

Unreadable gray eyes bored into her. How could she explain that if it had been just her, if she'd been the one with the terrible secret, she might have told him, might have confessed. Might.

But it was Jane's secret, Jane's reputation that would be forever destroyed, and it was Abby's duty to protect her sister. "It was not my secret to share."

There was a long silence. "Does my aunt know?"

"Yes, I told her everything before—"

"Before what?"

Abby raised her head and met his gaze. This part, at least, she was not ashamed of. "Before I accepted her invitation for us all to come and live with her."

Black brows snapped together. "She knew that three of you came from a brothel? And yet she claimed you as nieces and tried to foist you on the *ton*?"

"Yes," she flashed, her temper rising again. "And why not? Jane escaped from that place untouched, and I don't know about Damaris, but I do know that she hadn't been there much longer than Jane, and that she was brought in under cover of darkness, tied up and struggling—a victim as surely as Jane. Why should her life be forever ruined because of that?"

Max gave her a long, assessing look. "How did you get them out?"

"Daisy got them out."

"Daisy was a victim too?" That was stretching it. He'd bet the cheeky little cockney knew her way around all the rookeries.

"She was . . . she was taken there as a child. But no, she was a maidservant in the brothel, which made her able to come and go as the others weren't."

"A brothel maid, and you claimed her as sister?" He was incredulous.

"She *is* my sister!" Abby declared passionately. "Without her, Jane would be lost to me forever, and for that, yes, Daisy is my sister and will always be so. And so is Damaris! I will never deny them."

He couldn't fault her loyalty. Max ran his fingers through his hair. "Dammit, you women have a mighty flexible notion of kinship—you with your 'sisters' and my aunt claiming you as 'nieces.'"

"And do men not call some friends 'brothers'?" she retorted. "Brothers in arms, for instance?"

He considered that. "Yes, and brothers in adversity. I have several myself. Though in my case I claim them only in a metaphorical sense—you should appreciate that, with your literary bent."

She said nothing.

He rumpled his hair again. "I need a drink." He went to the

sideboard and poured two glasses, one in a large fat glass and the other smaller. He handed the smaller one to her. "Madeira— I didn't think you'd like brandy."

"Thank you." She took it and sipped gingerly. It appeared to meet with her approval, for a moment later she took another sip.

"How did you meet my aunt?"

She sighed. "I might as well admit it; you know everything else." She drank the rest of the wine and set the glass aside. "I climbed in through her bedroom window."

"You *what*?" It was the last thing he'd expected. Aunt Bea's bedroom was a good forty feet from the ground. What if she'd fallen? And why—?

"I was hoping to steal something."

"What?"

She shrugged wearily. "Anything."

"Why?" What would drive her to such an extreme?

"We needed the money. Jane was very sick and we had no money to pay a doctor."

There was a short silence. Of course. Risking herself to take care of others. He might have known. "What did you steal?"

"Nothing."

"Why not?"

"There was nothing to steal."

"And Jane got better anyway?"

"Yes." She looked at him. "Thanks to Damaris and Daisy. They helped me to care for her day and night."

Max got the point. The four girls had been through a lot together, and nothing could break the bond they'd forged.

Much like himself and Flynn and Ash.

He sipped his brandy thoughtfully. Her story still didn't quite make sense to him. "Are you telling me that my aunt, waking to find a burglar in her bedchamber, then invited you to come and live with her and bring your friends?" She'd always been eccentric, but this was mad. She must have been sicker than he'd realized.

"No, of course not. That first night we just talked. I . . . I liked her. And later—when Jane's fever had broken—I found myself worrying about Lady Beatrice, so I called on her. Her butler refused to admit me, so I gave him a note to give to her. And that night I went back—"

"You went back—again? At night? Through the window?" *Good God.* Risking her neck because she was worried about an old woman she'd met *once*?

"Yes, and it was as I'd suspected—she hadn't received any note or been informed of any callers, so I had to go back to ask her whom I could contact who would help her."

"She brought me soup." His aunt stood in the doorway.

"Soup?"

"Because my servants were starving me. And that's when I invited Abby and the other gels to come and live with me. Best decision I've ever made in my life."

"You knew where they'd come from?" Max was fairly sure of the answer, but he had to ask.

"Of course. Abby told me about the brothel, in case I wanted to change my mind and rescind the invitation. She's honest and good to the core, Max, and if you can't see that—"

He cut her off with a gesture. He didn't need anyone to tell him what she was. He stood abruptly. "I need to think."

Lady Beatrice called for tea. They drank it in silence. It was comforting, but Abby could have done with another glass of Madeira.

Her thoughts were in turmoil. He'd been shocked by her story, the brothel, the burglary most of all, and that she'd compounded it with lies—lies of omission, but still lies.

He'd lost all respect for her now. It felt . . . it felt like a kind of grief.

Featherby knocked and entered, looking worried. "Yes, what is it, Featherby?" Lady Beatrice asked.

"I thought you'd want to know, m'lady. Lord Davenham has just spent the last twenty minutes questioning Daisy and now he's taken her away in his carriage."

"Daisy? Why? Where's he taking her?"

"He didn't say, but"—Featherby shot Abby a meaningful look—"from something I, ahem, happened to overhear, I think he's taking her to a magistrate."

Abby jumped to her feet. "A magistrate? But why? Daisy's done nothing wrong."

But nobody had any answer.

"Sit down and drink your tea," Lady Beatrice told her. "Worrying never did anyone any good. My nephew's got a good head on his shoulders and a good heart—you'll just have to trust him to do the right thing."

But she didn't look particularly sanguine, Abby noticed. Oh, what was he doing with Daisy? Where had he taken her? And why?

Daisy, who'd always disapproved of the deception. Daisy, whose biggest fear was the threat of prison, or transportation to the other side of the world.

Part of Abby wanted to flee now, while they could, to get Jane and Damaris away, but that was just cowardice, she knew. She couldn't leave Daisy to her fate.

Lord Davenham wouldn't harm them, not really, she told herself. He might banish them from his house—and who could blame him?—but it wasn't that that Abby dreaded; it was seeing again the look in his eyes when he saw she didn't trust him.

And now here she was, not trusting him again.

Magistrate. She could think of only one reason to see a magistrate: to report a crime.

But Daisy hadn't done anything wrong. No more than the rest of them. Abby was the one who'd broken into his aunt's house—twice. The false name had been her idea too—the others had just followed along. And she was the eldest. She should be the one being taken to the magistrate, not Daisy.

"Abby, can we talk to you?" Jane and Damaris stood in the doorway.

"Yes, what is it?" She was still cross with them for slipping out and causing all the fuss in the first place, but she could never hold on to her temper for long, and they looked young and unhappy and troubled. "Come in," she said in a softer voice, and patted the chaise longue beside her.

"It's about the abductors," Jane said. "We've been thinking."

"We don't think it was Mort," Damaris said.

Abby blinked. "What? Of course it was."

Damaris shook her head. "If it was Mort, why only take Jane? Why not me too?"

Abby put down her cup. "How do you know they weren't after you as well?"

"One man knocked me to the ground while the other one grabbed Jane. The two of them were halfway to the carriage with her by the time I was on my feet again," Damaris said. "So obviously they didn't want me. But why?"

The three girls looked at one another.

It was certainly a conundrum, Abby thought. Perhaps they didn't recognize Damaris in her newly refurbished bonnet. But then, Jane was wearing a bonnet too. Perhaps they wanted Jane particularly because she was still a virgin. Or perhaps it was simply because Jane was beautiful, and Damaris was simply very pretty. Who knew how these evil people thought?

All Abby could think of to say was, "It's a mystery."

And all she could think of was, Where was Daisy? And how was she faring?

D aisy returned in the early evening. She came alone; there was no sign of Lord Davenham. The minute she arrived, they fell on her, hugging her in relief and pelting her with questions.

"Where have you been?"

"What happened?"

"Are you all right?"

"Gawd, have I died and come back from the dead or sommat?" she exclaimed. "Course I'm all right; why shouldn't I be?"

"But didn't Lord Davenham take you to a magistrate?"

"Yeah." Daisy grinned. "Where's the old lady? She'll want to hear this."

They hurried to the small sitting room, where Lady Beatrice was destroying a game of patience. "Well, about time! Come in, come in, my dear Daisy, and tell us where you've been all this time."

They all crowded into the sitting room, even Featherby and

William. A maid or two hovered in the doorway, but Featherby sent them away and shut the door firmly. Daisy pulled up an overstuffed stool and plopped down on it. She looked at all the waiting faces and grinned. "I could get used to this."

"Tell us everything," Lady Beatrice commanded.

"Well, after he'd been talking to you all, his lordship found me and asked me a heap of questions about the brothel." She shrugged. "I didn't see no harm in telling him, since Jane already spilled the beans. I hope that was right, Abby."

Abby nodded. "Go on."

"So then he said I had to tell it all to a friend of his."

"Who?" Jane asked curiously.

Daisy shrugged. "I never caught his name—some fat old toff in a big house. He give me a cup of tea and some cake and then I told him everything I'd told Lord D. And blow me down if he didn't turn out to be a magistrate! I just about died when his lordship told me."

"Then what happened?"

"So then the two of them went off into another room and talked, and then they took me to another old bloke's place—he was a magistrate too—and he gave me more tea and cake and asked me all the same questions again and a few more. I can tell you, I was getting right sick of it." She glanced at Featherby. "And them little cakes don't fill you up at all. I couldn't half murder a pie or something."

Featherby looked at William, who heaved a sigh and left. "Go on, Miss Daisy," Featherby said.

"Well, there was a lot of talking in corners and more blokes coming and going and more bloody questions—sorry, Lady B—and then Lord D put me in a carriage."

"Is that all?" said Lady Beatrice, disappointed.

"No, it's not," Abby said. She could tell by the brimming excitement Daisy was trying so hard to hide. "Something's going to happen, isn't it?"

"It's happened," Daisy said with the broadest grin yet. William came back with a pie, and they waited impatiently while Daisy took several giant mouthfuls. "Ah, that's better. They raided Mort's place this afternoon." She ate another mouthful. "I told them he paid blokes at Bow Street to warn him, so they used other people—I dunno who." Another mouthful. "But Mort's locked up right and tight in prison—his lordship let me watch from his carriage when they took him away. He looked blood—right miserable too." She laughed.

The girls all cheered and hugged one another. Lady Beatrice called for champagne. Daisy munched on her pie.

"Lord Davenham organized this? Today?" Abby couldn't believe it.

Daisy nodded vigorously. "You shoulda been there, Abby. Some of the old codgers wanted to hem and haw and consider the implications and form committees and investigate, but he wouldn't let them. He rousted them along, miss, like you wouldn't believe. Asked 'em what if their niece or granddaughter had been kidnapped on the way to school and was locked up in that house naked and waiting to be auctioned off to a roomful of randy old men—that got 'em going." She chuckled. "And then I said, all innocent-like, that if they waited until the evening, they'd be able to catch a whole lot of proper toffs in the house, and that really made 'em move. Don't reckon they wanted their friends embarrassed."

"Magnificent!" Lady Beatrice declared, raising her glass. "To the heroine of the hour, and my nephew." They all toasted Daisy. And the absent Lord Davenham.

Abby was breathless just thinking about it. Mort arrested and the brothel closed, and any girls imprisoned there would be free. All because Lord Davenham had known the right people to tell.

All her letters written in vain, and now in one afternoon the brothel was closed and the vile Mort in prison awaiting trial and punishment. It was a lesson in how the world worked.

She should have trusted him sooner.

"What's the matter, Abby?" Daisy asked her. "I thought you'd be pleased as punch."

"Oh, I am, I surely am." She smiled at Daisy. "I was just thinking. . . ."

"About the other places Mort has connections with?" Daisy said. "Don't worry; I told 'em about them too."

"Other places?"

"Didn't you know? He moves girls on to other places after

he's had 'em a while. Variety and all that. But I told them magistrates all about it, everything I know."

"Daisy, that's wonderful. You're a heroine, you know."

Daisy blushed. "Aw, get on with yer, Abby." She laughed. "You know, I used to be scared stiff of magistrates, but now . . ." She winked. "Without the wigs and the robes and fancy stuff, they're just old blokes, ain't they?" She ate the last bit of crust and wiped her mouth. "You know, I was thinking, if Mort hada left things the way his ma run the place, everyone there of their own free will . . ."

"If he had, would you have left?" Damaris asked curiously.

Daisy considered it. "Maybe. I dunno." She picked up a glass of champagne. "At any rate, I'm bloody glad I am where I am now. Who'da thought Daisy Smith'd be hobnobbin' with lords and ladies and takin' tea and cake with magistrates. And drinking champagne." She laughed and raised her glass again, and they all laughed with her and drank another toast.

Abby drank too. Her smiles were genuine, but she couldn't quite relax. Where was Lord Davenham, and what was he doing?

Max had had a busy day. He'd also had an epiphany. There were times in life when it seemed the heavens opened up and a ray of light shone down in a particular way and you suddenly saw everything more clearly than you ever had before, he reflected.

He'd had just such an insight when he realized how close to utter disaster Abby had been—and on more than one occasion. Brothels, sister at death's door, climbing up to his aunt's bedroom—twice! It couldn't be allowed to continue. And he knew just what to do.

A policy of a lifetime destroyed in an instant. What was more, he had no qualms about it.

He knocked on the door of the hotel room and waited. And waited. It wasn't late, not even seven o'clock. Had the Parsloes gone out for dinner?

He raised his hand to knock again when a woman's voice said, "Who's there?"

"Lord Davenham."

"One moment, please."

It was rather more than a minute when the door was opened by a maidservant. Behind her stood Henrietta, still dressed in day clothes, looking apprehensive.

"Good evening, Miss Parsloe, is your father in?"

"Papa has gone out to a meeting."

Damn. Still, what he had to say concerned her even more than her father. "May I come in? I have something important to tell you."

She exchanged a nervous glance with her maid. "I . . . I suppose so. But would you not prefer to come back tomorrow, when Papa will be here?"

"I will come back tomorrow, but first I need to talk to you," Max said firmly, and stepped inside. The maid looked out into the corridor and then closed the door.

"What did you want?" Henrietta seemed edgy, but quite composed.

"There's no easy way to say this, so I'll be blunt," Max said. "I've come to call off the wedding."

Her china blue eyes widened. "Papa said you'd never go back on your promise."

"I know. But I find I must. I am sorry for the upset this will cause you and your father, but I cannot marry you, Henrietta."

A thoughtful frown marred the smooth brow. "I see."

Max had braced himself for tears, recriminations, anger, even hysteria, but this calm acceptance baffled him. He said it again to be certain she understood. "I'm not going to marry you, Henrietta; do you understand?"

There was a flash of something in her eyes, some expression he did not quite catch, but all she said was, "I understand. But you haven't told Papa yet?"

"No, not yet." Did she imagine that her father would somehow be able to make him marry her; was that why she hadn't reacted? He supposed in Henrietta's world Papa made everything happen.

"Then will you promise me something?" she asked.

For whatever his promises were worth now. "What?" he asked cautiously.

"Will you wait until tomorrow to tell Papa you don't want to marry me?"

It was a small enough request. "Of course, if that's what you want." He supposed she wanted time to compose herself. Though she seemed quite composed to him already. She'd taken the news quite extraordinarily well, in fact. She hadn't even asked why.

"It is what I want." She held out her hand to him. "Thank you, Lord Davenham. Good-bye." Quite as if it were an ordinary call.

Bemused, Max took his leave. He ran down the staircase at the Pulteney feeling surprisingly lighthearted. He'd just broken his word, broken the principle of a lifetime. His honor was in the dust and yet he felt . . . wonderful.

Parsloe would be furious, of course, but Max didn't care. A weight had lifted off his shoulders. Breaking his word was wrong; yet at the deepest level of his soul, he knew this was the right thing to do.

Outside the hotel, he breathed deeply of the brisk evening breeze. He wasn't going to marry Henrietta Parsloe. He wanted to shout it from the rooftops.

He wanted to go home to Berkeley Square, to Abby, but he couldn't tell her, couldn't begin to court her properly until he'd settled things with Henry Parsloe. Only then could he come to her free and clear.

He'd planned it all out in his head when he'd had his epiphany—first tell the Parsloes, then tell Abby and see if he could read anything in her reaction to give him hope. And then tell the rest of the world, Aunt Bea, for a start—and wouldn't she crow? He smiled thinking of it.

But he couldn't tell Henry Parsloe till tomorrow, which meant he couldn't tell anyone. He went to his club and found Freddy there. For the first time in nine years he was free, but he couldn't even tell Freddy.

The two friends got quietly and companionably drunk.

Chapter Twenty

"I will be calm. I will be mistress of myself."

—JANE AUSTEN, *SENSE AND SENSIBILITY*

"Letter for you, Miss Abby." Featherby presented the silver salver.

"For me?" Abby glanced at the door—Lord Davenham would be down for breakfast shortly. She was nervous as a cat, waiting to see how he would treat her after the revelations of the day before.

She picked up the letter without much curiosity. Someone from the literary society, she supposed. Good-quality paper and addressed in a neat copperplate hand. Addressed—*oh, my God*—to Miss Abigail Chantry, and at the Berkeley Square address. And she'd seen that handwriting before, on a letter that was blank inside.

"How did this get here?" she asked Featherby.

"Pushed under the door this morning, miss. I did wonder when I saw how it was addressed—nobody else has seen it."

Abby broke open the wafer seal. This letter was not blank inside. Far from it.

To Miss Abigail Chantry and the filthy Whores she calls her sisters—

"Good morning, Miss Chance. Abby," a deep voice said from the doorway. "I'm sorry; did I startle you?"

"N—Good morning, Lord Davenham." Abby folded the letter hastily and slipped it into her sleeve. "Daisy told us what you did yesterday. It's wonderful news."

"Daisy? Oh, that. Yes."

Featherby glided in with a fresh pot of steaming coffee.

"And he, Mort, is truly in prison?"

Featherby hovered, tidying the dishes on the buffet.

"Yes, and further investigations are being made into the system whereby girls such as Jane and Damaris were abducted. He'll hang, you know."

Abby thought of all the girls whose lives Mort had ruined. "Good."

Lord Davenham looked at Featherby, who was now tidying the toast. "That will be all, Featherby."

"Yes, m'lord." He sent Abby an apologetic look and left.

A short silence followed. Lord Davenham fiddled with the saltcellar, turning it around and around in his big hands. Abby was uncomfortably aware of the vile letter in her sleeve. Who would send such a thing to her?

"Do you have any plans for this afternoon, Abby?" It was the second time he'd called her Abby. What did it mean? Was it a friendly kind of Abby, or did it signal a loss of respect?

She swallowed. "There's no meeting of the literary society this afternoon, if that's what you mean."

"Then I'd be obliged if you'd be available for, er, a discussion at three o'clock."

A discussion? What did that mean? Did he want her to talk to magistrates, as Daisy had done? Give evidence? But why her and not Jane? "Yes, of course."

The front doorbell jangled and Abby jumped nervously. Who would call at this hour? The letter up her sleeve. Abby felt cold, ill.

Lord Davenham gave her a searching glance. "Are you unwell?"

She forced a smile. "Just a slight headache."

"Abby . . ." He reached a hand toward her, then looked

around and said in quite a different tone, "Yes? What is it, Featherby?"

"Someone to see you, m'lord."

"Get rid of him." He turned back to Abby.

"It is Mr. Parsloe, m'lord, not looking very happy, I might say."

"Blast!" He gave Abby an apologetic look. "I'll have to speak to him. Three o'clock then?"

Abby nodded. The moment he'd gone she pulled the letter out of her sleeve and began reading.

*To Miss Abigail Chantry and the filthy Whores she calls
her sisters—*

Somehow the elegant copperplate writing made the words more horrible.

*Did you think you could pass yourselves off in society
as Decent Women? Whores from the lowest Brothel in
London?*

*What do you think will be said of Lady Beatrice Dav-
enham when it is known she claimed Filthy Whores as her
nieces? She will be reviled, scorned—at best a Laughing-
stock, at worst, a Pariah. The ton does not like to be made
Fools of. All those Ladies who come to your so-called Literary Society—do you think they will forgive the old lady
for making them Fawn and Dote on Whores? For causing
their Innocent Daughters to befriend you and their Sons to
buzz around you like flies buzz around Rotten Meat? And
what will they say of Lord Davenham, who keeps Whores
under his roof? Who knows what Depraved Appetites he
picked up in his years in the East?*

*You have until tomorrow to be gone from London, never
to show your faces in the city again. If you remain, All of
Society will be told exactly who and what you are. Proud
Lady Beatrice will be too ashamed to show her face in
public again, and Lord Davenham's honor will be in the
dust.*

The writing blurred before her eyes, but Abby continued to stare blindly at the letter. Who could have sent her this vile thing? Someone who knew her, knew her sisters and the life they lived here with Lady Beatrice. Someone who attended the literary society? The thought that it might be from someone who was pretending to be their friend sent her stomach churning.

She dragged her gaze off the elegant writing and with trembling hands refolded the letter. She felt nauseous, numb . . . frozen.

Her cup of tea sat at her elbow, cold now; she drank it all down, then poured herself another cup. It too was cold, and appropriately bitter. Slowly the numbness turned to something resembling calm. Yes, the letter was disgusting in its filthy interpretation of events, but really, did it make such a difference?

Didn't she know this day would eventually come? They'd been living under false names, masquerading in society as Lady Beatrice's nieces and hiding their pasts. And as all masquerades must, at some stage the masks had to be removed. It was a delusion to think otherwise.

It had come earlier than expected, and had happened in a horrible way, but there was an inevitability about it that she couldn't deny. No matter how much she wanted to.

They'd planned to leave before Lord Davenham's marriage anyway. And perhaps it would be easier to leave now, she told herself. At least she wouldn't have to endure watching—and assisting with—the preparations for his wedding.

Lady Beatrice would be upset, and would be bound to insist they stay, but she was shrewd enough to know, deep down, that it couldn't last, that it was, at best, a delightful pretense, a game that they'd all enjoyed.

And because it had been so wonderful, these weeks of pretending they were all one big, happy family, Abby had to ensure that their time together wasn't poisoned by the aftermath. Lady Beatrice had been kindness itself to Abby and her sisters, and so had her nephew in the end, and Abby would not . . . could not repay their generosity with scandal and humiliation and disgrace.

From the very beginning they'd planned to go to Bath. They didn't have enough money to go on as they'd hoped, or the range of clothing they needed for Jane to make a splash, but when she looked back at the desperate poverty they'd experienced before she'd climbed through Lady Beatrice's window, she was almost ashamed of herself for quibbling.

They were a great deal better off, materially and in many other ways; living with Lady Beatrice and mixing with her *ton*nish friends had given them a degree of social polish they otherwise wouldn't have.

Of course, they'd miss the old lady dreadfully. And Abby would miss—*No, better not even think such things*, she told herself fiercely. She wouldn't miss seeing him married to Henrietta Parsloe.

The thought was like a cold lump of iron in her chest.

There was no choice. Somehow she had to marshal the courage to leave, to pull herself together and do what she had to do. For the sake of them all, she had to be strong.

Desperately trying to overcome the cold desolation that filled her, she gradually became aware of voices raised in the entry hall. On legs that felt quite spongy, she walked to the doorway and looked out.

"It's your fault, I tell you!" Mr. Parsloe was waving a letter at Lord Davenham. Her throat froze at the sight of the letter. Had it started already? No, there was no reason for the writer of her letter, whoever it was, to write to Mr. Parsloe. Still, she had to be sure. She crept closer.

"Run off, damn you, run off with my own damned secretary! And him the younger son of a clergyman—what use is that, I ask you? Poor as church mice!"

Thank God, it wasn't about them at all.

Lord Davenham was trying to soothe him, speaking in a low voice. Abby couldn't catch what he was saying.

Mr. Parsloe wouldn't be soothed. "A gentleman? Pah! What use is that? Does he have a title? A fortune? Connections? I cannot believe my Henrietta would be such a fool! It's your fault, dammit—whatever you said to her yesterday has caused her to run off—it's all here."

Lord Davenham's voice rumbled again.

"What do you mean, planned it? How could she plan it?" Mr. Parsloe spluttered. Abby moved closer.

Of course she planned it, Max thought—you didn't organize

an elopement from London with a lad who lived in Manchester without some planning beforehand. She'd done it very neatly too. Henrietta had been ready to leave when he'd called last night, dressed in her traveling clothes, with her father away at a meeting, and nervous at Max's arrival because her lover was expected any minute. He'd been so caught up in his own thoughts he hadn't noticed. No wonder she hadn't wanted him to talk to her father that night.

"There are worse things than being married to a young, well-educated gentleman," Max told Henry Parsloe.

"Married? If she's married that young sprat I . . . I'll disinherit her! I'll disown her!" Max heard a gasp behind him. It was Abby, her face white and set, her eyes glittering.

Parsloe, unaware of the audience, ranted on. "They'll rue the day they flouted Henry Parsloe's wishes." He smacked Henrietta's note angrily. " 'Love more important than money'? Ha! I wish them joy of their poverty then! Let them beg in the streets; let them starve in their hovel. See how they like life without Henry Parsloe's money—they'll come crawling back soon enough, but it will be too—"

"How dare you!" Abby, her voice throbbing with anger, stepped forward.

"Eh?" Parsloe swiveled around to look at her.

"How dare you speak of your only daughter like that! How dare you wish her ill! It's . . . it's an obscene thing for a father to say!"

Parsloe looked down his nose at her. "Eh? What's it to you?"

Abby raged on. "I thought you loved your daughter!" She poked him in the chest with an angry finger. "You were as proud as punch of her when you came calling before—or was that a lie; was it? Are you really such a shallow popinjay of a man, the kind of petty humbug whose love is conditional, Manchester's answer to King Lear—"

"King who?" He looked at Max.

"—whose vanity is more important than the happiness and welfare of his daughter—his *only* child. Shame on you, Mr. Parsloe. Shame on you!"

"Listen here, lass—"

But Abby hadn't finished. "And how dare you blame Lord

Davenham—have you no finer feelings at all? How do you think he feels, being jilted by a silly little doll with no conversation?"

"Jilted?" Henry Parsloe looked a silent question at Max, who shook his head. He'd only just told Parsloe, so of course he hadn't spoken to Abby yet. But he wasn't going to interrupt; he was enjoying this too much. *Silly little doll with no conversation?* He hid a smile.

"Yes, jilted! You haven't given his feelings so much as a thought, have you? Because you're so horridly selfish you're only concerned about yourself."

"Am I indeed?"

"Yes. So think about this, Mr. Parsloe—how will you feel when you're old and alone with no daughter to care for you and no grandchildren to gladden your last days?"

"Grandchildren?"

"You hadn't thought of that, had you?" The anger was fading from her voice. She took on a more coaxing tone. "You wouldn't want your grandchildren living in poverty, would you? A man of your pride and standing in the community?"

Max understood where the anger stemmed from now.

She went on. "If this young man of Henrietta's is a gentleman, and educated, could you not teach him how to go on in business? He already works for you; he must be clever in that way, for otherwise you wouldn't have employed him."

Parsloe gave a cynical humph, but he was listening.

"Would not that be so satisfying? Every great man needs an apprentice to pass on his knowledge and wisdom to. And so what if he has no title—you did have your heart set on a title, I know."

Parsloe looked self-conscious. "And what's wrong with that?"

"Nothing, but for heaven's sake, you seem like a capable enough man—if you can build great manufactories and amass fortunes, I'm sure you could get yourself a knighthood if you put your mind to it. Would it not be better to be Sir Henry Parsloe than to have your own daughter outrank you?"

Parsloe's bushy eyebrows shot up, almost disappearing into his thinning gray hairline. His eyes grew thoughtful.

Max smiled. That had surely hit home.

"*Sir* Henry Parsloe," the man repeated. "Trying to soft-soap me, young woman?"

"A bit, but it's the truth." She added in an intense voice, "Mr. Parsloe, if you love Henrietta, really love her, you'll let her follow her heart and be happy, and with your support she can be happier still. But if you cut her off . . ." Tears glimmered in her eyes. "You have no idea of the misery that can result."

"Is that so?"

"I know it." There was both knowledge and despair in her eyes, as well as the tears she blinked back. "For that's what happened with my mother and father." She looked at the older man, all the passion gone now.

There was a short silence.

"We'd best get after that minx of mine," Parsloe said eventually. "I need to find her."

"And not cast her off?" she said.

He paused. "No, not cast her off."

"Or disinherit her?"

"No." He sighed. "What you saw, missy, was an old man in a foolish, frightened rage. I love my girl and I only want her happiness."

"I'm so glad," she said mistily, and kissed him on the cheek.

He turned to Max. "Will you come with me, my boy?"

With an effort Max dragged his gaze off Abby. "I will, sir."

"Then good-bye, Mr. Parsloe, and good luck." She kissed his cheek again.

She turned and held out her hand to Max, curiously formal. "Good-bye, Lord Davenham. I wish you all the best." She looked so pale and wan that Max wanted to sweep her into his arms then and there.

But there was one last thing he had to do to make things right with Henry Parsloe—help him find his daughter. Only then could he come to Abby free and clear and offer her his heart.

He'd waited all his life for her. A few more days wouldn't make any difference.

He took the hand she held out and kissed it, then turned it over and placed his mouth gently in the center of her palm. He hoped it would say the things he couldn't say in an entry hall with Parsloe and the butler looking interestedly on. Her fingers curled to gently cup his face around the kiss—an involuntary response or a brief caress?

He glanced up, hoping to read a message in her eyes, but they were full of tears again. "Good-bye. Take care," she whispered.

Max hesitated, but Parsloe was already at the door. "Come along, lad. They'll be halfway to Scotland by now."

"I'll be back soon," Max told her.

She nodded.

Max ran down the steps and climbed into his phaeton, where Henry Parsloe was already seated. "I hope you won't let that little lass get away," Parsloe said as they pulled away from the curb.

"Don't worry, sir; I have no intention of it."

"A grand little lass. The tongue on her!"

Max grinned. "I can see I'll have to watch my step."

Parsloe gave a huff of laughter. As they headed for the Great North Road, he said, "Sir Henry Parsloe, eh? What sort of a daft notion is that?" He gave Max a cautious glance.

"Not daft at all," Max said carelessly, knowing the older man was hanging on his every word. "I'd have thought it well within your capabilities. Might take you four or five years, though."

"As long as that?" Parsloe sniffed. "Aye, well, I might think on it."

Max smiled to himself. Two years at the most, he thought.

Abby stood at the foot of the staircase and watched him go. She held her hand cradled against her breast, her fingers still curled around his kiss.

She stood there long after Featherby had shut the door. He paused. "Are you all right, miss?" She nodded blindly, and he went away.

"Abby, are you all right?" It was Jane.

At the sound of her sister's voice, Abby's legs gave way. She sank down on the stairs and burst into tears.

M ax returned home five days later. It had taken them two days to catch up with the eloping couple, but at least they hadn't reached the border. When he'd left them, Henrietta and

Papa Parsloe had been enthusiastically planning a lavish spectacle of a wedding, to be held in Manchester, not London, and to take place rather more quickly than spring, the young couple having anticipated their vows. Henrietta Parsloe, like her father, left nothing to chance.

Max took the front steps two at a time. "Where's Abby?" he asked the moment Featherby opened the door.

"Not here, m'lord."

"Oh." *Damn.* He hadn't thought past taking her in his arms the moment he saw her. A letter addressed to him lay on the hall table. He picked it up, glanced carelessly at it and said, "Gone out, has she? When will she be back?"

"I think you'd better talk to your aunt, m'lord."

Something in the butler's tone caused Max to turn and look at him. "What is it? Where's she gone?"

"Your aunt is in the small sitting room."

Max stuffed the letter in his pocket and went in search of his aunt. He found her listlessly flipping the pages of a magazine. When she saw him she cast it aside and sat up. "About time! Where the deuce have you been? Preventing a marriage, I suppose."

"Yes, but—"

She made a disgusted noise. "Stupid boy! You should have been here, not gadding after that wretched Parsley chit."

He ignored that. "Where's Abby?"

"Gone."

"What do you mean, gone?"

"Is there more than one meaning to the word?" she said with asperity. "I mean gone—left—departed."

Gone? Max stared at her blankly. "Where to?"

She shrugged, her gaze accusing. "Your guess is as good as mine."

"Do you mean she's left here for good?" Max couldn't believe it. He ran his fingers through his hair. "But why would she leave? And without a word."

"Possibly because you went off chasing after that Parsloe chit."

He stared at her. "But she knew why I went. I had no choice."

His aunt snorted. He took a few restless paces around the

room, thinking furiously. And halted, thinking about that last, curiously formal good-bye Abby had made. "When did she leave?"

"The same day you did."

"All of them? Without warning?" She nodded.

"Then something must have happened to make them go—it can't have been to do with me going after Henrietta Parsloe. But what?" He paced around the room, thinking back over all the events leading up to his departure. "Was it the brothel arrests? Did she fear her sisters having to give evidence in a public court? Surely she'd know I'd protect them from that. Why did she think I took Daisy and not Jane or Damaris? No one would think twice about a cockney maidservant giving evidence—and besides, she used her real name—Daisy Smith, not Daisy Chance."

His aunt watched balefully as he paced back and forth, saying nothing. Clearly she blamed him for letting Abby leave, though how he could have prevented it when he wasn't even here . . .

After he'd exhausted every possibility, she said, "It was because of this." From the side of her chair she withdrew a folded sheet of paper, holding it disdainfully between finger and thumb.

He opened it, read the beginning and swore. "Who sent this piece of poisonous filth?"

She shook her head. "Anonymous, of course. Such cowardly things always are."

He read it again more slowly. "The bastard. The filthy bastard." He looked at his aunt. "She left to protect you."

"And you."

"I don't give a damn what people say about me."

"And you think I do?" she scoffed. "But Abby cares."

"I know," he said quietly. "It's what she does—cares." He sank, despairing, into a chair. "She should have told me. Dammit, why didn't she?"

"You were on the road to Scotland, chasing that stupid little—" He stopped her with a sharp look. She hunched a shoulder and said, "She couldn't wait; the letter gave her one day."

"She left without a word?"

"No, of course she told me, showed me that disgusting thing and wouldn't listen to a word I had to say. Hell-bent on protecting me from the consequences of her deception!" She snorted. "Deception. I wasn't deceived for a moment. But she's stubborn, that girl. Once she thinks what she's doing is right . . ."

Max nodded. He knew. But stubborn was the wrong word—she was strong, steadfast. "The last time I saw her she was trying not to cry. She must have known then. Blast it, I wish she'd trusted me enough to confide in me. I wouldn't have let her buckle under this sort of cowardly filth." He smashed his fist into his palm. "I thought—fool that I am—that the tears were about something else, something to do with her past."

His aunt nodded and in a voice that cracked with emotion said, "If you'd only seen her, Max, breaking her heart but so brave, trying not to show it, saying that all along she'd known this was just a lovely fantasy. But I'm no dratted fantasy, and I refuse to be part of one! It was real." She rubbed away a tear and added, "I love that gel and her sisters, Max."

"I know."

"Do you, Max? Do you?"

He said impatiently, "Of course I do. I couldn't care less about false names and burglaries—except that she shouldn't be living in such a blasted precarious fashion; it makes my blood run cold to think of her alone out there. Why didn't she tell me she was in trouble—surely she'd know I'd help her?"

"Why would she know it, dear boy?"

"Well, because . . ."

"Does she have any idea how you feel? Have you told her how you feel?"

"I couldn't, not until I got everything straightened out with—"

"Oh, for heaven's sake—spare me the thought processes of men!" his aunt declared acidly.

"I don't understand."

"No, you surely don't, you blockhead. You've been so busy dashing about, being the gallant knight, routing enemies and fighting dragons, that you forgot about the heroine."

"I damned well did not," Max said hotly. "Abby was at the

heart of everything I did—everything! She wasn't out of my mind for a minute."

Her expression softened. "Perhaps I should have said, you forgot to *talk* to the heroine."

"Talk?"

"Yes, dear boy, talk."

"But . . . she should have known. . . ."

"How?"

He stared at her blankly. He'd thought . . . He assumed . . .

"Think for a moment how everything unfolded that day: First someone tried to abduct Jane, and in the aftermath Abby confessed to you everything she'd been trying to hide all this time—the brothel, the false names, the burglary—"

"Yes, yes, what of it?" Max said impatiently. He knew all this; none of it mattered.

"When she'd finished telling you, what did you do?"

"I damned well went out and got that bastard locked up; that's what I did."

"Before that."

Max didn't understand what she was getting at.

"When Abby had finished telling you about the worst things she had done in her life—"

"Worst things? That girl is a heroine, Aunt Bea; can't you see that? All those things she did, the desperate circumstances she faced, the courage it took—if you can't see that she's the finest, bravest, most wonderful girl . . ."

"Oh, I see it, dear boy, but does she? And did you tell her so then, when she most needed to hear it from you—the one person whose good opinion she cared about? Or did you say, 'I need to think,' and rush out of the room? As if disgusted."

"Disgusted?" he repeated, appalled at her interpretation. "But I went out—"

"—to kill dragons, I know. But did Abby?"

Stricken, he stared at her. Abby couldn't have thought he was disgusted, surely? It was so much the opposite of what he felt for her, he could hardly imagine it. But his aunt's words made a ghastly kind of sense.

"And then you stayed out for the rest of the night, and in the morning, what must you do but go off chasing after that stupid fiancée of yours."

"She's not my fiancée."

"Well, of course, since she's run off—"

"I broke it off with her that same day."

"You what?" Her eyes popped.

He gave her a tired smile. "You should be pleased, Aunt Bea. That was why Henry Parsloe was so angry with me. He thought Henrietta had run off because I'd jilted her."

She made an impatient gesture. "I don't give a fig for the Parsleys. Max, you broke your word? For Abby?"

He nodded.

"You love her?"

"Of course I love her." How could anyone not?

"And did she know that?"

"No," he said heavily. "I wanted to tell her, but first I had to make everything right, so I could come to her free and clear. I needed—"

"To kill dragons."

He nodded. "I thought she knew how I felt." He sat down, despairing at the mess he'd made of things.

"My dear boy," she said gently, "women need to hear the words. They don't need the world conquered for them, but they do need a man to speak the words that are in his heart."

"I'll find her," Max said. "I don't care where she's gone or how long it takes; I'll find her. They would have left by stage-coach. Four pretty girls traveling together shouldn't be impossible to trace."

"They didn't go by stagecoach."

"What?" He gave her a sharp look. "How do you know?"

She snorted. "Do you think I'd let my nieces just disappear?" She snorted again. "I sent them off in the barouche with Turner and Hatch in attendance, of course."

Max stared at her in disbelief. "Then why the hell did you let me go through all of that?"

She shrugged. "For all I knew you were still betrothed to La Parsley."

He clenched his fists and said in a voice that was remarkably calm for a man who was itching to strangle a beloved but infuriating relative, "Where. Is. Abby?"

"She made me promise I wouldn't tell."

"Aunt Bea!" He couldn't believe his ears.

She laughed. "Oh, pish-tush, don't look like that, dear boy; you know what I think of stupid promises—and this is a really stupid one. Featherby has the address."

"Bless you, Aunt Bea." He kissed her on the forehead.

"So you'll bring Abby back for me?"

"No, I'll bring her back for me."

"Then you'd better have this." She dropped a ring into his palm.

Max stared at the gleaming emerald ring. "One of your rings? I thought they'd been stolen."

"I must have hidden them in the hollow post of my bed when I got sick. Featherby and William found them when we moved here." She nodded. "That one's my favorite. It's for Abby—don't look at me like that; you haven't bought her a ring yet, have you?"

He grinned and pocketed the ring. "Aunt Bea, you're a gem. All right, I'm going. Featherby!" he shouted.

"Yes, m'lord?" Featherby appeared right beside the door. "I took the liberty of ordering you a post chaise, m'lord. It's waiting outside."

"A yellow bounder?"

"Yes, m'lord, since you've been driving for days already. It'll be quick and you won't be so tired when you get to Bath."

"Bath? She's in Bath?"

"Yes, m'lord, safe and sound." Featherby pressed a small piece of paper into Max's hand. "Miss Abby's address, sir."

"Good man. Remind me to increase your wage."

As Featherby handed Max his hat and coat, he added, "I've packed your bag with clean clothes, and that and a basket with various victuals are waiting in the carriage for you. Godspeed, m'lord, bring Miss Abby home."

But Max was already running down the steps.

Chapter Twenty-one

*"In vain have I struggled. It will not do. My feelings will not
be repressed. You must allow me to tell you how ardently I
admire and love you."*

—JANE AUSTEN, *PRIDE AND PREJUDICE*

Bath was damp and cold, and the air was crisp with the
promise of winter when Max arrived. He'd driven through
the night, and it was midmorning. He took a suite of rooms at
York House, the best hotel in Bath, and quickly shaved, bathed
and changed his clothes before setting out in search of his
beloved.

He called in at her lodgings, a respectable enough place, but
faded, shabby. He vowed she wouldn't be there for long.

The young ladies had already gone out, their landlady told
him with a speculative look. He set off down Milsom Street,
heading for the Pump Room in the lower part of town, then
stopped dead. There she was, with her sisters, having an ani-
mated discussion in front of the window of a millinery shop.

She was in green. He liked her in green. He liked her in
anything except that gray dress of hers. When they were married he'd burn that gray dress. And the cloak.

He approached quietly. The sisters were intent on their conversation. Abby wore a small confection that he supposed was
a bonnet. It provided absolutely no protection from the misty
rain. Tiny jewel-like droplets of mist clung to her hair, like a
sprinkling of diamonds.

He stood for a moment, watching her tilt her head as she

examined something in the window, then shake it in disagreement. His heart was pounding. Every gesture, every movement was familiar and dear to him. He'd almost lost her because of his own stupid stubbornness. The thought chilled him to his spine.

Never again.

On that thought he stepped closer. "Abby."

She turned, her mouth forming a delicious O of surprise. She was pale, and her eyes, though beautiful, were a little heavy. He was not the only one who'd been losing sleep, then.

"Lord Davenham, how did you knmmph—" He kissed her right there in the street. At the first taste of her, a deep rush of hunger set his head spinning. He'd waited so long for this, for her. He thought he'd lost her, and now he'd found her.

"Max, what are you doinmmph—" He kissed her again, indifferent to the stares and muttering of the scandalized passersby. He'd feared he might never again hold her, taste her sweet, intoxicating . . . Abbyness.

"We need to talk," he told her when he'd released her again. She looked so adorably flushed and confused it took all his strength not to snatch her back and carry her off, regardless of the audience. "Not here in the street, nor . . ." He glanced at her sisters. "Morning, ladies, you'll forgive me if I take your sister back to my hotel." It wasn't a question.

"But if you take her to a hotel, won't she be compromised?" Jane asked.

Max nodded. "I certainly hope so."

Abby's eyes widened. A delicious blush colored her cheeks, but she didn't say a word.

Jane looked prepared to argue the point, until Daisy elbowed her firmly in the ribs. Ignoring Jane's surprised look, the little cockney winked at Max, turned to Abby and said, "Well, go on then, Abby; run along and let the nice man compromise you. You know you want to."

Max grinned. He'd always liked Daisy.

Abby spluttered with laughter, half shocked, half embarrassed. Oh, dear, was it so obvious? She'd tried so hard to hide her feelings.

And of course she didn't want to be compromised. No respectable girl would.

"Trust me, Abby." He slid his arm around her waist in a move guaranteed to set the Bath tabbies whispering again and pulled her hard against him. "Come with me."

His strength, his warmth, his certainty were so appealing.

She shouldn't do this. She shouldn't . . . She *knew* it wasn't possible.

She made no attempt to pull away

His hold on her tightened. "Ladies," he said, inclining his head to her sisters, and together he and Abby walked back up Milsom Street.

It was just a walk, she told herself, a walk in public. Quite respectable . . . except for the arm that encircled her waist. She loved the feel of him, the firm, possessive way he drew her against him, the way their bodies brushed against each other as they walked, the way he adjusted his long stride to hers.

But she wasn't going to any hotel with him.

The cobbles were damp, and the soot from the smoke of domestic coal fires that had covered the street was now, in the fine misty rain, collecting in the cracks, each wrinkle and crevasse etched in black. They walked in silence, hearts full, not knowing where to start because there was so much to say.

One question was at the forefront of her mind. "Henrietta Parsloe?"

"We caught up with them before they reached the border. It's all sorted. I left Henrietta and her father planning the grandest wedding Manchester's ever seen. She's a cunning little minx—that placid surface had us all fooled—she'd had this planned for weeks."

"I see." Abby didn't know what to say. An expression of sympathy was appropriate—he'd been jilted, after all—but her heart was singing. Oh, she had no right to be happy, no right even to think of possibilities. A connection with Abby would bring him worse disgrace and humiliation than mere jilting. Still, he was better off without Henrietta. He deserved a woman who loved and wanted him.

"Not that it mattered to me," he said, causing her to look up at him sharply.

"But I thought. . . I thought . . ."

"What did you think?" But he must have seen it in her

eyes. "You thought I'd marry her anyway? Even though she'd run off?"

"Yes. No. I don't know. Why did you go after her, then?"

"I owed it to her father to help. But there was no question of me marrying her. I'd already broken it off with Henrietta before she eloped—that's why her father was so angry with me. He thought it was why she'd run off. He didn't know—none of us did at that point—that she'd been planning it for weeks."

Abby gasped and stood stock-still. "You broke it off? But I thought keeping your word was so important to you."

"It is, but you're much more important." He brushed a lock of damp hair from her cheek.

"Me? But—" She stared at him, unable to think.

They'd reached York House. "All your questions shall be answered if only you'll come inside. Come on, sweetheart, it's started to rain and you're getting wet." He drew her into the doorway of the hotel.

Her heart thudding, she allowed him to lead her into the hotel. Further conversation was doused by the luxurious hush of the hotel lobby. She felt out of place, damp, bedraggled.

"How did you find us?" she asked as he led her up the stairs. It was not the question that tore at her but it was the easiest to ask in this lush environment.

He didn't respond.

She looked up at him. "Lady Beatrice? She promised she wouldn't betray me, but . . ."

He gave a small smile. "Betray you? Aunt Bea?"

"Then how did you know we were in Bath?"

"Featherby gave me your address."

"Featherby?" Abby exclaimed, hurt. She would have sworn Featherby would have remained loyal.

"Only because I threatened to beat it out of him."

She turned a shocked face to him. "You didn't! Threaten to beat poor Featherby? But—"

He laughed at her expression. "Of course I didn't. But Featherby knows where you belong better than you do, apparently. His last words to me were, 'Bring Miss Abby home.' And I intend to do just that."

Abby bit her lip and turned her face away. It was a lovely

thought, but it wasn't her home. That letter had ensured she could never go back.

At the top of the stairs he produced and key and unlocked a door. "Come in and hear me out, Abby," he said softly.

She hesitated. She shouldn't go in there, shouldn't be alone with him in his hotel room. There was no future for them, she knew it. She should leave, cling to what little respectability she still retained, return to her sisters. And yet . . . and yet . . .

What did he mean, saying she was more important to him than keeping his word?

For a moment Max was sure she was about to refuse, standing there in the corridor, her sweet face crumpled with doubt and indecision, her eyes troubled.

He took her hand and drew her inside, shutting the door behind them, shutting the rest of the world out.

"You wondered why I broke my engagement with Henrietta." He was drowning in her gaze. "Because I've found the one woman in the world I can't live without."

Her mouth trembled. "Oh, Max . . ."

He didn't wait. He couldn't. He hauled her into his arms and kissed her. She was stiff in his embrace at first, then he felt a shiver run through her and she softened, pressing herself eagerly against him, winding her arms around his neck as she returned his kiss. She tasted of innocence and rain, a hint of woodsmoke, and warm essence of Abby.

Her lips parted beneath his, and without warning the kiss spiraled out of control as he plunged into her sweet depths, the taste of her entering his blood like wildfire.

He hadn't planned for things to go this far, this fast.

"No, no—stop," she said suddenly, and pushed at his chest. "We cannot. I cannot."

"What is it? What's wrong?" Max took several deep breaths, struggling for control.

"I can't be with you. I can't go back to London. There was a . . . a horrid letter."

"Oh. Yes, I know." Of course she was worrying about that. Stupid of him not to deal with it earlier. With an effort he forced his body to behave. "Don't worry about it."

"You know about the letter? Then you understand why I can't go back—"

"Nonsense! Of course you can."

"But I couldn't bear it if you and Lady Beatrice suffered—"

"Nobody will suffer anything," Max told her firmly. "Not that either Aunt Bea or I care two hoots what anyone says about us—or you and your sisters—but the man who wrote that poisonous letter is in gaol. Sit down and I'll explain." He didn't trust himself to touch her again. He just wanted to haul her into his arms and kiss away all resistance and argument.

She removed the tiny piece of nonsense that passed for a bonnet, and placed it on the table. Her hair was damp from the misty rain; tiny dark tendrils spiraled along her nape and temple. He longed to touch them, to bury his face in her cool, tender neck. But she was a worrier, this little love of his, and when she came to him, he wanted it to be with a clear heart and no remaining doubts.

There was a decanter of something on the sideboard. He poured two glasses and handed one to her.

She received the glass absently. "You think Mort wrote the letter? But according to Daisy he can barely read, so I very much doubt—"

"Not Mortimer, someone else." He took out the letter he'd removed from the hall table the day before. He'd read it in the carriage on the way to Bath. "My friend the magistrate wrote to fill me in on what has happened in the last few days. It seems Sydney Mortimer—Mort, as you call him—on realizing he will undoubtedly hang, decided to take his partners in crime with him. He's been a fount of information, and as a result, a number of men—and some so-called gentlemen—are now in prison." He handed her the letter. "See if you recognize any of the names."

While she read, he sipped his wine, some kind of sherry. Not bad either.

She looked up in surprise. "Greevey? Sir Walter Greevey? But he's one of the governors of the Pillbury Home!"

Max nodded. "That, and a number of other charitable institutions for girls. According to Mortimer, Greevey's been personally selecting pretty orphan girls for abduction and sale to brothels for the last five years."

"How dreadful. I can hardly believe it—I never met him, but Jane said he was always so nice."

"The evidence is overwhelming. According to my friend, they discovered a pile of incriminating correspondence in his home. He'll hang as well."

She closed her eyes. "I can't bear to think of it, all those poor girls . . . What he did was cruel and evil, such a betrayal of his position of trust." She frowned thoughtfully. "You think he sent me the threatening letter?"

Max nodded. "It's the same handwriting as that blank one that you got that day you were attacked. My guess is it'll match that of the correspondence that was seized."

"So he sent that man after me with a knife? But why? He didn't even know me."

Max had given it some thought. "You're the reason Jane was able to escape the brothel—he mustn't have realized she had a sister, let alone one in London. And so he needed to get both you and Jane out of the way; the link between you girls and the Pillbury—and his crimes—was too clear. Your evidence could hang him."

"He arranged Jane's position at the vicarage and sent the carriage to take her there," Abby said. "It's sickening even to think of it—we were so grateful to him for arranging it, and all the time . . ." She shuddered. "I even wrote to him and the vicar and to Mrs. Bodkin, saying that Jane was safe with me—"

"Which is how he traced you and sent that villain after you with a knife."

"Mrs. Bodkin wasn't involved, was she?"

"The matron of the home?" Max shook his head. "No, she's now trying to trace every girl who ever left the Pillbury since he became involved—see, there." He pointed to the part of the letter that mentioned the matron.

"Oh, I'm so glad." She sipped her wine, grimaced and put it down. "It's such a relief that the author of that beastly letter wasn't anyone we know. It was so horrid wondering if any of our friends . . ."

Max slipped a comforting arm around her shoulder. "Don't think about it. It's all behind you now."

With a smile, she turned and, as natural as sunshine, lifted her face for his kiss.

He kissed her, lightly at first, then managed to say with some semblance of control, "Not yet. First there are things I need to tell you. Before we . . ." He swallowed and waved her back to her chair.

"What things?" She sat down, folding her hands like an anxious schoolgirl, so serious and pretty he wanted to kiss her again.

"The first and most important is that I love you and in a minute I'm going to ask you to marry me."

"Oh, Max—" She rose and took a step toward him, but he held up his hand.

"I'm not finished yet." He wanted to say it all, so there would be no misunderstandings before she accepted him. Or not. "First, I owe you an apology for not telling you back in London that I'd broken my betrothal to Henrietta. And after your sister was almost abducted, I should have explained to you what I was doing instead of rushing off."

"But I know now—"

"I should have told you at the time, not let you find out afterward, from other people. And the other morning, I should have explained exactly why I was going with Henry Parsloe in pursuit of Henrietta and her lover—and that it was *not* because I wanted to marry Henrietta. I owe Henry Parsloe a great deal, not just because he lent me money nine years ago."

Her eyes were shining. "Oh, Max, you don't need to explain anyth—"

"I do need to explain, because I think I hurt you and I didn't mean to. The thing is, I wanted to clear all the obstacles away first, so I could come to you free and clear. But I should have said—"

"Hush." She put soft fingers over his lips, silky and cool against his burning mouth. "It doesn't matter. And I think it's lovely that you wanted to make everything right first—it's one of the things I love about you, the way you always try to do things properly."

"One of the things?" He swallowed. "You love me?" She loved him!

"Oh, Max, of course I do, with all my heart." And she flung herself into his arms.

Her kiss was sweet and wild and slightly off-center in her enthusiasm. He wrapped his arms around her and held her against him, exploring the mystery of her, reveling in the graceful sinuousness of her body—the pure marvel of her, offering herself to him—as his mouth joined with hers in a dance as old as time. Abby.

His body ached for total possession but he forced himself to put her gently aside. His pulse was racing. He took a ragged deep breath, stepped back and produced the emerald ring from his pocket. "As you know, I like to be thorough in everything I do, so before we go any further . . ." He went down on one knee in front of her. "Abigail Chantry Chance Chancealotto—"

It surprised a choke of laughter out of her.

"Under whatever name you choose, would you do me the honor of becoming my wife? For I love you dearly and cannot imagine life without you by my side."

"Oh, Max. . . Oh, Max." Her eyes misted. "I'd be honored to. I love you so very much, so if you're sure . . ." He slid the ring onto her finger, rose to his feet, pulled her into his arms and kissed her again.

He stepped back almost immediately, putting two feet of space between them. It felt like a chasm. A cold gap that needed to be bridged immediately.

He was hard as a rock and aching with desire. "And now, I think you'd better leave, my love, before I do more than compromise you."

There was a short silence, and then a blush rose on her cheeks. Her gaze dropped. A tiny smile began to play on her lips. "Would you like some help with those buttons?"

His heart gave a lurch. As did other parts of his body. "Are you sure, love? I can wait until we're married."

"I can't." Her eyes were shining.

"You trust me?"

"Oh, Max, with all my heart." She reached for his waistcoat buttons. With fingers that tried not to tremble, she undid the buttons one by one—cloth buttons, hard to undo. Beneath the fine cloth she could feel his warmth, his strength, smell the dark, familiar scent of him. Smoke-dark eyes watched every move she made. She could not meet his gaze. She was not bashful, but emotions were swelling within her, and she felt so . . . exposed. They threatened to burst from her, like a sausage splitting its skin. It was not a pretty thought. So inelegant, at a time when she most wanted to be beautiful.

She wished she were more poised, more skillful, less ignorant, not such a fumbling fool. She wanted it, wanted him, more than she could ever believe possible. *A consummation devoutly to be wished* . . . So where did these nerves come from?

"Would it be easier if I did this?" He leaned forward and brushed his mouth across her lips. Her fingers instantly became thumbs.

"Or this?" He trailed kisses along the line of her jaw. Like a cat she raised her face to give him better access, and shivered deliciously as he laved her skin with his tongue.

All she could do was to clutch feebly at the fabric of his waistcoat and give herself up to the luscious, shimmering sensations that washed through her with every touch.

She had never imagined it could be so with a man.

He nibbled her behind the ear. She shuddered and arched against him and felt him smile against her skin.

"Come, let us move to the bedchamber." He took her hands and she stood and took a couple of wobbly steps; her legs felt strange, as though her knees were about to dissolve.

With a swift movement he swung her into his arms. She gasped and wrapped her arms around his neck as he carried her into the bedchamber—carried her. She hadn't been carried since she was a child, but there was nothing childlike in this. She felt entirely womanly, desired and desirous.

He laid her down on the bed like some precious gift, then stepped back and, keeping his burning-ice gaze on her, he quickly stripped off his waistcoat and neck cloth. He bent and pulled off his boots and she admired the lean, elegant line of his thighs and the firm masculine buttocks in the tight buff breeches.

He turned and caught her looking, and she blushed furiously, but could not help but smile at the same time.

It felt deliciously wanton to be lying on a man's bed, admiring his person so blatantly, knowing she had every right to look as much as she wanted. He *loved* her. Loved *her*. All the lonely years . . . and now . . . this glorious, wonderful, magnificent man. Her man.

She watched as he unfastened the fall of his breeches and pushed them down his legs. He was still wearing his shirt, so all she could see was long, bare, well-muscled legs. Her face was so hot, it was just as well.

"Now you," he said, and, feeling tongue-tied and self-conscious, she sat up and moved to unfasten her dress but he knelt before her and slipped off her shoes, one by one. Then his hands slid up her calves, seeking the ties of her garters. He undid them by feel alone, his hands hidden, moving under her skirts, an oddly erotic sight. His long, strong fingers were deft and quick as he dealt with the ties, then slowly rolled off her stockings one by one, brushing down her bare legs, stroking her, gently caressing her feet with his big, warm hands. With every movement, tiny shivers of pleasure arrowed to the core of her. She was melting under his touch.

She watched, mesmerized, as he laid the stockings neatly on the chair, side by side.

He straightened. "Do you need a hand with that?" His voice was deep and a little husky, and she realized she hadn't done a thing to remove her dress, she'd been so taken up with the way he'd removed her stockings.

Hurriedly, breathing in quick, small gasps, she plucked at the fastenings of her dress.

"Let me," he said, and in a few movements her dress started to fall away from her shoulders. "I like this dress," he told her as he seized the hem and pulled it up. "Lift your bottom." It was almost prosaic, except that her dress was whisked over her head and was gone. He shook it out and draped it carefully over the chair. While his back was turned she hurriedly undid her stays.

And then there was just him in his shirt and Abby in her chemise. Should she take that off too? She was suddenly frozen with anxiety. She wasn't very . . . womanly. What if he found her disappointing? She folded her arms across her breasts, trying to disguise her lack.

"You are beautiful," he said softly, and bent to take her mouth with his, and she forgot everything else, all her small, pointless worries burned to ash under the onslaught of his mouth against her senses.

She couldn't think, only react, only feel. She tasted desire, and hunger and a bone-deep loneliness in him that some long-buried part of her recognized instinctively. She wrapped her arms around him, returning each kiss, each caress. She buried her fingers in his thick, closely cropped dark hair, and briefly wished he were still her wild, long-maned Viking.

Through her chemise he caressed her breasts, her belly, her limbs. Everywhere he touched, the abrasion of hands over fabric left her melting and quivering with pleasure.

And all the time he gazed at her, making love to her with his eyes, his smoke-hot, mist-dark eyes. How had she ever thought him cold?

He pulled off his shirt and a moment later her chemise went the same way, without apology, without regret. She hardly noticed she was naked and exposed; she was eating him up with her eyes. So beautiful, so strong.

And when he worshiped her breasts with lips and tongue and hands and the masculine abrasion of his jaw, she almost burst with the pleasure of it. Lacking? She felt powerful, helpless, beautiful. Triumphant.

She pressed herself hard against him, her limbs twining around him like a vine. The sensation of body against body, skin to skin, was exhilarating. His strength, his power, the fierce intensity of his desire ignited her. She felt lit from within.

She gloried in the hard, strong planes of his chest, running her palms over his skin, exploring the tiny male nubbins with delicate fingers, caressing, possessing and learning how it pleased him. So much pleased him.

He arched and writhed beneath her touch, growling his pleasure, telling her she was his love, his beauty, his soul. And all the time he was kissing her as if he would never, could never stop. He kissed her as she were the water of life itself, and he dying of thirst. And she blossomed beneath his touch.

He nudged her legs apart and caressed her there, his long, strong fingers insistent, knowing, skillful. She writhed restlessly beneath his ministrations, shivering with pleasure, aching and desperate for something, but not knowing what.

She was melting; she was strung as tight as a violin wire; she was shaking with need.

She looked at him, at his hard masculine part that jutted out so forcefully. It was strange; it was magnificent. She reached for it to give him the same pleasure he'd given her. And the same frustration.

"No," he said, catching her hand before she could touch him. "Not this time, my love. I'll explode if you touch me."

"You too?" she wailed.

He smiled, though he was gritting his teeth as if in pain. "Not much longer."

He moved, pressing her down into the bed with his body. The weight of him crushed her, but, "Yes, yes," she muttered. This was it, what she wanted, some part of her recognized. She wrapped her legs around his waist, wanting to pull him closer, hold him tighter. She felt the hard heat of him nudging at her entrance and gasped as it pushed against her.

"It's not going to fit," she panted.

"It is." He didn't move.

She stiffened, wanting suddenly to shove him off her. She pushed at his chest, but in the same instant he entered her in a long, slow thrust that left her rigid with discomfort. The burst-sausage image came to mind again.

"I told you it wouldn't fit!" But even as she spoke the words, she felt her body softening around him, adjusting to fit him, and suddenly she wasn't quite so uncomfortable. It felt strange, and there was a slight stinging, but that was all.

He started to move and she stiffened in preparation for more discomfort, but no . . . It was all right. He was moving more rhythmically now, and she was almost . . . feeling . . . something. . . . She strained for . . . whatever it was, and then his fingers slipped between them and sensation arced through her like a flame, like a meteor.

She shrieked, arching and bucking beneath him, and he thrust and thrust, and she was moving with him and oh, it was glorious, and suddenly she was teetering on the edge of unbearable ecstasy, and it built and built until, with a loud groan, he gave one final thrust and shuddered deeply as she shattered gloriously around him.

When Abby woke, she was tucked into bed, curled against something big and warm and hard. She stretched luxuriantly, enjoying the sensation of skin against skin.

She didn't feel at all like a burst sausage; she felt like a flower that had split open its plain, hard gray case and opened tender new brilliantly colorful petals to the sun. She felt safe; she felt warm; she was loved.

"Abby?" A deep, anxious male voice rumbled in her ear. "Are you all right?"

She opened her eyes and found herself confronting a worried smoke-gray gaze. A most beloved gaze.

She smiled, feeling full of joy, yet at the same time close to tears. She blinked them back, knowing he wouldn't understand happy tears. "That was . . . I had no idea . . ."

"You're all right?"

She snuggled against him, laying her cheek against his bare chest and wrapping her arms around him. "Just wonderful." She sighed happily.

His arm circled her and he kissed her lightly. "It will be better the next time, I promise."

She smiled against his skin. "I don't see how it could be, but I'm happy to let you convince me."

He gave a quiet huff of amusement and she felt him relax. He stroked one arm lazily, his long, clever fingers evoking delicious trails of remembered sensation. She hadn't expected what passed between a man and a woman to be so. . . emotional, and at the same time, so very . . . animal. And yet so right.

She lay curled against him, in a half-awake, dreamy state, listening to him breathe, feeling the steady thud of his heartbeat under her cheek.

It was so intimate, lying here in this quiet room, skin to skin with the man she loved.

Outside it started to rain, cold pellets beating against the windowpanes. A leaden gray light filled the room. It was early afternoon, but it felt like nightfall. The room filled with shadows and Abby wondered whether they should dress and return to her sisters. She didn't want to go anywhere.

"I'll get us some light." With a surge of blankets he rose from the bed and, naked, padded to the fireplace where a fire had been laid. He took down the tinderbox and set about making a flame. He seemed entirely unself-conscious.

Abby had never seen a fully naked man before. At first she felt as though she should avert her gaze, but then. . . he was to be her husband. And he was already her lover. It was silly to be shy. She watched him, admiring the ripple of corded muscle across his back, the line of his spine, his taut buttocks, his long, hard thighs. Male to her female. Her Viking.

He set tinder to the fire and soon bright flames danced in the grate. With a long sliver of burning kindling he lit half a dozen candles. She stared, unable to look away when he turned and she saw the full masculinity of him, the part that had been inside her. Sensation rippled through her body at the sight of him.

Such a magnificent man. Emotion filled her throat. What had she done to deserve him?

Seeing her watching him, he smiled, and the smile told her he understood she was still a little shy, and that he liked it, and more than liked her. It warmed her to her toes.

He loved her.

He crossed the room and drew the curtains against the cold light outside. Rain beat on the cold glass panes; inside it was warm and bright and cozy as Max slipped back into bed.

"You don't want to leave yet, do you?" he murmured and when she shook her head, he took her in his arms once more.

And if the first time they made love was a hungry claiming of frantic, aching flesh, this second time was slower, deeper . . . surer.

It was a vow.

Afterward they lay twined together in the warm light, talking in murmurs to the sound of crackling fire and rain outside. He told her of the mess his uncle had left him, of his first trip to sea and the desperate misery of seasickness.

In turn she told him about her parents and the places they'd lived, and how they died.

And of Laurence. He'd held her tightly then and later told her of the woman he'd had a long-term liaison with, a Chinese widow who had no desire to marry again.

Later the talk turned to their plans for the future. He told her about Davenham Hall, his property in the country, and how he'd managed to keep it—just—out of all the properties his uncle had owned. It would need a lot of work to rebuild the estate, and he had no idea what condition the house was in.

"Would you mind living in the country for a good part of the year?" he asked her. "I know a lot of people don't like—"

"Mind? The opportunity to create my very own home? Don't you know how precious that would be for me?" Her eyes filled with tears. She tried to blink them away. "I've never had a home of my own before."

His embrace tightened. "I haven't either," he said, his voice husky. "Not really."

Abby thought of the small boy who'd waited and waited to be collected from school, and never was, the boy who, when he'd finally been invited to his uncle's house, had found it cold and formal, despite the warmth of his aunt. He might own the house in Berkeley Square, but he'd bought it for his aunt, and it was furnished with her things.

"We'll create a home together," she promised him. "For us and for our children."

Epilogue

"I must learn to be content with being happier than I deserve."

—JANE AUSTEN, *PRIDE AND PREJUDICE*

"In the *country*?" Lady Beatrice declared. "You can't possibly mean to get married in some poky little church in the country when you can marry in St. George's, Hanover Square. It's *the* place to be wed."

Abby smiled. "The chapel at Davenham Hall is perfect. We don't want a big wedding, and it seems so right to be getting married there, beginning our new life in the place where we'll live it." Abby had fallen in love with Davenham Hall at first sight. Their carriage had crested the hill and they'd stopped to look down at the ancient stone house nestled in a green valley. The house was surrounded by a tangled garden and half hidden by trees, which at this time of year were starting to show signs of scarlet and gold and copper and green.

Abby had explored the rambling old house eagerly. It was dusty, but perfect, almost like something out of a fairy tale, with turrets and gothic windows and a fireplace in the hall large enough to roast an ox. And the tiny sixteenth-century chapel was exquisite—perfect for the wedding of two people who didn't have a large family. Yet.

Lady Beatrice turned to Max. "Max, this is your doing!"

He shook his head. "It's not, you know. If I had my way I'd marry her out of hand with a special license."

His aunt made a disgusted noise. "You'd let the gel get married in rags, I suppose. Men!"

Max grinned and slipped his arm around Abby's waist. "I'd marry her in nothing at all."

Abby leaned her head on his shoulder. The waiting was hard on both of them. She longed to have the freedom to lie with him in his big bed, making love the way they had that glorious wet afternoon in Bath, but it wasn't possible. Not here, where it seemed there were curious sisters, beady-eyed aunts and butlers underfoot at every turn.

Abby didn't really mind what she wore to her wedding, but Daisy had set her heart on making her a special dress and Abby wasn't going to disappoint her, especially since Max had given them the freedom of his silk warehouse. It would be the first dress Daisy had ever sewed using all new fabric.

"This is Abby's notion," Max said.

"It's what I want, truly," Abby assured the old lady. "It's beautiful, just wait until you get there. The autumn colors are just starting and by the wedding, they'll be stunning. And when we've finished with the house, it will look beautiful too. It just needs a good cleaning and some rearrangement."

"Abby and I are going to travel ahead to Davenham Hall," Max told his aunt. They'd planned it the night before. "We'll get the house and chapel ready, and the wedding preparations under way."

"We'd like to take Featherby and William with us," Abby said quickly, before Lady Beatrice had a chance to object. "And a maid."

"For a chaperone," Max said.

Lady Beatrice raised her brows. "Not a sister?"

Abby shook her head, hoping her blush wasn't too visible. "No, Jane and Damaris want to stay here and help Daisy." That was true enough, but it was also true that she didn't want her sisters underfoot, observing Abby behaving scandalously with her betrothed. She had every intention of repeating her Bath experience at Davenham Hall.

"Taking my butler too, I see." Lady Beatrice sniffed. "Barefaced piracy."

"It's just that he's so good at organizing people," Abby

coaxed. "He'll return after the wedding, I promise. I can't imagine Featherby taking to country life permanently, can you?"

"Well, if you must, you must—oh, get along with you, Miss Burglar," she pretended to grumble as Abby hugged her and planted a kiss on her cheek. "I suppose when love is bursting out of you, you have to kiss someone."

"It is," Abby agreed softly, and glanced at Max. "And I do."

Abby and Max's wedding day dawned mild and sunny. Jane and Daisy and Damaris helped Abby to get ready. Her wedding dress was in heavy cream silk, and so simply and beautifully cut it took Abby's breath away when she saw it. Gathered from a square neckline, it was caught under the bust by a wide satin bow, the only piece of decoration in the whole dress unless you counted the tiny puffed sleeves. When she walked, the sumptuous fabric flowed around her like water.

"Oh, Daisy, it's beautiful. I feel like a princess."

Daisy grinned and nodded. "You know, Abby, I was that nervous when I went to cut the material—real silk it is, and never been touched—me hands were shaking. Still, it's turned out all right, ain't it?"

"It's utterly beautiful and you know it," Abby told her. "I should have chosen St. George's, Hanover Square after all, so the *ton* could see this dress. Once they see it, they'll be lining up for you to make them dresses, wait and see."

Daisy grinned. "Don't you worry about me, Abby. You just go off and get yourself married to that man of yours. Everything ready?"

Abby checked. She wore the beautiful square-cut emerald ring that Max had given her, that Lady Beatrice had inherited from her own mother. She touched the pearl and diamond necklace she wore around her neck, a gift from Max. Tucked beneath her satin waistband was a small lace handkerchief given to her by Lady Beddington, "Because one always cries at weddings, even one's own." A saucy pair of blue satin garters held up her silk stockings, a gift from Featherby and William, and on the table beside her sat the posy she would carry, fashioned by Damaris's clever fingers.

All were tokens from the people who loved her. Abby knew she was blessed. It was foolish to wish for some small item from her mother or father to wear or carry on this most important day, but they'd paid for Mama's funeral with her wedding ring and there was nothing else.

"Come on, Abby, you don't want to be late," Jane said.

Abby looked up at her sister and smiled. Of course, how could she forget? Here was her most precious gift from Mama and Papa—her sister Jane, smiling and beautiful, the very image of Mama.

She smoothed on her long white gloves. "I'm ready."

Every inch of the church had been scrubbed and polished, from the ancient oak pews glowing with beeswax, to the decorative brasses and the glittering stained glass windows. Since it had been an unseasonably cold summer, and there were only a few flowers left, the church had been decorated with sprays of autumn leaves, huge silver vases filled to overflowing with crimson and gold and copper and rust, glowing in the candlelight and filling the small stone church with light and warmth and the clean, earthy fragrance of the forest.

Every pew was filled, for not only had all their friends from London traveled down for the wedding, but most of the local villagers and Davenham tenants had turned out too. Abby recognized most of the faces that turned to smile at her as she entered the church, her sisters behind her. These people had all helped with the massive job of readying Davenham Hall for the event. Apart from Featherby and William, Max had insisted on employing only local labor. It had been a bad season for crops and people needed the income, he'd explained.

Now they'd all come, shyly filling up the back rows, dressed in their Sunday best, with scrubbed faces and polished shoes and slicked-back hair, full of smiles and nods and even a few tears as Abby walked slowly down the aisle.

Abby blinked back some tears of her own. This was her future, her people. Her home.

More and more people turned to smile at her, members of the literary society, Lady Beddington and her friends, Featherby and William—Featherby sobbing already.

And in the front pew, leaning on her cane, a most magnificent old lady who'd taken in a burglar and claimed her as her niece. She nodded at Abby, gave a smile that wobbled, and blew loudly into a handkerchief.

Her family.

And there by the altar, standing tall and somber and magnificent was her love, his gray eyes burning in the dark little church as he waited for her, for plain Abby Chantry, who in the light of his gaze felt utterly beautiful. Her beloved Viking.

He held out his hand to her. Her eyes misted. She was home.

FROM
JULIANA GRAY

A Gentleman Never Tells

Six years ago, Elizabeth Harewood and Lord Roland Pen-hallow were London's golden couple, young and beautiful and wildly in love. Forced apart by her scheming relatives and his clandestine career, Lilibet and Roland buried their passion beneath years of duty and self-denial, until a chance holiday encounter changes everything they ever knew about themselves . . . and each other.

But Miss Elizabeth Harewood is now the Countess of Somerton, estranged wife of one of England's most brutal and depraved aristocrats, and she can't afford the slightest hint of scandal attached to her name. When Roland turns up mysteriously at the castle where she's hidden herself away, she struggles to act as a lady should, but the gallant lover of her youth has grown into an irresistibly dashing and dangerous man, and temptation is only a single kiss away . . .

PRAISE FOR JULIANA GRAY

"Juliana Gray has a stupendously lyrical voice
unlike anybody else."
—Meredith Duran, *New York Times* bestselling author

"Juliana Gray is on my auto-buy list."
—Elizabeth Hoyt, *New York Times* bestselling author

julianagray.com
facebook.com/JulianaGray
facebook.com/LoveAlwaysBooks
penguin.com

An imperfect pair . . .
perfectly matched.

FROM THE *USA TODAY* BESTSELLING AUTHOR

JENNIFER ASHLEY

The Duke's Perfect Wife

Lady Eleanor Ramsay is the only one who knows the truth about Hart Mackenzie. Once his fiancée, she is the sole woman to whom he could ever pour out his heart.

Hart has it all—a dukedom, wealth, power, influence, whatever he desires—and every woman wants him. But Hart has sacrificed much to keep his brothers safe, first from their brutal father, and then from the world. He's also suffered loss—his wife, his infant son, and the woman he loved with all his heart though he realized it too late.

Now, Eleanor has reappeared on Hart's doorstep, with scandalous nude photographs of Hart taken long ago. Intrigued by the challenge in her blue eyes—and aroused by her charming, no-nonsense determination—Hart wonders if his young love has come to ruin him . . . or save him.

M1053T0212